Readers love Anna Romer

Praise for *Lyrebird Hill*

'Brooding and mesmerising, this is an absorbingly written and richly atmospheric novel combining suspense, intrigue and mystery' – *Book Muster Down Under*

'Beautifully written, richly characterised and intricately plotted, *Lyrebird Hill* is one of those books that draws you in and doesn't let go . . . I read it in one sitting. It captivated me, held me in its thrall' – *Write Note Reviews*

'An absorbing and atmospheric tale, beautifully told' – *Book'd Out*

'A real page-turner by one of our favourite authors' – *New Idea*

Praise for *Thornwood House*

'Packed with tension, intrigue, suspense, romance, Aboriginal folklore, the quaintness (and peculiarities) of a small town and hidden truths. I can't recommend this book enough! – *The Australian Bookshelf*

'An impressive debut from Anna Romer . . . I will definitely be picking up her next book.' – *Book'd Out*

'A truly captivating and haunting read, *Thornwood House* made me dig out one of my favourites, *Rebecca* by Daphne Du Maurier, another gothic tale of obsession and secrets . . . It made me want to read another book by Anna Romer. Soon.' – *Write Note Reviews*

Also by Anna Romer

Lyrebird Hill
Thornwood House

Beyond the Orchard

ANNA
ROMER

SIMON &
SCHUSTER

London · New York · Sydney · Toronto · New Delhi

A CBS COMPANY

BEYOND THE ORCHARD
First published in Australia in 2016 by
Simon & Schuster (Australia) Pty Limited
Suite 19A, Level 1, Building C, 450 Miller Street, Cammeray, NSW 2062

10 9 8 7 6 5 4 3 2 1

A CBS Company
Sydney New York London Toronto New Delhi
Visit our website at www.simonandschuster.com.au

A cataloguing in publication record for this title is available from the
National Library of Australia

Creator: Romer, Anna, author.
Title: Beyond the Orchard/Anna Romer.
ISBN: 9781925184426 (paperback)
           9781925184440 (ebook)
Subjects: Family secrets – Fiction.
           Families – Fiction.
Dewey Number: A823.4

Cover design: Christabella Designs
Cover image: Rekha Garton/Trevillion Images, Madlen/Shutterstock,
             Valentin Agapov/Shutterstock
Typeset by Midland Typesetters, Australia
Printed and bound in Australia by Griffin Press

The paper this book is printed on is certified
against the Forest Stewardship Council®
Standards. Griffin Press holds FSC chain
of custody certification SGS-COC-005088.
FSC promotes environmentally responsible,
socially beneficial and economically viable
management of the world's forests.

FSC
www.fsc.org
MIX
Paper from
responsible sources
FSC® C009448

*To my mum Jeanette,
for your wisdom and kindness,
and for always believing in me*

The cave you fear to enter holds the treasure you seek.
Joseph Campbell

Such a clever, golden-haired girl. Sandy freckles danced on her cheeks, and her watchful eyes were as dark as the wild kelp that grew beyond the shore.

'Found in a seashell,' the fisherman claimed.

The Queen clasped her hands to stop them trembling. A child washed up on the beach, all alone in the world, in need of a mother; and she, the Queen, with empty arms and a heart that ached to be filled.

—The Shell Queen

1

Bitterwood, 1931

With infinite care, he lifted her into his arms and staggered through the dark house, out into the garden. She weighed almost nothing, as though her living soul had been the only thing giving her substance.

Treading heavily across the grass, he went downhill towards the orchard, through the weeping mulberry trees she had loved. The stars were brilliant, the garden black with shadows. When he reached the leafy hollow where the icehouse lurked unseen, he paused, breathless.

Drinking in the night air, he blinked to clear his eyes, clutching her to him, wishing he could turn back time, wishing . . . But no, he would not let his mind revisit what he had done. Later, in the dusty quiet of his room, among his books and familiar things, he would crumble. But not here, not now.

The trees around him blurred, the sea breeze blew icy on his cheeks. He pressed his lips to her forehead, a familiar, comforting gesture – but the chill in her skin, the clammy stickiness of sweat and blood, and the vague dark odour of death brought the realisation crashing down.

He had lost her.

The linchpin that held the fragments of his world together, the singular ray of hope in his grey life; she was gone. He could only blame himself. He had tried to contain her in the prison of his love, but instead he had smothered her. He had wanted to keep her safe, protect her, give her the life he had envisaged for her, a good life. Instead, he had clipped her wings, stolen from her everything she held dear.

No one could know. If anyone asked, he would say she had moved on, gone back to her family. Returned to her old life, the life she had lived before him. The life he had always resented so bitterly—

A murmur drifted from the darkness. His breath came quick as he searched the pale smudge of her face in the moonlight. Shadows danced over her features, playing tricks with his mind. He prayed for a sign – another murmur, a whisper of forgiveness, the faint utterance of his name. Not that he would have heard it; the booming pulse in his ears was deafening. Minutes ticked away. His ears and eyes began to ache, so keenly alert were they, but still he could not move. The sound came again, clearer this time. Hope ebbed away. It was not her breath he had heard, not her whisper, merely the scratch of dry leaves along the brick path in the orchard.

Regathering her against him, he forced his numb legs to take one measured step after another. Slowly, he made his way through the darkness to the icehouse.

'You'll be safe now, my darling. I'll be here to watch over you always.'

The keys were in his pocket. He fumbled them out and then somehow forced them into the lock. The door creaked, opening into deeper dark. A gust of damp billowed out, and with it came the smell of earth and stone, of air undisturbed for many years. Air that would, as of this night forth, remain undisturbed for many more years to come.

2

Melbourne, June 1993

Winter had arrived early. It was only five o'clock, and already the night sky had settled black over the city. Trams rattled across the junction, churning up a slipstream of chip wrappers and dust. The air smelled of diesel exhaust, and faintly of the ocean.

As the streetlights blinked on along Dandenong Road, I hurried up the footpath towards the Astor Theatre. On the bill tonight was a Hitchcock double feature. *Rear Window* I had seen a thousand times, but *Rope* was new to me. Critics deemed it Hitchcock's masterpiece and I was abuzz to see it.

A short balding man in his sixties with a shaggy beard stood near the entryway stairs at the tail end of a queue. He wore jeans and a cardigan, and clutched a beaten old briefcase. The cold evening air had flushed his ears pink. I wanted to run to him, fling myself into his arms the way

I'd done as a little girl, smother his round cheeks in kisses. Instead, I trod silently up behind him and tapped him on the shoulder.

He whirled around and beamed, but then his face fell. 'Lucy, you look terrible.'

I gave him a quick hug. 'Thanks, Dad. It's great to see you, too.'

He peered into my face. 'Been getting enough sleep?'

'It's only jetlag. I'll be fine.'

'How's Adam?'

I tried to sound cheery. 'He called last night, he's good.'

'Has he changed his mind about joining you?'

I gazed along the street and forced a smile. 'He's flat out at work, otherwise he'd be here. Don't worry, he's still keen to meet you.'

Dad shook his head and sighed. 'Why do I get the feeling there's more to the story than you're telling?'

I dug my hands into my pockets, thinking of the letter. It had been on my mind since I received it back in London a month ago. It was more a cryptic note really, hastily scrawled in my grandfather's shaky hand. *I have something for you*, he'd written. *It will explain everything, but I can't post it . . . Any chance of a visit?*

Now was not the time to tell Dad about it. There would be a row, and he'd try to stop me seeing the old man. I would tell him after, I decided. After I had visited my grandfather and learned what this mysterious 'something' was.

'Missing him already, are we?' Dad said.

Backtracking, I realised he was still talking about Adam. 'Hmm,' I said noncommittally, and then nudged his arm as we shuffled forward in the queue. 'The place is packed. I hope we get good seats.'

Dad narrowed his eyes. 'You sure you're okay?'

'Stop fussing.' Regretting my sharpness, I tried to make amends. 'How's the new book?'

Dad brightened. Sliding a bundle of papers from his briefcase, he gave it to me. 'Finally finished. I managed to turn a deaf ear to Wilma's nagging today and get the ending written. I hope you like it.'

'Wow, Dad.' The letter and Adam both forgotten, I turned the manuscript over in my hands. Suddenly I wanted to be at home, curled in a comfy chair, a pot of scalding tea by my side as I lost myself in the warped and wonderful world of my father's latest creation. 'Let me guess, Rumpelstiltskin?'

Dad nodded, latching his briefcase. 'I couldn't resist turning him into the love interest. He got a rum deal in the original. He helps a damsel in distress and then they weasel out of paying him.'

'He wanted their firstborn,' I pointed out.

Dad shook his head. 'A deal's a deal, Luce. If you can't afford to lose, then don't gamble.'

'Trust you to tell the gritty side of the story.'

He scratched his beard, eyes twinkling. 'The underdogs of the fairytale kingdom always get a bad rap. The so-called evil stepmothers and wicked witches, the trolls under the bridge – they were only doing what they thought was best. Tell me, why are baddies always so misunderstood?'

'Umm,' I bit back a smile. 'Because they're *bad*?'

Dad's round cheeks glowed. 'Everyone's a hero in their

own story. Even the crooks. They're all struggling to get along in life, find a measure of happiness, just like the next guy.'

I couldn't help smiling as we went up the Astor's wide front steps into the entry foyer. I had missed our talks. London was on the other side of the world, and although Dad and I talked on the phone most weeks, the physical distance had brought back the hairline fractures in our closeness.

I hugged the parcel to my chest. 'It's good to be back.'

Dad gave my shoulder a gentle squeeze. 'Things aren't the same without you, kiddo. I'm glad you're here, but the next month will fly. I wish you and Adam would move home.'

'London *is* home for Adam.'

'But not for you.'

'It is now,' I murmured, then instantly regretted how bleak my words had sounded. Dad seemed on the brink of commenting, but the queue progressed suddenly towards the ticket booth and, to my relief, the moment was lost. Our odd little silence reminded me that things between us hadn't always been so sweet. We still skirted around certain topics – my grandfather, for instance – and we still knocked heads over my decision to live in London. For the most part, though, we were stable – all thanks to Dad's stories. His publisher marketed his novellas for young adults, but he had fans of all ages, from five to ninety-five. He rewrote fairytales, turning the classics on their heads: a wicked Thumbelina who climbed into little boys' ears and drove them to evil deeds, a kindly Bluebeard who locked himself in the cellar to escape his henpecking wives, Red Riding Hood as a shape-shifting villain. I loved Dad's topsy-turvy world. My happiest moments were always those I spent bringing his twisted fairytales to life with pen and ink.

We had been a team for almost a decade, since I was seventeen. One day, cross with Dad after another of our rows, I had defaced one of his manuscripts with angry little sketches, which he later found. He'd begun to cackle and soon he was laughing full-belly.

'You caught it,' he marvelled, wiping his eyes. 'Damn it, Lucy, you caught the ogre's expression exactly. Talk about funny! And look at the prince's feeble chin, it's perfect.'

A few weeks later, his publisher called, asking to see a folio of my work. I had sketches from my art class at school, and other doodles I'd done in my textbook margins. To my surprise, they loved them. When Dad's next book came out, his legion of young fans were overjoyed to discover it illustrated in full colour. That edition did so well the publisher commissioned me to illustrate the new editions for all Dad's earlier books. Almost overnight, it seemed, my father and I had become a team. For the first time in years, we had common ground. The arguments petered out; our silences gave way to discussions about character sketches and colour palettes. Dad seemed to regard me through more appreciative eyes.

We bought our tickets and made our way up the grand staircase. We were early. The first film didn't start for twenty minutes. Still time to settle ourselves, grab a bite to eat and locate our favourite seats.

'Uh-oh,' Dad muttered as we reached the upstairs foyer. 'Here's trouble.'

I followed his gaze. At first I didn't recognise the striking young man on the other side of the circular balustrade. He was standing with a group next to the chandelier, and when he turned to acknowledge one of his companions, the light caught the side of his face.

My stomach knotted. Coby Roseblade had filled out in the past five years. His chronic skinniness was gone; he'd clearly been working out. The snug fabric of his pullover left just enough to the imagination to make any red-blooded girl's mouth water. He'd cropped his hair short, which accentuated his broad cheekbones and square jaw.

'What's he doing here?' Dad said.

I swallowed. 'No doubt he's come to see the double feature, like us.'

'I'm sorry, Luce. If I'd known he was a Hitchcock fan, I'd have suggested we do something else tonight. Want to leave?'

I shook my head. 'I was bound to run into him eventually. He wasn't the reason I left, you know.'

Dad didn't look convinced. 'You realise I'll have to go over and say hello.'

'It'd be rude not to.'

'You coming?'

'Actually—' I gazed around for a suitable excuse, and spied the queue of people at the kiosk. Digging out my wallet, I forced a bright smile. 'I'll get us both a choc top before they sell out.'

Dad looked back at me. His face softened. 'Since Wilma's not here to witness my depravity, you'd better grab a packet of chips as well.'

I stood in the kiosk queue for an eternity, fighting to control the butterflies swarming my ribcage, determined not to let my attention stray over to the group near the chandelier. My gaze didn't wander, but my thoughts did. The first time Coby Roseblade declared he wanted to marry me, we were nine. He was a skinny freckle-faced boy, newly fostered and insecure, in need of a friend. I'd shrugged and told him, 'Sure, why not?' The second time he asked, five years ago, I'd been twenty-one. I'd made my feelings clear in the only way I'd known how: I packed my bags, and without explanation booked myself on the next flight to London.

I collected my chips and ice cream, relieved to see that my father had returned to our spot near the stairs. On my way back, a woman crossed my path. A tall, beautiful woman with sleek dark hair and the bluest eyes I'd ever seen. She stopped abruptly in front of me, covering her shock with a smile.

'Hey, Lucy.'

My stomach flipped. 'Nina.'

She looked radiant. Her cheeks were rose-petal pink, her full lips stained dark red. She had always been striking, but in the five years since I'd seen her she'd transformed into a goddess.

'I was hoping to run into you,' she said warmly. 'How long are you staying?'

'Only a few weeks. I'm housesitting for one of Dad's friends.'

Her dimples came out as she smiled. 'A soon-to-be married woman,' she said with a husky little laugh. 'Who would have thought?'

I found myself smiling back. 'Least of all me.'

'I'm dying to meet him. Adam, isn't it?' She peered over my shoulder. 'Is he here?'

I shook my head. 'Still in London, I'm afraid. He works for Amnesty, and his hours are horrendous.'

'What a shame. He sounds interesting.'

I shuffled my shoes. 'Dad told me you finally set up your shop. How's it going?'

She rolled her eyes. 'Remind me never to start a business again while the country's going broke. I had a bumpy start, but things are slowly picking up. Thank goodness.'

'I wish I could sew. Your clothes are amazing. I know you'll do well.'

She seemed taken aback, her eyes suddenly shiny. We stood that way for a moment, as though unsure how to proceed. Then I took a breath.

'How're things with Coby?'

Nina hesitated, but then smiled and wrinkled her nose. On anyone else, the expression would have looked silly, but Nina Gilbert, my one-time best friend, managed to look even more adorable. 'We're great, never better. He's following Morgan's footsteps into uni, a history major. I'm really proud of him.' There was an uncomfortable beat, and then she leaned nearer and asked quietly, 'Is it too weird? You know, that Coby and I hooked up so soon after you left?'

'Maybe a little.' Then I sighed. 'Of course not. It's not weird at all. Coby and I were never together, you know that. Besides, it was me who ran off.'

She brushed her fingers down my arm. 'He misses you, Luce. So does Morgan.'

I tensed and drew back. A shadow crossed Nina's beautiful face, and she smiled with such sadness that it tore my heart. I hadn't meant to flinch away, to react so strongly to the mention of his name. *Morgan*, I thought bitterly. Coby's foster father. The man who'd come between us in the end. I felt a shiver starting and rubbed my arms. Morgan's role in my sudden departure for London might have been unintentional, but it didn't make him any less to blame.

Suddenly, I wanted to tell Nina everything. The real reason I'd left, the real reason I'd stayed away for so long. The real reason I'd abandoned her and Coby, my two closest friends. I wanted to grab her by the hand and drag her out into the cold air of the street, and tell her the whole long sorry story.

'How are you?' I said instead.

Her smile was luminous. 'Really good. Amazing, in fact.' She moved her hand protectively to her midriff, and something made me glance down. She'd gained weight, I saw, taken a small step from the realm of voluptuous, into fleshier territory. But as I admired the sapphire–blue vintage dress that clung to her hourglass figure, I noticed how the folds under the bodice gathered delicately over her belly . . . her rather swollen belly.

'Oh,' I blurted.

Nina blushed – not the sort of harsh veiny redness that afflicted me, but a pretty flush of colour that danced lightly on her cheekbones.

'Yeah, who would have thought? Me having a baby, insane isn't it? A little girl,' she added with a hitch of excitement. Patting her bulge, she smiled warmly into my face.

'We're thrilled. I'm so looking forward to holding her for the first time, can you imagine? And Coby's really stoked, he's—'

She caught herself, and pressed her lips into one of those smiles that said, *I've gone and put my foot in it, haven't I?*

'Coby always wanted kids,' I said quietly.

'Tons of them,' she agreed, widening her eyes. Then she added wistfully, 'Family equals security for him. Nine years in the foster system will do that to a person.'

'He'll make a great dad.'

Nina grasped my hand. 'Oh Lucy, it's so good to see your face.'

This time I squeezed back. 'Yours, too.'

Then she grimaced. 'I *really* have to wee. Will you promise me something?'

'What?'

'Don't be a stranger. Come and visit. Please?'

'Sure.'

'Hey, Sunday's curry night at our place – what do you say?'

'Sounds good. I've missed your curries.'

'Great! Come at six, we're early eaters. Lucy, it's amazing to see you. I can't wait to hear all about your adventures. And all about Adam,' she added with a gleam in her eye. Dipping towards me, she placed a butterfly-soft kiss on my cheek and then hurried away. Knots of people stepped aside for her, opened their little groups to allow her fleeting access, and then watched her with admiring glances.

A sticky trickle of melting ice cream leaked onto my hand. I headed back to where Dad and I had been standing near the balustrade. As I shuffled around the perimeter of a tightknit group, something made me look across the foyer towards the chandelier. Coby tilted his chin, a cautious acknowledgement. I lifted my hand in a wave, and then hurried back to Dad.

'You look peaky,' he said as I delivered his ice cream. 'How was Nina?'

'She's pregnant, actually.' My words came out stiffer than I'd intended. 'I guess it must have slipped your mind?'

Dad winced. 'Sorry about that, kiddo. I was scared you might jet off again if you knew.'

I sighed. 'It's okay, Dad. Coby and I were never really an item . . . He thought we were, but it wasn't that way with us. You know?'

'I know he had a hell of a time after you went AWOL. Morgan said he stayed in his room for six months brooding to Metallica.'

My cheeks burned. I felt hot and weak again. Tearing the cellophane off my ice cream, I cracked the hard chocolate topping with my teeth and devoured the cold sweetness in a couple of bites. The sugar hit revived me.

'Nina wants me to visit,' I told Dad.

'I think you should. She's missed you, you know.'

I busied myself crunching through the last of my cone.

Dad's eyes narrowed. 'What's with you tonight? You usually wait until the movie starts before you even take off the wrapper.'

Balling the cellophane, I sighed. 'I was hungry.'

Dad took the rubbish from my fingers, gave me his hanky, and scouted around for a bin. When he came back, he looked at me.

14

'You won't like hearing this, but I have to ask. Are you certain you're not rushing into this? Marriage, I mean. You're only twenty-six, you've got your whole life ahead of you.'

I frowned at him, mystified. 'Why the sudden grilling?'

'You don't seem quite yourself. And it's not jetlag. Not getting cold feet, are you?'

'Why would I? Adam is a really lovely guy.' I wiped my hands on his hanky and passed it back. 'He's got all your books. You'll like him.'

Dad sighed. 'I'm sure I will.'

I glanced towards the bright spot near the chandelier. Coby and Nina and their group of friends had moved along. My encounter with Nina had left me feeling as if I'd found something precious that had been lost, and now it was gone again. I twisted the ring on my finger, Adam's ring, its big square-cut diamond warm from my skin. I was more like Coby than I cared to admit. I understood his hunger for security. More than anything else, I craved a safe harbour, a place to drop anchor and drift quietly through life, knowing I was sheltered from any storms that might blow my way. Adam, with his soft-spoken humour and gentle strength, was my harbour. There was no fiery passion between us, no tempest that might blow me off course, but rather a solid alliance built on loyalty and respect. For me, that was enough.

'Did I tell you about Morgan?' Dad said suddenly.

I regarded him warily. 'Umm . . . no.'

'He and Gwen finally got divorced.'

A rush of heartbeats, a vaguely giddy sick feeling overtook me. I forced myself to focus on Dad's face, forced myself to sound natural.

'What a shame. They were married forever.'

'Almost two decades,' Dad agreed. 'They're still friends, although Gwen's living in Canberra now with her new partner. Funny,' he added wistfully, 'how things turn out, isn't it?'

'How do you mean?'

'Gwen and Morgan were always firm friends, but there was never any real spark between them.'

I wondered if he'd overheard my thoughts, and felt my defences prickle. 'What's so bad about that? Sparks are over-rated. They don't last.'

Dad looked at me. 'You used to light up when Morgan came into the room, you know.'

I shot him a warning glare. 'I was a kid.'

'Crazy, isn't it? Young Coby falling for you, when it was always his father you liked.'

'Foster father. Besides, I didn't *like* him. It was just hero worship.'

Dad scratched his beard and smiled. 'You and Morgan always had a bond. As a kid, you thought the sun shone out of him. Then when you were older, I seem to remember a crush. These days you're barely on speaking terms with him. What happened?'

My words came out harsher than I'd intended. 'I grew up.'

'Did I tell you he's been helping Wilma at the historical society? He restored their photo collection, all those old prints from the war. Did a superb job. He blew up copies for the Red Cross auction, they were a huge hit.'

'Great,' I murmured.

'He printed off a snap of your mother, too. Taken that

last summer, while she was sitting under the big old tree at . . . Well, you remember it. A pity,' he added, almost to himself, 'I haven't had a chance to get it framed.'

The rawness in his eyes threw me off guard. He was doing his best, I reminded myself. My mother, Karen, had been his soul mate, his great love. Sixteen years had passed since we lost her, but it seemed like no time at all. Dad had fallen into a black depression after she died, his grief an entity in itself, a shadow-creature living right there in the house with us. I spent my early teenage years tiptoe-ing around him, running and fetching to keep him happy, hiding in my room when rage and despair drove him to seek oblivion in the bottom of a wine cask. Years later, after the breakdown that sent him to Banksia House, Wilma came on the scene and everything changed. We began to rub along as a family. Dad rediscovered his smile, and we found the common ground of his stories and my illus-trations. Yet the shadow lingered, mostly ignored, a dark whisper of reproach wedged subtly between us.

I took a deep breath. 'You were telling me about Morgan.'

Dad nodded. 'He's a professor now. A brilliant one, too. Hard to believe he started out as a skinny, half-starved kid who didn't even finish high school.'

I stayed silent. I'd known Morgan since I was four. Dad met him at university when Morgan was a down-and-out history student, and Dad a disillusioned lecturer. They'd recognised each other as kindred spirits, struck up a friend-ship, and had remained close over the years, through the hard times, and then as both their lives took turns for the better. Morgan had no family of his own – or so I'd assumed when he started coming home with Dad for the holidays. He never spoke about his past, at least not to me. My mother took him under her wing and he became the son she'd always longed for.

The year I turned eight, Morgan announced he was getting married. My parents were beyond thrilled. They insisted he bring the lucky girl over for dinner. Gwen Larkin was another one of Dad's students. She was tall and slim, as pale as a moonbeam, a staunch women's libber with a passion for saving the environment, the underdog, the downtrodden. She was everything I aspired to be, and I might have been as smitten by her as everyone else was, but for one glaring flaw: she was about to marry the man I adored.

Dad looked at me. 'He's always had a soft spot for you, Lucy. Now that he's single, maybe . . .'

I held up my hand, wiggling my fingers so my engagement ring – my very expensive diamond engagement ring – twinkled conspicuously. 'I'm already spoken for. Besides, Morgan's too old for me.'

'Ouch. You young people can be really cruel sometimes.'

I couldn't hold back a smile. 'Your choc top's melting.'

Dad examined his ice cream. Condensation bubbled on the hard chocolate coating and threads of cream snaked over his hand. Taking out his rumpled hanky, he mopped the leaks thoughtfully.

'I just want you to be happy, kiddo.'

'I am happy.'

Dad looked dubious. 'If you could have anything at all, what would it be?'

'Rub a magic lamp, you mean?'

'Or wish on a star. Yeah.'

I blinked. That was a no-brainer. I'd wish for what everyone else wished for: a perfect body . . . a million dollars . . . a life that wasn't a shambles. Gosh, where to begin?

I tucked my diamond ring away from sight. 'I've got everything I need,' I told my father crisply. 'What about you? What's your burning desire?'

He smiled wistfully. 'To hear my little girl laugh more often. It's such a pretty laugh. Not to mention how damn cute she sounds when she snorts.'

I frowned. 'It's not like you to be sentimental.'

'I'm just getting the vibe that your life isn't as rosy as you want everyone to think. I mean, why are you here alone? You've half-blinded me with that diamond a dozen times, but the man himself is conspicuous in his absence. What's really going on, Luce?'

I couldn't meet his eyes. The air in the old theatre seemed suddenly stale, unbreathable. I gazed towards the stairwell, wanting to be out on the windy street, breathing the damp night air. Wishing I were back at the house, propped in bed with hot cocoa, pondering the mystery of my grandfather's letter, or losing myself in Dad's most recent manuscript.

Instead, I flashed back to the time *before*. Before I ran away to London. Before I stuffed things up so badly I could no longer bear to show my face. Before I severed ties with everyone I loved. I'd been different then, bright-eyed and quicker to smile, not so guarded. Life had seemed straightforward, ripe with opportunity. I'd believed that all you had to do was identify what you wanted and then just reach out and take it. Although, of course, that particular bubble of naivety had quickly popped.

Heat crept into my cheeks. My ears began to burn. I braced myself for Dad to continue prodding.

He must have sensed my defeat, because he said nothing more. A moment later, the gong sounded. The first feature was about to begin. I did a quick scan of the foyer and, satisfied Nina and Coby were nowhere in view, I linked arms with Dad and steered him towards the welcome darkness of the theatre.

Elegant golden curtains slid back from the screen and the film began. As the opening music flooded the auditorium, I settled back in the seat and retreated inside myself to brood over my father's words.

Gwen and Morgan were always firm friends, but there was never any real spark between them.

The divorce had been a long time coming, I mused. They had always been an on-again, off-again sort of couple. Gwen was stubborn, and Morgan quick to storm off; tension simmered between them even during their good times. They had done their best to keep it amicable for Coby's sake, but he always seemed to get caught in the crossfire. As Nina said, family was everything to Coby and it had troubled him that his own was so often unstable.

The year I turned twenty-one, Morgan and Gwen separated yet again. Coby had been devastated, and we began spending more time together. Not dating, at least not in my mind – just hanging out, listening to records, or walking for endless hours along the esplanade while Coby talked his parents' latest split out of his system. We grew closer, much closer than we'd ever been.

The night of my birthday party, Morgan had seemed distant. While I danced away the hours with Nina and Coby and our group of friends, I kept glimpsing him from the corner of my eye – talking to Dad and Wilma or replenishing the cooler, fixing a string of blown fairy lights. After my friends left, I found him alone in the garden. He was sitting in the shadows on an old timber bench, his back resting against the shed wall. His hair was raked about, his face craggy with tiredness, dark circles under his eyes. He must have heard me approach, because he looked around and smiled.

'Who's this gorgeous creature?' he said with a wink. 'What have you done with my little Lucy?'

When I didn't say anything, his smile fell away. 'You okay, sport?'

'Dad's going to kill me,' I blurted.

Morgan cocked an eyebrow. 'What've you done?'

I sat beside him on the bench. I wore my usual jeans, Doc Martens on my feet, my fair hair loose around my shoulders. Nina had helped me choose a short dress to wear as a top, a glittery red sheath with spaghetti straps and a low-cut neckline that made me look shapelier than I was. I let the lacy wrap fall away from my shoulders. It was November, the night warm. The garden was mostly dark, except for the fairy lights that Wilma and I had strung from the trees earlier that day.

In the gloom, I saw – no, not *saw* exactly, rather, *felt* – Morgan's gaze linger on me. A slow, appreciative gaze that set my blood alight. Feather-soft, that gaze took in my bare arms and danced its way across the skimpy neckline. It trailed up my throat and then, as warm as honey, settled for one intoxicating moment on my lips. When his eyes finally met mine, a shadow crossed his face. His jaw tightened. Then he tried to mask the tightness behind a smile.

'What have you done?' he asked again, only now his voice was strangely soft.

'I got a tattoo.' I lifted my shoulder for him to see. The design inked into my skin was still a little inflamed, but no longer sore. 'It's kind of a birthday present to myself. What do you think?'

Morgan looked at my shoulder and whistled. 'A little mermaid. She looks just like you.' He smiled, and the garden seemed suddenly very dark, as though even the fairy lights had dimmed. The stars grew dull, the round face of the moon faded to a hazy thumbprint. Morgan, on the other hand, glowed.

'I love you,' I whispered. 'I always have, Morgan. Always will.'

His smile faltered. He tilted his head, as though uncertain he'd heard correctly.

I was possessed, I must have been. The heat he had ignited in me with his lingering, appreciative glance must have short-circuited the logical part of my brain. As though watching from a distance, I saw my hand float towards his face. I saw my fingers gently cup his cheek. I saw myself lean against him, my face turned upwards like a sunflower seeking the light. I watched my younger self with a mix of mortification and dread, as I slid my other arm around his neck and pressed my lips against his mouth—

'No!'

Jolting back to the dark cinema, I realised I'd spoken aloud. Not just spoken – I'd virtually yelled. My father shot me a startled look, but then must have assumed a tense moment in the film had taken me off guard. He smiled indulgently and settled his attention back on the screen.

I sank into my seat. My cheeks burned. I thought of Coby and Nina, somewhere in the dark theatre, perhaps sitting nearby. They would have recognised my voice, known the shout had come from me. I imagined them casting each other sideways looks in the flickering gloom, Nina digging Coby with her elbow, the two of them laughing a little and rolling their eyes.

I sank lower, resigning myself to sit out the rest of the film in shame. Then, from somewhere behind me, a woman cried, 'Oh!'

The man on the other side of Dad jumped, and then gave a sheepish snort. A few people tittered.

'Bloody Hitchcock,' I heard Dad mutter. 'Nightmares all round, tonight.'

3

A man stepped from the shadows of my front verandah. He wore jeans and an old leather coat, biker boots that thudded on the stairs as he came to greet me, his stride no less confident because of the slight limp.

Climbing from my van, I let the door slam shut.

I had dreaded this moment for nearly five years, yet in a secret corner of my being, I'd been yearning for it too. I found myself drinking in the sight of him, cataloguing the familiar features. The windswept dark hair, the striking face and intense pale eyes. The mouth that was, even now, quirked up in the enigmatic half-smile that, I realised regretfully, still had the power to tie my stomach in knots.

'Lucy,' he said, with a hint of accusation.

I stood my ground, watching him warily. 'What are you doing here?'

'I want to talk.'

I glanced at the house, its windows clamped tight against the night. I took in the straggly hedge enclosing the yard, the deep shadows along the verandah. Finally, I braved Morgan's eyes – the pale grey of the moon on a stormy night, yet fierce as those of a wolf. 'I've got nothing to say.'

'Don't worry, I've got plenty.'

'Morgan, I'm tired. Can we do this another time?'

'And risk you absconding from my life for another five years?'

'I didn't *abscond*. I went to live in London.'

'You didn't even say goodbye.'

I pushed past him, gripping my keys, intending to escape into the house, but he grabbed my arm.

'A letter would've been nice.'

I shook free and continued along the path, only turning back when I reached the verandah. 'I'm sure Dad filled you in on all my goings-on.'

Morgan gazed after me, his expression lost in the shadows. Behind him, the street lamp burned dull yellow, painting a ragged halo about him. He might have been the villain from a book or movie, a pirate poised on the deck of his vessel, solitary, ever so vaguely heroic. Exactly the way I had conjured him so many times in my imagination.

'You ran off that night,' he said gruffly. 'Before I could explain.'

'Your explanation was clear enough.'

He shuffled, his boots scraping the brick path. 'It came out all wrong. I made a mess of it, and by the time I'd collected myself, you'd gone. I'm sorry I hurt you,' he added softly. 'It wasn't my intention.'

I wanted him to move into the light so I could see his face. I wanted to watch his eyes when I said the words I had travelled halfway across the globe to tell him. *I don't love you, Morgan. I made a mistake. It wasn't love, after all. A girly crush, nothing more. You're well and truly out of my system. Besides, I've met someone else, someone amazing, and we're getting married . . .*

I took a breath, but then he shifted into the lamplight and the words died on my tongue. There was that almost-smile again. The curve of his lips, the eye contact. The slight leaning forward as though drawn to me by gravitational force. I shoved my hands deeper into my pockets.

'I'm not inviting you inside, if that's what you're hoping.'

'Then will you walk with me?'

I almost said no. I almost turned and let myself into the silent house, escaped into the unfamiliar darkness. Almost. But here was an opportunity to hear the words I'd suspected all along. Words that would cure my Morgan fixation forever. I shrugged and went back down the steps, along the path, past my van and back out onto the deserted street.

We walked the block in silence. I drank in the damp air. Bright winter stars glittered overhead, and our shadows leaped along the footpath ahead of us, Morgan's bearlike, mine willowy.

'I'm listening,' I prompted.

Morgan gave me a sideways glance. 'I wish I could take back what I said to you that night. I wish we could forget it happened, start over. Go back to how things were before. I've missed you, Luce. Five years is too long.'

My words came out in a rush, my carefully rehearsed

speech forgotten. 'How can we ever go back? I'm not that smitten girl anymore, Morgan. You can't give me the brush-off the way you did back then. All that stuff about the gap, about being old enough to be my father. I was twenty-one, not twelve. It was humiliating.'

He tried to take my arm, tried to swing me around to face him, but I shrugged him off and kept walking.

He caught up, kept pace beside me. 'I wasn't giving you the brush-off. It was more complicated than that. We had a past together. I'd known you since you were little. You were like family. Besides, you'd always been—'

'A kid sister,' I said bitterly.

'Out of reach, I was going to say.'

The way he said it, the wistful catch in his voice. I almost dropped my guard. *Out of reach?* Stupid, how desperately I wanted to believe him. 'Apology accepted,' I said tersely. 'Let's just forget it ever happened.'

'If that's what you want.'

My skin began to flush hot and cold. A trembly sort of dread was setting in. I twisted my ring around so the diamond sat hard and solid in my palm. I gave it a reassuring squeeze, like a talisman.

'It's ancient history, okay? Water under the bridge. Anyway, I've moved on. Met someone, Dad must've told you? I'm getting married.' My cheeks burned. Grateful for the dark, I put my head down and kept walking, but I could feel Morgan's eyes on me.

'So we're good, then?' he wanted to know.

'Yeah.'

'And you really love this guy?'

'Why else would I be marrying him?'

'Ron thinks you're making a mistake.'

'Oh, great. My father and my self-appointed big brother sitting in judgement of my life, how reassuring. For your information, I've known Adam for two years. He's kind, intelligent, rich, and thoughtful. He has a good sense of humour—'

Morgan lifted a brow.

'—and,' I continued, flourishing my fingers as we passed beneath a streetlamp, 'he bought me a freaking great diamond. What's not to love?'

Morgan stopped walking and grabbed my hand, pulling me around so I had to look at him. He barely gave the diamond a glance, but searched my face.

'Why are you trying so hard to convince me?'

'I'm not.'

He was very near. When he spoke, his voice was low, his gaze intent on mine.

'What really brought you home, Lucy?'

The ocean murmured in the bay, and a distant truck rattled along Elsternwick Road. I thought of the letter sitting on my bedside back at the house, my grandfather's spidery writing barely legible. I thought of the object he had tucked into the envelope, and I shivered.

'Just a visit.'

'I think there's something you're not telling me.'

'Why should I care what you think?'

Morgan let me go. 'You *shouldn't* care. Not if you're certain Adam's the man you really want.'

'He is.'

'Then I sincerely hope you'll be happy together.' He continued walking, shrugging deeper into his heavy coat, patting his ribcage as if absently searching his pockets, a sign he was deep in thought.

The action jogged a memory. A beach picnic, some years ago. A glimpse of Morgan's perfectly flat stomach, tanned and hairy above the frayed waistline of his Levi's. Not exactly a ripped six-pack, but an impressive effort for a man approaching forty.

I blinked away the vision. Morgan was now forty-three. Seventeen years and two months older than me. I didn't need to calculate. Each year on my birthday, my first thought was always the *gap*. The gap mattered to me, because it mattered to Morgan. It had drawn a line in the sand that he simply would not cross.

I'm old enough to be your father, he'd told me that long ago night in the garden. *Seventeen years is too much. You're the same age as my son . . . besides, there's still a chance to fix my marriage. Oh hell, Luce . . . we can't do this, you know. Not now, not ever—*

Eventually I had realised the truth. Morgan's argument about our age difference was an excuse. A gentle way of breaking the news that he didn't feel the same way, that he didn't love me, would never love me, couldn't. Weeks later, he and Gwen patched things up, and by then I had fled to the other side of the world.

Morgan stopped walking. 'Did you hear that?'

A mournful yowl drifted from somewhere beneath us. Going over to the curb, he crouched unsteadily on the road-side. I joined him, and together we looked into the drain.

A large whitish cat peered back at us. Morgan went to his knees and reached in. Grasping the animal by the scruff, he drew it out. Ribs and hipbones jutted from its filthy fur, its ears were bitten and bloodied. It struggled feebly, but made no attempt to scratch or bite. Morgan got to his feet, cradling the cat in his arms. It paddled its paws for a moment, but then settled against his chest.

'It likes you,' I said.

'They don't call me the cat whisperer for nothing.'

He looked so pleased with himself, and the cat seemed so quickly at home, that I almost laughed. Warmth flooded through me. I touched my fingers lightly to the cat's soft belly. 'Morgan, they don't call you the cat whisperer, full stop.'

Our eyes met for a second, and then Morgan looked down at the cat. 'Someone needs a good feed,' he told it. 'Here you go,' he added, delivering the creature into my arms. 'My wedding gift to you.'

I started to protest. I didn't want a cat. I was only here for a month and there was no way I could take it back to London with me. Besides, Adam was allergic. Then I gazed into its enormous green eyes. It was cold and half-starved, frightened. I drew it against me. It squirmed but then curled in the warm crook of my arms, burrowing against my chest. An unfamiliar feeling came over me. Tenderness, I realised. My arms tightened protectively, and the cat began to purr.

By the time we reached my verandah, it was sleeping.

Morgan unlocked the front door for me. I couldn't quite see his face in the semi-dark, just the outline of his features etched silver in the moonlight. I took back the keys, but he lingered.

'It's good to see you, Lucy.' Reaching over, he cupped the side of my face. His hand was calloused and warm, his touch distantly familiar. He traced his thumb across my cheekbone, and then leaned in to press a light kiss on my forehead. 'I hope everything works out for you. You of all people deserve to be happy.'

I shivered, instinctively raising my face, but Morgan was already retreating across the verandah, his shadow briefly eclipsing the moonlight as he went down the stairs, into the yard. A moment later, his motorbike roared to life and he was gone.

For the longest time I stood there, watching the gap in the hedge, imagining what would happen if he reappeared. What would happen if he rushed back to me, pulled me into his arms and kissed me properly. Of course, he didn't. I touched the place above my eyebrow where he had pressed his lips, and shivered again. Morgan was my first love. I would probably never forget him. But the last five years had changed me. The naive young girl was gone. In her place was someone less trustful, someone who guarded her heart more carefully.

I went inside and shut the door. Dad's friend who owned the house was an artist, and all her rooms smelled vaguely of Venetian turpentine, which I found reassuring. Her walls were crowded with artworks and the rooms furnished with a comfortable jumble of second-hand finds and battered old antiques. Breathing in the sweetly tart air, I carried the cat upstairs to the sunroom, where I made him a nest from a cardboard box lined with an old jumper. I fed him tuna straight from the can, and then watched him sniff around his new home. Ten minutes later, he was curled in the box, purring noisily.

I stood at the sunroom window, my fingertips resting on the cold glass as I gazed over the treetops and houses, across Port Phillip Bay. The water looked icy and desolate. A small thornlike pain pricked my heart. *If only*, it seemed to say. *If only you hadn't rushed off that night. If only you had waited, bided your time, maybe then . . .*

'Sparks are overrated,' I reminded myself.

Beyond the window, the stars and moon disappeared behind a bank of clouds. The water in the bay turned black. Tiny lights glittered along the esplanade, houses and streetlights, and there in the distance, a solitary vessel inched its way slowly out to sea.

4

Victorian coast, 1929

Orah huddled beside her mother in the belly of the lifeboat, thigh-deep in water, freezing fingers clamped to the crossbench. Staring over the rim, she searched the moonlit waves. Splintered planks swirled like matchsticks in the black water. Barrels bobbed among the wreckage, a suitcase and a small chest swirled past. Once, she glimpsed something white that might have been a man. It turned out to be an empty nightshirt. The current churned the shirt on its foamy surface, and then sucked it away.

Hot tears stung her eyes as she looked for the shore.

'Mam, we're drifting out to sea!' She hadn't meant to sound so small and frightened, not when she'd made a private promise to be brave. They only had one oar, and no rope nor anchor. Not that it would have mattered. A weaving woman and her thirteen-year-old daughter from the cobbled heart of Glasgow were no match for the sea. The *Lady Mary*'s captain and his crew had gone down. The strong labourers, the midshipmen, the navvies and stewards – all of them gone. Orah and her mother were the last survivors, and the sea was hungry for them too.

Mam grasped her hand. 'We'll be all right, love. The coastguard will find us, and before you know it we'll be with your pa, snug in warm blankets, sipping sugary tea.'

When Mam pressed her lips to Orah's brow, Orah began to weep. The kiss was warm, the only warmth apart from her tears that Orah had felt in hours. She clung to her mother, and Mam stroked her cold face. Orah found herself drifting into an uneasy stupor, rocked by the swell of water beneath them, cradled in Mam's arms . . .

But then Mam cried out.

Orah lurched up in time to see an outcrop of rocks loom out of the water into their path. Mam flung herself to the edge of the boat, grappling for the oar, but she was too late. The lifeboat struck the rock. The impact threw Mam off balance, and before her daughter's frozen senses could react, she had gone overboard.

Orah launched after her, but the vessel lurched violently and almost sent her into the water too. Mam surfaced and Orah reached down and grasped her hand, but she was too heavy to drag over the rim and back into the boat.

Orah clutched her tightly. 'Mam!'

'Hold on, Orah,' Mam said. Clamping her free hand on the edge of the boat, she tried to heave herself up, but again the little vessel listed dangerously, sinking lower in the water.

'Let go of my hand,' Mam ordered.

Orah let go. The boat sat low in the water, rocking and dipping wildly as Mam struggled to pull herself up over the side. Her arms shook and her wet dress dragged her backwards with each wave. Orah gripped her under the arms, but again and again the swell threw them off balance. Mam was growing tired. For a while she rested her head against the rim of the boat, panting. When she looked up again, her eyes held a glimmer of her old fire.

'Hold tight,' she instructed. She edged along the boat and grasped the bow, then began to paddle with one arm. Slowly, the lifeboat began to move through the water towards the shore.

Just when Orah thought they were safe, the swell retreated and another bank of submerged rock broke the surface nearby. The current foamed and swirled, rushing the lifeboat towards it.

Orah screamed.

Mam wrenched around. Her face was chalky, her eyes widened when she saw the rock. Her mouth opened in a silent cry as the wave hollowed out and sucked the boat swiftly towards the rock. Her body struck it soundlessly. She buckled like a rag doll, and the tide dragged her under.

Orah threw herself to the front of the boat and straddled the edge, somehow managing to grasp Mam's sleeve, then her wrist. Mam's skin was slippery, and Orah almost lost her. Then their hands locked and Mam's face broke the surface.

She gasped. 'Orah . . . Orah!'

Orah hung on hard. Her hands were strong. After Pa's departure for Australia six years before, Mam had kept them in food and board by spinning raw yarn and weaving woollen cloth for a tailor. Orah had helped to spin and card the yarn, a job she had come to love. It had given her the gift of physical strength, which until now she had taken for granted.

She tightened her grip, but seawater found its way through her fingers, into her palm, weakening her hold. Mam's lips moved. As if from a great distance, her voice spoke softly in Orah's mind.

My clever girl, one day you'll leave the nest and make a great life for yourself. When you do, remember that whatever else changes, your old mam will always love you.

Mam locked her gaze on Orah. Her fingers slackened. 'My darling girl, I love you so.'

'No,' Orah cried. What was Mam doing? 'No, no!'

Mam released her grip. Her eyes widened as she slipped from Orah's grasp. Mam cried out, a single word, a final haunting wail that was lost forever as the black water claimed her and took her under.

Orah couldn't remember how the lifeboat had capsized, only that the lower half of her body was now in the water. She grasped the splintered hull with frozen fingers. Debris bobbed past, chests and lifebelts, scraps of wood. Black waves slapped against her, foul-smelling and oily.

She wanted to sink into the darkness and be with Mam. She was so very tired. The effort of staying alive was wearying, and she wished it over. All she had to do was let go. The seawater would rush in and fill her lungs, all the bubbles of her breath would escape, and she would sink down and join her mother in slumber.

She glared at her fingers, willing them to loosen. *Mam, wait for me. Don't leave me alone.* Tears began to burn down her cheeks. Her brain was punishing her, throwing out sweet memories that here, in the vast cold hell of the sea, made her ache with longing: Mam's lips on her brow, Mam's gentle voice, her big soft-bodied embrace, her reassuring presence. Only now, there were other memories: Mam's worried eyes, Mam in the water, the slow horrible slide as Mam slipped through Orah's fingers and away. If only she were still here. Orah screwed up her eyes, searching the dark water, wishing hard. Perhaps Mam had surfaced again, too far away for Orah to see. Perhaps she was, at this very moment, searching the wreckage for a sign of Orah.

'Mam!' she shouted. 'Where are you?'

Orah's cry ended on a shriek as something nudged her shoulder. She wrenched around, alight with frantic joy. *Mam's survived. She's not dead at all, and now she's found her way back to the lifeboat, back to me—*

But it wasn't Mam.

It was a boy. Treading water an arm's length away. His brown face peered at her through the half-light. Wild wet hair jutted from his head, and his straight brows furrowed over midnight eyes. Eyes so dark they surely belonged to a devil risen from the deep.

'Give me your hand,' he said sharply.

Orah's mouth opened, but the scream stuck in her throat. She tried to thrash away from the boy, but lost her hold on the broken hull and slid into the water, swallowing a mouthful. She began to cough so hard she couldn't breathe.

The boy grasped her arm. She shoved away from him, spluttering and gasping, managing to scramble back to the upturned boat. He tried to take hold of her again, but she lashed out, clawing at him with frozen fingers.

'Let me help,' he said more gently. 'Put your arms around my neck and hold on. I'll swim you to shore.'

He pointed to the headland, and finally Orah's fearful mind began to jostle together a sort of sense. She looked at him. He was no devil from the deep. Just a boy, not much older than her. He patted his shoulder and said, 'Here, climb on my back. Hold tight. Don't be afraid. I'm a good swimmer.'

Orah made no move to let go.

'Will you let me help?' he asked.

She nodded.

With one hand, he gripped Orah's fingers and prised them from the hull. His skin was a shock of warmth. Orah wondered vaguely why the chill had not taken hold of him as it had taken hold of her. She slid into the water, clumsy with fear, but the boy did not let her sink. The lifeboat drifted out of reach. She twisted, trying to splash after it, but the boy held her firm.

He drew her to him and pulled her arms around his neck. She clung to him, letting her cheek fall against his head as he swam towards the shore, his muscles bunching and lengthening, his lean body warm through the sodden cloth of Orah's dress. He crested the swelling waves with ease, pushing strong and swift through the troughs. Soon the shadows of the headland loomed over them. Orah saw a cut of deeper darkness at its base, and realised with a pang of sorrow that Mam had been right. A tiny cove lay at the foot of the headland, with a narrow stretch of gravelly beach curving along the water's edge.

They reached the shore and the boy laid Orah on the sand. She rolled onto her belly, retching. When the spasms stopped, she hunched into a ball to catch her breath. Finally, she looked up.

The boy was crouched beside her, his eyes fixed to her face. He wasn't alone. A girl knelt next to him. She was dark-skinned like the boy, and her wide eyes shone in the gloom.

'Come on.' The boy put out his hand.

Orah brushed him away and struggled to her feet. She stood shakily, then pointed to the water.

'Mam's out there. You have to help her.'

The boy studied her face, his brows drawn. He looked at the girl, and back at Orah, then nodded solemnly.

For the next hour, he dived and searched. Orah shivered on the shore, straining to see. The girl stood motionless at Orah's side, her skinny frame ghostlike in the gloom. From time to time, Orah heard her speak, her words as melodic as birdsong. Orah couldn't make out what the girl was saying. The roar of the ocean still rang in her ears, and her heart thumped too loudly. The boy was a shadow in the predawn light. Paddling in circles, swimming along the surface of the waves, and then diving deep. At times, he was gone so long that Orah thought the current had pulled him under, drowned him like all the others. Finally, he swam back to shore, emerging from the surf panting, his head held low. He collapsed on the sand next to her.

Orah dropped to her knees. She had bitten her lips, and the sticky ooze of blood mingled warmly with the salty crust of dried seawater around her mouth. She drove her fists hard into her temples, as if that would somehow stop the pain. She pressed her face into the sand, the cry inside her trapped, her body rigid.

'Warra,' the girl cried. Her small hands fluttered over Orah's frozen skin like warm moths. 'Oh, Warra, look at her!'

The boy took Orah's hand. After a while, he helped her to her feet and led her along the beach. They entered the shadows of the headland. The girl hurried along behind them, and from time to time, Orah heard her speaking or singing quietly as they walked.

'Watch the rocks,' she called to Orah. 'Uphill now, mind your feet.'

Orah had no care where she trod, no care that the stones cut her bare heels and bruised her toes. She cared nothing for where the boy might be taking her. She simply stumbled along beside him, following like a lamb, her heart in tatters. They climbed up into the rocks, and worked their way along a steep path. As they climbed, the ocean's roar became a muffled, hollow moan. Several times, Orah had to stop and rest until the trembling in her legs subsided. Each time they stopped, the boy waited without a word.

His grip on her hand never wavered, his fingers strong and warm around hers. The girl stayed close, a dark butterfly flitting along behind Orah and the boy, sometimes beside them, sometimes ahead, never far.

Orah thought their climb would go on forever. The sun broke over the horizon and bathed them in its first yellow rays. Still they climbed. Rocks gave way to grasses. They entered a thicket of stumpy trees with small leathery leaves, and a while later broke through the other side onto flat ground.

Soon after, Orah lost her sense of place, of time. She walked blindly, as if walking was all she knew. She placed one foot in front of the other, dragging herself through a sludge of seconds, minutes, perhaps hours. In the swirling sea storm of her mind, she saw the ocean, the lifeboat, the wild rolling waves, the crash of water. She relived the giddying fear. Now, rather than the boy's warm fingers, she was holding Mam's cold ones. Clutching them for dear life, praying that this time, *this time*, if she only held tightly enough she would be able to save her.

5

Melbourne, June 1993

Cold hands closed around my ankle, dragging me deeper into the water. A voice murmured in my ear. *Why did you lie . . . Why, Lucy?*

Black water, so deep; a bottomless abyss without light or hope. Just like my guilt. I struggled, but the grip on my foot would not let go. In my mind, I could see those hands clearly: long-fingered and freckled, strong and lean, the nails blunt and neat. My mother's hands.

You lied, and now I'm trapped here, here in this dark place . . .

I tried to break the surface, to rouse myself, but the hands were too strong. My mother's face shimmered in the water below me. Her blonde hair clung to her cheeks, her mouth curved in an almost loving smile, but there was no warmth in her eyes. Blue as the water she was drowning me in, cold and unblinking. Somewhere behind her, the ocean roared.

You lied . . .

Dreaming, I told myself. The same old dream. Just open your eyes and you'll see the bedroom window with its yellow curtains, the dresser with the fresh roses, last night's clothes on the chair. All you need to do is open your eyes.

I reached for the bedside lamp, but instead my fingers grazed cold, clammy stone. I felt my body – strangely insubstantial, as thin and small as a child's – sliding away from me. I was falling, not down into the sea, but backwards in time, along a tunnel of almost pure black. *If only you hadn't lied*, the voice whispered in my mind, *I'd still be with you, darling . . . but now I'm trapped under the weight of all this water and it's very cold here, Lucy . . . very cold indeed . . .* The whispers grew more urgent, rising in pitch to a scream—

I kicked free and swam to the surface, woke up. Flicked on the bedside lamp. Placing my palms over my face, I breathed through my fingers until the panic ebbed. My cheeks were damp, my throat dry. The air felt sub-zero.

I checked the clock: 3 a.m.

My quilt was bunched at the foot of the bed, half-dragged to the floor. I yanked it back up around me and burrowed into its soft folds. Noises drifted in from the garden: night birds softly calling, branches creaking. The distant wash of water in the bay that seemed, at that moment, unutterably sad. Closer sounds – the rustle of bedclothes, the manic drumbeat of my pulse – were suddenly loud and invasive. Wanting distraction, I found myself remembering that moment on the verandah, Morgan's palm against my face, my breathless anticipation as he leaned towards me, and then the sting of disappointment as his lips grazed my brow.

Outside, an owl shrieked.

There was no point trying to sleep. My mind was buzzing, my limbs jittery. I reached for my water glass and took a swig, and then spied the manuscript Dad had given me the night before. Eager to dispel the aftertaste of my nightmare, I picked up the pile of papers and settled back against the pillows. Dad had titled his newest story *Fineflower and the Man of Shadows*. Within minutes, I had forgotten my dream and became submersed in the world of my father's story.

Marriage to the old King was not what Fineflower had expected. Before their wedding, he had been tolerant and fatherly, but lately he'd grown cold.

Fineflower stood at the window, rocking her son in her arms. Gazing down on the waves that crashed against the foot of the cliff below the castle, she sent her mind back, trying to pinpoint the beginning of the change. Six weeks ago, perhaps, when her son was born? Or the long lumbering months before the birth, when she had craved nothing but fish? She had barely seen the King in those days, caught up as he was with his imperial undertakings.

Then she remembered.

Market day. Three weeks earlier.

The day she had seen the soldier.

Her soldier, as she now thought of him. He had been standing on the edge of the crowd, so fine in his blue jacket with brass buttons and golden sash, his shiny black boots. His eyes had sharpened when he saw her glance his way and Fineflower thought she'd seen him smile. In surprise, she had smiled back—

Warmth flushed her cheeks.

Perhaps the King had observed the admiration on her face. Perhaps he'd seen the brightness in her eyes, noticed the subtle quickening of her breath. Perhaps he had even witnessed that fleeting smile. Fineflower pressed a kiss to her baby's forehead. Why should the King care? He was always preoccupied with important matters that he said were of no relevance to a woman. He rarely spoke to her, and then only to criticise.

Fineflower drew her shawl around her shoulders. The King had no right to be jealous. He had not minced his meaning when he said that Fineflower was a trophy wife, nothing more. A means to an end, a union between two kingdoms. A chattel.

She pinched her lips together. If anyone should be angry, it was her. She hadn't wanted to marry the elderly King. All she cared about back then was tending the roses in her garden. Her nostrils flared. How she craved the sweet heady scent of her blooms, but all she could smell was brine and the damp castle walls and the stink of rotting fish that wafted from the fishermen's cove below. She bent her head over her sleeping child and breathed his scent instead. The milky sweetness, a hint of cinnamon. Her agitation eased. The boy was all she cared about now. And perhaps—

Her thoughts flew back to the soldier. How handsome he'd been, how proud; a brave soldier with knowing eyes and a secretive smile. In another life, perhaps Fineflower would have chosen a man like that to wed. Then again, perhaps she would not. She did not believe in love. Giving away your heart was a dangerous thing. It made you weak. It made you do things, and think things, and worst of all *feel* things that were not at all sensible.

The dinner gong sounded.

Fineflower sighed and drew away from the window. Another dreary meal with the King. Another tedious night with his dull courtiers. Another night of nodding and smiling, of stifling her yawns, of daintily nibbling her modest portions of salad, while she longed to fill her grumbling stomach with fish and potatoes.

After placing her little prince in his cot under the watchful gaze of his nanny, she went downstairs. When she reached the dining hall, she was surprised to see the King sitting alone. His spotted old head rested in his hands and his bony shoulders shook. Muffled sobs echoed off the high walls. The piteous sight stirred Fineflower's heart.

'My lord,' she called from the doorway. 'Are you unwell?'

The King shot out of his chair, startled. He twisted around, his hawkish face shiny with tears. He stalked across the hall to where Fineflower stood, and grabbed her by the arm.

'Betray me, will you?' he cried. 'Wretched girl, you have broken my heart. I thought you were different, but I see now that you are cut from the same cloth as all the others.'

'Others?'

The King did not answer. He marched her through a doorway and into a shadowed corridor. They descended a flight of seemingly endless stairs, where torches shed feeble light. Water dripped from the walls, rats ran from their path, and the darkness echoed with the roar of waves below. The stairwell was cold, but the dungeon in the dark belly of the castle was colder.

'Here you'll stay,' the King told her, 'until you make the spindle leap and dance and fill this room with gold. If you succeed, I will grant any wish you desire. If you fail, I'll hang you from the rafters and drain your blood.'

The door slammed on her cell.

'What of my son?' she cried after the King, but he did not reply.

Fineflower gazed around in dismay. Moonlight wafted through a high little window, barely piercing the darkness. Nearby sat a spinning wheel. In the corner was a mountain of white cocoons. Looking closer, she saw millions of silk-worms, their pale bodies wriggling in the moonlight. Worms, around her feet, rustling in the straw mattress by the door, in the shadows – and there, lingering in the dank air, the faint fetid smell of mulberry leaves being slowly devoured.

As her eyes adjusted to the gloom, she noticed four figures beneath the window. They hovered just above the floor, swaying gently, as though in a breeze. With a jolt of terror, Fineflower understood the King's words.

I'll hang you from the rafters . . .

The figures turned out to be maidens of similar age to Fineflower. Their arms dangled limp at their sides. Shadows made thumbprints where their eyes should have been, and their faces glowed waxy pale, the skin bloodless. Their feet did not touch the ground, Fineflower saw, but moved slowly this way and that, this way and that. On the flagstone floor beneath their stained silk slippers, their shadows shifted restlessly.

Setting the manuscript aside, I climbed from the bed. The night seemed unnaturally black. The air pressed against my skin, large soft fingers of darkness that made me shiver.

My father's story had unsettled me, but I didn't understand why. It seemed familiar, like an echo from the past that I recognised but could not quite place. Grabbing cardigan and slippers, I wandered along the hall to the sunroom. The cat was asleep in his box, a mound of white fluff that began to purr when I kneeled to stroke his back.

Downstairs in the kitchen, I brewed coffee and took it outside. Silver clouds etched the sky. A full moon sailed overhead like a hazy penny. Beyond the trees that sheltered my temporary haven, the city of Melbourne rumbled through the early hours. A siren wailed in a distant street. Traffic mumbled along Dandenong Road. Bats twittered in the fig trees that grew along the fence and the smell of onions and late-night sausages sat greasily on the ocean air. I breathed deep, savouring the familiarity of these sounds and smells of home, surprised by the longing they inspired in me.

Crossing the garden, I let myself into an old timber shed. The front garage area housed my former pride and joy – a Volkswagen camper, classic green and white with a split windscreen and every mod con from the 1960s. The van had languished in Dad's garage for the last five years.

He swore he'd been unable to find a buyer, claiming that no one was splashing out, thanks to the recession. Secretly though, I suspected, he hoped my old van might eventually lure me home.

At the back of the shed was a room that the owner had converted into a painting studio. In anticipation of Dad's manuscript, I had brought the tools of my trade with me from London. Paintbrushes, several blocks of Arches water-colour paper, and a lovely old pottery water jar that Adam had given me. Dad had lent me copies of our books – twelve hardbacks to date, all written by him and illustrated by me. Six had won awards. I selected one and took it over to the big worktable, switching on the lamp.

My bright drawings tumbled across the page, spilling over the edges. Liquid ink, watercolour pencil, dots of gold leaf. The typesetting had a handwritten look about it, which suited the exuberance of the artwork. The finished illustra-tions appeared swiftly executed, but first impressions were deceptive. I had spent many hours sketching and re-sketching, erasing and sketching again until I deemed the illustration perfect. It was my way of making sense of my father's pande-monium of words. If I could not fully understand the man, then I would content myself with understanding that part of him he poured into his stories.

Years ago, Dad had rewritten the Rapunzel tale, only rather than a castle, the girl had been trapped beneath a lake. She had flung up her long hair like a fishing line to snare the unsuspecting Prince and pull him to her. My drawings for that one had been very dark, arising from my memories of the summer my mother drowned. I asked Dad about it later, and he explained that his Rapunzel had been a kind of therapy.

Writing stories is how I work through things I don't understand, he'd said. *Karen was everything to me, you know that, Lucy. When we lost her, I fell apart. The Rapunzel tale, probably the other stories too, was my way of keeping her alive.*

I thought of Mum with her regal height and large-boned frame. She had towered over Dad. *My little dumpling*, she had called him, at which he would pretend despair, but anyone could see how he adored her. It seemed impossible that a woman like her, invincible in my eyes and perfect in Dad's, had been taken from us so quickly. One wrong step on some slippery rocks was all it took to change our lives forever.

I sat at the drafting table, shivering in pyjamas and cardigan. The coffee was hot and sweet and quickly warmed me. For the next few hours, I escaped into the zone, surrendering myself to the swirls of jewel-bright inks and watercolour that flowed from my brush. The only sounds were the clink of my pens in the inkbottle, the whisper of paint washing across the paper, and from somewhere beyond the doorway the quiet drip of dew from the trees.

By the time the sun rose, I had done a day's work. Buckled sheets of watercolour paper littered the studio floor, ten full-colour sketches, created in a frenzy. But as I gazed at them, my heart sank. The images were good, that wasn't the problem. What depressed me was the figure they depicted.

In several, he held a cat. In others, he stood on a low brick wall staring out across the sea, his wild hair tugged by the wind. There was even one of him sitting in a dark garden surrounded by fairy lights and winter roses. And beside him – tiny and ghost-like, insubstantial – was a sad little figure in a red dress.

I tore that one up.

The others I collected and squashed into the bin. I felt no regret, just annoyance that I'd wasted so many hours, so much paper and ink and effort. Spending time with Morgan was a bad idea. Best to avoid him. Besides, I was only here for a few weeks. How hard would it be? Going back to the table, I took out a fresh sheet of Arches, swirled my brushes clean in the water jar, and tried to summon inspiration, but nothing came.

I stood up, suddenly cold. I'd been sitting too long. My joints were stiff, my hands and feet numb.

My failed drawings weighed on me. In them, I saw all my other failings: my fearfulness, my guilt . . . my habit of running away when the going got tough. I longed for security, yet also suffered from a horror of being trapped. No wonder my relationship was on the rocks.

Wedding jitters, Adam had called it back in London. *Cold feet*. 'It happens all the time,' he'd reassured me. 'Why don't we take a holiday in Spain, just the two of us, give those frosty little toes a chance to thaw out?'

But it was more than just nerves. A whole lot more.

I agreed with Fineflower, I realised. Giving away your heart *was* dangerous. I had tried it once, and my heart had ended up broken. The best way forward was not to let it happen again. Ever.

Dad's voice drifted back to me.

If you could have anything at all, what would it be?

As the morning sun glimmered over the horizon and turned the clouds to gold, a face came to mind, a man's face with light grey eyes and a quirky half-smile that made my pulse race. It was a face made rugged by time, etched with laughter lines, framed by windswept dark hair. A face I'd known so long, it was almost as familiar to me as my own.

Becoming the custodian of a stray tomcat had thrown out my plans. It was Saturday, which I'd been intending to spend with my grandfather. I had dialled his number countless times in the last week to alert him to my visit, but he wasn't answering. I was reluctant to show up out of the blue. He was in his nineties and a shock like that could be fatal. I decided to try ringing again in an hour. Meanwhile, there was a skinny, flea-bitten stray in urgent need of a makeover.

In the bathroom, I laid out towels, Betadine, eardrops from a quick visit to the vet, and tar soap. I ran tepid water and when the tub was a quarter full, I broke the bad news to the cat.

Surprisingly, he went into the bath with good grace. He squirmed and tried to make a dash for it when I brought out the soap, but then stood stoically as I lathered away the dirt and grime and blood from his matted fur. When I patted him dry with a fluffy towel, he lifted his luminous green gaze and looked right into my eyes. Then he began to purr.

The tips of his ears were in tatters, his delicate pink nose covered in scars. The fur had rubbed away around his neck, exposing the skin. Not a pretty boy, but my heart went out to him. It would take longer than four weeks to fatten him up and bring the lustre back to his coat, heal his wounds. But a month was all I had. After that, if I failed to find him a home, he would probably end up in a shelter.

I settled him in a patch of sunlight, but he wanted to shake himself and run about. His tail fluffed up, making me laugh, making me think of a fox's feathery tail.

'Basil,' I decided to call him. 'Basil Brush. What do you think?'

He ran into his cardboard box, but then reappeared a moment later, pink nose twitching. He wound himself around my ankles, tickling my shins with his whiskers.

'Basil it is,' I said softly, crouching to smooth my hand over his sleek head. Naming him was probably a bad idea, but under the circumstances, the dignity of a name was the least I could do for him.

Adam would say I was getting attached. He would shake his head and chuckle indulgently. Putty in my hands, an onlooker might think – but beneath his tousle-haired boyishness, Adam was all steel. He had to be, it was part of his job as an advocate for Amnesty. A job he excelled at; he worked tirelessly to raise money for people wrongly imprisoned – artists, writers, political activists. We had met at a charity dinner. Adam joked later that he'd paid the guest sitting next to me £50 to swap seats, and then set out to charm me with his most interesting stories. He needn't have bothered with the chair swapping or the stories. At first glance, I'd liked him. He had a strong, interesting face and sandy hair that refused to sit straight no matter how much he combed it. When he spoke about injustice, he had a way of punctuating his sentences with a sharp inhalation, almost a gasp, as though the words caused him actual physical pain.

In the two years since we'd met, we'd been mostly happy. The nightmares I'd suffered since childhood ebbed away. Adam's calm presence soothed my bouts of agitation. I had drifted along on the surface of my life, finally able to ignore the shadow-shapes that swarmed below in the depths. Adam proposed, and soon after that I moved into his Camden Town apartment. London was a beautiful labyrinth, especially with Adam at my side. I drifted through it as though in a dream. The hectic pace dazzled me, the constant stream of restaurants and charity dinners and theatre shows made my head spin. I was giddy with life, and I didn't want it to stop. It made me believe that my life as a surface dweller was real; it made me hope that, in his quiet way, Adam was my saviour.

That was, until my grandfather's letter.

I have something for you . . . It will explain everything.

Upstairs in the bedroom, I took out the charm he had tucked inside the envelope with his note. A gold heart the size of my thumbnail, dented on one side, its edges worn smooth. I had recognised it instantly as the charm from the bracelet he had once given my mother. A bracelet I'd fiercely coveted as a child. The same bracelet that Dad insisted went into the sea with her.

I weighed the small heart in my palm. It was as light as a leaf, almost insubstantial – but to me it felt heavy, leaden with guilt. I pushed it back into the envelope.

It will explain everything . . .

Soon after the letter arrived, cracks began to appear in my perfect world. Adam's presence was no longer quite so soothing; rather, he began to irk me. His long rambles about injustice and political freedom, his late nights on the phone or hunched over his desk drafting petitions and letters of appeal; the way he woke red-eyed in the morning barely able to string his words together until that first coffee.

Slowly, my nightmares trickled back. Cold fingers tugged me from sleep, and I woke drenched in sweat and tears, gagging on the smell of ocean air. Tired all the time, I found fault with Adam, picking arguments over trivial things. The shadow-shapes returned, resuming their gentle bump-bump below the surface. I threw myself into my work, but it didn't help. My heart felt full of holes, through which seeped all the darkness I'd been suppressing for years.

The doorbell rang, bringing me back to the present. 'Go away,' I muttered, sliding the envelope out of sight beside my bedside lamp. 'I'm busy.'

The bell buzzed again, and then someone hammered. I padded downstairs and yanked open the door.

Morgan stood there. His eyes were hollow and dark-circled, his jaw bristling with stubble.

'What's happened?' I said.

'Your father's had a fall. A broken hip, he's at the hospital.' He moved nearer and cupped my elbows, as though to steady me. 'Wilma said she tried to call. There was no answer so she asked me to come over.'

'A fall? How did he—' I broke off and frowned. 'He was drinking, wasn't he?'

Morgan nodded.

With a muttered curse, I ducked inside to get my wallet and car keys, my jacket from behind the door. After locking up, I pushed past Morgan and went to my van. I saw Morgan's old Harley propped near the gate, but wasn't surprised when he climbed into the passenger seat beside me. I started the motor before he'd even buckled up, and a couple of minutes later we were roaring along St Kilda Road towards the hospital.

I kept picturing Dad at the Astor the night before, his cheeks flushed from the cold, pleased about finishing his book. What could have turned his mood around so drastically? A broken hip was bad; that he'd been sozzled enough to fall over and break it was far worse. A memory came to me: Dad reeking of booze a few months after we lost Mum; armed with a baseball bat, he'd run out onto the street in front of our house and started taking swings at passing cars—

'What would send him over the brink like that?' I wondered aloud. 'He's been dry for fourteen years, not a drop in all that time. What could it be?'

'No idea, Luce.' Morgan stared through the windscreen. His face was serious, his eyes burning up the road ahead. 'But I expect we're about to find out.'

The city sped past. The chaos of rattling trams and buses and cars, the drifts of rubbish in the gutters and clouds of exhaust, the throngs clustered at pedestrian crossings, all seemed suddenly overwhelming. I clung to the steering wheel, my knuckles white, my arms rigid. Dad had promised. Fourteen years ago, he had made me a promise.

As far as I knew, he had kept it. Until now.

Suddenly the answer came to me. There was only one reason he would go back on his word, one reason he'd fall off the wagon. The same reason he had started drinking in the first place.

A face appeared in my mind's eye. A thin face, peering from the past. The skin pulled tight over prominent bones, the brow creased in permanent worry. The eyes so dark they seemed black, an animal's eyes, watching furtively as though a hunter lurked around every corner.

'Edwin,' I murmured, and the sound of his name, the sound of my grandfather's name, sent a chill prickling over my heart.

6

Bitterwood, May 1993

Once, he'd been tall, almost freakishly so. Now, time had bent him, buckled him into an old man who cared only for the company of shadows. He shuffled across his bedroom to the window and gazed out at the moonlight. It was time, he decided. He did not have long now, and it was time to cover his tracks.

Down in the kitchen, he rummaged through the utility drawer, found the matches, and then retrieved a jerry can of kerosene from under the sink. Outside, he went along the brick path, past the rearing house. Once, he had spent hours sweeping leaf litter from around the old barn. He had polished its windows and hung them with curtains, and kept it free of cobwebs and dust. Now, the place was little more than a storehouse for memories, overgrown and unkempt.

He hurried into the shadows of the orchard. The path ran downhill, beneath the cave-like overhang of mulberry trees. Their limbs were mostly bare; just a few stubborn leaves remained, rattling dryly in the night air. At the bottom of the orchard, he emerged into a shady clearing. A high grassy mound overlooked the clearing, shadowed by the remains of an enormous old oak tree. Two decades ago, lightning had struck and killed the tree. Each year since, Edwin had expected it to fall, but it never did. Perhaps it was waiting for him to go first.

He approached the mound and came to an overhang of ivy, which he pushed aside to reveal a heavy wooden door.

The door was three inches thick and reinforced with steel, specially designed to keep the cold in and the heat out. Behind the door, support beams bolstered a series of passageways that led to an underground icehouse.

In the early days, Bitterwood Park had been a thriving resort, attracting wealthy city people. During the summer months, trucks had transported enormous blocks of ice to Bitterwood, delivering them to the cool room inside the icehouse where they would store unmelted for many weeks. Edwin's mother had given him the job of ice boy. His task was to go along the passageways into the cool heart of the place where the ice slabs were stored. He would chip ice into his bucket and take it back to the house, to keep meat and other perishables chilled during the hot weather.

Jangling the keys from his pocket, he unlocked the door and went inside. Unscrewing the jerry can lid, he splashed kerosene around the support beams and onto some wooden shelving until the reeking fumes sent him back out into the open air. He shut the door behind him, locked it, and then pressed his ear against the wood. He thought he heard a murmur from the other side. It might have been a leaf scratching on the flagstones, stirred by a draft under the door. It might have been a sigh, a soft utterance. But of what? If she could speak to him now, what would she say? And what would he say to her? That he had once killed for love and in light of that, telling one small lie should have been nothing?

He hung his head. Some nights he stood here for an hour or more, perhaps quietly weeping, or just lost in the maze of his thoughts. Anything to prolong returning to the lonely hole of his life. Yet tonight he must not linger. He wanted the sanctuary of his room, where the sound of his heartbeat would echo on the walls. He wanted to hide beneath his pillow while the past caught alight and burned.

He struck a match. It flared brightly in the darkness. The flame seemed alive, eager to leap and spread, impatient to sizzle. He drew it to his lips, savoured the tiny barb of heat against his skin.

The human heart was a dim, unwholesome place. Clarice had taught him that. Like the small flame dancing on its match-head, his passions had led him through the secret unlit chambers of his own heart. There he'd forged a path through darkness that at times seemed impenetrable. He had navigated poorly, for the most part. Let others dictate to him, permitted the gradual erosion of those fragments of himself that had once been decent.

The match went out, so he struck another. This time he didn't hesitate. He released the match from his trembling fingers, caught his breath as it hit the edge of the kerosene trail he'd splashed under the door. The flame guttered and almost went out, but then whooshed suddenly as the kerosene caught alight.

His pulse hammered unsteadily, his legs turned to water. He went to stumble away, but something kept him. He did not press his ear to the door this time, only bowed his head before it as if in prayer. On the other side, he heard the roar of fire.

'Forgiveness,' he whispered. 'That's all I ask.'

He hadn't expected a reply, of course. So when a branch creaked in the old dead oak above him, he flinched. Probably an owl or nightjar alighting on a bough, but when it hooted suddenly – a soft and eerie sound that pricked gooseflesh across his naked skull – he would have sworn on his mother's Bible that somewhere in the darkness behind him, a woman was quietly sobbing.

7

Victorian coast, 1929

Laughter invaded her dreams. Strange, harsh laughter. The sound rose in a squawking frenzy, crested to a high note, and then dropped away to a lazy *haw-haw*, as if the joke had finally worn thin.

Orah burrowed back into sleep. The ground began to pitch beneath her. The wind lashed the waves into frothy peaks. Cries shattered the night as the great ship swung onto the rocks and its underbelly tore away. The water was so terribly cold. Mam's face was pale and bleeding, her eyes big pools of fear. When the black water took her, she cried out—

Orah . . . Orah!

Orah lurched upright. She lay in a small shelter made of branches and sticks, covered by a thin blanket. Beyond the shelter was a clearing surrounded by thick bushes and ferns. She could still hear the ocean, but its

62

roar seemed distant, as though muffled by the densely growing trees.

A few feet away, a fire crackled. Plumes of smoke drifted on the air. A breeze brought the smell of roasting meat unlike anything Orah had known before, rich and dark, strange. Her stomach rumbled. She hadn't had a bite to eat in what felt like days. Bread and mutton, and sweet tea from tin cups that Mam had begged from the galley—

Mam.

Desolation washed over her. She had the urge to smash her hands on her legs and bruise the skin, to claw her neck and draw blood. Her eyes streamed and stung, and when she dashed her hands to her face, a swirling giddiness overtook her. Rolling onto her side, she retched. A trickle of seawater puddled on the dirt.

Oh, Mam. No.

She couldn't be gone. Orah needed her. Needed her so badly that her brain and body ached. She balled her fists to strike herself, this time for certain, but something stopped her.

Perhaps she was wrong. Perhaps the ocean hadn't swallowed Mam after all. Someone might have rescued her, just as the boy had rescued Orah; or perhaps the current had washed Mam ashore. Perhaps Mam was sitting, at this very minute, safe and dry in her own rough shelter, wondering what had become of her daughter.

Orah wiped her face on the blanket, drew her knees to her chest. It was easier to think of Mam that way. Sitting on the beach beneath a shady tree, gazing along the sand, pondering her lucky escape. It was easier to picture her alive, her fair hair drying in the sun, curling at the tips as she wrung out the salt water and raked the strands with her fingers. Waiting patiently for help to find her. Waiting for her girl.

Orah let out a breath. Once she found Pa, she would tell him about that beach. They'd return there and find Mam. Mam would catch sight of them and wave happily. She would run up and sweep Orah into her arms, weeping for joy. They would take her back to Pa's house in Melbourne, and feed her cake and cups of sweet tea. They would celebrate Christmas together, the three of them reunited at last. They would be a family again, just as Orah had always dreamed.

Rubbing her eyes, she looked beyond her shelter. The sun was high. Birds whistled and chirped. The sound of laughter came again, but it was distant, as if the merrymakers had drifted away. Orah was glad. Laughter was supposed to be a happy sound, but something about that noise hollowed her out, made her afraid.

Near the campfire sat a tent-like construction of sticks over which her sodden dress and petticoats hung to dry. She realised she wore only her undergarments, still clinging damply to her body.

The boy approached with an armload of wood.

Orah watched him, her eyes growing large. He had saved her from the water, risked his life for her; he had walked beside her for miles, never letting go of her hand . . . but now she saw him as though for the first time. He was beautiful, brown-skinned with wind-shocked hair and liquid dark eyes. He wore shorts and a grey shirt. His feet were bare. When he looked at her, Orah felt her heart beat a little faster.

'Are you all right?' he asked.

She nodded.

He threw down his bundle and crouched to tend the fire. 'Sleep a bit more. Later, we'll eat.'

Orah opened her mouth to tell him about her plan to find Pa, and about Mam waiting back at the beach. She wanted to ask him to bring her dress and petticoats, even though they were still damp. It occurred to her, as her stomach growled again, to enquire about the delicious smell drifting on the air, but forming the words seemed too much effort. The fire blazed, warming her. Her eyelids grew heavy.

'I heard someone laughing,' she murmured sleepily.

'Just birds,' she heard the boy say, as though from far off.

She frowned. No bird could make such a sound. Perhaps the boy had misunderstood. She tried to gather the will to argue, but instead felt her eyes sink shut. She would rest, she decided. Just for a moment. Just until her strength returned. Taking one last look at the boy, satisfied he was near, she dragged the rough blanket back up over her and settled on the grass bed, quickly sinking into sleep.

She woke at intervals through the day, eating morsels of food the boy brought her, drinking the water he provided, but mostly escaping into an uneasy listlessness. Strange half-dreams washed around her. One moment she felt the giddy rise and fall of waves, and heard the cries of people drowning. But then a sense of calm took hold. There was just the crackle of the fire, and the wind in the trees. Eventually, night came. With a sigh, she let herself slip down into the soft leaf-scented darkness.

In her dream, her parents were arguing. Their angry words drifted up the stairs and along the hall to Orah's room, finding her ears despite her retreat beneath the covers.

It's everything I have, Mam said. *I'll not let you take it all.*

Pa rumbled, *I'm not asking for your last penny. Simply enough money to get me across the sea to the colonies and set me up for a few months until I make my fortune. The boys on the docks, even the sailors, they're all talking about Australia. It's the place to be. There's wealth beyond imagining, gold under every clump of earth, all free for the taking.*

What rot, Hanley, Mam said. *Your mind's been addled by talk. I'll not have it, do you hear? I'll not have you taking every cent of our savings and frittering it away on a dream.*

Their voices grew quiet, and then stopped. An exhausted silence settled on the house. Orah didn't want her father to leave. She didn't want him to travel to another land, chasing a dream. Yet she couldn't stop her heart from racing as she remembered his words.

Wealth beyond imagining, gold under every clump, all free for the taking.

The voices started up again. This time they didn't belong to her parents. They were strange musical voices. Whispering urgently, close to her ear.

'Wake up. Quickly, we have to go.'

Someone was shaking her, pulling her upright. Lurching from her dream, she flailed about, fearing the dark ocean waves had claimed her once more. Tiny bright stars still glittered in the sky, but daylight was edging up over the horizon, slowly invading the darkness. In the gloom, two young faces watched her.

'Come on,' the boy said, taking her hand. 'Don't make a sound.'

He hauled her to her feet, leading her away from the camp and into the trees. She trudged beside him, irritable after her dream, still groggy from sleep. So thirsty, her tongue glued itself to the roof of her mouth. She looked back over her shoulder. The girl collected Orah's clothes and blanket, kicked earth into the fire pit, and then ran after them.

'Hurry,' the boy said, tugging Orah's hand.

Behind them in the dark, a horse whinnied. A man's voice rang out, calling to someone. Orah glanced over her shoulder, and into her mind flashed her father's ruddy face.

'Pa!' she yelled, trying to twist out of the boy's grip. 'Over here, Pa!'

A deafening report split the silence, the night seemed to explode. Strong fingers clamped over her mouth. The boy pulled her after him into the bushes, and held her steady against a tree trunk.

'That was gunfire,' the girl whispered. 'Old Mister's feelin' nasty tonight.'

For a hushed eternity, they crouched in the bushy shadows, listening. The clop of horses' hooves and the quiet call of male voices drifted nearer, but then the noises faded away. Finally, they disappeared.

The girl tugged Orah to her feet and they stumbled away through the dark. After a while, she gave Orah's hand a gentle squeeze. 'No more funny business,' she warned. 'Those fellas aren't who you think they are. If they catch us, we're in strife.'

As the sun rose, Orah sat in a patch of sunlight watching him. He was crouched by the fire he had built, feeding sticks into the flames. Wisps of smoke drifted up to the sky.

She had thought him her age, but now saw he was a year or so older. A faint shadow darkened his jaw and upper lip, and he moved about with confidence. When he glanced over, she did not smile and he offered none of his own, but Orah sensed a silent conversation unfolding between them. As long as he was near, she would be safe; somehow, he knew this, and his frequent glances held reassurance.

The fire died down. Still Orah sat, watching.

When the boy got up to collect a handful of leaves, she followed him with her eyes. When he went behind a clump of bushes and out of her sight, she got up and stood where she could see him. His dark hair had dried into corkscrew curls, and Orah remembered the softness of it against her face as she'd clung to him in the water.

He returned to the fire, and Orah went back to her patch of sunlight. The boy rummaged in a canvas sack and took out a bag of flour, which he emptied into a pannikin. He added water and kneaded the mixture with his fingers. Rolling the dough into a clump, he laid it on a flat stone at the edge of the fire. He cleaned the pannikin with dirt, pulled a rag from his pocket and dusted it out, then carefully filled it with water from a flask. He positioned the pan over the glowing embers, and then glanced at Orah.

Orah burrowed into her blanket.

Her head spun. Their run through the bush had left her feet bruised and bloodied. Insect bites covered her legs, and her pale skin stung from the sun. She wished she were back in the quiet stillness of her bedroom in Glasgow, with Mam in the kitchen, cooking breakfast. There would be porridge bubbling on the hearth, and the smell of lanoline from the newly spun wool, and the spicy aromas of indigo and woad dye lingering in the warm air.

She shut her eyes. The earth pitched and rolled beneath her, one moment lifting her to the clouds, the next dragging her down into a dark trough. She smelled the salty panic of her body, heard her mother's last cry as the ocean dragged her under—

Orah blinked and saw the girl standing before her. Up close, she looked to be Orah's age, twelve or thirteen. She wore a shapeless dress of blue homespun, and her feet were bare and dusty. Her hair fell to her jawline, kinked with soft waves, streaked with tawny lights where the sun had touched it. Her eyes were dark and kind, and freckles danced across her brown skin. In her arms was a bundle of clothes – Orah's clothes, dry and fragrant with sunlight.

'Feelin' better?' the girl asked, placing the bundle on the blanket.

Orah reached for her clothes with a murmur of thanks, but then fumbled when she tried to pull them on.

'I'm Nala,' the girl said. She picked up Orah's petticoat and shook it out, then held it against herself, as if taking its measure. 'I was on the beach, remember?'

Orah nodded.

Nala handed Orah the petticoat and helped her slip into it. She pulled the skirt over Orah's head, brushing her fingers over the creases, and then buttoned it into place. 'You nearly drowned,' she said gravely. 'Warra saw you in the water. You were lucky.'

Orah looked across at the boy. He was kneeling beside the fire, prodding the embers with a stick. The bread he'd made was scorched on one side but golden on the other. He broke it into three pieces and set it on a flat rock to cool. A delicious doughy fragrance wafted on the air.

Nala helped Orah into her blouse, brushing out the wrinkles as she'd done with the skirt, and picked a grass stalk off the sleeve.

'What's your name?' she asked.

'Orah.'

Nala beamed. 'That's pretty. What's it mean?'

'Mean?'

'All names mean somethin'. I got mine 'cause Mum said I sounded like a grass wren, always chattering.'

Despite the gloom in Orah's heart, she felt the beginnings of a smile. 'I don't know what my name means, but I'm glad you like it.'

From where he crouched near the fire, Warra called a string of quick, musical words to his sister. Nala went to him, and returned to Orah with a plate of food. Bread, an enormous lump of roasted root vegetable caramelised by the fire, and some charred leaves that were fat and succulent. Nala and Warra settled nearby on a log with their own plates. They ate in silence. The bread was crusty and good. The vegetable was similar to potato only sweeter. The leaves burst like grapes and filled Orah's mouth with fresh tartness. When the last morsel was gone, she sat back. Her face burned from the heat of the fire, and a deep bone-weariness crept over her.

A hush settled on the day. The birds fell silent. There

was just the pop and crack of the embers and a soft clatter as Nala collected their plates.

'I thought I heard my father's voice last night,' Orah said suddenly. 'That's why I cried out.'

Warra frowned. 'Was he on the ship?'

Orah told them, haltingly at first, but then in a breathless rush, everything that had happened to bring her here. When she got to the part about Mam she hung her head, embarrassed by her tears.

Nala nestled beside her, her skinny arm sliding around Orah's shoulders. 'Poor thing, you miss your mum.'

Orah hadn't wanted sympathy. She hadn't meant to cry. By nature, she was a foot stomper, a shouter, a puller of grim faces. She had used all manner of tantrums to get her own way with Mam in the past. Yet never tears.

Nala continued to croon and pat Orah's arm. After a while, her murmured reassurances began to take effect. The fire dried away Orah's tears. She let out a hiccup, and then took a breath.

'I have to find my father,' she said. 'He lives in Melbourne.'

Warra studied her, his brows creased. 'You better ask Mr Briar.'

'Mr Briar's our boss,' Nala clarified. 'He runs a guesthouse with his wife. Warra and me work there. I cook and help clean the guest rooms, and Warra does the outside chores. Bitterwood, it's called. A good place. They're kind people, the Briars. They'll help you find your dad.'

Orah's spirits lifted. Warra went to the fire and returned with a tin cup, which he placed in her hands.

'Thank you, Warra,' she said quietly.

His eyes held hers, and the corners of his lips twitched. Not quite a smile, but it came close enough. Orah hid her blush in the cup, blowing on the tea. Steam rose off the green liquid, but it didn't smell like any tea Orah recognised.

'Emu-bush tea,' Warra told her.

She sipped, then made a face and pushed the cup back at him.

'Drink,' he said. 'You'll feel better.'

There was such kindness in his voice that she did as he said, almost without thinking. The hot liquid burned all the way down, then sat warm in her belly.

'Who was following us last night?'

'Old Mister,' Warra said.

'Mister Burke.' Nala pulled a sour face. 'He reckons all this land belongs to him. Says he don't want us crossing it, that we got no business here. But our family lives up there.' She twisted around and pointed back the way they had come, to a line of distant hills. 'Two days' walk from Bitterwood. Mrs Briar lets us go home every couple of months. We stay a few days with Mum and our aunties, and then walk back.'

'We walk along the beach, mostly,' Warra added. 'Then we cut across Old Mister's land. He don't like it, but it's quicker.'

'Lucky for you,' Nala added quietly, squeezing Orah's hand. 'When that storm came the other night, we were on the headland. We took shelter in a cave. Early next morning, Warra went to find dry wood to build fire. That's when he saw you.'

Warra took her empty cup. He looked at her, his pupils shining like black glass. 'Rest again now. You'll feel better after a sleep.'

Orah wanted to stay awake, talk more to Warra and Nala, but she was suddenly yawning, unable to keep her eyes open, as though her body was obeying Warra's soft command. Warmth flooded her toes and fingers, her feet and legs. She looked over at Warra, who had returned to the fire. He saw her looking, and once again almost smiled. This time Orah smiled back. Then, reassured by the crackle of flames, and secure in the nearness of the boy who had saved her, she nestled back under her blanket.

8

Melbourne, June 1993

D ad was sleeping when we arrived. Tucked tightly into the hospital bed, frail and deflated, a different the man to the one I'd laughed and chatted with at the movies the night before. He stirred as the door whispered shut behind us, but seemed unable to keep his eyes open.

'It's the painkillers,' Wilma explained. She huddled at the bedside, clutching my father's hand. Her dark curls were unbrushed, fraying around her pale face.

I took the chair on the other side of the bed. Dad's fingers felt clammy. I chafed his hand between my own, but his skin refused to warm.

'He's cold,' I told Wilma.

Morgan brought over a blanket and helped us tuck it around my father. Dad's skin was waxy, pasty white but for twin heat spots on his cheekbones. He stirred again, but quickly sank back into a doze. Wilma settled back at the bedside, clasping Dad's hand again between her own. Her lips began to move. She'd never been religious. If she worshipped anyone, it was Dad. I guessed she was silently talking to him, encouraging him to rest well, to heal.

They'd been together for thirteen years. Wilma was a psychologist at Banksia House in Melbourne when Dad was admitted there after his breakdown. All his life he had struggled with depression, which had contributed to his addiction to booze. When Karen died, he'd been lost. He spent six months in Wilma's care, detoxing and learning how to deal with his grief. When he left the institution, they stayed in touch for a few years. Letters, phone calls, occasional catch-ups. Dad liked to say theirs was a great friendship that bloomed into love. As a happy side effect, Dad's episodes of depression became less frequent, less intense. In the past few years, he had stopped his medication, managing his illness with yoga and organic food. Wilma could be sharp-tongued with lesser mortals – namely me – but she was Dad's guardian angel.

Today she wore no make-up, and I realised I'd never seen her without it before. Her face was round, patterned with delicate lines, her eyes soft blue. Without the strong lipstick and dramatic eyeliner, she seemed younger, almost vulnerable.

'Wilma,' I whispered. 'You look tired. Have you eaten?'

She shook her head. 'I'm all right, Lucy. My only concern at the moment is Ron.'

Morgan slipped out the door, leaving us alone.

'Dad was fine last night,' I said. 'What happened?'

Wilma untucked a hanky from her sleeve and blotted her

cheeks. 'I woke this morning and found him on the bathroom floor. He was groggy, disorientated, couldn't remember what had happened. I called the ambulance straightaway, despite his objections. At first I thought he'd just fallen, hit his head. He didn't say anything, just gripped my hand. His fingers were like a vice – he must've been in dreadful pain. It was only after the X-rays that I learned about his hip.'

Morgan returned with sandwiches and three cups of coffee. Wilma hunched over her coffee, taking quick little sips until she'd finished. I took it from her fingers, and then passed her mine. We liked it the same, lots of milk and sugar. She drank that too, and accepted one of the soggy kiosk sandwiches Morgan apologetically offered.

Once she'd eaten, she seemed brighter. Reaching into the bag slung over the back of her chair, she withdrew a crumpled letter.

'It's from your grandfather's solicitor,' she said quietly. 'Ron forgets to check the mailbox, and it was among the pile I left on the table for him last night. I found it this morning, crushed on the bathroom floor. I presume it's the reason he . . . he was upset.'

Her fingers trembled as she passed the letter across the bed to me.

I took it, but my eyes were suddenly swimming. It had to be shock setting in, the fright of my father's accident. Fear, perhaps, that Edwin had written to my father after all, told him that he had contacted me and sent me my mother's gold charm . . .

Morgan took the document from my fingers, scanned the contents and read it aloud. '". . . regret to inform you of the death of Edwin Albert Briar of Bitterwood Park in Stern Bay. I'm under instruction to tell you that the deceased has left his estate in its entirety to you, Ronald Gordon Briar. Please call this office and make an appointment to discuss probate at your earliest convenience . . .'"

I looked bleakly at Morgan.

He passed the letter back. 'Sorry, love.'

A sense of unreality washed over me. I waited for the grief, for shock, but none came. In truth, I wasn't entirely sure what I should be feeling. My mother's death in 1977 had torn apart the already fragile relationship Dad had with Edwin. After that, we never mentioned my grandfather's name; it was an unspoken law between us. I'd never really understood the animosity between Dad and Edwin, only that their grievance had its roots in a row they'd had when my father was a teenager. Their falling-out had sent Dad running from his family home, not to return for almost thirty years.

I stared at the solicitor's letter in my hand. Edwin was gone. Whatever explanation he had meant to give me was gone too. Now I would never know how he had come to possess my mother's gold charm. I'd never know why, after years of silence between us, he had suddenly wanted to see me.

'Mad old buzzard,' Dad murmured, and then opened his eyes, looking blearily around at us. 'I've been here all along, you realise, listening in.'

I scrambled to my feet, the letter forgotten. I pressed my forehead to his, breathing him in. The whiff of antiseptic brought a lump to my throat. There had been a time when my father smelled of wonderful things: ink and old paper, dusty books and binding leather, candle wax and polished wood. Calming smells that even now, in the sterile hospital room, stirred in my memory.

I had intended to scold him for scaring us, for turning to the bottle when he should have confided in Wilma or me or Morgan, but my words got tangled somewhere between my brain and my lips.

'Oh, Dad,' I whispered. 'I was so worried.'

'Sorry about that, kiddo.'

He held my gaze, his eyes suddenly intense. I suspected his apology was less about worrying me and more to do with breaking his long-standing promise.

'You got a shock,' I said, remembering the letter crushed in my hand. 'No wonder you were upset.'

Dad eyed the crumpled letter.

'It was unexpected,' he said hoarsely. 'Edwin and I hadn't spoken in years, not since we lost Karen. I'm not surprised he's dead, living in that damp place by himself. He was in his nineties, you know.' He cleared his throat, and shot a glance at Wilma. She nodded, and Dad looked back at me. 'Lucy, there's something I need you to do.'

I nodded. 'I'll ring the solicitor on Monday morning, see if I can get an appointment—'

'Wilma can take care of that side of things. The favour I want from you is, unfortunately, a little bigger.'

I leaned closer. 'Anything.'

'Once probate goes through, Edwin's guesthouse will need to be sold. The furniture is straightforward, the auction house can see to that. But the household goods – Edwin's

papers and personal items will need boxing and label-
ling, sorting through. Lucy, I need you to take care of it
for me.'

I hesitated. Heat rushed to my cheeks, but the rest of my
body turned cold. Carefully I folded the letter I still held,
and kept folding until it resembled an origami failure. I
barely noticed when Morgan took it from my fingers and
passed it back to Wilma.

'Sort Edwin's things?' I said in a small voice.

Dad nodded.

My chair creaked as I shifted my weight. Despite the
intrigue of my grandfather's letter, I had been dreading my
visit to Bitterwood. Now, with Edwin gone, the prospect
of returning to his drafty rabbit warren of a guesthouse
alone was suddenly daunting. 'Could the auction place deal
with it? Or a company that specialises in clearing deceased
estates? They do everything these days. I'm sure they'd
gladly take on the guesthouse and ship everything off to
the auctioneers.'

Wilma leaned forward. 'Lower your voice, Lucy. You're
in a hospital.'

I sighed. 'It's a big job.'

'Ah, Lucy,' Dad said. 'I'd have tackled it myself, if it
weren't for my blasted hip. And once I'm out of hospital,
I'll need Wilma at home with me. There's no need to wait
for probate. I already have the keys. You can go down this
weekend, get it over with.'

I was clutching at straws. 'Is that even legal?'

'Bitterwood was my home once. As far as I'm concerned,
probate's just a formality. Besides, I want to put Edwin

behind me. The only way to do that is to sell the old place as quickly as possible.'

My palms were damp. I opened my mouth to argue further, but from the corner of my eye I saw Wilma shake her head.

'Anyway,' Dad went on, sounding tired. 'There's something I want, something Edwin has hidden away. I need you to find it for me.'

I sat back heavily in my chair. Before today, Dad had never asked anything of me. There had been a time – so long ago now that it shimmered in my memory like a half-remembered fairytale – when my father's clear voice had led a little lost girl through the darkness and back out into the light. A whisper from one of his stories had given me hope, promised me that the weak ones could fight back and become strong. Then I remembered the gold charm that had once hung from my mother's bracelet, and Edwin's letter claiming he had something for me, something that would explain everything . . . whatever *everything* meant. Perhaps there were answers for me at Bitterwood, after all.

'What do you want me to find?'

Dad looked relieved. He accepted the glass of water Wilma offered, took a long swallow, and wiped his lips with the back of his hand.

'There's a photo album. Bound in black leather, with a crest on the spine. It's full of old family snapshots. Your Grandma Dulcie gave it to me before she died, but Edwin took it, insisting that it wasn't hers to give. Over the years I offered to have copies made, but Edwin guarded it like a hawk.' Dad reached for my hand. His grip was so firm it almost hurt. He caught my gaze and held it. 'Now that he's gone,' he added in a ragged whisper, 'I want it back.'

'Velocity is what you need right now, Luce.' Morgan crossed the yard to his Harley. 'It always clears my head. What do you say?'

I wandered after him in a daze. Just now, driving home from the hospital, I kept flashing back to Dad's drunken bouts and eventual breakdown. I understood that losing Mum all those years ago had sent him over the brink, and that getting sober again had been a long struggle. What I couldn't fathom was his apparent devastation over the death of a man he claimed to despise. A man he had shunned most of his life.

I looked at Morgan. If I asked, he would draw me against him and hug me tight, pat my back, comfort me the way I had seen him comfort Coby growing up. Bad idea. I needed to clear the fog of emotion from my head, not muddle it further.

'A ride sounds perfect.'

Morgan gave my shoulder a gentle squeeze. 'He'll be all right, you know.'

I nodded, but I didn't know. Not really.

Morgan helped me settle the bike helmet over my head, and then buckled it under my chin. I adjusted the strap and snapped down my visor. The outside world dulled. I felt trapped inside the bubble of my helmet, my thoughts noisy. My father's hip would heal. What worried me most was his relapse into drinking. As I'd kissed him goodbye at the hospital, he'd promised that his bender had been a one-off and wouldn't happen again. Despite his assurance, my old fears resurfaced. Dad had made promises before, and I had watched him break them one after the other, watched him slide back into his old drinking habits. *Alcohol will kill him eventually*, one of the Banksia House doctors had warned, *unless he deals with the issues fuelling his addiction.*

'All right, Lucy?' Morgan wanted to know.

'Sure. Let's go.'

Morgan fitted his own helmet and straddled the bike. I climbed on after him, locking my arms around his waist. In the old days, before I'd revealed my feelings for him, we had done this hundreds of times. According to Morgan, a fast bike ride was the cure for anything. Failed exams, quarrels with my father, high school dance jitters.

The ignition rumbled and Morgan nudged the throttle. The bike veered out of my driveway and onto the road. Morgan's back was warm through his coat and the intoxicating scent of him enveloped me: motor oil, warm leather, and a hint of fresh sweat. It made me cling tighter, made me wish, just for a moment, that things between us had turned out differently.

Hennessy Avenue disappeared behind us. We rode down Dickens Street and then along Mitford, weaving through the heart of St Kilda before turning onto Beaconsfield Parade. When the traffic lights were behind us, Morgan increased the throttle and the powerful bike surged forward.

The wind blowing from the bay was icy. Morgan shivered. My own body responded, but whether from cold or Morgan's proximity, I couldn't be sure. His muscles flexed as he manoeuvred through the traffic, my hands warm around him despite the freezing wind. A car horn blared as we sped past. Suddenly I was fifteen again, under the spell of the rush, the dizzying thrill of the ride, my heart pounding in time to the Harley's pulsing engine, my mind free. The sea air flushed away the chemical hospital smells; I forgot to worry about my father, forgot the surreal half-sorrow of my grandfather's death. All I knew in that moment was the intoxication of travelling so fast that my breath caught in my throat.

And Morgan. Rock solid Morgan, his muscles rigid as the Harley crept over the speed limit, as he leaned into the curves. As he sped me away from the chaos of the city and out along the open stretch of beach road.

A while later we pulled onto a gravel verge opposite the old Seamen's Mission building. Waves lapped a tiny beach below us, and a little pier jutted out across the grey water.

I got off the bike and removed my helmet. Morgan unbuckled his chinstrap, pulled off his own helmet and then raked his fingers through his flattened hair. We stood that way, me breathless, Morgan gallant and intense as he regarded me.

'Better?' he asked.

'Thanks. I needed that fresh air after the hospital.'

'A ride never fails to clear my head,' he agreed. He weighed his helmet in his hand and then wedged it against the bike seat, did the same with mine. As we walked to the end of the pier, he added, 'By the way, I'm coming with you. To Bitterwood, I mean.'

I stared at him. 'What? No.'

'You don't have to do it alone.'

I shook my head remembering my vow to avoid him. Today didn't count – Dad's fall and the news about Edwin had shaken me . . . but my promise to myself still stood. 'I don't need your help clearing the place.'

He caught my gaze. 'I'm not talking about packing up your grandfather's belongings. The last time you were at Bitterwood, you rang me to collect you. I thought it was about your mum, but it wasn't, was it? When Gwen and I picked you up, you were more distressed than I'd ever seen you. But you refused to tell us what had happened.'

'I got spooked. That's all.'

Morgan frowned. The afternoon sun caught the ginger in his stubble, turned his grey eyes almost blue. 'I've never seen a kid look more haunted.'

'I'm not a kid anymore, Morgan.'

He shifted closer and smiled almost grudgingly, a crooked smile that parted his lips and made him look suddenly boyish.

'So I see.'

Heat rose to my face. I turned to look back along the pier to the mission across the road. Bare paddocks surrounded the old building and a few straggly gum trees did their best to shelter its art deco lines from the wind. The chapel's stained-glass windows gleamed in the sunlight, several broken panes hinting at the empty darkness within.

'Besides,' I went on, 'I need to focus on finding Dad's album.'

Morgan laughed softly. 'I promise I won't distract you.'

I glared at him. 'Thanks all the same, but I'd rather do it alone.'

He nodded, and then asked, 'Why do you think Ron's so keen to retrieve this album? It's not like him to be sentimental. He and Edwin weren't close.'

'It's probably just a bunch of old family shots,' I agreed. 'Nothing to get excited about.' I shrugged for good measure, hoping Morgan hadn't heard the flutter in my voice.

Photos. No big deal. Most people had them. Most people . . . but not *us*. Of course, we had plenty from when Mum was alive. Holiday snapshots at our beachside cottage near Bitterwood, and endless childhood Polaroids of me with my parents. But there were few of other relatives. My mother had lost all her family photos in a flood, while Dad had only a shoebox of loose pictures, mostly of Grandma Dulcie and himself as a little boy. The prospect of poring through an old family album made my pulse fly. Especially one my grandfather had been so reluctant to part with. Had he kept it from my father out of spite, or because there were photos in it he didn't want Dad to see?

Besides, the old man might have left something for me at the house. A package with my name scrawled on it, perhaps. A letter in his spidery handwriting, enclosing the answers he'd promised. Or even just a note explaining how he had come to possess my mother's charm, when it should have been lost in the sea.

Morgan shifted closer. 'It'll take forever on your own.'

I pulled my gaze back to him. 'I'll be fine.'

He lifted an eyebrow. 'I expect you will. That's the thing about you, Lucy. When you really want something, you don't let fear stand in your way of getting it.'

He turned his attention to the horizon, squinting into the brightness. Far away in the distance, the ghostly silhouette of an ocean liner nudged across the edge of the world. It looked so peaceful, so intent on its journey. A tiny fleck of grey moving across the vast ocean, unaware of the shadow-shapes that bumped through the deep waters below.

I rubbed my arms. The idea of returning to Bitterwood was suddenly a mixed bag. I was burning to find the album, and possibly discover links to the past. My father's past and my own. Perhaps even a link to my mother's past, as well. At the same time, the thought of searching my grandfather's gloomy old guesthouse gave me the shivers. Morgan was right to suspect that something had once happened to me there. I told him I'd been spooked, but it was more than that. Much more.

His words lingered in my mind. *When you really want something.* And I *did* want this, I realised. I wanted to know why Edwin had sent me the charm, why he had insisted I visit. I wanted the explanation he'd promised. Mostly, though, I sensed that returning to Bitterwood might some-how help me close a chapter of my life that I'd been trying to outrun for the past sixteen years.

At my request, Morgan dropped me off in Acland Street outside a vintage clothing shop. I hesitated in front of the window. Behind my reflection – fair hair pulled back, frown lines, wide worried eyes – was a display of antique sewing machines arranged among gorgeous handmade dresses. I had a flash of a dark-haired girl bent over her latest creation, stitching late into the night, and me sitting nearby reading to her from a magazine, the two of us laughing. The memory made me yearn for those simpler times. The past and present, I thought, each unable to exist without the other. At that moment, London seemed dreamlike, while Melbourne, with its wintry sea air and rattling trams, its echoes of another life, was suddenly very real.

Taking a breath, I opened the shop door.

A bell tinkled as I went inside. Nina looked up from the counter. She had plaited her dark hair back from her face, and her cheeks were pink from the heater burning nearby. Rushing over, Nina gathered me in a bear hug.

'I'm sorry about your grandad,' she whispered against my cheek. 'And poor Ron. Is there anything I can do?'

'All under control. But curry night's off, I'm afraid.'

'Coby'll be disappointed. He was looking forward to seeing you. He felt like a goon for not coming over to say hello last night.'

'Are we okay, then? The three of us, I mean.'

She sighed. 'You know what Coby's like. He took it hard when you left. He had a massive crush, but that wasn't what hurt him. You're his family, he felt abandoned. But he loves you, Lucy. We both do. We miss having you in our lives.'

I bit my lips to stop the sudden tremble. 'I didn't mean to hurt him. I didn't mean to hurt any of you, I was just . . .'

'You had a few things to sort out.' She gave my arm a squeeze. 'Nothing wrong with that. Besides, now that you're back you'll have to put up with me using every trick in the book to keep you here permanently.'

I smiled. 'Dad wants me to clear out Edwin's guesthouse. I'm leaving in the morning.'

Nina's brow wrinkled. 'By yourself?'

'I work better that way.'

'Ask Morgan to go with you. He's been chirpier since you got back.'

I ignored the last bit. 'I'll be fine.'

'He's good in a crisis.'

I almost laughed. 'It's not a crisis, just a clean-up.'

'It's a huge job!'

'It'll keep me busy for the next week or so. Take my mind off . . .' I stalled, realising my blunder.

Nina's eyes sharpened. 'Take your mind off what?'

'Oh, you know.' I shrugged, trying to sound offhand. 'Wedding jitters.'

Her smile fell away. Taking my hand, she dragged me towards the back of the shop. Pushing me onto an over-stuffed lounge, she settled beside me.

'Come on, Bub,' she said in a low voice, 'spill the beans.'

The old nickname made me smile. 'What do you mean?'

'You and Adam. What's really going on?' She picked up my hand, turning it this way and that as though consid-ering it for one of her displays, making my diamond twinkle under the light. 'Has something happened between you?'

'We're fine.' I tried to pull back my hand, worried she might feel how damp it had suddenly become, but she wouldn't let go.

'You've fallen out, haven't you? That's why you're here alone.'

I shifted uncomfortably in my seat and looked longingly at the door.

Anna Romer

Nina tickled the top of my hand. 'Steady on, old Bub. You're not jetting off just yet. Since I won't get the opportunity to pick your brains tomorrow night, I need some answers now. Please, Lucy. Tell me what's going on.'

I sighed. 'Things got a bit rocky with Adam. Quarrels, you know what it's like. My nightmares came back. I was tired from lack of sleep. Nothing major, but we agreed to have some time apart.'

'The wedding's still on?'

'Yes. I think . . . I don't know, Neeny. I really don't know.'

A dark brow shot up. 'Do you realise how long it's been since you called me Neeny?'

'Five years?'

She looked into my face. 'Bub and Neeny. Are we back, then?'

My smile was a little wider than I'd intended. 'Seems that way.'

She chafed my cold fingers between her warm ones. 'You'll figure this out.'

'I've made a mess of it all,' I admitted.

'No . . . you just have unfinished business.'

I looked at her, my old anxieties creeping back. 'Coby, you mean?'

She shook her head. 'I think you know who I'm talking about. Someone you used to love. You know, Bub, you can't make a fresh start in London with Adam until you've properly settled things here.'

I searched her dark eyes, wondering how much she knew. Or, at least, how much she had guessed over the years. I'd been naive to think that my closest friend hadn't noticed all the longing looks, the stolen glances, all the blushing and stumbling around I had done in Morgan's presence.

'Don't worry,' she said, as if reading my mind, 'your secret is safe with me.'

'Does Coby—?'

'He suspects.' She got to her feet, hauling me after her. 'Now, when's your grandad's funeral? I'm coming with you.'

'Been and gone,' I said. 'According to the solicitor's letter, Edwin wanted a private cremation. We didn't get the chance to go.'

Her face crumpled in sympathy. 'What a god-awful day you've had, poor sweetheart. Are you sure there's nothing I can do?'

It was worth a try. 'Know anyone in urgent need of an old tomcat?'

She laughed. 'Morgan already tried to offload him. We've got five critters at last count. And one more hungry little person on the way,' she added, patting her belly. 'I'll ask around, though. What'll you do with him when you go down the coast?'

'Take him with me.'

'In the van?'

'I can't abandon him.'

'Butter on the paws,' Nina suggested. 'Mum swore by it. The butter distracts the cat while it adjusts to a new environment. If all else fails, just keep the van doors and windows shut. You probably will anyway, Stern Bay's freezing at this time of year.'

'It might get a bit pongy with the litter tray.'

'I'm sure you'll cope. You used to survive at my place, and I only had three cats back then.'

'I'd hate Basil to stress. He's had a hellish life so far.'

'Basil?' Nina's expression melted into a smile. 'You love him already, don't you?'

'Of course not.'

'I predict he'll win your heart. Then you'll have to stay. You'll be trapped here forever.'

I smiled at her scheming. 'My heart belongs with Adam in London.'

'Oh, Bub,' she said wistfully. 'I do wish you were staying. For good, I mean. Now that I've got you back, I don't think I can bear to lose you again.'

'You won't,' I said, as we hugged goodbye. 'Next time, we'll stay in touch. That's a promise.'

Deep inside the castle walls, the child worked tirelessly. The spindle leaped and danced, the spinning wheel hummed. Room after room filled with gold, but still the Queen was not happy. She had more wealth than she could spend in a lifetime, yet the one thing she did not have – the one thing, the only thing she longed for with all her heart – could never truly be hers.

—The Shell Queen

9

France, 1917

He was thinking of her when his pistol went off; or, more precisely, he was thinking of her lips. Wondering, with the frantic preoccupation of a man who wished with all his heart and soul that he was anywhere but here – here, on this godforsaken brink of hell with its screaming noise and stench of blood and rotting flesh – wondering if lips really could taste like cherries. His brother had kissed her, he reasoned. If anyone knew, it would be Ronald. Hadn't he taunted Edwin with the knowledge, laughed at the hunger he had surely seen in Edwin's eager eyes? And Edwin hanging off his every word, unashamed, so desperately did he long to know for himself—

A shell went off somewhere to the left of him. He staggered sideways, and when the aftershock struck him in the chest he crashed to his knees. For a moment, all he could hear was the sluggish *whomp* of his heartbeat, dull and slow, as if drifting to him from underwater. He shook his head. His ears popped and noise exploded back around him. Shouting behind, then rapid rifle fire. A shrill scream as a strafe cut down the man beside him. Edwin struggled to his feet, his body numb, his mind ablaze with fear.

Dear God, he was on the brink. He clutched at sanity. Cherries, he thought. Remember the taste: sour–sweet, rich with sunlight, bursting in the mouth with such impossible goodness that your hunger for them increased tenfold. He had spent every summer in the orchard, gorging on mulberries and cherries, eating his fill of grapes and passionfruit, laughing at his mother's scoldings for leaving so few strawberries for her afternoon tea. He should have remembered the taste of sun-warmed fruit, he should have been able to imagine – but he was cold and afraid and he itched from lice. And men, men he knew, were dying around him. All he could remember was the taste of mud, the acid tang of fear and blood. No matter how he tried to conjure it, the sweet wild flavour of cherries eluded him.

He tightened his grip on the pistol. His hand was trembling so hard he could barely feel the weapon's weight in his palm, let alone the touch of the trigger. Yet when a figure loomed up suddenly ahead of him, he reacted without hesitation. His fingers constricted on the grip, and the handgun wavered. He choked on a sob and took unsteady aim.

'Fire!' someone shouted, close to his ear. The captain, he thought, though it was hard to be sure. His ears still rang from the blast, but there was been no mistaking the urgency in the captain's voice, as though he too was on the very edge of panic. '—Fire, damn you!'

A blood-streaked face burst from the smoke haze ahead. Edwin barely registered the mud-encrusted uniform, the wild eyes, the helmet knocked askew—

An inner voice whispered, *For the love of God, hold your fire* . . . but it was the voice of a person Edwin had abandoned years ago. A person with a liking for piano music and books and cool dark places into which he could escape. A person he had shed the moment he stepped off the wharf and onto the gangway of the great grey battleship that would sail him to the other side of the world. A person who no longer existed. A weakling, Ronald had called him, a nancy-boy with no right to carry arms. Well, Edwin would show him. He'd prove his worth as a soldier and show Ronald up as a fool. Ignoring the voice, Edwin gritted his teeth and whispered her name.

Clarice . . . Clarice. The girl he loved. *Beautiful, kind Clarice.*

The girl who would, once the nightmare had spent itself and, God willing, they were shipped off home, marry his brother. His taunting, boastful, undeserving brother Ronald.

The pistol bucked in his hand, he tasted the squirt of cordite at the back of his throat. Before him, the man with the blood-streaked face twitched mid-stride and then crumpled to his knees. As the man hit the ground, a greyness descended on Edwin. The mayhem around him faded, his senses tunnelled. A waft of breeze delivered the scent of overripe fruit, gaggingly sweet, turned to rot by the sun—

He snapped alert as the dim blare of shouting erupted nearby.

'My God, man. He's one of ours. Move aside, you mongrel. Someone call a medic!'

Later, that moment would return to him in dreams. The cries, the blast of weaponry, the choking smoke, the whistle of shells; and beneath it all, the barely audible footfall of the blood-faced man as he scrambled incoherently towards Edwin, his arms thrust forth. He carried no weapon, Edwin now understood. Rather, his hands were outstretched, empty, his fingers splayed as though imploring Edwin to grasp them.

In these dreams, other details surfaced. Edwin clearly heard the captain's call. *Hold your fire!* he had cried. *Hold your fire, damn you!* A thousand times Edwin had replayed that moment, and a thousand times he had despaired. How had he failed to hear the captain's warning? How had he not seen behind the man's blood mask? How had the mud and fear and noise obscured what hindsight now clearly showed him to be true? A face he had seen day after day throughout the long balmy summers and icy winters of his childhood, a face as familiar to him as his own.

The face of his most hated enemy.

His brother's face.

Kyneton, 1918

She sensed her mother's presence in the sitting room, but did not turn around. What was the point? There was nothing Mother nor anyone else could say to change what had happened. There was no one in the world blessed with the ability to bring him back.

'Clarice, darling,' her mother said carefully. Shoes shuffled on the Persian carpet, and the rustle of skirts seemed overloud in the dusty stillness. 'A young man is here to see you.'

Hope spiked in Clarice's chest, but quickly died. A young man did not mean *her* young man. She ignored her mother. If she sat very still, she felt in control of the pain; it became a solid burn, hollowing her slowly from the inside, unbearable but by no means lethal. The moment she moved – the twitch of a finger, the flare of her nostrils, the too-sudden intake of breath that lifted the position of her rib cage – the grief rose up and threatened to consume her.

'Oh, darling, he's travelled here especially to see you.'

'Go away,' Clarice murmured. 'All of you. I shan't see anyone.'

'He's brought something for you,' her mother persisted, and then added pleadingly, 'It's Edwin.'

A memory knocked softly on the windowpane of Clarice's closed mind. She flashed on the image of a tall, awkward boy with a pasty face and serious eyes. Eyes that made her think of a rabbit or a fox squirming in the steel jaws of perpetual humiliation. With the memory came laughter; not just any old chuckle or snort, but *his* laugh, dear Ronald's laugh – a rich, slightly mocking honey-warm rumble that always made her want to join in. She swivelled her head.

Her mother nodded, her small, sharp-featured face suddenly flushed. 'He says he has a parcel for you. It's from . . . Oh, my dear, will you not see him, just for a moment?'

Minutes later, the boy was sitting stiffly on the edge of her mother's good sofa. He was as thin as Clarice remembered, and just as awkward, only now he wore a soldier's uniform. The jacket rumpled around the shoulders, frayed at the cuff, the trousers hung too short at the ankle. He was gazing at Clarice with those large damp eyes she remembered. *More rabbit than fox*, she thought absently. Yet there was something hungry in their brown depths, as though the poor creature needed a decent feed. In his sweaty hands, he clutched a small package.

'Is that for me?' she managed.

The boy swallowed noisily. 'He wanted you to have them . . . his medals. He made me promise, if anything happened—' Edwin's brows furrowed suddenly, and now he was hawklike, wary. Reaching over, he placed the parcel on the edge of the lamp table, as though eager to rid himself of its burden.

Clarice frowned. How had this poor scrap of humanity survived, while Ronald – dear, brave Ronald with his fine strong body and sharply intelligent mind – how had he been lost? With a sinking heart, she found herself cataloguing their differences. Ronald was outgoing and cheerful, gifted and witty, while his younger brother seemed to hover on the

100

edge of life like a frightened sparrow. He had never joined in their lively conversations, never coped with their teasing banter. Rather, he had retreated, preferring the anonymity of his own company. If Clarice had been the sort of woman to accept a wager, she'd have placed her last shilling on the odds that Edwin Briar would most certainly have been one of the war's first casualties. Yet here he was, perched on her mother's sofa, gazing back at her in apparent terror. Alive and well, while Ronald—

Clarice swallowed. She dragged in a breath, expecting the pain to shred her, but to her surprise, she no longer felt quite so brittle. Taking another breath, this time venturing to draw it all the way into her lungs, she heard herself say in a rush, 'You were there, weren't you, Edwin? What did you see? Did he—' Her throat closed as the swirling force of her grief tried to break free, but she managed to rein it in. 'Did he mention me?'

Edwin drew his fingers into fists on his knees, as though pulling them out of harm's way. At this strangely vulnerable gesture, Clarice felt her pity for him blossom.

'I'm sorry,' she said hastily, 'I'm being rude. You've travelled all this way and I haven't even offered you tea.' She began to stand, but Edwin reached out and caught her sleeve in his pale fingers. It was just a gentle tug, but enough to startle Clarice into sitting back down.

Edwin leaned nearer. 'My brother loved you very much, Miss Hopeworth. I'd never known him to be as happy as he was in those times he spent with you. I can't imagine your pain, and I'm truly sorry for it. If you like, I can return in a day or so. It might comfort you to speak of him. Not,' he hastened to add, 'what happened over there. Rather, the way he used to be with you . . . when he was happy.'

Clarice sat back. She had never heard the boy speak so many words in one breath, nor had she expected such kindness. If she were perfectly honest, she would have to admit that something about his presence calmed her.

She took the parcel from the lampstand and placed it carefully, almost reverently, on her lap. Medals. How she wanted to throw them in the fire, be rid of them. Yet she also longed to hold them to her heart, cling to them, bathe them with her tears. They were her last vestige of Ronald. She looked at the boy. Perhaps the medals were not her last vestige of Ronald, after all. From some forgotten place inside her, a tiny smile emerged and settled hesitantly on her lips.

'I think I should like that,' she murmured. 'I'd like it very much indeed.'

10

Stern Bay, June 1993

A cold wind chased leaves and grit along the main street of Stern Bay. The smell of wood smoke and frying fish swirled through the chink in my van window, bringing with it a whiff of diesel. It was late morning and I guessed the fishing boats were returning with the night's catch.

Part of me was in a rush to get to Bitterwood, to search Edwin's gloomy old rooms in the hope of finding the explanation he'd promised. But another more fearful part kept stalling. Being there alone, among the shadows and echoes of the past, would be like sliding back through time into the landscape of my nightmares. A landscape I wasn't entirely sure I felt ready to face.

I'd skipped breakfast, so decided to have an early lunch. As I manoeuvred into a park outside the town's only takeaway shop, I saw the red postbox on the corner across the road.

Memory engulfed me. I was ten years old again, standing on that windy corner, the card I'd written to my father clutched tight. *Get well soon, Daddy. I miss you.*

Edwin had provided envelope and stamp, and printed the address of the hospital where Dad was staying. He called it a sanatorium, a special hospital, he said. He turned away quickly after he said this, but not before I had noticed the tears in his eyes. Later, when he drove me to Stern Bay to send off my card, he was quiet, and his mood infected me. I had lingered beside the postbox, unable to drop the envelope through the slot. That card linked me to Dad, who in turn linked me to my mother. He was the only other person in the world who missed her as terribly as I did, who understood the pain of losing her. I stood there for a long time, the salt breeze flushing my face, before I mustered the courage to let the card drop from my fingers and break the link. When it did, I rested my ear against the postbox. I fancied I could hear all the other letters and cards whispering to the newcomer in their papery voices, asking where it was going and what news it contained.

I walked back along the street to where Edwin waited in the car, my legs leaden, my heart empty as a seashell. It was only later – many years later, long after I had buried my memories of Bitterwood in the darkest corner of my mind – that the broken link between my father and me had finally begun to heal.

A door clanged open up the street, and the smell of fish and chips cut through the softer smells of seaweed and ocean air. Basil meowed in his crate beside me.

'My sentiments exactly,' I said. Grabbing my wallet, I climbed from the car and made a beeline for the takeaway shop. Ten minutes later, I was back in the van with my greasy armload: chips, two large fillets of whiting, three dim sims and a milkshake.

It was too windy to sit on the beach, so I parked on the foreshore and sat in the van, gazing through the windscreen at the waves. The hot oily saltiness of the chips made me feel better. Peeling the batter off the second piece of fish, I let it cool and offered a morsel to Basil. He nibbled daintily at first, as if astonished that something could be so delicious. Within minutes, the entire piece of fish was gone. He peered at me through the slender bars, and I smiled to myself.

'Plenty more where that came from, boyo.'

Settling back with my milkshake, I gazed across the wintry beach. In the distance, a dark speck moved slowly along the shoreline. Someone was collecting shells or pebbles, or flotsam – and the sight of them drew me back in time.

When I was a kid, my family had holidayed near here, in a tiny cottage a mile or so from Bitterwood, right on the beach. Christmas time meant a hamper of sandwiches, cold drinks, fruitcake on the sand. Once or twice we had come midyear, which left indelible memories of huddling out of the wind, scalding our tongues on the sickly sweetness of my mother's hot chocolate sipped from tin mugs.

The summer I turned ten, all that changed.

In my mind, I could see my mother just as she looked that last day. Her blonde hair tied back from her face, her cheeks pink from the sun. She wore her favourite jeans and her threadbare blue cardigan. She adored that cardigan despite the loose cuffs and odd buttons, and refused all my father's admonitions to throw it away. I could still see her hurrying along the beach, clutching her sunhat to her head with one hand, its brim flapping like a wounded bird. I tried to keep her frozen there, but the inevitable always followed: her fall from the slippery rocks, her plunge into deep water. Her last breath, not of her garden or of the lavender hand cream she wore to bed, or of chocolate cake fresh from the oven, but of salt air, and rotting seaweed, and deep water – smells I knew she tolerated only for my father's sake. Mum had been a country girl, preferring the gentler atmosphere of mountain air and river water, but had brought us to the coast every year in the hope of repairing Dad's relationship with Edwin.

In the years that followed her death, I read anything I could find on the subject of drowning. I learned about people who thrashed so violently they broke ribs or dislocated major joints, or inhaled debris deep into their lungs. Those images of her were the worst. I asked Dad about it years later, when I thought it might have finally been safe to mention her. Dad studied his hands, turning them palm-up, his fingers curled like a limp sea creature.

'It would have been quick,' he reassured me.

Yet I knew from his hollow voice that quick did not mean pain-free. At ten – and then eleven, twelve, thirteen – I refused to see how dying would be painless. How could it be, when those left behind suffered so terribly?

At first, Dad bore up to the strain, but weeks later, when

they found her washed up miles from where she'd gone in, my father's resolve to be strong for me crumbled. The shadow of my mother's absence folded around us, took over our lives. My father lost his way and ended up at Banksia House.

As for me, I had gone to stay with my grandfather.

At Bitterwood, where I'd learned to jump at shadows.

The ocean had turned grey. Dirty sea foam capped the waves. Overhead, big bruised clouds pushed across the sky. The distant shell collector had vanished, leaving the shoreline windswept and bare.

Rain was coming. Not just rain, but a storm. The ocean road would be too dangerous to navigate in wild weather, so I buckled up and headed out of town.

I drove west along the coast, leaving behind the village of Stern Bay as my van rattled and clanked around the tight bends of the Great Ocean Road. The road was a grey ribbon, winding along the edge of steep hilly bushland that dropped away to wintry beaches and wind-carved headlands. Beyond that, the vast aquamarine waters of the Bass Strait swept out towards what seemed a deep blue eternity.

I gripped the steering wheel, trying to squeeze the tremor from my fingers. I switched on the radio and jabbed through the channels, hoping to find some music or a talkback show to distract me. My thoughts kept circling back to my grandfather. I had tortured myself for weeks over whether or not to tell him about my wedding. He was too old to travel, I silently argued. He would barely remember me. Yet not inviting him seemed rude.

Then, his reply. He wished Adam and me a happy life together, and quoted a line of Emily Dickinson. *Exultation is the going of an inland soul to sea.* Odd for a wedding sentiment, which puzzled me ... until I found the small object he'd included with the letter. Perhaps as an afterthought, he had wrapped the little gold heart in tissue paper and slipped it in. Had he found it washed up on the beach, I wondered, near the rocks where my mother had fallen? Or was there a murkier explanation?

I have something for you . . .

A mile or so from Bitterwood, I passed the beachside cottage where my family had holidayed in the seventies. A car was parked in the drive, and the place looked neat and freshly painted. Only the old pine in the front yard had grown taller and stragglier, and seeing it gave me a pang. Mum had loved to breakfast in its cool shade. As the cottage disappeared behind me I pictured her sitting there, smiling in her thoughtful way, her face turned to the sea, the endless blue-green body of water reflected in her eyes.

The main road veered away from the coastline. I left it and turned onto a narrow lane, which I followed around the back of the headland. The bitumen became dirt, and the roadside trees thinned out, replaced by an avenue of gnarled banksias.

Bitterwood appeared. It was a tall sandstone building with iron lace verandahs and a black tiled roof set back in a rambling garden. The shuttered windows and creeping arms of ivy made it seem otherworldly, a place torn from the pages of a dark fairytale, a porthole to another time.

I pulled up in front of the huge rusty iron gates and

got out. Beyond the gates, a gravel driveway led around a turning circle where an old birdbath mouldered in the dappled light. Large trees dominated the garden. Magnolia, fig, bare limbed maples and soaring pines. It was early afternoon, but the atmosphere beneath the trees seemed nocturnal, as though my grandfather's realm was one of shadows and night.

Once, this had been a magical place. I had loved nothing more than exploring the front garden, or escaping to the sheltered orchard down behind the house, nestled out of the wind where the trees grew lush and strong. Lofty mulberry trees whose fruit I ate in mushy handfuls and then wore the purple evidence on my hands for days afterwards. Quince trees and sour plums, cherries and apples, fuzzy peaches that tasted like sunlight, luscious black figs.

Inside the old guesthouse was even better. The maze of upstairs rooms had seemed to me an Aladdin's cave of treasures, and my grandfather had happily indulged my eagerness to explore. There were six guest rooms, which, according to my father, had been constantly booked out during the guesthouse's heyday. Now, they lay empty and dusty. I used to imagine that the only living creature to visit them, aside from the rats and possums and birds nesting in the walls, was me. My grandfather lived in the seventh room, and there was another small private wing once inhabited by servants. Directly above these rooms was an attic the length of a runway, narrow and filled to the rafters with tea chests and boxes, suitcases full of musty papers, debris left behind by the receding tides of the past. Bitterwood was a storehouse of memories . . . not all of them rosy. And somewhere inside was an album of photos that Edwin had not wanted my father to see. With luck, there was also a note or parcel for me, containing Edwin's promised explanation.

I hauled open the gates and drove through.

Beside me in his cage, Basil yowled uneasily.

'It's just for a few days,' I reassured him. My voice was reedy, a little breathless, and it didn't convince either of us.

I parked around the back, and then returned to the front verandah, keys in hand. Taking a breath, I unlocked the door and let myself inside.

The entryway was icy. I rubbed my arms. Ahead stretched a dim hall leading to the back of the house, to the kitchen and laundry, a supply store and Edwin's office. To my left was the formal sitting room. I went in and gazed around. Wintry sunshine splashed through rips in the curtains, but the room was dark. Going over to the high bay window, I dragged aside the dusty drapes.

Once, this would have been a majestic room. Tall glass fronted cabinets displayed beautiful old tea sets and china-ware. A big grandfather clock stood silently against the far wall, and curvy armchairs made graceful silhouettes in the half-light. Framed watercolour prints hung on the walls, brightly coloured birds and insects, exotic flowers and seedpods. Those prints had kept me spellbound as a child. As I stood before one of them now – a tiny hummingbird hovering on the lip of a bell-shaped flower – it made me itch to take my colours into the garden, spend the afternoon drawing and painting.

But first, there was a house to search.

Crossing the room, I went through the drawers of a long redwood sideboard, but found only tarnished cutlery and yellowing linen napkins. Hands on hips, I surveyed the room. I felt in the grip of a powerful yearning . . . but for what, I didn't quite know. It had to do with my mother's charm, Edwin's letter, and Dad's urgency for me to find the dusty old album of photos. It was a barely-there voice in the back of my mind, calling me to follow. Echoes from a dream, urging me towards . . . *something*.

Returning to the hallway, I hurried down to the kitchen. It had always been the most welcoming room in the house. Full of warmth and baking smells, with a large picture window overlooking the back garden.

It hadn't changed much. The high ceiling with exposed wooden beams, the huge scarred table in the centre, the old Warmray wood heater with its blackened hotplate and copper flue. The faint smell of stewed fruit sent me reeling back through time. I pictured a small, slender woman with huge black-rimmed glasses. Edwin's housekeeper, I couldn't recall her name, only that I'd liked her. She knew every bird in the garden: rosellas, currawongs, gang gang cockatoos, little grey fantails, and had a story about each of them. Every morning for breakfast, she'd served thick delicious pancakes with homemade jam.

Something drew me to the window.

The mulberry trees had shed their leaves, their bare branches mottled with lichen, black in the afternoon light. Down the hill at the bottom of the orchard was a shady spot where mushrooms grew beneath a dead oak tree and soft grass carpeted the slope. And there, built into the slope, was a low door. Behind the door lurked my grandfather's icehouse, a subterranean cave of shadows where, a long time ago, large blocks of ice had lasted through the summer in the cool darkness. Where, long after the last of the ice had melted and been replaced by refrigeration, I had once hidden as a child.

Morgan's words drifted to me. *That's the thing about you, Lucy. When you really want something, you don't let fear stand in your way of getting it.*

Yet I *had* let fear stand in my way. Not just once or twice, but repeatedly. My fear was like an iceberg, barely visible on the surface, while the immense frozen bulk of it lurked below. And no matter how much I tried to escape it – no matter how far or fast I ran – it always seemed to catch me in the end.

Dusk crept across the garden. Trees disappeared into the shadows. The air turned damp. I crossed the yard to where I'd parked the Volkswagen on a shady gravel patch at the back of the house. Once, it had been the parking lot for guests, but was now weedy and overgrown.

Sliding open the van hatch, I climbed in. Cool air flowed through the half-open windows. Basil was where I left him, curled snug on an old mohair jumper on the bench seat. He yowled when he saw me, and then began to purr. Sitting beside him, I made sandwiches from the supplies I'd bought, and gazed through the window while I ate.

A feeling of unreality came over me. Maybe it was Bitterwood's isolation from the rest of the world, or maybe the rush of memories that assailed me at every step. Or perhaps it was simply a delayed reaction to my grandfather's death and my father's relapse. Whatever it was, I couldn't seem to shake the feeling that the quest for Dad's album, and my hope of finding Edwin's promised 'something' were incidental. As if another, greater, darker force had drawn me here.

Back in the house, I went along the hallway to Edwin's office. The cold air wrapped around me, giving me the shivers. The house was utterly silent, not even the distant murmur of waves or birdsong from the garden seemed able to penetrate the tomblike stillness. There was just the whisper of my breath, and my shoes echoing on the wooden boards.

Pushing open the office door, I stepped inside . . . and let out a cry when I saw the man standing behind the desk. Then I breathed out. It wasn't a man. Hand on my chest, I laughed weakly. A large portrait hung on the far wall. One of many that turned Edwin's office into a grim gallery of patriarchs. It came back to me then, how I'd hated this room as a child. All those stern faces with disapproving eyes. They gave me the creeps as much now as they had then.

Only one face seemed friendly.

I went over to the portrait of my grandfather.

It showed a tall man standing disembodied against a black background. He was lanky as a scarecrow, his long sallow face creased with worry, his overly large, wet looking eyes gazing, almost fearfully, at something only he could see.

When I stayed at Bitterwood, he had spent all his time indoors. Upstairs in the little library or down here in his office, bent over a ledger, his pen scratching furiously. He never remarried after Grandma Dulcie died. He must have been lonely. For fifty years his only real company was his housekeeper, and for a time, once a year on holidays, my parents and me. What sort of secrets would a man like that be hiding? Surely nothing too dreadful.

In a bookshelf, I noticed a row of familiar books. Going over, I took one out. It was a twisted version of Riding Hood, the cover showed a girl in a red cape with smug, knowing eyes. It was one of Dad's early editions, before I'd started illustrating. The pages were well thumbed, and as I went along the row, I found Dad's other books. All of them, each worse for wear, as though Edwin had read and reread them countless times.

An ache of warmth went through me. I glanced back at the portrait, and my grandfather's sorrowful eyes held mine for an instant. *You see*, they seemed to say, *I never forgot you*. I wondered if he'd also sensed the echo of my father's life written into his stories. I suspected he had, and it made me wish with all my heart that I'd managed to get here before he died.

I went through the desk. In the top drawer, I found a ring of keys, mostly duplicates of the ones Dad had given me. I pocketed the keys, but there was little else of interest, just pens, letter opener, a dried up inkbottle. The battered old filing cabinet in the corner yielded only dusty documents, years out of date. A chair, a desk lamp, a pile of boxes in one corner. No hint or clue that Edwin might have left something here for me.

The enormity of my task washed over me. The old

guesthouse was a labyrinth of rooms, all of them crammed with clutter, honeycombed with possible hiding places. Searching through it was going to take forever.

I leaned in the doorway, frowning.

I didn't have forever. But I did have my remaining three weeks. And so I made a silent promise that by the time I was ready to return to London – to Adam and the new life I'd forged there – any unfinished business here would be done, dusted, and resolutely left behind in the past where it belonged.

The following day, I started searching the upper floors. My plan was to begin at the top of the house and methodically work my way down, filling rubbish bags, and setting aside anything of value that we could sell.

The attic was smaller and more cramped than I remembered. It was full of wooden tea chests, piles of dusty books, the buckled remains of a bicycle, a mountain of cardboard boxes, abandoned furniture.

I went over to an old wardrobe. Its doors hung askew, its mirror so tarnished that my reflection was barely more than a ghost. On the floor of the hanging compartment, I found a cardboard box littered with mouse dirt. Inside was a stack of rectangular glass pieces. They were old photo negatives, haphazardly packed one on top of the other and crusty with grime. I began sliding out the box, but was stopped by the crack of breaking glass.

I sat back. Dad hadn't said anything about negatives, so perhaps there was nothing of interest among them. I lifted out the top plate, blew away some of the dust and held it to the light.

It showed two young men and a stout woman. The woman was leaning against one of the men, her arms around his waist. The other man stood a little apart, and something about his stance – lanky, somehow ill at ease – made me think of the portrait downstairs in Edwin's office. It may have been my grandfather, but I couldn't be sure, his features obscured by the eerie inversion of bright and dark. The woman's mutton sleeves were tight around her chubby arms, her collar buttoned under her chin, her face set in a frown. Both men wore military uniforms, and the longer I looked the more I began to see a similarity in their angular features. They stood beneath an archway formed by the heavily laden boughs of a mulberry tree. In the background, I recognised the edge of a familiar building: my grandfather's rearing house.

Taking the plate over to the window, I held it up to a bright patch of light and studied the picture for a long time. It was him, I felt sure. He was younger, straight-backed with thick hair, but the narrow face with its huge eyes and feeble chin was undeniably familiar.

'Edwin,' I whispered.

As his name left my lips, an image opened in my mind. Deep in the forgotten dungeon of a fairytale castle, a young woman daydreamed about her soldier love. And then my father's voice. *Writing is how I work through things I don't understand.*

I searched the grimy negative, tilting it this way and that in the light, wondering. If the thin young man was my grandfather, who were his companions? His mother, a brother? Dad had never mentioned an uncle, but that meant nothing. My father's distant past was a closed book. He often sang Grandma Dulcie's praises, but rarely mentioned his life growing up with Edwin.

I stood there for a long time, gazing at the image, my thoughts on fire. If the castle in Dad's fairytale was Bitterwood, and the old King was my grandfather, then who were the other players? Was one of these young men the soldier Fineflower had loved? And if so, who was Fineflower? Who were the other wives strung from the rafters and drained of blood? Was that detail purely fiction, or did it also contain reverberations of the truth? I couldn't help wondering if my father knew more than he was telling. At least, more than he was telling *me*.

Placing the glass negative back in the box, I dusted my hands on my jeans and ran downstairs to retrieve his manuscript from my van.

Night settled across the land. The moon rose, and one by one bright stars pricked the sky. Deep in the heart of the King's gloomy castle, Fineflower huddled in her cell, thinking about her little boy. Was he crying for her, missing her warm cuddles, hungry? She folded her empty arms about her chest, but the ache of loneliness only deepened.

Behind her, the mountain of cocoons seemed to have grown. Some of the silkworms had hatched into butterflies. A few had flown away, escaping between the window bars and vanishing into the night; most had perished in the shadows. Fineflower felt the weight of despair settle on her. Each day she picked at the cocoons, trying to peel away the weblike threads of silk. She thought of her son and worked until her fingers bled, but each day she failed.

Unravelling silk was one thing, but turning it into gold? She was doomed.

The cell grew darker. The other wives swayed, their shadows bumping beneath their slippered feet. Fineflower felt them watching her, the blind hollows of their eyes beseeching, but for what she did not know. She offered them water from her cup, but they did not drink. She sang to them while she worked, but they did not seem to hear. It was only when she told them about her little boy – six weeks old with bright button eyes and hair like thistledown – that their interest pricked. She thought she heard them whispering among themselves, and the sound made her shiver.

She rested her head in her hands. She did not love the King. She had seen his real face, the face he kept hidden from the outside world. He cared nothing for her, and perhaps he cared nothing for her child. His only passion was gold – and if Fineflower failed to spin it, she would join the other wives in their silent dance beneath the window.

'I'd give anything to see my son again,' she whispered fiercely. 'Anything to hold him again in my arms.'

A shuffle came from the darkness. Looking up, she blinked in surprise. A man stood before her. He wore a blue jacket with brass buttons. A soldier, she realised – *her* soldier, the same young man who had caught her eye in the marketplace.

What a glorious smile he had. His eyes glowed like black fire, his teeth shone straight and white. Dimples bracketed his lovely lips. He stood tall, his fine military coat snug around muscular arms, his hair glossy as an eagle's wing, his limbs sturdy and strong.

'Who are you?' she asked, with a catch of wonder in her throat.

The man did not answer. He swooped to her side, and for one wild reckless moment, she thought he meant to pull her into his arms for a kiss. Instead, his quick fingers plucked a silk thread from her sleeve.

Fineflower flinched at his touch. 'Won't you tell me your name?'

The man held the strand up before his eyes. 'My name is not important,' he said in a voice that sent tingles of fright and desire across her skin. 'All that matters is getting you out of here. Alive,' he added, gazing pointedly at the ghostly wives.

'All favours come with a price,' she said warily. 'What is yours?'

Dusting the silk from his fingers, the soldier looked into her eyes. His gaze was fathomless as a subterranean cave. When he spoke, his voice was full of hunger.

'Your willing heart.'

Fineflower shuddered and drew away. 'I can't give you that. I don't believe in love. But my gown is sewn with jewels. You can have those, if you like. Sapphires. Rubies. Diamonds?'

The man of shadows shook his head. 'I have no need of baubles.' He glanced at the mountain of cocoons, and sighed heavily. 'A task such as this demands a high price. The heart is a treasure, nothing of greater value exists in this world or the next. My offer stands. Your heart . . . given willingly.'

11

Bitterwood, 1929

Nala let out a whoop. As they crested the hill, the ocean burst into view. Not the bruised black depths and rolling grey waves of Orah's memory, but a glittering blue sheet pulled tight behind a coastline of grassy green hills. A dusty road meandered along a cliff edge, and further back, on the very top of the bluff, was a large house.

Orah felt a thrill of wonder. In the dying afternoon light, it looked like a magical fortress plucked from the pages of a fairytale book. She remembered Nala's words. *They're kind people, the Briars. They'll help you find your dad.*

Twenty minutes later, Warra was leading them along a grassy path and around the side of the house, through a tunnel of camellia bushes, and under an archway smothered in climbing roses. They emerged into a private, neatly kept yard that resembled a miniature farm.

A colony of brown hens scratched around a vegetable garden, and black-faced sheep grazed in a small paddock. Grassy avenues cut between rows of sprawling mulberry trees, while further down grew apples, quinces, persimmons, cherries, and lemons.

As they approached the back of the house, a woman stepped from the shadows of a long verandah. Her light green dress shimmered in the sunlight as she walked towards them, hugging her slim figure, and complementing her red-gold hair, which she wore pinned back in a loose bun.

Orah held back, staying by Warra's side.

Nala pushed forward. 'Mrs Briar, this is Orah. She came from Scotland with her mum but the ship was wrecked in the storm. Warra pulled her from the water, but she's all alone. Her dad lives in Melbourne, but she doesn't know how to find him—'

'Nala, please. Slow down, you sound like a lorikeet. Shipwreck, you say?'

Nala nodded frantically. 'Everyone drowned.'

Mrs Briar's frown deepened. Her gaze travelled over Orah's tattered dress and bare feet, the cuts and purple bruises on her arms, the knotted hair. 'Edwin rang this morning. He said there'd been a wreck further up the coast, but I had no idea it was so close. Are you quite sure?'

Orah moved closer to Warra. She had been looking forward to meeting the Briars after hearing so much about them, but now that she was here, she felt awkward and shy.

Nala seemed unable to contain herself, and raced off again. 'We were on the cliff and saw her in the water. Warra swam out through all the wreckage and saved her.'

'You brought her straight here?'

'Yes, missus.'

'Did you see anyone along the way?'

Nala shook her head and launched into a lengthy description of their journey through the bush and along the sea cliffs.

Orah stopped listening. The woman, Mrs Briar, was like no one she had ever seen. A film star, or a queen from the fairytale book she had left behind in Glasgow. Her hair was polished copper, glowing pure gold where the sun struck it. Her skin was creamy white, as smooth and flawless as fresh milk. The blueness of her eyes made Orah think of sunlit water.

'We thought you would know what to do,' Nala finished.

Mrs Briar pondered Orah for the longest time. When at last she spoke again, her voice had changed, become gentle.

'Did you say your parents were on board the ship?'

Orah opened her mouth to speak, but her heart beat so hard she couldn't breathe.

Warra said softly, 'Her mother.'

'Did she survive too?'

Warra shook his head.

Mrs Briar looked at Orah. 'What about your father?'

Again, Orah stalled. She was suddenly, horribly aware of her ragged dress and knotty hair, and her face and hands stiff with salt and dust.

Nala came to her rescue. 'He lives in Melbourne, missus. Orah remembers his address. She's hoping,' she added quietly, 'that you could help find him.'

Mrs Briar was shaking her head, as if the story of Orah's

survival was finally sinking in and proving too far-fetched to believe. Her gaze softened on Orah.

'What did you say your name was?'

Orah swallowed and her throat made a clicking sound. 'Orah Dane.'

Mrs Briar reached out and plucked a dry leaf from Orah's hair. Pinching the leaf between her forefinger and thumb, she examined it, as if it might contain the solution to this unexpected dilemma. With a sigh, she let the leaf fall, and her blue gaze followed it to the ground. She looked back at Orah.

'Well, Orah Dane, I'm ever so sorry about your mother. When my husband returns next week, we'll talk further about what to do. Until then, you must stay here as our guest.' She looked at Nala. 'Go and clean yourself up, then bring us some tea and sandwiches.'

'Yes, missus.'

'Warra, start fetching the bottles from storage. We'll begin preserving tomorrow.' Mrs Briar gestured to Orah. 'Come along inside. You must be starving. While you eat you can tell me more about this shipwreck.'

Orah followed Mrs Briar to the front of the house where they entered a spacious sitting room.

The furniture was elegant, chairs with curved legs and glass-fronted cabinets displaying chinaware, and a tall grandfather clock with a gilded face stood near the window. Botanical pictures hung on all the walls, and Orah would have liked to observe them more closely. Birds and butterflies, and strange prickly flowers.

Mrs Briar settled herself on a couch. She beckoned Orah to sit beside her. Orah hesitated, before perching at the far end.

The grandfather clock ticked loudly in the silence. Nala brought in a tray of bread and jam and tea things, which she placed on a low table. As she poured tea, she met Orah's eye and winked.

'Thank you, Nala,' Mrs Briar said. 'Have you started dinner yet?'

'It'll be ready at six, missus.' Nala smiled at Orah, and then hurried back into the hall.

Mrs Briar passed Orah a plate and a linen napkin. 'You must be starving. Eat up.'

Orah took the plate. Mam said it was rude to eat in front of someone who wasn't eating too, but as she breathed in the delicious smells, her hunger overcame her good manners. Bread made crusty over the fire, wedges of butter that melted and ran between her fingers, sticky plum jam.

Orah forced herself to chew slowly, savour every mouthful. After washing it all down with a long thirsty swallow of tea, she mopped her lips with the napkin, and quietly thanked Mrs Briar.

The woman nodded. 'Now, will you tell me how you came to be here? Start at the beginning so I can get a clear picture of events.'

'Yes, Mrs Briar.'

'Please, my dear, call me Clarice. We don't stand on ceremony here.'

Orah nodded, stealing a glance at Mrs Briar from beneath her lashes. Mrs Briar was unusually lovely, with her creamy skin and blue eyes. Taking a deep breath, Orah began to talk, softly at first, barely able to push the words from her throat, wobbly and halting, but with Mrs Briar's encouraging nods she soon found herself relating her story with more confidence.

At its end, Mrs Briar leaned forward and placed her fingers lightly on Orah's shoulder. The woman's eyes had turned glassy with unshed tears, and they seemed to bore into Orah as though she were drinking in her hurt, recognising the distinctive flavour of grief.

'Your poor mother,' she whispered. 'You must feel so very lost without her.'

Orah's lips trembled. She *was* lost. Cast adrift in a world she knew nothing about. She went to speak, but there were no words. Hanging her head, she clenched her body tight around the pain.

Mrs Briar murmured in sympathy. Her fingers slid to Orah's wrist and she gently tugged the girl towards her. Orah wanted to surrender, to sink against Mrs Briar's softness and absorb the warm comfort of her embrace. She wanted it so badly her bones ached. Yet she held back. This woman wasn't her mother. She couldn't even remember the name Mrs Briar had insisted she call her. Her mind was fuzzy, her thoughts tangled. She frowned, as if recalling Mrs Briar's name was suddenly the most important thing in the world. *Posie*, she kept thinking. Which was silly. Posie was her mother's name. And Mrs Briar – despite her kindness, despite her beauty and soft ways, and the liking she had clearly taken to Orah – was not Mam.

Embarrassed by Mrs Briar's patient scrutiny, Orah drew away.

'I remember Pa's address. Mam wrote to him there, it's a boarding house in Victoria Street in Melbourne. Do you know of it?'

Mrs Briar smoothed her hands together on her lap. 'I'm afraid I don't, but Edwin might. Melbourne's several hours from here. My husband travels there every second month on business, but he only left a few days ago. He's too busy to make a return journey so soon, especially with Christmas less than a month away. Which means you'll have to stay here for a while. That is, unless you have relatives you can go to?'

Orah shook her head. 'Mam's family turned their back on her when she married my father. Pa's parents died when he was a boy. There were distant cousins in Glasgow, but we never saw them. There's no one. Not in Glasgow, and not here.'

'You're all alone, then?'

Orah swallowed. Mrs Briar's words echoed in her mind. Alone. All alone. Her shoulders began to shake. Her body buckled over. A sob choked out of her, shaking loose the invisible threads she had stitched around herself to hold in her grief.

This time, when Mrs Briar gathered Orah into her arms, the girl did not resist. Mrs Briar was bony, her breasts small, her arms slender and insubstantial. She had none of the cushioning comfort of Orah's mother; none of the fleshy security Orah had taken for granted would always be there. Now that Mam was gone, Orah craved her tenderness. Mrs Briar was warm and sweetly scented, and in her own way, somehow needy. She held Orah so tightly, almost desperately, that Orah began to shake. Despite her fear and shame at coming apart in a stranger's arms, she buckled into Mrs Briar's embrace, grateful for any small comfort offered freely by this blindingly beautiful woman whose name she could not remember.

The room was small, a cocoon of darkness. Immediately Orah felt at home. A narrow single bed jutted from the wall, with a plump pillow and soft mattress, a cheerful patchwork quilt. Beside the bed was a table with washbasin and jug, and a brass candlestick. A pretty dress and undergarments in Orah's size were folded over the back of a chair, while on the bed lay a crisp white nightdress.

She crossed to the window. Below was an enormous parklike garden. It looked wild and unkempt, nothing at all like the house's grand entryway with its circular stone drive and guardian trees. In between the foliage, she glimpsed a shed roof. Warra and Nala sometimes slept in one of the outbuildings, they'd told her, but Orah could see no lights or movement. She knotted her fingers together, wishing she were with them. This was the first time they had been apart since the wreck.

The moon drifted behind clouds, plunging the garden into darkness. Orah turned away. Months would pass before Mr Briar could look for her father, and the thought filled her with heaviness. She longed to lie on the bed and fall asleep, but she knew there would be no rest for her until she found her father.

A knock sounded on the door. Mrs Briar poked her head into the room, and then entered. 'I've just come to tuck you in, Orah dear. I hope the room is to your liking?'

Orah nodded. She slipped into bed. Mrs Briar tucked her in and then sat on the edge of the mattress and smoothed cool fingers over Orah's brow. Her dress crackled pleasantly, and a scent rose from her skin, roses and sugar syrup.

'Shall I tell you a story?' she said.

Orah nodded again. She liked stories. They always soothed her. She settled under the covers, but the moment she closed her eyes, she saw her mother's face and all the memories of that terrible night rushed back. A tear leaked from her eye. She turned her face to the pillow, hoping Mrs Briar hadn't seen.

'. . . a Chinese princess,' Mrs Briar was saying, 'who loved nothing more than walking in her garden beneath the trees, sipping her tea as she pondered the landscape. One day a cocoon fell into her hot drink and began to unravel. As she fished it out, the princess noticed that this thread was finer than any she'd ever seen.'

Orah blinked around, her sorrow forgotten. 'What was it?'

'Why, darling girl, it was silk. And that was how the world discovered the most delightful material ever to clothe our human skin. Here,' she added, extending her sleeve, encouraging Orah to touch it. 'Exquisite, isn't it?'

Orah ran her fingertips lightly along Mrs Briar's sleeve. She found she could not remove her hand. But it wasn't the silk that kept her touch resting there, although that was very fine, just as Mrs Briar had said. What made her linger, what kept her fingers curled lightly around the woman's elegant wrist, was the human warmth. It soothed her, made the band of worry on her brow loosen and disappear.

Mrs Briar placed her hand over Orah's and stroked her fingers. She gazed at Orah for the longest time, and then smiled. 'Perhaps while you're here, I'll teach you to spin.'

Orah found herself nodding sleepily. Her last image was of a small white cocoon plopping into a teacup, and the princess's eyes – light blue rimmed with grey, just like Mrs Briar's – peering curiously over the rim.

The following day, Orah found herself in the midst of a jam-making flurry, jostling elbow to elbow in the kitchen with Nala and Mrs Briar – Clarice, as she was learning to call her. The annual church fete was still a few months away, Clarice explained, but the fruit was ripe now and needed bottling.

Enormous pots of sticky syrup bubbled on the stove, filling the kitchen with fragrant steam. Nala cored and peeled, while Warra gave Orah a tiny paring knife and showed her how to pit the cherries. Warra delivered a seemingly endless supply of fruit to the kitchen table. Mulberries, apples, figs, peaches. Orah watched him come and go, and found that if she positioned herself near the window she had a clear view of him. As long as he was near, the sea stopped rolling beneath her and the roar of waves in her mind became quiet.

For the next few days, they worked tirelessly. Soon they had made enough jam to fill sixty jars. Not only jam, but also bottled vegetables, and preserved whole fruit in syrup. They brewed up any leftover parings with the summer tomatoes and made spicy relish.

'Just in time,' Clarice announced as she entered the kitchen one evening. 'Edwin's arriving home in the morning.' She grabbed the kettle and hauled it over to the sink. 'Come on you lot, back to work. I want this kitchen spotless before bedtime.'

Orah was in the garden early next morning. The air was brisk and she tugged her wrap about her shoulders, hurrying around the house and down the slope towards the orchard.

She had hoped to see Warra, but he and Nala were nowhere about. There'd been talk of fishing last night, so they were probably down on the beach. As the sky began to lighten, she walked between the trees, following the grassy avenue downhill. At the edge of the orchard, she found a weatherboard building with a steep gabled roof. Going over to a window, she cupped her hands and peered in.

The lofty cathedral ceiling made the space appear cavernous. Four tables dominated the room. On the tables were large wooden trays that looked, from her vantage point at the window, to be full of leaves. There were strange shelves against the far wall, seemingly made of sticks—

'Hello there,' a voice said behind her.

Orah whipped around.

A man stood in the patchy sunlight. Lanky and thin, more of a scarecrow than a man. Mam would have called him a string bean. He wore a shabby black suit that was too short at the ankle and frayed at the cuff.

'I'm sorry I startled you,' he said. 'You must be Orah?'

She nodded.

'I'm Edwin Briar. Clarice said you've come to stay with us. How did you find your room?'

'Good, thank you.'

The first skeins of sunlight picked through the treetops, illuminating his features. His long face was made striking by the sharpness of his cheekbones and brow. It was an odd face, pinched by a frown, yet somehow still friendly. His dark hair had been worried into a cockscomb that jutted in disarray from his head. He nodded towards the rearing house.

'Want to see inside?' Taking out a ring of keys, he unlocked the heavy wooden door, and then pushed through.

Orah followed him in. 'Why is it called the rearing house?'

'It's where we rear our little workers.'

She stared at him, mystified.

Mr Briar seemed pleased. He beckoned her over to the nearest table. Orah saw that she'd been right: the trays were full of leaves. Mr Briar brushed a handful of leaves aside, and gestured her nearer. Bending closer she saw thousands of tiny wriggling white bodies clinging to the underside of the leaves.

'What are they?' She wrinkled her nose. 'Maggots?'

Mr Briar had a soft laugh, a throaty chuckle that made her think of sun-warmed honey. 'Silkworms. My mother started farming them just after the war. Her brother brought back a bag of silkworms from the Orient, along with instructions on how to care for them. The rest she learned herself through many years of trial and error.

Orah pointed to the far wall. 'What are those shelves?'

'Nesting frames. When the worms are big enough, we transfer them there. They attach themselves to the sticks while they spin their silk cocoons, and when they're done with that, they turn into moths.'

Orah remembered Clarice's story about the Chinese princess. 'You make silk?'

'Silk thread. Clarice spins it from the short fibres leftover when the moths emerge. She hasn't the heart to boil them.'

'Do you make a living from it?' Orah wanted to know.

Mr Briar laughed gently. 'It's more of a hobby, really. Clarice loves to sew, but there's no fine fabric around these days. And no money to spend on luxuries. There's a mill in Geelong where they weave our thread into cloth and dye it. They keep a bolt of fabric for their troubles, and give us what's left. Usually enough for Clarice to make a dress or two.'

Orah smiled at this. She remembered long cosy days in Glasgow with her mother, twirling her spindle, watching it bulge with newly spun yarn. Silk, she marvelled. How much finer it would be than the coarse fluffy fibres of wool.

'Our main living,' Mr Briar went on, 'comes from the guesthouse. Although lately, things have slowed right down. No one has the money for holidays. We only had a handful of people last year, and this season we've had just one couple.' He drew a breath and rubbed his hands together. 'But the slump won't last forever. The new ocean road is already attracting people to the area. In the meantime, we get a modest income from produce. Fruit and preserves, eggs and meat. Speaking of which, have you sampled Nala's pancakes and homemade jam?'

Orah nodded, and to her horror, her stomach grumbled.

Mr Briar laughed again in that soft liquid-honey way he had. 'Hmm, I'm quite sure I can smell the sizzle of something marvellous on the hob. Would you do me the honour?'

He smiled at Orah and offered his arm, as though she were a lady and he a fine gentleman – rather than a girl with bare feet, and a string bean in a worn-out suit.

Orah felt like giggling. Wildly, nervously. Instead, she adopted a haughty look and took his arm, which made him smile widely, his eyes gleaming with pleasure, and perhaps a little surprise.

Orah was surprised too.

Her ordeal on the ocean had crippled her, stolen the joy from her life, stolen her mam. It had abandoned her on the shores of a strange country, bereft and alone and filled to the brim with sorrow. She had believed, with a strength of conviction that ached deep inside her, that she would never laugh or smile again.

Yet here she was, barely more than a week later, giggling like a five-year-old in the company of a man she had only just met. A man who, in some unidentifiable way, made her remember another man, a flushed-faced bear of a man who had romped and skylarked and play-acted with her, all the way back in those dreamlike childhood days in Glasgow.

12

Bitterwood, May 1993

He hadn't meant to startle her that day, but she'd been so absorbed in her thoughts, standing in the early morning light, her face pressed to the rearing house window, a glorious child. Freckles sprinkling her nose, a high forehead framed by golden locks, skin the colour of clotted cream, eyes the deep velvet blue of spring violets.

Later they laughed about it, made a joke of how he'd shaved a few years off her young life. Even Clarice had chimed in, teasing that the girl might soon discover a few grey hairs among the gold.

Yet even as they laughed and bantered, Edwin kept seeing another little fair-haired girl, and the likeness between the two made his heart ache.

He shook his head, banishing them all to the shadows. Unlocking the rearing house, he went in, bypassing the tables to stand at the back of the room where the light barely reached. He had built the nesting shelves soon after the first war. The dark time, he called his post-war days. While his mother grieved for her favourite son, Edwin had almost worked himself into an early grave, planting new trees and pruning the old, applying himself to maintenance around the guesthouse until there was not a window that creaked, not a door that jammed in its frame, not a pane of glass besmeared by grime. Madness, his mother had called it. In Edwin's mind, it was penance.

In those days, it had been just him and his mother, following her dream to help pioneer the silk boom she predicted would soon sweep Australia.

'Silk is the warmest fibre on earth,' she used to say. 'You don't need acres of land, just a grove of mulberry trees and a sheltered place for the worms to spin in peace. Once you get the knack of caring for the worms, production is cheap and easy. A child could do it.'

Edwin smiled.

She had been short and stout, with the rosy-cheeked face of a cherub. Even when she was in her eighties, there was something of the delighted child about her. It may have been her enthusiasm, her impish smile, or the waxy skin that never seemed to age. Edwin pictured her striding between the trees in her coveralls and gumboots, sawing leaves from the trees with the long-handled blade she had made especially for the job.

She had warned him about Clarice. Warned him that he would never make her happy, that her heart would always belong to Ronald. Gently, in her kind way, she had explained that a quiet, bookish man like Edwin was out of his depth with a passionate girl like Clarice. 'You're too different,' she had warned. 'Give her up, Edwin. Find yourself a plainer girl, someone who can be content with your ways. Who will,' she'd added softly, 'take care of you when I'm gone.'

Edwin sighed. As always, his mother was right. He had known he was rushing headlong into dark waters. In the beginning, he had considered himself a good enough swimmer. From the moment he'd first seen Clarice, he had wanted her. Even when she'd belonged to Ronald, he had wanted her with a passion he hadn't known possible. What red-blooded man wouldn't? She was beautiful, like a Hollywood star with her cherry-red lips and high heels and sleek satiny dresses that whispered around the curves of her body when she walked. Edwin lost his head. Seeing her with Ronald had been torture. The thought of possessing her – having what other men desired, proving wrong the people who looked down on him – was too great a temptation. He used to daydream about strolling through town with Clarice on his arm, her beauty inspiring envious glances from all who saw them.

Shaking free of the spell Clarice always cast on him, he shuffled over to one of the large feeding tables that dominated the rearing house. The silkworms were gone. Nothing remained but empty trays and leaf dross. Outside, a breeze lifted the branches of the lemon tree, scratching them against the window, casting ghostly shadows on the walls.

If he had listened to his mother, his life would have taken a different path. He often conjured the woman his mother had described to him, the strong, reliable girl who knew her way around the kitchen, who, in another version of his life, would have taken care of him. Dulcie had fitted that bill, but he had found her too late. By the time Dulcie had come along, Edwin was tainted. His blood still burned for Clarice, his heart and soul bore her imprint so indelibly that he could barely see another woman, let alone love her.

If only they had never met. If only Ronald had not brought Clarice home that long-ago Sunday. If only she'd been plainer, less dazzling, perhaps then Edwin would have stood a chance. Perhaps tonight, instead of loitering in the abandoned rearing house conversing with ghosts, he'd be sitting around a bustling dinner table amid the happy babble of voices. The voices of his children, his grand-children and of his goodhearted wife. And he'd be raising his glass, giving thanks for the full life he had led.

A chill ran over his skin.

It was a heartless fantasy. So real in his mind, yet so removed from reality.

He sighed. No amount of bitterness or regret had ever managed to rewrite history. His crime would eventually surface. One day, the truth would come out. He only hoped that by the time it did, he would be gone.

His brain dislodged an image. A golden-haired girl rushing ahead of him through the avenue of trees, her basket piled with mulberry leaves that jostled free as she ran, swirling behind her in the luminous afternoon . . .

He hung his head. Perhaps if the children had chosen a different day to return. Perhaps if they'd lingered with their family at the camp or decided to take the long way back to

Bitterwood. Perhaps if Edwin had not been so quick to offer their young companion a place in his home. Perhaps then, their lives would have taken a different turn.

He still blamed Clarice. From the moment she had first seen the pretty violet-eyed child and learned that she was alone in the world – motherless, her father's whereabouts uncertain – she had begun to scheme. Like Edwin, she had yearned too strongly for something more, something to fill the aching, terrible void.

Edwin could have told her early on that nothing good ever came from a lie. But he'd always lacked the power to make her listen.

Fumbling for the keys, he went to the rearing house door. Locked it behind him and shuffled along the path towards the house. The only power he'd ever had was the power of forgetting. And there were times, like tonight, when even that eluded him.

13

Bitterwood, June 1993

A gust of wind shook the old Volkswagen. I drew back the curtain. It wasn't yet dawn. Watery moonlight silvered the upper branches of the mulberry trees in the orchard, but beneath them lurked dark shadow. Thunder rumbled overhead, and the first spots of rain began to patter the van roof.

I returned to my little table, where I'd been drinking tea and doodling some illustration ideas for Dad's manuscript, pondering his story. The chapter I'd read last night before bed had not yielded anything concrete to bolster my theory that Dad's characters were based on real people. The old King clearly resembled my grandfather, and the castle reeked of Bitterwood, but I was still attempting to puzzle out how Fineflower and the other wives factored into our family tree – if at all. Before me on the table, arranged like evidence, were my grandfather's letter, the little gold heart, and the glass negative of the two soldiers I'd retrieved from the attic. My attempts to link them had failed, but I couldn't get Edwin's words out of my mind.

I have something for you. It will explain everything.

Explain . . . explain what, exactly?

I sketched a woman's face. Square-jawed, with full lips, and wide cheekbones dotted with freckles, framed by waves of shoulder-length blonde hair. My mother's face. She was part of the puzzle, but when I placed my drawing on the table beside my collection of objects, she only seemed to add to the confusion—

A deafening crash overhead sent me flying to my feet.

Sliding open the side hatch, I stepped out. A branch had fallen on the van roof. I dragged it off and hurled it into the trees, then checked the roof for damage, relieved to find none. Heavy clouds were now smothering any moon or starlight. The house loomed like a dark fortress against the mottled dawn sky. Further down the slope, blacker shadows gathered beneath the bare twiggy limbs of the mulberry trees.

A spear of lightning ignited the horizon, followed by a thunderclap. From the corner of my eye, I glimpsed a pale shape dart from the van and streak away into the night.

'Basil!'

I saw him at the edge of the orchard, just before he vanished. The rain fell harder; droplets dampened my hair and shoulders, sending a cool chill along my scalp. Grabbing my torch from the van, I ran down the slope towards the trees. I looked around, calling his name, but the cat had gone.

I stood in the darkness, listening. The garden seemed

full of stealthy creaks and rustlings, joined now by the increasingly loud patter of raindrops.

I shivered, suddenly aware that I was miles from town, barefoot in pyjama bottoms and T-shirt on a winter night in the rain. I weighed up running back to the van for jeans and a cardigan, shoes. But by then Basil might be long gone.

The rain began to fall more heavily. I was soon soaked to the skin. Raindrops danced in the torch-beam, and all around me the garden teemed with wet shadows.

'Basil?'

I continued down the slope, shining my light into the tree trunks, calling. When I reached the bottom of the garden, another flash of lightning illuminated the old dead oak tree. Its contorted branches raked the sky, its trunk rising from the steep mound that sheltered my grandfather's icehouse.

I hadn't meant to venture so close. The shock of seeing it jogged a memory. I was ten years old, creeping through the orchard on another night exactly like this one. Moonless, rainy and wild. I had taken my grandfather's keys from the pantry lintel and unlocked the icehouse door, stepped inside and ventured along the passageway into the dark. I never really knew what drew me there that night. Curiosity. The thrill of the forbidden. The excitement of the unknown. Then a gust of wind had grabbed the door and slammed it behind me, the force so great the broken handle shot off and bounced away into the shadows. For the longest time I stood staring into the gloom, my knuckles pressed to my mouth, my breath ringing in my ears. Then, a familiar voice called softly through the blackness—

'Lucy?'

I jerked around as memory and reality collided. I began to run. Up the hill, through the maze of fruit trees with their wet shadows and mouldering leaves, back towards the safe haven of my van—

Straight into the arms of a large rain-soaked man.

My scream could have shattered glass. The man flinched away, but then he gripped my shoulders.

'Lucy, it's me.'

Warm hands, I registered. Strong fingers. He knew my name.

'Morgan?' I squinted at him in the half-light, going limp with relief. He was large and solid, reassuringly familiar after my sprint through the rainy trees. But as my shock ebbed away, I felt the first stirrings of annoyance. What part of *I'd rather do it alone* hadn't he understood?

He drew me under a tree where the dense canopy formed a natural shelter. 'You okay?'

I was shaky, my limbs suddenly flushed with heat. I stepped away from him.

'I was, until you gave me a heart attack. Why are you here?'

'Ron got worried. He saw a storm warning on the weather report, asked me to pop down and check on you.'

'Pop down? It's a two-hour drive.'

Morgan shrugged. 'All in a day's work.'

'So, now you've checked you'll be heading straight back will you?'

'I might stick around a day or two, help with any heavy lifting.'

'Don't you have classes?'

'They owe me leave.'

His hair was wet, raked back from his face. Raindrops gleamed on his skin. The sky behind him lit up suddenly. In the brightness that followed, his image burned itself into my eyes. His face shadowed, his hair glittering with raindrops, his shoulders hunched slightly against the downpour.

I stepped away. Instinct told me to get rid of him as quickly as possible, send him back to Melbourne, keeping my promise to avoid him. But another part of me, the naive girl who had once kissed him under the party lights in her father's garden and had her heart broken, was secretly glad. Perhaps spending time with him would break the spell of the kiss, get us back on even footing. Set me free.

'It's early,' I pointed out. 'You must have left in the middle of the night.'

He shrugged. 'I wanted to avoid the downpour. That road is deadly in a storm, especially on a bike. Anyway, Ron didn't want you being alone.'

I hugged my arms around myself, and frowned down the hill.

'Basil's out there somewhere. The thunder scared him, I forgot to shut the van door and he ran off.'

'Basil. The cat?'

I nodded. 'You think he'll be okay?'

'He's probably nice and dry in a hollow log. He'll be back in time for breakfast, you'll see. Cats generally don't wander far.'

I looked at him. 'Sage advice from the cat whisperer?'

He smiled. 'Something like that.'

'Great. I'll mention it to Basil, if he ever returns.'

'We need to get out of this rain.'

I ran over to the van. In my rush to chase the cat, I'd left the sliding door open. Even in the gloom, I could see puddles gleaming inside on the floor.

'Damn,' I muttered. Slamming shut the hatch I whirled to face Morgan. 'I don't suppose the cat whisperer has any quick fixes for a saturated campervan.'

He laughed quietly. 'As a matter of fact, he does.' He led me towards the house. 'Tea and toast. A blazing fire. Some dry clothes. And maybe, if you're very good, a long hot shower.'

The cat whisperer kept all but one of his promises. As I stood shivering in my grandfather's dark kitchen, Morgan located a teapot and caddy of tea leaves, then set a kettle of water on the gas stove to boil.

I retrieved dry clothes from the van, and stood about sipping tea, waiting for Morgan to get the fire blazing. Beside the old combustion heater, he found a wooden box full of newspapers and kindling, matches. Then he crouched in front of the firebox and opened the door. 'What's this?'

At first glance, it appeared to be a book. All that remained was the spine and partial, scorched pages. As I kneeled beside him for a closer look, my heart sank.

'It's a photo album.'

Morgan reached into the ash, shook the album free, and flipped through what remained of the pages. The photos were mostly burned away. Only the edges closest to the spine had survived. Some still clung to the page by paper hinges, but most had fallen loose and were buckled and charred beyond recognition. Several showed people. An elderly woman against a background of roses, a smiling Aboriginal girl holding a basket of apples, and a man on horseback. Others were no more than empty skies propped by the edges of buildings.

'Wait,' I said. 'Go back.'

The photo that caught my eye was little more than a ragged strip. It showed the edge of a weatherboard building, possibly a church, cast deep in shadow. A woman stood in the foreground, bathed in light. Her hair shone as if electrified, and her striking face seemed to glow with an inner fire.

Morgan bent closer. 'Definitely a relative. Do you recognise her?'

'No.'

She wore a light-coloured dress belted at the waist, with puffed sleeves and soft bow collar. The style was 1930s, the design demure, but the fabric enfolded her slender curves in a way that must have seemed, at the time, almost sinful. Beside her stood a man, rigid and formal in a suit and hat. His face had been lost in the flames, but his bearing made me think it could be my grandfather. My attention went back to the woman. The back of my neck tingled. I knew her. At least, that's how it felt. My sense of recognition was so strong, that I wondered if the photo had a duplicate in Dad's meagre collection. But the more I studied it, the more certain I became. I had never seen this woman before, but still . . . I *knew* her.

'Are you sure she's not your grandmother?' Morgan wanted to know.

'Grandma Dulcie was dark-haired,' I said absently, unable to tear my gaze from the woman's face. The more I studied her, the more I saw Morgan was right. She *did* resemble me. Not the me I saw in the mirror every day, but another version. A brighter, more captivating version who gazed, with evident displeasure, from the pages of my grandfather's past.

'She looks unhappy.'

'Almost haunted,' Morgan agreed.

'I wonder who she is.'

'Ron must know.'

I closed the charred album and looked at the spine, rubbed my thumb over the emblem stamped in the leather. 'This is the album he wanted. What's left of it.'

I imagined my father sitting in the sunroom at the back of his house. Not writing, not watching television, and perhaps not even talking to Wilma. Just waiting for me to return with the album of memories he'd sent me to find.

'Why would Edwin burn them?' I said softly.

Morgan picked up a charred photograph and shook off the ash. 'I guess he didn't want Ron to have them.'

'It's such a shame.'

Morgan dropped the photo back into the ashes. 'I wonder if he destroyed the negatives too. Most people hang onto them. We might have to ransack the place.'

'Negatives?' I smiled, remembering what I had found upstairs in the attic the day before. A battered cardboard box, a stack of glass slides. Suddenly I was certain that among them would be more pictures of this woman. Fumbling open the album, I flipped the pages until I found her. The intense eyes, the magnetic gaze, the lovely figure, the elusive way she resembled me but could not have been more different. A strange excited chill washed over me.

'No need to ransack,' I told Morgan. 'Follow me.'

Watery morning sun streamed through the attic window. The light was grey and overcast, doing its best to push through the grime-coated panes. Dust motes whirled in the stuffy air, disturbed by our intrusion.

Opening the wardrobe, I showed Morgan the box of negatives.

'I didn't dare take them out, in case I smashed the lot. The box is crumbling away.'

Morgan kneeled in front of the wardrobe and began to slide the box carefully out of its niche. As he placed it on the floor between us, I heard the crackle and pop of breaking glass.

We exchanged glances, mine wincing, Morgan's apologetic. The top negative was in five pieces. It showed a landscape with a farmhouse in the foreground, barely visible beneath a thick fuzz of dust and mouse dirt. Morgan got to his feet.

'I'm guessing the damage at the bottom of the box is worse. Those plates lower down will have been under the weight of all the others. Whoever put them here clearly wasn't fussed about preserving them.'

I brushed a finger gently over the surface of the top negative. 'They'll need a good soak to get all this filth off, but I'm guessing we can't just pop them in the dishwasher, even if Edwin had one.'

Morgan made a sound, too grim to be a laugh. 'I've cleaned up plenty of negatives before, but never ones so poorly retained.'

He scanned the room, and then frowned at an old dining table mostly hidden beneath an enormous mountain of boxes.

'What are you looking for?' I asked.

'We need a flat surface to lay the negatives out on. That way we can see what we have, and pick the ones we want to develop. There's a darkroom at the uni. That's where I do all the developing for the historical society. Although I'm reluctant to transport these plates to Melbourne, they're too fragile. Be good find somewhere local, a hobbyist or professional willing to lend me his darkroom.' Wandering over to the table, he lifted off one of the boxes and placed it on the floor. 'Once we sort them, we'll have to wrap each one separately. Want to give me a hand?'

While we worked, I watched him from the corner of my eye. The lines around his mouth and eyes were a little deeper than they had been five years ago. Most people dreaded getting old, but I was looking forward to it. I liked the way life etched itself into a person's features, it seemed that age brought the soul closer to the surface. There were times I looked at Morgan and saw a man so beautiful it made my chest ache; other times I couldn't move past the eyes that were too intense, the brow knotted constantly with worry, and the mouth that hovered on the brink of a smile but never quite got there. Aside from my father, he was the person I knew best in the world. Yet there were times, like now, when I felt I didn't really know him at all.

As we lifted boxes, moving in and out of each other's space, the memory of my disastrous birthday kiss filled my mind's eye. I could still feel his lips against mine, how surprisingly soft they'd been, yet how firm; his first startled pulling away, and then the shock of heat as he kissed back, a man's kiss against my fumbling inexperience, a jolting intimacy that took my breath away . . . and was still taking it away now, five years later—

The sun broke from behind the clouds. The light in the room turned from grey to yellow and then bright white, and it was in that sudden, intense illumination that it struck me. I'd been hoping to prove to myself that I was over Morgan, that I'd shaken off my schoolgirl crush and that somewhere, in the span of the last five years, I had finally grown up. But standing there in that brilliant sunlight brought a moment of clarity that was almost painful. Rather than diminish my feelings for Morgan, my time in London – attending art school, meeting Adam, getting caught up in the whirl of theatre and galleries and museums, the excitement and history of that magical city – had somehow only served to deepen them.

I glanced at him, relieved to see that while I stood immobilised by my thoughts, Morgan was shaking out an old sheet, spreading it across the table, preparing a surface to lay out the plates so we could examine them.

I began sorting through the box of negatives. After

brushing off the worst of the mouse dirt and dust, I arranged them on the table and we looked over them.

Against the white sheet, the images leaped from the glass, fragments of the past captured in the ghostly emulsion. Many turned out to be landscapes or shots of the guesthouse, some from an elevated perspective, as if the photographer had climbed one of the nearby hills. There were more church photos similar to the fragment we had found in the album, as well as other snaps equally as intriguing. Family portraits and a series of less formal images that showed children working in the orchard.

At the bottom of the pile, I found the negative I'd been searching for, the couple in front of the church. They stood near the apse, its tall narrow leadlight window catching a flare of sunlight. The woman's serious expression was lost in the inverted lights and darks, but even so she intrigued me. Once again, I had the tingly feeling that I knew her, that she was somehow important. That maybe, just possibly, she was the reason my father had asked me to find the album.

Dad's phone was engaged when I tried to ring later that morning. Morgan had gone into town in search of a darkroom, so I started clearing the attic. I decided to store anything good down in the sitting room, and fill the empty car space beside Edwin's clunky old Toyota in the garage with stuff destined for the tip.

By mid-morning, the rain had blown away, leaving the sky clear blue. I went looking for Basil, and found him stretched in a patch of watery sunlight on the verandah. He yowled when he saw me and sprang to his feet, running delicately to greet me, making me laugh. I picked him up and brought him inside, making a nest for him by the heater and leaving the laundry door open a crack so he could come and go as he pleased.

When Morgan still hadn't returned that afternoon, I accepted that he'd be staying the night at Bitterwood. I prepared one of the guest rooms, sweeping and dusting, dressing the bed with fresh sheets and pillows, hanging several thick blankets on the verandah to air. That done, I hurried down to the kitchen, keeping myself busy, not wanting to think about Morgan sleeping upstairs while I tossed and turned all night in my van.

Just before five o'clock, Dad finally answered his phone.

'Your line's been busy all day,' I said by way of greeting.

'Sorry about that, kiddo. Wilma's been sorting legals all day.'

'How are you feeling?'

'Glad to be home. Any luck with finding that album?'

I hesitated. Outside, I heard the growl of a motorbike. My gaze flew to the window, watching for Morgan. He was a blur as the bike coasted down the gravel drive and vanished around the side of the house.

I took a breath. 'Bad news about the album, Dad. I'm afraid Edwin tried to burn it.'

Dad made a choking sound, so I hurried on. 'But I found a box of old negatives in the attic. The album photos are all there. Morgan's going to develop them.' A grumble on the end of the line. I decided to get to the point. 'Dad, there's a woman in some of the photos. She's with Edwin in most of them. Any idea who she is?'

'That'll be your Grandma Dulcie,' Dad said.

'No, it's not Dulcie. The woman in the photo is slim and fair-haired. She looks like me.'

'Ah.'

'You know her?'

There was a silence. I knocked the toe of my shoe against the skirting board, frustrated by my father's lengthy pause.

Dad coughed, and finally said, 'She's Edwin's first wife. Clarice.'

My toe stopped knocking. My breath became shallow. *Edwin's first wife.* I thought of the resemblance we shared, the eerie feeling of seeing my own features gazing back at me from an old photo. Realisation settled over me.

'She was your mother.'

'Yes.'

Heat flooded my veins, but my skin turned to ice. Grandma Dulcie had died when Dad was a teenager; I knew her only from photos. Yet I found myself disappointed, almost bitter. I tried to dredge up her image, but it slipped away, and in its place emerged the face of a stranger.

'Why didn't you tell me?'

Dad sighed. 'What was the point? She walked out when I was a baby. Just left in the night like a thief. I never even knew she existed until after Dulcie died. She never bothered to make contact, no letters or birthday cards. Nothing.'

'You never even mentioned her.'

'Talking about her wasn't going to change what she did. Or who she was.'

'What do you mean?'

A pause. I could picture him sitting in slippers and dressing gown, stooping towards the phone, as though poised to catch every nuance of the voice on the other end of the line.

He sounded strained. 'She walked out on us, Luce. Left Edwin with a newborn to care for. Tell me, what sort of woman leaves her husband and baby, and never looks back?'

I became aware of the grime clinging to my skin, the dust powdering my hair, a vague grubby feeling of anxiety. In the back of my mind, a small voice asked, *What sort of person leaves her friends and family, escapes to London, and never looks back?* I had the urge to argue with my father, to defend Clarice, but the words wouldn't come. Instead, I went on the attack.

'You let me believe Dulcie was my grandma.'

'And so she was.' Dad cleared his throat. 'Dulcie was there since I was a tot. The best mum I could have hoped for. Clarice meant nothing to me. She might have bewitched Edwin and left him incapable of loving anyone else, but I've forgotten about her. So should you.'

'Then why did you send me after the album?'

A pause. 'Just sentimental, I guess.'

'Not about Edwin.'

'I thought there might be some pictures of Dulcie.'

I frowned, remembering his plea in the hospital, the way he'd gripped my hand, locked his gaze to mine. *I want it back.* I understood then. Our circumstances were different, and a gap of many years lay between our separate sorrows, but here was a missing piece of my father's puzzle. I had lost my mother, too. I knew what it felt like to wish she was still with us.

'You *want* to know Clarice,' I told him. 'That's why you asked me to find the album. You want to see your mother's face and try to understand her.' There was a pulse of silence. I could hear my father breathing. 'Come on, Dad,' I prodded. 'You must have been curious. Didn't you ever wonder *why* she left? Didn't you want to know—'

Dad's cough cut me off. 'Look, Lucy, can we talk about this later? Wilma's just about to serve up dinner.'

I glanced at my watch: quarter to five. Dad and Wilma never ate that early, but I didn't have the heart to argue. Daylight was fading fast. The sound of clinking pots and cutlery drifted along the hallway from the kitchen, and I could hear the low murmur of Morgan's voice.

'We can talk more when I see you,' I told Dad.

He gave a wheeze, and something clunked against the receiver.

My heart flipped. 'Dad, are you all right?'

'Lucy, it's Wilma. What's going on?'

'Where's Dad?'

'He's having a coughing fit. What did you say to upset him?'

'Nothing, I was just—'

'Lucy, I have to go. Your father's fine, at least he will be once I've made him a warm drink. I really wish you wouldn't badger him at the moment. You know how unwell he's been.'

The line went dead. I held the receiver hard against my ear, as if my father might return, but there was just the dial tone.

Perhaps it was my imagination, but the sitting room grew darker. Cold settled around me. The light through the window was fading.

Morgan's voice drifted from the kitchen. I wondered absently if he was talking to the cat. He laughed, a warm gravelly sound that filled me with longing and loneliness. All I had to do was replace the receiver in the phone cradle and walk along the hallway, join him in the kitchen. A simple action, but my body had frozen, trapping me here in the twilight, with the echo of a dial tone ringing in my ear.

I'd always regretted that Grandma Dulcie had not survived long enough to be a part of my life. It seemed futile to mourn someone I'd never met, but my conversation with Dad had plunged me into a mood that felt very much like despair. Suddenly, without warning, his revelation had disconnected me even further from my family. I was someone other than the person I'd always believed myself to be. Not the granddaughter of Dulcie Briar. Rather, the descendant of a woman who had abandoned her loved ones – just as I had abandoned mine.

She bewitched Edwin, my father had said. *But I've forgotten about her . . . so should you.*

Despite my father's warning, I could not forget her. My sudden knowledge of her was like a thorn in my heart, aggravated by the slightest movement. The more I worried it, the more it hurt. Yet I couldn't help wondering. Who was she really, this woman who resembled me? Why had she abandoned her husband and child, broken Edwin's heart and left her son to grow up embittered?

As I stared across the room at the fading daylight beyond the window, I saw in my mind the scrap of half-burned photo. Saw Clarice Briar's intense dark gaze. And I knew one thing for certain.

She had bewitched Edwin. Now, she had done the same to me.

14

Bitterwood, 1929

Orah stared at Clarice, unable to believe her ears.

They stood in the cool shadows of the rearing house. The nesting frames at the far end of the room were empty, but tufts of pure white fibre still clung to several of branches where the worms had spun their cocoons. Clarice stood near the window, holding in her arms a beautiful dress of rose-pink silk that shimmered in the muted sunlight. Orah had been fingering the hem, marvelling over the exquisite colour, the impossible sheen, the delicious rustle under her touch.

'A single dress requires three yards of silk,' she said, trying to anchor the facts in her mind.

Clarice nodded. 'That's right.'

'So, to grow enough silk to weave three yards of fabric, you need nine *thousand* cocoons.'

Clarice bit her lips, and then burst out laughing. 'Oh

darling, look at your face! If I hadn't seen the clear blue sky out there for myself, I'd think there was a thunderstorm on the way.'

Orah tried to shake off the frown, but she still couldn't believe that Clarice would go to such lengths for a single dress. In Orah's mind, such an extravagance was unthinkable. 'But Clarice, nine *thousand*? It seems enough to fill the entire room. Perhaps the entire guesthouse. Perhaps—' She couldn't think of anything larger, and her eyes goggled with the strain.

Clarice smiled widely, sweeping an elegant hand in an arc to encompass the long tables. 'Each tray contains a thousand worms,' she declared. 'And sometimes we keep twenty trays in operation.'

Orah scrunched up her eyes at Clarice, baffled. '*Twenty* thousand cocoons? I thought you only needed nine?'

Clarice laughed. 'I've learned the hard way to accommodate for the whims of ladies' fashion. Any excess silk I have from year to year goes into the making of—' and here she lowered her voice to a whisper, 'rather comfortable bloomers.'

Orah's eyes went wide, and Clarice laughed again. 'Come on, my pet, there's something I want you to see.'

Orah followed Clarice outside and then down through the orchard. Tall trees blocked the sunlight, casting the grassy mound housing the icehouse into deep shade. Clarice pushed open the door and they went inside. While Clarice lit the kerosene lamp, Orah looked around. High narrow shelves lined the walls, packed with dozens of bottles, their store of preserved vegetables and fruit. Clarice held the lantern aloft and led the way along the passage, down some steps, and further into the dark. They reached a narrow doorway and ducked through into a small square room. There were more shelves here, only wider than the ones in the passageway. Instead of jam jars, these shelves were packed with narrow wooden boxes. Clarice retrieved a box and removed its lid, then held the lantern high so Orah could see inside.

At first they looked like sheets of wrinkled paper – leaves from the Bible, Orah thought – but then she noticed that each sheet was covered in tiny black dots.

'Silkworm eggs,' Clarice told her. 'We keep them cold in here until we need them. Then we bring them into the relative warmth of the rearing house so they can hatch. That way we can produce batches of silk all year round.'

Orah shivered. She stepped away from the box, suddenly eager to be back out in the sunlight. She looked at Clarice and found the older woman smiling back at her. It must have been the oily lantern light, or perhaps the dense darkness; it might have been the lack of air, or the dull pervading cold. For whatever reason, Clarice seemed faded, her vibrant beauty somehow dimmed.

Later, much later that night, Orah woke from a dream. She sat up, but didn't switch on the light. Usually she forgot her dreams on waking, but this one had roused her from sleep, and she knew there would be no forgetting. In the dream, she'd held Clarice in the palm of her hand – not the real Clarice, of course, a tiny version, her very own Thumbelina with Clarice's face and shining red hair, dressed in one of Clarice's fine silk dresses. Orah had carried tiny Clarice to the icehouse, down the dark steps and along the narrow passage to where the egg boxes waited. Sliding the cover from one of the boxes, she popped Clarice inside. When the cover went back on, little Clarice began to cry – forlornly, desperately, a sobbing so ragged it tore at Orah's nerves. The wretched sound followed Orah back along the passage-way, past the bottles of preserves, through the heavy door, and back out into the garden. She could still hear it now, echoing in the back of her mind as she sat in her moonlit bedroom – the muffled mouse-like weeping. On and on it went, on and on, as though that tiny hidden heart must surely break.

As the weeks passed, Clarice found herself looking forward to that quiet part of the day when the chores were done, the children's school lessons were learned, and everyone was fed and left to their own devices. Night had fallen by then, and in the hours before bedtime, it became customary for Clarice and her girls, as she thought of them, to light the lanterns and congregate in the rearing house.

The girls were in there now.

The night was hot; the weather had become muggy in the days leading up to Christmas. On her way back from the kitchen with a tray of cool drinks, Clarice paused to look in on them, unseen, from the window.

Orah sat at the old spinning wheel, pumping the treadle with her foot as her nimble fingers teased out the fluffy silk she held in her hands. Nala provided a steady supply of raw downy fibre to Orah's lap basket, making sure it never emptied. Spinning silk thread, as opposed to simply unravelling the cocoons, was a tricky business, yet Orah had delighted Clarice with how quickly she had learned the skill. Clarice had set aside time each evening to instruct her, a special part of her day.

'You're a natural,' she'd told Orah.

'Mam was a spinner,' Orah explained. 'She showed me how, although I've only ever used a spindle and wool, never silk.'

Within a week, the girl had mastered a skill it had taken Clarice nearly two years to grasp. Edwin's mother had been against the boiling of cocoons to harvest the silk – a method that killed the worms inside. It was cruel, she'd said, and Clarice had agreed wholeheartedly. Instead, Susanna Briar had taken instruction from one of her Chinese friends in Ballarat, and learned to spin silk from the short strands left behind when the worms broke from their silken nests. To maintain the strength of the silk, double strands must be spun into the one thread, requiring two hands – and sometimes, in a pinch, Nala would provide a third.

Clarice's heart filled with warmth. They were such good girls; they never bickered or complained, and Clarice so enjoyed having them around. Of course, Nala already had a mother, but Orah was all alone in the world, in need of a mother – while she, Clarice, had empty arms and a heart that ached for love. Was it so very wrong, she wondered, to want Orah to stay?

Clarice's breath fogged on the windowpane, and she drew away. Something made her glance over her shoulder, in time to see Edwin approaching. She held a finger to her lips, and then motioned to the window. Edwin joined her, and after a little while, he murmured, 'My mother would have loved her, wouldn't she? She's taken to that spinning wheel like a duck to water.'

Clarice smiled. Edwin's comment had been casual enough, but it made her see that he wanted it too. He wanted them to be a family. The warmth in Clarice's heart began to glow, and for the first time in many years, she reached up and gently touched Edwin's cheek.

'Do you promise? Orah hadn't meant her voice to come out quite so sharply.

It was now February. Almost two months had passed since her arrival at Bitterwood. Christmas had been and gone, a solemn day for Orah despite Edwin and Clarice's attempts to cheer her. It was her first without Mam, and in the wake of it, her longing to find Pa had grown almost unbearable.

Edwin patted his pocket. 'I've written down your father's address. It's right here. Victoria Street, Melbourne.'

'Will you telephone to let us know?'

'We'll see. I'll do everything in my power to find him, Orah, but do you remember what I told you?'

She slumped. 'He might have moved on.'

'It's a possibility.'

Her voice turned small. 'He might . . . he might have died.'

'Don't lose heart, little Orah. We'll cross that bridge when we come to it.' Edwin smiled. 'Are you happy here with us, my dear?'

'Oh yes. You've been ever so kind.'

'If . . . if it turns out that he's – well, if your father can't be found, would you like to stay with us at Bitterwood? Forever, I mean.'

Orah didn't want to think about that. It meant giving up on Pa, and worse, accepting that Mam was gone too. Besides, forever was a long time. Truth be told, she loved the guesthouse and its big rambling garden. She loved the rearing house with its warm musty smells and beautiful silk moths. She had grown accustomed to the perpetual boom and swish of the ocean on the cliffs below. In so many ways, her life here was richer and more interesting than ever it had been in Glasgow. But Pa was Pa, her flesh and blood. What could be more important than finding him?

Her gaze strayed down the slope towards the orchard. A ladder rested against one of the tallest mulberry trees, and Warra balanced halfway up, reaching into the branches. Below, Nala held a basket to catch the fruit he dropped. From time to time, their shouts and giggles or soft chatter carried on the balmy breeze.

As if sensing her attention, Warra looked around and smiled, and Orah felt her face flush with happiness.

Yes, she thought. *I could live here forever.*

She looked back at Edwin. 'You'll try your best to find Pa, though, won't you?'

'Of course, my angel. I'll head off in the morning and should arrive in Melbourne after lunch. The supplies will take a couple of days, but after that I'll start making enquiries. Visit this place in Victoria Street, see if I can flush him out.'

She knew he'd meant to cheer her, to lighten her worries and put her heart to rest, but as he turned away, Orah thought she saw the sudden gleam of tears in his eyes. Perhaps it was the sun, or the dust, or the salt air, or any number of irritants bent on making a person's eyes water. Besides, why would the prospect of finding her father upset Edwin?

She'd been mistaken, she decided, hurrying down the slope towards the orchard. When Warra glanced around again and waved, the hypnotic warmth of his smile made her forget about Edwin, forget about what she'd seen. Her heart leaped and she ran the rest of the way to the trees to join her friends.

Voices woke her. Midnight voices, perhaps the echoes of a dream.

Orah stirred in her bed.

For the first few groggy moments, she thought she was in her old bedroom in Glasgow, in the days before Pa left for Australia. It was him and Mam she could hear, their hushed utterances drifting up from the room below. They spoke softly, yet urgently, with the edge of reproach they always used when arguing.

You can't let her go, Edwin. I won't let you.

It's the law.

The voices sounded a long way off, disembodied in the darkness, the way they might in a fever dream. Distinct one moment, muffled the next.

The law be damned. Even if he's alive . . . I pray you never find him.

I have to try.

Orah shook herself awake and sat up. Tilting her head, she listened, holding her breath the better to hear. It was no dream. The voices – those of a man and a woman – continued, but the words became indistinct.

Abandoned them . . . What right has he . . . No claim . . .

She's his child.

Why can't she stay . . . We've always wanted—

I can't—

Climbing from the bed, Orah went to the window and peered between the curtains. A draught whispered through a crack in the pane. From somewhere outside, a light was shining, the bright yellow gleam of a kerosene lamp. As she watched, the light moved slowly through the gloom. There, moving side by side like slow shadows, were two figures. One was slim and shapely, appearing then disappearing between the tangled confusion of shadowy tree trunks. The other was tall and angular, shambling through the dark with the graceless bearing of a scarecrow.

The lamplight fluttered, and the figures melted into the dark trees. The quiet insistence of their voices lingered for a while in the warm air, but finally even that faded into the night.

Orah rested her forehead on the window. Her breath clouded the glass, and the sea air blew across her shoulders. Edwin would find her father. She couldn't say why she believed this so intensely, just that she knew it in her heart. Quiet, clever Edwin; he wouldn't give up. After all, he had promised.

She strained to hear the voices, but there was nothing now. Just the melodic hoot of an owl down in the orchard, and the distant murmur of the rolling, washing sea.

15

Bitterwood, May 1993

With trembling fingers, he opened the wardrobe and lifted out a silk dress. It almost slithered from his grasp, its shiny folds taunting, as if to say, *See? See how lovely I still am, while you, old man, have all but crumbled to dust.*

The silk looked black in the moonlight, but he knew that if he flicked on the bedside lamp the colour of the fabric would leap and shimmer like a splash of blood.

Scarlet, she'd called it, with a prim emphasis on the 't'.

He raised the dress to his lips. Even now, her scent lingered in the fold. Cherries and sugar syrup. Mulberry leaves, and a warm musk that was somehow all her own. He breathed deeply, letting the aromas of the past settle around him, comforting and – even after all this time – agreeably familiar.

At last, his heartbeat slowed. His breathing became less erratic. A figure materialised from the dark. She stood before him, her long copper-bright hair cascading over her shoulders, gleaming against the deep red of her silk dress. Her eyes were so clear and blue he wished he could drown in them.

How he loved her.

He could still picture her the way she'd been that late summer night in the orchard, before his departure. The night the rift had finally swallowed them. She had glared at him in the lantern light, shifting her body impatiently, making the dress flare around her shapely hips.

God help him, that red silk dress.

Clarice had reared the silkworms that spun the fibre to make that dress. She had fed the worms three times a day, bundled them into the nesting frames so they could spin their cocoons. Later, she had collected basketsful of wooden spools, wound around with thousands of yards of silk thread. Edwin had driven those baskets of thread to the mill in Geelong. There, skilled labourers had hooked the thread into their machines and woven it into bolts of fabric so fine and silky a man could die of joy just to run it through his fingers. Then the dyeing, where the bolts were plunged into bubbling cauldrons of mauve, forest green, pale pink.

And her favourite, the deep bright scarlet.

To everyone's surprise, she had proved herself an exceptional seamstress. Bent over his mother's old Singer sewing machine, her legs pumping the treadle, her long fingers manoeuvring the fabric this way and that until, with a final flourish, she would hold aloft an exquisitely tailored skirt or blouse.

Or, perhaps, a dress.

He saw it now so clearly. The way it had shimmered in the lantern light beneath the orchard trees, teasing him, rendering him helpless. Reminding him of what he had lost.

Clarice had spoken fiercely. 'He abandoned them, his wife and his little girl. What right has he to claim her now? No claim, I tell you.'

'She's his child,' Edwin had countered.

'Why can't she stay? We've always wanted another daughter. Just tell her you were unable to find him. Please, Edwin.'

'I can't do it,' he'd told her. 'I can't lie to her.'

'You must.'

'Clarice, I cannot.'

'Please, Edwin. My heart will break.'

Around them, the mulberry trees seemed alive. He was not aware of the breeze, but the leaves fluttered as though stirred by invisible hands. The boughs creaked nervously. A lone owl hooted somewhere in the branches over their heads, its song shrill with warning.

'I'm sorry, my love. I can't betray her trust.'

'So instead, you betray your wife?' Clarice wiped a tear from her cheek. 'What sort of a man are you?'

The words struck at his heart. Edwin's brother had often asked that very same question. Edwin's thoughts flew to Ronald, to that morning in France. The crack of gunfire, the stink of mud and fear. The captain's shout in his ear, *For the love of God, hold your fire!*

After the war, he'd been a shell of a man. Withdrawn into himself, disillusioned by the cruelty and pointless waste he'd seen on the battlefields. Bowed beneath a guilt so heavy he knew it must eventually crush him. Then, miracle of miracles, Clarice had accepted his fumbling proposal. Back then she had been a bright butterfly in his colourless world, a creature of whimsy and aching beauty who had helped him forget.

'Your happiness was all I ever wanted,' he said.

'Once I thought I could love you, Edwin.' Her tone was low and accusing, but her voice trembled. 'You were sweet and sincere, always kind. Now, I see what you were all along. Weak, spineless. The sort of man I find so easy to despise.'

She turned suddenly as though to rush away, but in her distress stumbled over the gnarled root of a tree. She hit the ground hard, and the air left her lungs in a breathy grunt. Burying her face in her arms, she began to sob.

Edwin might have fallen to his knees beside and begged her forgiveness. It struck at his heart to see her there, crumpled in the dirt as she wept her bitter tears. But he heard movement behind him.

Twisting around, he stared into the trees. It hadn't been a noise, not exactly. Rather, a disturbance in the air. An indrawn breath. A sigh that rustled the leaves. The blink of watchful eyes. Then he saw it. A shadow, a man's shadow. Brass buttons glinted in the lantern light as the shadow reached its arms towards Edwin, its fingers splayed as though beseeching. Edwin inhaled sharply, and the scent of rotting cherries filled his lungs.

The orchard faded back into the past, making way for the dim and somehow unappealing light of reality. Edwin stared across the cavernous expanse of his bedroom. The dark had grown deeper, the moonlight from the window gone.

So many memories. So much to ponder before he died. How could he bear to leave it all? The answer was simple. He could not.

At least, not yet.

Carefully, he placed the dress back on its hanger, returned it to the wardrobe, and tucked it away from sight.

Below the walls of the great castle, the waves whispered and sighed as they beat their watery fists against the rocks. The ocean was angry, the Queen knew. Angry, and impatient to reclaim what she had stolen.

—The Shell Queen

16

Bitterwood, June 1993

'What's this?' Morgan called from the bottom of the orchard. 'Some kind of fallout shelter?'

I paused on the path. Sleep had evaded me last night. Every time I closed my eyes, I saw Morgan in the upstairs guest room, tucked into the bed I'd made up for him. His light was on until after midnight. I saw it blink out, leaving the house in darkness. Leaving me restless, tossing and turning, burning with guilt, eventually tumbling into sleep, and into dreams of deep water and forgetting how to swim.

I gazed along the path meandering through the trees. Wintry afternoon sunlight shone through the branches, casting twiggy shadows on the damp ground.

I had spent the morning cleaning up the glass photo negatives, while Morgan rode back into town to continue his search for a darkroom. He had returned with good news. A portrait photographer in Queenscliff, further east

175

along the coast towards Melbourne, had offered the use of his set-up in return for print copies and permission to include them in his archive of historical images. Morgan had agreed to be there the following day. In the meantime, I was giving him a guided tour of my grandfather's garden.

'Lucy?'

Reluctantly, I went along the path through the copse of mulberries, bypassing quinces and lemons and plums, down towards the shady hollow on the lowest level of the garden. It seemed a thousand years had passed since I had entered this dank, secluded corner. Yet the big old oak and the grassy mound, the tall trees smothered in vines, were all just as I remembered. As I joined Morgan in the little clearing, I had the eerie feeling of time unravelling, of being a child again, of standing here with the icy weight of keys in my hand, shivering with anticipation.

Morgan gave me a curious look. 'Fallout shelter?' he asked again.

I glanced at the door, then away. 'It's the icehouse.'

'Ever been inside?'

'Edwin kept it locked.'

'Do you know where he stashed the keys?'

I shook my head. An icy gust howled in the back of my brain, bringing with it the distant echo of a child sobbing. Rubbing my arms, I stepped into a patch of sunlight.

Morgan walked over and joined me. In the sun, the lines around his eyes looked deeper. 'Tough old time for you back then, wasn't it?' he said quietly.

I shrugged. 'It seems like someone else's life now.'

'You were so lost when you came to stay with us. First your mum, and then Ron's breakdown . . .'

I gazed up at the twisted old oak, past its naked silvery branches to the blue sky. 'Dad did his best.'

Morgan watched me for a moment longer and then when I turned away he wandered back over to the icehouse door. 'Your grandfather really liked his fires.'

I braved a closer look. The icehouse door was blackened around the edges, the iron reinforcements along its length buckled. At some time in the recent past, flames had escaped under the door a short way, charring the stone step. The smell of old smoke lingered in the damp air.

'There used to be a kerosene lamp hanging in there,' I said. 'Maybe Edwin left it burning and it caused a fire.'

Morgan kicked the door. Soot puffed out of the crevices. 'I wonder how badly damaged it is inside.'

'Maybe all burned out,' I said hopefully. 'All the beams were wood, the roof has probably collapsed.'

Morgan tested the door handle. 'I wonder if Edwin set it alight deliberately, like he did with the photo album.'

'Why would he do that?'

Morgan lifted his brows. 'Maybe he had something to hide.'

I took a step back. An image flashed into my mind, a drawing. It was one of my preliminary sketches for Dad's story, only now I saw the final version in full colour. The dungeon in the depths of a castle, its violet shadows retreating from a row of suspended figures. Four ghostly women, their bloodless faces darkened by the holes of their eyes . . .

Maybe he had something to hide.

'What is it?' Morgan came over, searching my face. He placed his hands lightly on my elbows, the way he had when he'd told me about my father's fall. 'You've gone white.'

I shrugged away from him, but something kept me near. 'It's nothing.'

A stretch of silence followed. Rather, a stretch of time when neither one of us spoke, because it was far from silent. A magpie warbled overhead, and the raucous chatter of lorikeets drifted from the orchard. In that quiet beat, a memory surfaced.

Treading gently into the dark. The sensation of wrongness, that I was unwelcome, that I had no right to be there. Yet still I stumbled deeper along the passageway, my torchlight jittering about, catching shards of glass on the floor, sweeping across a ceiling thick with cobwebs. I heard the shuffle of my feet, the noisy huff-huff *of my breath . . . and then a whisper from somewhere nearby—*

'Do you know what I think, Lucy?' Morgan frowned, his eyes bright despite the shadows. 'There's another reason you've come back here.'

Goose bumps pricked along my arms. 'What reason?'

'You stayed here after your mum died. It's only natural you have uneasy memories of the place. Maybe the universe has led you back here to confront your demons.'

I met his eyes briefly, then looked away. Over the years, Morgan's beliefs had shaped the way I looked at the world. He voted green, even before it was fashionable, he was vegetarian, had a soft spot for the elderly and an enduring passion for anything historical. There was just one ideology I'd never been able to get my head around: Morgan believed in fate, in the playing out of some cosmic scheme that connected us all. My leanings were more towards the existential side of things: we were born, and we lived our lives. When we died, we turned to dust. I just couldn't align with Morgan's view that our souls were eternal, that death was just a doorway through which the spirit flew like a bird, circling for a time in a heavenly place, before returning to earth in a different form.

Maybe the universe has led you back . . .

Shivering, I rubbed my arms. 'I don't have any demons.' Before he could reply, I turned and hurried away, heading uphill along the path to the orchard, back into the dappled sunlight.

The lie was still haunting me the following morning as we stood in the driveway. Morgan was about to drive to Queenscliff to develop the photos. I had insisted that he take my van, to preserve the box of fragile glass plates secured on the front seat. We had wrapped each plate individually in newspaper, padding the box with old clothes I'd found in one of the guest rooms. The box looked ready to withstand a nuclear blast, but I wanted to give the negatives their best chance.

'They'll be fine,' Morgan reassured me, taking the car keys from my hand. He climbed into the driver's seat, buckled up and started the ignition. 'I'll guard them with my life.'

Still I hovered, strangely reluctant to see him go. 'Try not to blow the speed limit,' I added, patting the van roof. 'I'm kind of fond of this old girl.'

'Are you sure you won't come with me?'

'Quite sure.' I stepped back, gave a little wave. I had told him I would stay and make headway on clearing the guest rooms. This was partly true, as I was keen to continue my search for the mysterious something Edwin had promised me in his letter. But I'd planned another activity, one I had to do alone.

Morgan revved the Volkswagen to life and cruised away along the road. I dragged shut the gates. For a while, I stood gazing out at the ocean. The water was light blue-grey in the sunlight, the exact colour of Morgan's eyes. I imagined swimming out as far as I could, losing myself in the vastness, letting the tides wash away the uneasy feeling that had dogged me since my return to Bitterwood.

The universe has led you back here, Morgan had said. The words haunted me. In a way, they were true. The universe – or at least, my grandfather's letter, and then my father's request to find the album – had indeed lured me back. But for what eventual purpose, I didn't know.

I retreated along the drive to the house.

With my van gone, I felt strangely desolate. In an emergency, I knew how to ride Morgan's Harley, or there was Edwin's ancient Toyota in the garage. My clothes and toiletries waited in my old room at the top of the stairs, just in case Morgan had to stay overnight in Queenscliff.

I sat in the kitchen, restless.

Basil had devoured a can of tuna and half a bowl of kibble, and now paced hopefully at the back door, waiting for me to let him out. I hadn't needed to butter his paws. He seemed reluctant to stray far from my side. But I didn't want to open the door. Not yet. I kept glancing at the window, watching the trees sway in the morning breeze. Morgan's words echoed in my mind.

The universe has led you back.

I got to my feet. From under the sink, I retrieved a torch. As though in a trance, I went to the pantry. Ducked behind the door and reached up onto the lintel ledge where Edwin concealed his keys. There were two keys on the ring. One large, the other short and stubby with a square head.

From the safety of the kitchen, with its blazing fire and cosy warmth, my plan seemed foolproof. I only had to walk to the bottom of the garden, unlock the icehouse door. Poke my head in, acknowledge that my horrors were nothing but dust, and then return, fulfilled and somehow stronger, to the house.

Demons confronted.

With a sigh, I replaced the keys on the lintel. Retreating to my spot at the table, I took Dad's manuscript from my satchel. Flipping through, I found my place and escaped back into the story.

The man of shadows waited patiently for Fineflower's answer.

Your heart . . . given willingly.

Fineflower listened to the rustle of silkworms as they chewed their leaves. She listened to the creak and sway of the wives in their everlasting dance. Time ticked away. In a few hours, the King would return. He would discover her failure and hang her from the rafters, drain out her blood. She would never see her baby son again.

'All right,' she told the man of shadows. 'I'll give you my heart.'

'Willingly?'

She nodded.

Around her in the cell, the shadows shifted. The man stepped nearer, and smiled. Fineflower recognised that smile, she had seen it that day in the marketplace; it was the smile that had begun all her troubles. As she pondered the soldier's face – the eyes like black fire, the straight white teeth, and the dimples pushing the edges of his lips – she knew she could not be angry. Instead, she began to melt a little, to bask in the glow of that smile and let her fears unravel.

Reaching into her bodice, she drew out a crimson handkerchief that had once belonged to her mother. It was Fineflower's most treasured possession.

The man of shadows took it gently from her fingers. He drew it to his nose, breathed its scent, and then tucked it into his pocket. He sat at the spinning wheel. Scooping up a handful of cocoons, he moistened them with his breath and pricked away the fine sticky thread. He wound three silken lengths around the flyer and began to pump the treadle; the bobbin spun and the thread gathered quickly around its shank, only now the silk was no longer white – but pure gleaming gold.

While he worked, the soldier bowed his head and began to sing. His song was sorrowful, and Fineflower felt the darkness gather heavily on her chest. Her empty chest. She pressed her hands to the place where her heart had once been, and felt the stillness there. It was a fair price, she reasoned. Soon, she would see her little son.

Gold and bright, sang the soldier, *darkest night,*
Seek the spinner in the light.

An hour passed. Two hours. Three.

The moon rose, drifted across the distant sky, and then began to set. The first rays of dawn trickled through the small high window above. Fineflower blinked awake and gazed around in joy. Her soldier had kept his promise. Wooden reels sat in piles around the cell, their bellies fat with gold thread that glimmered brightly in the early sunlight. Fineflower went to the soldier and spoke her thanks. He gazed at her through weary eyes and took her hand.

'Forget the King,' he told her. 'Leave with me now, we can start a new life together.'

Fineflower shook her head. 'Not without my son—'

Before the soldier could reply, footsteps sounded in the corridor. The door burst open. In marched the King. When he saw Fineflower standing at the spinning wheel with her soldier, he drew his sword and shouted for his men. He rushed at them, but the soldier was faster. He drew his knife and drove the King back towards the doorway. Then the King's men arrived and surrounded the man of shadows. With savage cries, they dragged him to the floor and laid into him with their boots. Moments later, they were hauling his motionless body away along the corridor, leaving Fineflower alone in her cell with the angry King.

Rather than calm me, Fineflower's story had made me more restless, made me realise I was teetering on the edge of a precipice.

I had two choices. I could continue to ignore the darkness building in the back of my brain; continue to ignore the nightmares, the sweaty guilt that prodded me awake in the night. Or I could leave the cosy warmth of the kitchen right now and venture into the garden. I could walk along the path through the orchard, open the icehouse door and march into its shadowy heart with my torch blazing. I could prove to myself that what I had seen – or *imagined* I'd seen – as a frightened ten-year-old was nothing more than a pile of disused bricks or a harmless bundle of old rags.

My time at Bitterwood as a kid had thrown me off kilter, causing me to view everything from a place of uncertainty, a dark place where frightful things lurked in every shadow. I could put an end to all that.

Getting to my feet, I went to the pantry and retrieved Edwin's keys. Collected the torch, opened the back door and stepped out. Breathing deeply of the cool night air, I crossed the verandah and hurried down into the garden.

The smell of damp grass, rotting leaves. The chill of the overhanging trees as I walked beneath them. Branches creaked in the wind, unseen creatures rustled in the shadows; the back of my neck prickled. Through the orchard I went, following the path down the slope to the dank clearing beneath the dead oak. The old tree gleamed white in the morning sunlight, its bleached branches stark against the cloudless sky.

I stood in front of the icehouse door.

Singling out the big key, I forced it into the lock. The brass doorknob was cold under my fingers, slick with last night's rain. I pushed the door open. Its base squealed against the flagstones and a burnt smell rushed out. I found a brick to chock the door, and then stepped inside. The scorched smell intensified, acrid and stale, and as I shone my light around I saw that the bases of all the beams were blackened and burned away in sections. Smoke had discoloured the rock ceiling, and I was suddenly aware of the weight of stone above me. Tree roots had grown through between some of the supports, and pockets of grit had crumbled away.

Further inside, the reek of charred wood gave way to other smells. Mould and dust, dampness. As I took a shuffling step forward, my outstretched hand collided with something hard and cold, a wall. My dream flashed back. The cold, clammy stone beneath my touch, the freefall back through time, my mother's urgent whisper. *If only you hadn't lied.* I hunched my shoulders against it and walked on. My torchlight fell on rows of shelving, several stacked with dusty Fowlers jars and some old wood boxes. Broken glass littered the floor beneath.

Go back, said a voice in my mind. *The place is unstable, the beams half burned away . . . The roof could fall, go back.* Instead, I went deeper, but then hesitated when I came to a short flight of steps. Four narrow wooden risers led down into a darkness that was so dense I could almost taste it, almost feel its dampness on my skin like fog.

Go back.

Slowly, I descended the steps. Gritty things crunched beneath my shoes, dirt and insect husks, years of dead leaves blown under the door.

My torch beam seemed diminished, unable to penetrate the heavy gloom more than an arm's length ahead.
At the bottom of the steps, I paused again. My breathing
sounded harsh and overloud, as though I wasn't the only
person present. I listened, straining to hear beyond the roar
of blood in my ears.

Suddenly the roar became my father's voice. *It's not her,*
he had cried in the foyer of the morgue. *That's not my wife
in there, you've made a mistake . . . I'm telling you, it's not her—*

I kept going. My body seemed to be folding in on itself,
growing smaller. My feet taking littler steps, my fingers
curling protectively. I was ten again, and as I pushed along
the passageway, a feeling of wrongness overcame me, a
sense that I was unwelcome, out of bounds.

The police had explained to my father that two weeks
submerged in water changed a person's physiology. They
knew how difficult it must be for him, but he was the only
one who could identify her body without question. He must
see beyond the bloating, the injuries and violent discolouration, see beyond his own horror and grief, look only at the
features, identify them, and try to find peace in the fact
that her remains were no longer adrift.

But it's not her.

While my father ranted, while he tried to drown his last
vision of her in a wine cask, I had curled in a ball at the foot
of my bed, hands pressed over my ears, hot tears leaking
into my hair. If Mum wasn't at the morgue, I had wondered,
then where was she?

I took another step into the darkness. Something whispered around my legs, a gust of breeze from outside bringing

with it the smell of damp grass and rain. Dead leaves stirred around me, their rasping voices taking on a familiar tone.

I'm in here, Lucy . . . Drowning all over again in this damp darkness.

A flush of heat surged through me, and then I went cold. I saw her then in my mind's eye, slumped on the floor in the dark inner chamber ahead of me, frighteningly still. Her skin had turned black and withered away, her features melted into bone, her hair – her lovely blonde hair – a mess of dust littering the flagstones beneath her fractured skull—

I began to back away, sick with dread. It wasn't her, it couldn't possibly have been her. What I'd seen that night in the dark heart of the icehouse when I was ten had been nothing more than the wretched imaginings of a grief-stricken girl. Abandoned rubbish, perhaps, like the broken preserve jars and old bottles in the passageway behind me. A pile of bricks, a roll of mouldy carpet. Better yet, not real, merely a figment, a trick played by a young mind pushed to its limits.

You lied, Lucy . . . and now I'm trapped here . . .

Turning, I fled back along the passage and up the stairs, crashing against the wall in my haste, almost tripping. Bursting from the icehouse, I staggered out into the garden, dragging shut the door and locking it tight, the keys gripped in my trembling fingers. For the longest time I stood on the path, jangled and shaking, wanting to laugh at myself, how foolish and scared I'd just been, startled by shadows. But I didn't laugh, I couldn't. I just waited for the quaking to stop, and then trod unsteadily back up the path, through the copse of mulberry trees, back towards the house.

Basil stretched on the lawn near the verandah steps sunning himself in a patch of sunlight. His eyes were half-mast, his body relaxed into a long white sausage. I fell onto the grass beside him, burying my fingers in his thick coat.

'Clever old boy,' I muttered. 'Soaking up the sun, not a care in the world . . . unlike your silly mistress here, jumping out of her skin at shadows.' I tickled his belly, which made him purr happily and squirm onto his back. Resting my face against his fur, I breathed in the sweet sunshiny scent of him. Soon, his kitten-talk surrounded me, the soft vibrations anchoring me, drawing me up through time, out of the past and into the brighter light of the present.

17

Bitterwood, 1930

Her argument with Edwin had left her shaken, bruised after her fall. Betrayed. She hurried inside and along the hall, glad the children were asleep, glad there was no one to witness her distress.

The stairway was dark, but Clarice didn't bother to switch on the light. She knew her way through this house by touch alone. As she went up to the bedroom, she kept seeing Edwin poised in the orchard denying her, resisting her pleas; she kept seeing the stubborn jut of his lip, kept hearing his hateful words.

I can't betray her trust.

He spoke so easily of betrayal, but that had not been Clarice's intention. She wanted only what was best for the girl, which meant keeping her here at Bitterwood with them. Orah was growing happier by the day, settling in, flourishing as part of their family. Her father – provided he was even alive – was an unknown quantity. He had abandoned Orah once when she was a vulnerable seven-year-old; how could he be trusted to stand by her now she was a girl of thirteen? Clarice burst through the doorway into the room she shared with Edwin, and stood in the stillness, her hand pressed over her thumping heart.

A man who abandoned his child did not deserve a second chance. Why could Edwin not see that?

She had presumed he shared her feelings about the girl. She had seen it in him, the adoration, the willingness to please. He had been the same way with Edith. A witty buffoon, a tireless playmate, a surprisingly gracious clown. Clarice hated to admit it, but he was the perfect father. Perhaps a better father than even Ronald would have been, and this thought pained her greatly. If only Ronald had lived. If only he had fathered her children, stood beside her to watch them grow. And they would have grown. With Ronald at the helm of their family, no tragedy, no mishap, no misfortune would have dared to tiptoe over their threshold.

Not that she blamed Edwin for the loss of their daughters. He would have gladly died if it meant saving them. She did not doubt his devotion. But he had hurt her deeply tonight, failed to keep his promise.

You're my life, Clarice. I'll stand by you, come what may.

Dragging a suitcase from beneath the wardrobe, she placed it on her bed and began to fill it with clothes. She didn't care what she packed, flinging her good dresses in with her old ones, her stockings knotting up with her scarves and gloves, toiletries thrown into the mix with hasty abandon.

She would take some money from the safe, where Edwin

kept his reserves. Then she'd pack the Ford, leave straight away for Melbourne, and take Orah with her. They would find a modest establishment in the city where no one asked questions. Even if anyone did, who would doubt a loving mother and her daughter?

Hot tears clung to her lashes.

He knew how she had suffered when they lost Edith and Joyce. Edith's poor little body succumbed to diphtheria, while Joyce was born with fluid in her lungs. One loss would have been intolerable, but two . . . There were days when Clarice could not breathe from the unfairness of it. Buried in the same grave, along with the last shreds of her sanity – at least, so it had seemed at the time. She had fallen into despair, a black pit from which there was no escape. She had surrendered to the darkness, allowed the pain to pick away at her mind until it felt like a carcass, useless and spent.

But two months ago, the ocean had yielded them a gift, a beautiful golden-haired girl. Clarice already loved her. It was cruel of Edwin not to see this, cruel of him to refuse what she asked.

The tears spilled, burning wet tracks down her cheeks. A memory came to her, a long-ago morning in the orchard. She and Edwin had frolicked with Edith. Such cheerful times, it pained Clarice to realise she would never know such happiness again. She stared at the mess of clothes in her suitcase. Bitterwood was full of such memories. Perfect moments of love and joy untainted by the shadow of what was to come.

With a sigh, she considered her jumbled things. Was she ready to leave it all behind, to sever ties and start a fresh, somewhere out there in the unforgiving world?

The shadows shifted. Her tears began to dry. Closing her eyes, she listened to the whispers of the past. Edith's footfall on the stairs; baby Joyce's soft murmurs as she nursed; Edwin's dear old mother Susanna shuffling along the hall at midnight with her candle; and the barely-there shouts of Ronald as he raced through the orchard on his way to the cove, hair tousled lovingly by the wind. Ronald had been a terrible tease, he'd ragged poor Edwin nonstop, but hidden beneath his swagger was a keenly compassionate heart, a heart Clarice knew well, because he had given it utterly, eternally, to her.

Clarice untangled her stockings and refolded them into her dresser drawer. She replaced her scarves and gloves in the pearl-inlaid box Edwin had given her. She retrieved her dresses one by one and placed them back on their hangers. With the suitcase once again tucked under the wardrobe, she stood in the quiet room with her fingers pressed to her lips. She would stay, and make her peace with Edwin. She would say no more on the matter, not even when he departed the following day. Bitterwood was too full of memories for her; she could not bring herself to forsake them. Those memories were like chains keeping her bound to the place. Bound to Edwin. She sighed. Once, she had fancied that within Edwin's lanky form dwelled the soul of a rabbit: soft and pliable, timid and weak. What a fool she'd been. Edwin had proved tonight that he was less the gullible pushover, and rather more the scheming fox.

Ballarat, 1930

Edwin barely noticed the heat as he climbed from the Ford and surveyed the dusty street. In his suitcase, he carried several changes of clothes, a silver tin with travel-sized shaving gear and soap, and his portable ledgers. In the breast pocket of his jacket was a knotted handkerchief containing two pound notes. He carried this reserve at Clarice's insistence. She liked to know that in the event of a stolen wallet or lost bag, Edwin would have enough money for decent lodgings and a meal. This small kindness had made him ache at the thought of leaving her. He always hated going, but this time seemed worse. Their farewell had been chilly, Clarice barely able to look at him. If only she hadn't asked the impossible. Edwin had never refused her anything before, but her request, even now, made him lightheaded with shame.

He took a room in a hotel overlooking the junction of two wide dusty streets. He paid several day's board in advance, although he suspected his undertaking would be over before then. The old boarding house in Victoria Street, back in Melbourne, had closed years before, the building now condemned, but a chance meeting on the footpath outside with the former proprietor had inspired Edwin to continue searching. The man remembered the big boastful Scotsman, and suggested he try the goldfields of Ballarat. *There's been no mining and no gold for many years now,* he'd told Edwin, *but I've heard of a camp out near Black Hill where the desperates still congregate.*

Edwin went up to his hotel lodgings, changed out of his dusty travel clothes, and then, after a hearty meal in the dining room downstairs, he ventured into the public bar. Two elderly gents were sitting at a table near the window, smoking and looking into their beer glasses. Otherwise, the bar was empty. Edwin approached the counter and ordered a neat brandy, which he drank in a single swallow. He struck up a conversation with the barmaid, a stout woman by the name of Mrs Mallard. She peered at him through well-polished spectacles, rambling for a while about the heat and the dust, about the slowness of business since the economy's downturn.

When she paused to repolish the counter, Edwin took his chance.

'I've heard there's a camp of drifters out at Black Hill.'

'Then you've heard right,' Mrs Mallard agreed.

'See many of them in here, do you?'

She screwed up her doughy face. 'Those fellas don't have two pennies to rub together. If they want grog, they brew it themselves, or flog it. Poor blighters. You'd feel sorry for them, except the whole country is in a bad way. Out of work, travelling to earth's end in search of employment. Begging for food, stealing when they can.'

'I'm looking for someone,' Edwin said at last. 'A Scotsman by the name of Hanley Dane. He immigrated here in 1923, lived for a time in Melbourne. The boarding house proprietor there told me he caught the gold fever and came to Ballarat.'

Mrs Mallard shook her head. 'The gold's gone. They closed up the mines years ago. Of course, the fields are still full of fossickers and hopefuls, trying their luck in the creeks or sifting through the dross left by the miners. Occasionally someone gets lucky. Just the other day a man came in with a nugget the size of a knucklebone. But mostly they're on the drift, and a more broken bunch of men you've never seen.'

Edwin wet his lips. 'I wouldn't mind taking a drive out to Black Hill.'

Mrs Mallard studied him. 'What's he done to you, this Hanley Dane? You seem ever so keen to find him.'

Edwin cleared his throat, glanced towards the doorway. 'It's a personal matter,' he said quietly. Sliding out his wallet, he paid for the drink, and turned away from the bar.

Mrs Mallard called him back. 'You know,' she said, her eyes sharp behind the gleam of her spectacles, 'a while back, some of the fellas out there hitched a lift in a truck to Wonthaggi, down on the south coast. They were hiring at the coalmine.'

'When was this?'

'A couple of months ago.'

Edwin pictured another long car trip ahead of him, and sighed. 'Wonthaggi, did you say?'

Mrs Mallard leaned on the counter, and shook her head. 'You won't find him there.'

'Why's that?'

'A dreadful place, the Wonthaggi mine. Living conditions are bad, but the mine is worse. The ground is unstable, cave-ins happen all the time. Lives lost, but the men are too desperate to care. Eleven drifters climbed onto that truck. Now, I'm not saying your Scotsman was among them. But do you know how many returned?'

Edwin stared at her, frozen in place. He could barely hear her words, so loudly did his pulse thunder in his ears. It was hope, he realised. Wild, overwhelming hope.

Mrs Mallard took off her glasses, polished them on her apron. Slid them back on and narrowed her gaze at Edwin. 'None of them,' she said with grim satisfaction. 'All lost beneath the coal and rubble. Buried alive.'

Bitterwood, 1930

Monday was normally the quietest day of the week, but today was an exception. Orah was up at dawn, raiding the garden with Nala for tonight's feast. There would be baked potatoes, fresh peas, huge springy Yorkshire puddings and pork gravy to smother them with. Warra chopped wood and stoked the range, then caught one of the fattened ducks. They scrubbed floors and polished windows, spread the beds with fresh linen, and placed huge jars of wildflowers throughout the house.

Orah worked quickly, trying to lose herself in the day's chores, but her mind wanted to stray. Edwin had not telephoned with news of Pa, but she couldn't stop the butterflies in her belly, couldn't help the anxious excitement from bubbling through her. *Soon*, whispered a small hopeful voice in her head, *soon I'll be seeing Pa, and we'll be a family again.*

When the sound of the Ford utility finally rumbled along the road at six o'clock that evening, they ran out to greet it.

Edwin alighted the truck. As he approached the verandah, he paused and looked up, surveying his surrounds, shaking his head as though in wonderment. As though, rather than spending a mere fortnight away, he had been absent for years.

'Bitterwood,' Orah heard him murmur as he gazed

along the shadowy rooftop. 'Dear old Bitterwood, how I've missed it.'

Orah tried to catch his eye, but he only smiled vaguely and headed inside.

After a wash and quick change of clothes, he took his position at the head of the table. Clarice sat at the opposite end, gesturing for Warra and Nala to seat themselves across from Orah. Edwin bowed his head, thanked the Lord for the beautiful spread of food, and recited the blessing.

Orah watched him through her lashes.

He looked different. There was a dark flush to his normally pale complexion. He had lost weight; he had been thin before, but now his flesh looked stringy, his skin stretched too tightly over his bones.

Orah barely touched her food. While the others ate hungrily, she chased a slice of duck breast around her plate with her fork. She longed to leap up from the table and drag Edwin to a quiet corner, demand that he tell her what he'd learned about her father. Had he found him? Was he well? Would Orah see him soon? Edwin seemed reluctant to speak of his journey.

'What did you think of Geelong?' Clarice wanted to know. 'Were the roads clogged with automobiles? What were the women wearing? Did you meet anyone of interest?'

Edwin deflected her enquiries, and instead kept steering the conversation back to the guesthouse. Had Warra remembered to mend the garage roof? Were the chickens laying well? Was Nala looking forward to seeing her mother and aunts at the end of the month? How was Orah settling into life at Bitterwood?

After their meal, Warra excused himself to set a possum trap in the orchard. Nala collected the plates, and when Orah rose from the table to help her, Edwin motioned for her to remain seated. Tiny beads of sweat had collected on his temple. The flush in his cheeks had drained away, leaving his skin ashen. He ran a hand through his hair, and as he lowered his arm, his elbow struck the table edge. Teacups clattered and a rose in the centrepiece vase shed its petals.

Clarice slumped back in her chair with a sigh. 'Edwin, please. Orah is sick with waiting.'

Collecting one of the rose petals between thumb and forefinger, Edwin rubbed the velvet cup until it bruised to mush. Finally, he looked at Orah.

'I found the boarding house in Victoria Street. According to the proprietor, your father hadn't lived there for years.' He lowered his gaze back to the fallen flower petals, edging them into a pile with his fingertip. All the while his mouth moved, as if chewing over words he could not bring himself to say.

'Pa must have moved on,' Orah prompted, ignoring the hollow feeling that was opening in her chest. 'Did you—' She gulped a breath, unable to continue.

Edwin nodded. 'Your father did move on, to the gold-fields of Ballarat. I went in search of him there, but—' The dark flush had returned, and moisture glistened on his temple. Finally, he looked at Orah. 'I'm sorry, my dear. Your father's gone.'

Orah went rigid. 'Gone?'

Edwin's nostrils flared as he inhaled. 'A few months ago, he travelled to a town called Wonthaggi, and found employment in the coalmine. There was a terrible accident. Part of the mine collapsed. Some of the miners were killed. I'm so sorry, my dear, but I'm afraid your father was among them.'

Clarice went to Orah, crouching by the chair and opening her arms, trying to gather Orah into them.

Orah flinched away. She continued to sit rigidly, staring at Edwin's face. Finally, she dropped her gaze, taking sudden interest in the way the skin on her knuckles wrinkled when she pressed her hands flat against the table. She sucked in tiny sips of air, unable to expand her lungs fully enough to breathe deeply. She kept very still, knowing that if she moved too suddenly, breathed too deeply, allowed herself to think beyond the moment, she would fall apart.

I'm alone, she thought. *Alone in a land where I don't belong.* A frightening thought, but she wasn't afraid. She wasn't *anything*. She felt no fear or sorrow, just an empty sort of numbness. Perhaps she had turned to stone. The air around her grew cold. For what seemed an eternity, the breath caught in her lungs, congealing into an unbreathable solid. The room vanished, along with its fine furnishings and rich hardwood floor. Orah floated in a grey mist, where the only sound was the harried *ratta-tat-tat* of her heart.

As if from a great distance, she heard Clarice sigh.

'Edwin, ring for Nala. We'll have tea and biscuits. And some warm milk with brandy for Orah.'

'Wait.' Orah finally looked up. Her voice was a mouse-like whisper. 'What will happen to me now?'

Edwin glanced at Clarice, and a stillness fell upon the table.

'Clarice and I considered this possibility before my departure. We spoke at length about what would happen if my quest to find your father failed. If we delivered you to the authorities, they would find you placement in an orphanage. But if you would rather . . . I mean to say, if you decided . . .'

The mist folded back around Orah, closing her off to Edwin's words. The hollowness in her chest grew colder and darker. She did not breathe. Her heart refused to beat. *Orphanage?* Until now, she had never considered such a devastating possibility. Even in her darker moments, she had managed to turn her thoughts around. To imagine Pa striding out of the gloom, his laugh booming as she rushed into his arms, and him lifting her in a bear hug, swinging her around, rubbing his beard against her cheek and mumbling in his gravelly way, *Orah, my Orah . . . My little girl, where have you been?*

Clarice reached for Orah's hand and clasped the girl's cold fingers in her own.

'What Edwin is trying to say is that we want you here. At home, with us. We've grown to love you, Orah. We . . . we would like you to be part of our family.'

Orah's gaze went to the window. There was nothing to see, just the darkness. From the distance came a dim hammering sound, and she wondered if Warra was still out there laying a trap for the possum who had decimated several of the trees.

She was so tired.

She looked at Clarice. The woman's beautiful face seemed rumpled, like a chemise forgotten at the bottom of the laundry basket. She seemed on the brink of tears, her lips bitten to a deep cherry red, her eyes glassy bright and small with silent pleading.

Orah looked at Edwin. He had the pasty complexion of someone who spent all his time indoors, yet his hands were rough and knotted at the joints, freckled and hairy like those of a worker. He spoke little, and when he did, he chose his words carefully.

They were kind people. They had taken Orah in, given her shelter and food, clean clothes. They had made her welcome in their home, as if she were a long-lost relative rather than a stranger.

Beyond these walls was a world she knew nothing about. She remembered her desolation as she lay beside the campfire that first night after the shipwreck. Despite the warmth of the flames, a cold emptiness had settled over her. For the first time in her life, she was alone. The only people she knew here were Warra and Nala . . . and now Clarice and Edwin Briar. If she didn't stay here, where else would she go?

She found herself nodding. 'Thank you,' she murmured, just before her throat closed.

Clarice seemed to melt, as if her bones had turned to jelly under the enormity of sudden relief.

'You'll be happy here with us, dear Orah. So very happy, I promise. Edwin and I have come to love you as a daughter. You are ours now, darling. Our very own.'

18

Bitterwood, June 1993

Even in the warmth of the kitchen, my chills lingered. I brewed hot chocolate and sat watching Basil groom himself on a dusty mat in front of the wood stove. I tried to push away my thoughts of the universe and the demons it had lured me back here to face, but all I could see was that dank passageway in the icehouse, the steps leading down into black nothingness, the charred-smelling air alive with echoes of the past.

Venturing in had been a mistake. It held too many associations with the year I lost my mum. Confronting the past might work in theory, but chasing shadows was getting me nowhere. I needed concrete answers.

Taking out my collection of items, I assembled them once again on the table: my grandfather's letter and the gold heart charm, the sketch I'd made of my mother, Dad's manuscript, and the remnant of burnt photo showing one half of a woman's face. On a whim, I added the icehouse keys. The glass plate negative of the two young soldiers was with Morgan, but I hadn't forgotten it. Instinct told me that the developed photos – along with the other items – were all pieces of a much larger puzzle.

I picked up the heart-shaped charm. Dad had insisted that Mum's bracelet had gone into the sea with her. Yet here it was, part of it anyway, resting on my palm, gleaming in the cool morning light. Had Edwin found it washed up on the beach . . . or was there another, less innocent explanation?

Closing my fingers around the charm, hiding it from sight, I thought of that long ago day. Mum had left the cottage early, kissing me goodbye and waving as she set out along the beach to Bitterwood. An hour later she'd come rushing back, calling for my father, clearly shaken. On the brink of tears. There were scratches on her arms, I remembered. And mud smears on the knees of her jeans. Urgency in her voice.

Where's your father?

Dad used to joke that it would take a nuclear blast to rattle Mum's calm. Something must have happened that day. Had she and my grandfather argued, was that why she'd been so upset, so desperate to find Dad? I picked up my drawing, studied her strong face. The old ache returned. The guilty hollowness, the regret. My father's voice raged in the back of my mind. *What was she doing there, anyway? Those rocks were slippery after the rain, she should have known better . . .*

I had a flash of her in the garden at our old house in Brighton, deadheading the roses she loved. Her favourite was a pink rambler that smothered the archway over the front gate. We were crouched beside it, examining its thick trunk, me looking on while Mum snipped away the shrivelled blooms. She wore her best dress, pale blue with a narrow black belt, teamed incongruously with gumboots. It must have been her birthday. In her view, good enough reason to wear her Sunday best in the yard. She had found a dried rosehip, and for some reason it delighted her. She pulled me close, nuzzled my cheek, making me laugh so hard my head filled with the scent of roses.

I replaced the drawing on the table and went upstairs. In a back room, I found a sewing basket and hunted through, retrieved a length of ribbon. I threaded the charm onto the ribbon and tied it around my neck. Tucked it under my shirt, against my skin.

There was only one way to dispel the heaviness in my heart, and that was to get moving. Edwin had promised me answers, and I was suddenly impatient to discover what they were.

It took several hours to transfer the contents of the pantry and cupboards into oversized garbage bags. I swept the cobwebs from the kitchen ceiling and windows, and rolled up the mouldy old carpet runner in front of the sink. I brushed the wood stove clean, and then swept up the ash and stray matches that had fallen down behind it. A corner of paper poked out from under the stove, and I wriggled it free. It was an envelope, badly scorched, that must have escaped the flames. The stamp was old, franked eight years ago, in 1985.

It was addressed to my grandfather. I tossed it into my bag of recyclables and finished cleaning the back of the range.

A while later, I returned to the bag, dumped in more rubbish, hovered a moment – and then gave in to my curiosity. Retrieving the envelope, I pulled out a letter.

> *Edwin,*
> *Much time has passed since that terrible night, but I still think of her every day. For years I was able to drown my guilt at the bottom of a bottle. These days I am dry, but my cowardice haunts me no less. I can't bring her back, but a question torments me, and only you know the answer. How was it for her, Edwin? At the end, her last breath – how was it? Did she slip peacefully into the next world? Did she, perhaps in a moment of forgiveness, speak my name? A note is all I ask. If you can bring yourself to use the telephone, my number is at the top of this letter. Please Edwin, take pity on a man you once wronged. If not for my sake, then for hers.*

Taking the letter over to the table, I sat down heavily and reread it. Then read it again. It was signed *Sincerely yours*, but the name was charred and unreadable. The return address was a Salvation Army office in Geelong.

Questions erupted in my mind like mushrooms after rain. Who was the woman to Edwin and how had she died? Had my grandfather replied to the letter, and if so, what had he said? What wrong had Edwin once done, and why had the man written to him in hope of forgiveness?

Nearly a decade had passed since the letter was written. Edwin was dead. Perhaps the sender was gone too. It might be a red herring; then again, it might provide a lead to understanding my grandmother's disappearance.

I hurried down the hall to the sitting room, picked up the phone and dialled the number at the top of the letter. A woman answered.

I introduced myself and took a breath. 'I'm tying up my grandfather's affairs, and I've just found a letter. The sender's name has been burned away, but they gave this number as a contact. The letter is old, so I realise it's a long shot—'

'You want to know who sent it.'

'Is there any hope of finding out?'

'We're only a small office here, so it's possible. Who was it addressed to?'

I gave Edwin's name and address.

'Hold on, dear. I'll ask around.'

I heard muffled voices, and then a man talking at length. When the woman came back on the phone, she was apologetic. 'No one in the office knows anything, I'm afraid. We have a lot of volunteers coming and going, so I'll spread the word . . . but after all this time, your letter-writer might not be around anymore.'

I left my contact details, thanked her and hung up. I hadn't pinned my hopes on discovering anything – the half-burned remnant of letter had been an unexpected wildcard – but I went back to the kitchen in a slump.

I placed the letter on the table with my other puzzle pieces. I had travelled halfway across the world to learn the solution to a mystery that, until a month ago, I hadn't even known existed. My grandfather's cryptic note had sparked my curiosity. What had he meant, *explain everything*? Where was his mysterious 'something'? As my collection of clues grew larger, that curiosity ignited and began to burn in earnest. I was being drawn into a vortex where past and present existed simultaneously. It made me giddy, made my pulse thunder in my ears, made my skin damp with anticipation. Made me ever more determined to find the explanation my grandfather had promised me.

At four o'clock, I finished sweeping the kitchen. On my way upstairs to wash off the day's dust, I saw Basil flopped in a patch of sunlight on top of a bookshelf in the hall. He seemed perfectly at home, outstretched on his back, his belly fur exposed to soak up every last ray of sun. I stopped to scratch his ears, still pondering the letter I'd found, and wondering what connection it could have to my grandfather's explanation. Wondering, too, where Edwin might hide something meant for me. In that moment of stillness, warmed by fading sunbeams, I realised there was one place I hadn't yet looked.

Edwin's bedroom was expansive and sun-filled, but paint flaked off the walls and the cracked ceiling – with its plaster mouldings and glorious art deco light fitting – was a nightmare of dusty cobwebs. A cast-iron single bed faced the door, its mattress bare, its pillows naked. On the wall behind the bed hung a cheerful painting of the orchard, a dappled symphony of golden sunlight, green leaves, flecks of blue sky, and purple shadows nesting beneath the trees:

an oasis of colour and light that leaped from the drabness of my grandfather's room.

Next to a tall wardrobe stood a dressing table with a swing mirror, and beside that a large overstuffed chair. Piles of books and papers littered the floor, creating untidy islands on the dark red carpet.

At the far end of the room was a tall bay window. Its glass was foggy with grime, so I rubbed a spyhole in one of the panes and looked out. Twilight was lapping at the edges of the garden, the trees already sunk in their nocturnal shadows.

My gaze lingered on the gate. I wondered if Morgan had decided to camp overnight in Queenscliff. I pictured him bent over a tray of developer, watching faces from my grandfather's past reveal themselves on the photographic paper. He seemed as engrossed in our project as I was, and I sensed that it wasn't all due to his loyalty to Dad. He had changed in the five years I had been away, grown quieter, more reflective. The divorce, I mused. That sort of stress and heartbreak would dampen anyone's spirit. Yet it was more. I sensed it when he looked at me, the way his gaze sharpened as if puzzled. The way he moved around me, sometimes as though on eggshells.

Probably terrified I'd try to kiss him again.

I stepped around a pile of books and slid open the bedside drawer. It contained only basic essentials. Cufflinks, a comb, bottles of medication that rattled around like loose teeth. Inside the wardrobe hung dark suit jackets and matching pants, a dozen or more shirts, most of them grey from wear. I was about to close the door, when a flash of colour caught my eye. Tucked at the end of the rack, gleaming seductively among my grandfather's drab clothes, was a red dress. Not just red. Blood red, ruby red. A deep shimmering crimson that seemed alive. The fabric, pure silk, floated across my palm, magic against my skin. My first thought: Nina would love this, I'll set it aside for her. My second thought came on a possessive rush.

I wonder if it fits.

Stripping to my underwear, I stepped into the dress and buttoned up the front. I was a jeans and T-shirt kind of girl, unadventurous when it came to style, happy just to pull back my fair hair in a simple ponytail. When Nina and I were teenagers, she had itched to give me a makeover. Once, I'd let her put me in a skirt and blouse, twine a glittery string of beads around my neck, and paint my lips and cheeks. She had teased my hair and pinned it back, letting the length hang forward over my shoulders. When I teetered over to the mirror in borrowed high heels, I had expected to see a new person in the glass; one who would take control, succeed where I failed, be the sort of person I had always longed to be.

Instead, I'd encountered a smaller, thinner, plainer version of Nina: a little Goth girl with teased hair and racoon-eyes of Kohl. Thanks to Nina's clever way with make-up and fashion, I looked good – I just didn't look like *me*. That was when I realised I was most comfortable blending into the background, being the girl that everyone noticed second. Besides, the new girl, that mini Nina in a short skirt and platform heels, deserved attitude. She deserved to be someone big at heart, someone outgoing and confident who could make the most of a situation. I'd scrubbed off the make-up, handed back the clothes and shoes, combed the knots and gel from my hair, and retreated into the duller, more comfortable me.

As I approached the mirror now, I was half expecting the same. My eyes widened. There in the glass was the *other* version of myself. The version I had found two days ago in a scrap of charred photograph. It was *her* dress, I realised. Clarice's dress, it had to be, for there she was reflected in the mirror, her hair tangled around her shoulders, her feet bare, and her eyes wide and enquiring.

Illusion, of course.

Out of my uniform of jeans, I looked different, that was all. I stepped closer. The silk skimmed my scant curves, giving them substance. The deep crimson hue drew a rosy flush from my skin, made my hair seem milkier, my face more alive. I was still me, only somehow enhanced. I went nearer, studying my reflection. If I squinted, I could almost see her.

'What happened?' I whispered. 'Why did you leave?'

The back of my neck prickled. I looked over my shoulder, certain I was no longer alone. The room was empty, of course, and I let out the breath of a laugh. *Crazy . . . Next you'll be hearing voices.*

Instead of voices, I heard the rumbling of an engine.

Going over to the window, I looked through my grimy peephole into the yard below. The gates were open. My van nosed through. Morgan got out to haul shut the gates.

My heart began to race. I hugged my arms about my chest and shivered. The photos, I told myself; I was excited about the photos, eager to see those ghostly faces drawn from their negative world into a visual form I could more easily identify.

I lingered at the window. Morgan was returning to the van. Shadows darkened his eyes, and his limp seemed more conspicuous, the uneven gait making him appear oddly fragile, drawing from me a pang of protectiveness. I rarely thought about the limp. It was simply part of the Morgan package, another layer of his enigma, a souvenir from his youthful obsession with fast bikes. Late one night, returning from a party at Mount Macedon, he had leaned too boldly into a curve and lost control, causing the bike to skid off the road and drag him with it, shattering his leg from ankle to knee.

Morgan made to climb into the van, but then paused. He glanced towards the house, right up at the window where I stood. I was sure he couldn't see me – dusk had fallen, Edwin's room was now dark, the windowpanes cloudy with grime. Yet something told me he knew I was there, standing in the shadows watching him. The bolt of awareness was so swift, the spark of yearning in my heart so intense, that my breath caught. My pulse began to hammer. I shivered and pressed my palm flat on the glass.

If Morgan saw me, he made no sign. Hauling himself into the van, he drove towards the house and disappeared around the side.

Standing at the back door, I watched Morgan thump along the verandah towards me, oblivious. His head was down, as if he was battling a windstorm; he seemed deep in his thoughts. Tucked under his arm was a parcel.

He almost reached the door before he saw me.

The frown turned into a smile. His gaze flew over my arms, my shoulders, and then finally met my eyes. The jolt I'd felt upstairs hit me again, but it had morphed into something more reckless than simply pleasure; a flush of warmth sped through my veins, and a giddy yearning overtook me. The fading sunlight dulled, the afternoon sky receded, and the trees became a blur. Only Morgan seemed alive. I had the urge to reach out and touch him, pull him into my arms and savour the warm weight of him, just as I had the night of my party when I'd wound myself around him and pressed my lips to his—

Morgan grinned. 'Going out for dinner, are we?'

I snapped back to reality. 'What?'

'Great, I'm starved.'

I glanced down at the dress. It seemed far skimpier than it had upstairs among the chaste shadows of my grandfather's dusty room. 'It's Edwin's,' I blurted.

Morgan's brow went up. 'Not sure I wanted to know that.'

I scowled, but then remembered the parcel he carried. 'That's them?'

Smiling mysteriously, he brushed past me into the kitchen.

I stared after him, gathering my wits. I felt naked in the dress. The fabric was too thin, too shimmery. My skin was too hot. My pulse tapped irregular beats all over my body. The slipstream of Morgan's warmth, the scent of him, his big bear-like presence seemed to wash around me, creating a whirlpool of what felt disturbingly like desire.

Wrong, wrong, wrong.

I shut my eyes, trying to conjure Adam's face. I returned in my mind to the photo I kept in my wallet: Adam in one of his less formal outfits, pants and a blue cotton shirt, leaning in the doorway of our favourite pub in Camden Town, smiling sexily.

The photo of Adam dissolved.

In its place appeared an old Polaroid from the seventies I had glimpsed once. A young man leaning rakishly against a battered vintage Harley, helmet under his arm, bike jacket straining across his chest, snug Levi's marked with motor oil and frayed at the knees. He glared unsmiling at the camera, and his face – not the craggy, lived-in face I knew now, but rather the face of a fierce, angry young man – seemed to mock me from the past.

We can't do this . . . not now, not ever.

I had made a mistake, I realised. I should never have come back. I should have burned Edwin's cryptic letter, put it from my mind, stayed in London and tried to be happy—

'Lucy?'

I trailed him into the kitchen, grabbing my old cardigan, which I'd left on the servery. Slipping it over the dress, hugging it around me, I joined Morgan at the table. He took a penknife from his pocket and cut the string tied around the parcel. As he tore the wrapping open, a faint chemical smell wafted up and my misgivings evaporated.

Elbowing past him, I began to spread the photos out, barely looking at one before moving on to the next. 'Beautiful,' I murmured. 'Oh Morgan, they're just beautiful.'

'Take your time,' he said. 'I'll get the negatives from the van.'

I shuffled through the prints, spreading them across the table. The landscapes I placed in a pile to one side, then added all the groups and portraits of people unknown to me. Morgan had minimised the effects of cracking and discolouration, sharpening the focus so the details popped, and underdeveloping slightly so that the faces peering from the past were bright and clear.

One face in particular.

'Clarice,' I whispered, sliding into a chair. There she was at the church in front of the apse. Frowning intently, her eyes full of dark fire. The sky was cloudless, summery. Nearby, a flock of native ravens had lifted into the air from the branches of a tree, as though startled into flight by the force of Clarice's aggravation. I had been right. The man beside her was my grandfather, smart in a suit and hat, his long bony face lit by a gentle smile. I gazed at him a long while. I had never seen him smile like that. The grandfather I had known briefly was sour-faced, his wrinkles falling naturally into frown lines, his brow perpetually knotted. Not this younger version; he looked almost handsome. Morgan had also enlarged some of the unbroken slides to capture certain details in close-up. The writing on the banner pinpointed the location and date: *Stern Bay Presbyterian Church Fete 1930.*

Another close-up showed Clarice sitting on a bench in the garden smiling at a young girl, who looked to be about thirteen. The girl was striking, with her heart shaped face and large eyes. She wore her hair long and loose at a time when all the other girls wore theirs bobbed to chin-level.

I added these to my keepers pile, which now contained a dozen photos of interest. In all of them, Clarice seemed to glow. Not in a joyful way, because in the photos her expression was too sombre. Rather, she stood out from the crowd, as though the camera had been pulled into perfect focus on her alone.

I heard Morgan step into the kitchen, heard him kick the door shut and walk past my chair. He laid the box of negatives carefully on the sideboard and then joined me at the table.

'Who's the kid?' he said, picking up one of the fete shots.

'I wish I knew.'

I sifted through the photos until I found one of the three of them. Clarice was smiling at the girl, her expression all fondness, warmth. I did a quick calculation. 'She'd be in her seventies now. If she's still alive, I'm sure she'd remember Clarice. She might even know what happened to her.'

Morgan rubbed his jaw. 'There's something about her. The look on her face, it's familiar.'

I looked at him, hopeful. 'You've seen her before?'

He shook his head. 'Not *her*, but definitely her expression.'

'Where?'

'War photos. Many of the returned servicemen and women had that same look. Haunted, as if they were still seeing or hearing things they'd hoped to put behind them. Not something you'd notice at first glance, but after hours in the darkroom watching their faces materialise on the paper, I started picking it straight away.'

He looked at me, and for a moment – barely two heart-beats – I lost track of our conversation. His face was near, the overhead light giving his eyes a blueness that made me think of the ocean. *Be careful*, whispered a tiny voice, *you're drifting into dangerous territory*. I realised I was staring, and glanced back at the photo.

'You think she's shell-shocked?'

'Traumatised, maybe.'

'From an accident?'

He met my gaze, held it. Said softly, 'I once saw the same look in your eyes. It was just after you lost your mum.'

Drawing away, I shuffled through more photos, found an enlargement of the girl. I pretended to examine the image, but inside my heart skipped unsteadily. It touched me that Morgan had once looked into my ten-year-old eyes and seen my deep sorrow. It touched me even more that he remembered. But it also bothered me. I wasn't ten anymore. Not that he seemed to have noticed.

I peered closer at the girl. 'So she could have lost a parent?'

'It's possible. Edwin and Clarice might have taken her in. Unless she's a sister Ron doesn't know about.'

'No, Dad was definitely an only—' I broke off. Snatching up the enlargement, I tilted it to the light. The girl sat with her hands fisted on her knees, her sleeves not quite covering her wrist bones. Peeping below one sleeve cuff, captured in crisp detail, was a familiar looking bracelet.

Morgan leaned nearer. 'What've you found?'

Through the thin silk of my dress, I felt his body warmth. I should have moved away, but couldn't take my eyes off the photo.

216

'Look at the girl's wrist.'

'The bracelet?'

'My mother had one exactly like it,' I murmured. 'Edwin gave it to her.'

'You think it's the same one?'

I nodded. 'I used to pester Mum for it. She let me wear it once or twice, but always made me give it back. I nagged and nagged, but Mum stood firm. It was a gift, she explained. A sort of peace offering from Edwin, although at the time I didn't know what she meant by that. It would have been rude of her to give it away, she said. Even to me.'

Morgan was watching me. 'I remember you coming back to Melbourne after your holidays here. Ron was always hung over. Karen was usually chirpy with news. And you,' he added with a smile, 'were inevitably sunburned.'

'Hmm.' I slumped. Earlier, on the verandah, I had thought – for one electric moment – that I'd glimpsed lust in Morgan's eyes. I'd been wrong, of course. The only lustful thoughts had been the ones swirling inside my own foolish head. When Morgan looked at me, even dressed as I was in figure-hugging silk, all he saw was a kid sister.

Pushing down my disappointment, I went back to the photo. 'Mum told me her bracelet once belonged to Edwin's mother. She said Edwin had been saving it to give to his daughter, and that since Mum was like a daughter to him, he gave the bracelet to her.'

'Which means,' Morgan said, 'this girl could be Edwin's daughter after all. A sister Ron never knew about.'

Two days ago, I might have argued. Now, after Dad's revelation about his real mother, Clarice, I was no longer sure about anything.

'If not a daughter,' Morgan mused, 'then maybe a cousin, or the child of a close family friend or neighbour. The possibilities are endless.'

'I don't want possibilities,' I said. 'I want facts. Only I don't quite know where to begin.'

Morgan smiled. 'Then you're in luck. Digging up the past just happens to be my specialty.'

The charm tied to the ribbon around my neck suddenly felt heavy. I had fled to the other side of the world to escape it, but it had crossed the sea in an envelope to find me. Now, hidden beneath the neckline of my grandmother's silk dress, it pressed on my skin, a reminder of the lie I had once told.

I'm here, it whispered. *Trapped down here in the cold darkness. Waiting for you to dig deep enough to find me.*

That lie had changed my life forever, and although sixteen years had passed and my mother was long gone, the burden of her death continued to haunt me.

19

Gull Cottage, 1977

Opening the bedroom door a crack, Karen looked into the dimness. Lucy's favourite book, *Charlotte's Web*, was open on the bedside table. The pillow, as usual, lay on the floor half under the bed. A compact lump lay curled beneath the sheet, head hidden, like a little animal in hibernation.

'Lucy?' Karen whispered, unable to help herself. She went in and bent over the child, placed a soft kiss on her head. 'Darling, are you awake?'

Of course, there was no answer; the girl was clearly lost to the world. Karen smiled, and retreated to the hallway. She shut the door and trod silently along the hall into the kitchen. It was midnight. She often woke at this time, unable to go back to sleep. Edwin had once told her that his mother was the same, stalking around at night, her candle chasing shadows up the walls. Dear old Edwin, he always seemed to have a story to ease her occasional flights of anxiety. She could never understand why Ron disliked him so. Karen had never met anyone quite like Ron's father – Ron said he was cunning and manipulative, but Karen couldn't see it. She found Edwin to be old-fashioned and charming, chronically courteous with occasional bursts of gentle humour. Yet beneath his well-mannered mask was sadness that Karen sensed ran deep.

She took a glass of water and stood in the doorway watching her husband sleep. She was now fifty-two, six years older than Ron, although the difference had never bothered either of them. They were a good match, academics both, madly in love with art and music, literature . . . and, surprisingly after nineteen years, still with each other. Their happiest moments – aside from the ones they spent with Lucy – found them engaged in heated discussions about a movie they'd seen, or a book one of them had read. Cheese and wine nights, Ron called them, always with a wink that made Lucy roll her eyes and Karen smile knowingly.

'Ron, honey,' she whispered from the doorway, 'I'm just going out for a bit. A walk on the beach might help me sleep.'

Ron rolled over and murmured something unintelligible. Karen caught the faintest whiff of alcohol. Rats in paradise, she thought grimly. She hated to admit it, but Ron's drinking had overstepped the boundary of normal.

She wondered if she were to blame. She had encouraged him to make peace with Edwin – for Lucy's sake, she'd insisted at the time; the girl deserved to know her grandfather, it wasn't right to deny her. Which was the truth, but not all of it. Karen thought it cruel to keep punishing Edwin for whatever rift had sent Ron running from his family home at the age of fifteen. Almost thirty years had passed since then, which, by Karen's reckoning, was long enough to hold a grudge. So, she'd organised for them to stay a little cottage near the beach, a twenty-minute walk from Bitterwood. Each year in July, when the sea was stormy and the beaches cold and windswept, they would travel two hours from Melbourne and spend a week, maybe ten days, at the cottage. A couple of years ago, they had begun visiting in summertime as well, and last year they'd spent Christmas there. Bitterwood had long since ceased operation as a guesthouse. Edwin had become too frail to manage on his own, and after his housekeeper went to live with her daughter in Bentleigh, he'd refused to hire anyone else.

Karen hurried along the track down to the beach, breathing a sigh as her feet sank into the damp sand. She drank in the salty air, relishing the crash and hiss of the moonlit waves as they broke against the silvery shoreline.

She picked her way carefully along the beach towards the dark mass of the headland. *That'll be my turning-back point*, she planned. *Forty minutes should do it. By the time I'm back here, my head will be clear and I'll be ready for sleep.* But as she approached the headland, she glimpsed a bright star burning in the darkness. Not a star, she realised, a tiny wavering light, and it was coming from Bitterwood.

There was enough moonlight to see the path that led along the side of the headland and up onto the dark verge above. The going was slow. Karen knew that parts of this beach and its surrounds were cordoned off due to accidents in the past. Rockslides, or unstable banks caused by king tides. She had walked this path up to Bitterwood hundreds of times, and although she felt confident even in the dark, she wasn't the sort of person to take risks. By the time she reached the top, she was panting softly, her body dampened by a light layer of perspiration.

The tiny light still burned. On even ground now, she hurried towards it. She imagined Edwin in his library, poring over his books, or perhaps in the kitchen brewing a cup of tea. He had told her that once he reached eighty, he rarely slept. Two, three hours per night, that was all he seemed to need. *What do you do with all that time*, Karen had asked enviously. Edwin had smiled, and a shadow of sadness had darkened his eyes. He had hooked his arm in hers and taken her to see something in the orchard, a new lime tree, or the rhododendron in flower, Karen couldn't remember. What she did remember, later, on reflection, was that Edwin hadn't answered her question.

Perhaps tonight she'd find out.

She hadn't bothered to put on shoes when she left the cottage, and her feet were feeling bruised after her journey up the rocky path, so she found herself treading along the soft grass, around the side of the house towards the kitchen. She climbed the steps onto the verandah, and walked along a little way, her feet padding softly on the weather-worn decking. Edwin was in the kitchen, she glimpsed him as she passed the window. He was hunched over the table, his head sunk in his hands, his knotted fingers digging into his bare scalp.

Karen moved closer to tap on the glass, but caught herself in time. She didn't want to give the old boy a heart attack. He seemed so intent on the book spread open in front of him – a photo album, she now saw, some of its photos removed and scattered about the table.

Edwin looked up suddenly. He seemed unable to see through the glass into the blackness beyond, unable to see Karen. His face – his dear old face with its liver spots and craggy terrain of wrinkles, the huge shrubby eyebrows that shadowed his deep-set eyes – his face was twisted in anguish, his cheeks wet with tears.

Karen stepped back.

Edwin must have sensed the motion, because his expression changed instantly. 'Who's there?' he cried, pushing back from the table. The chair legs scraped against the wooden boards, overly loud in the silent night. 'Clarice . . . is that you?'

Karen had a flash of herself trying to explain her presence: why she'd been standing in the darkness peering in through Edwin's window, not making herself known despite his state of apparent vulnerability. Spying, she thought guiltily, and saw ahead to that moment when the fragile bridge of trust she'd so carefully built between Edwin and her family would crumble, irrevocably. Without really knowing why, other than to save face for both Edwin and herself, she turned and ran.

'What do you expect me to do,' Ron said crossly the next morning, 'pull a rabbit out of a hat?'

Karen was brewing coffee. She glanced towards the lounge room where Lucy was watching cartoon reruns on the TV. She lowered her voice. 'Aren't you the least bit worried about him?'

'Why?' Ron's tone was ever so vaguely challenging. 'Because the silly old coot was having a sob fest?'

'He wasn't just crying. His poor old face was twisted up, his cheeks were streaming. I've never seen him so upset.' She hadn't meant to sound accusing, but Ron's expression became hard. His brows – already woolly and unmanageable, so like his father's – drew sharply together.

'What do you expect, at his age?' he growled, heading for the fridge. 'Probably lost his marbles. Gone senile. I knew it was a mistake.'

'What?' Karen asked, unable to keep the edge of anger from her own voice. 'What do you mean, a mistake?'

Ron clenched his jaw, as though attempting to bite back a torrent of unsavoury words. Then he gave a strangled sigh, and spun on her. 'Coming here year after year after flaming year. Pretending everything's okay, and that Edwin's nothing more than a harmless old grandfather. I know you blame me for the rift. But honestly, Karen, you don't know the full story.'

'Not through lack of asking.'

Yanking open the fridge door, Ron glared at the contents neatly arranged on the shelves – leftover meatloaf, a container of lettuce leaves, cheese, apple juice – and his frown deepened. 'Edwin deserves every single one of those tears you saw him shed last night.'

'That's just cruel.'

'No, Karen, it's the truth.' He sounded tired all of a sudden, flat. 'We're out of beer, I see.' It was his turn to sound accusing.

'You're the only one who drinks it, Ron.'

He slammed shut the fridge, then spent a moment rattling through his trouser pockets. Drawing out a handful of dollar notes, he shuffled through them with a scowl. 'You know, Karen, you're always going on about being open to the truth, about seeing behind the mask. Getting to the bottom of things. Well, last night you caught a glimpse of the real Edwin, the Edwin I knew as a kid. The selfish old fruitcake so caught up in his own affairs that he failed to see what was right in front of his nose. He had a doting wife and a son who idolised him, but do you think he noticed? Do you think he even cared? Oh no, not dear old Dad. He was too caught up in the past to pay any sort of attention to what was going on around him. Mad old buzzard, there's likely more than one skeleton hiding in his closet – skeletons he's probably buried there himself.'

Cramming the notes back into his pocket, Ron stalked to the door. He wrenched it open, but then glanced back, his round cheeks flushed, his ears pink. 'Next year we might head up to the Gold Coast – I hear it's nice this time of year. The change might do us all good.'

'Where are you going?'

'I need to clear my head.'

She trailed after him, at a loss. She hadn't expected such vitriol. A lack of interest, maybe. Perhaps even a touch of feigned concern. But not the anger, the avoidance, the storming out; his reaction befitted a hormonal sixteen-year-old boy, not a middle-aged man who knew better.

'I'm going to talk to him,' she told the back of Ron's head. 'I'm worried about him. I'll go up this afternoon and see if he's all right. He's too old to be so isolated, rattling around those big empty rooms by himself. All that solitude, it's not healthy for a man his age.'

Ron glanced back. 'Do whatever you like, Karen. Just as long as you don't involve me.' Then he was hurrying away, his sandals slapping the footpath, his hands dug deep in his pockets, his shoulders hunched as though beneath the weight of the world.

20

Bitterwood, June 1993

We breakfasted beneath a vine-covered pergola in the garden, at a wrought iron table once part of an outdoor dining area. Most of the leaves had fallen off the vine, and beyond the bare sinewy branches, the sky was a clear lapis lazuli blue.

I had lain awake again the night before, tucked in my van, gazing up at Morgan's window. At midnight, his light had finally gone out. I wondered what he'd been reading, and what thoughts had kept him from sleep. I wondered if he might have glanced occasionally at his own window, and thought of me snuggling warm in my van somewhere below. It wasn't until later, into the early hours, that I had startled from my musings. What was I doing, lying awake sifting over every conversation I'd had with Morgan since my return? I wore a diamond on my finger that symbolised the promise I had made to another man. Guilt, then.

Electrifying guilt that kept me awake for another few hours until finally I fell into a restless sleep.

I finished my coffee and stood up.

'I have a surprise.'

Morgan narrowed his eyes.

'It's not really a *surprise*,' I hurried on, 'just something . . . of interest. Being a history buff, I thought you'd like to see it.'

He cast me a sideways look. 'Not another bomb shelter?'

I smiled, and then found myself laughing. A giddy joy took hold and I almost skipped along the grass. Perhaps it was the fragile winter sun melting my defences, or maybe my night of tossing and turning, of sleeplessness and half-remembered dreams. Not my usual dark dreams, but rather soft sunny glimpses of hearts on ribbons, of churchyards and charred photos, forgotten letters, and lost things returning to their rightful owners. At some time during the night, I had flashed on what felt like a dream, but was actually a memory. Me at age ten, sitting in the orchard, trying to solve the puzzle written on a tree.

The same tree we now approached, a huge old bare-limbed cherry with a wrought iron bench beneath it. I tugged Morgan over and made him sit, then settled beside him.

His gaze lingered on my face. 'This is your surprise? A garden seat?'

'No . . . the tree behind us.' In a moment of daring, I took his hand and guided his fingers across the scarred trunk where, a lifetime ago, someone had used a sharp instrument to carve into the bark.

'When I was a kid,' I explained, 'I used to sit here all the time. It's out of view of the house, like a secret grotto. This scarring on the trunk was what I loved most about it. I used to trace my fingers over the squiggles and lines, puzzling over whether they had once been words, or if they were just marks made by an insect.'

Morgan peered closer. 'Like on a scribbly gum tree.'

'Exactly, but last night I had a revelation. It's a name.'

Morgan's fingers were warm in mine as I guided them over the scars cut into the bumpy bark. 'It says *Clarice*. Don't you see? Edwin tried to burn away all evidence of her, but she carved her name on this tree and it's still here. Amazing, isn't it?'

The sun was making me tipsy. I felt like a teenager again, high on life. I shifted my position on the bench, swinging around so my knees rested ever so lightly against Morgan's leg. Sitting there in my grandfather's timeless garden, I sensed the rest of the world dissolve behind a veil of fog. While the sun shone in the orchard, darkness descended over the rest of the globe. Melbourne seemed an eternity away, and London – with its busy streets and historic alleyways, and the mod apartment I shared with Adam – seemed to exist in another lifetime.

I was still holding Morgan's hand. His fingers curled around mine, gently, without pressure. He watched me, perhaps a little warily, perhaps waiting for me to let him go. Hastily, I did.

Morgan rested his elbow on the wrought iron seatback. 'You need glasses.'

My glow winked out. 'Why?'

'You're mistaken about the name. It can't be Clarice. The first letter is an O. Next is R.' He frowned at the scar. 'Can't make out what's next, but that last is definitely an H.'

I slumped, frowning at the tree. The letters I'd been so sure of a moment ago were muddled again. Jumbled, turned back to a mess of swirls and wavering lines; insect scribbles, after all.

I huffed, unwilling to give in. 'You're the one who needs your eyes checked, Morgan.'

He sighed. 'You only see what you want to see, Lucy. That's always been your problem. You have a strong mind, and if you believe something to be a certain way, then that's exactly how it appears to you.'

I pulled back, glaring at him. The fog lifted. The outside world began to intrude. The crash of waves at the foot of the headland was suddenly loud, joined by the drone of a distant car speeding along the Great Ocean Road. Ridiculously, I felt the prick of tears. 'There's nothing wrong with my eyesight.'

'I'm not talking about your eyes.'

The knot between my shoulder blades tightened. I sensed, even before Morgan spoke, where this was going. Morgan lifted a brow and regarded me through narrowed eyes. I knew that look; growing up, I had seen it a thousand times. *You're not going to like hearing this*, the look said, *but it's for your own good.*

Morgan didn't quite smile. 'You're about to blunder into the worst mistake of your life, but you can't see it. You've created a fairytale life for yourself over there in London, even furnished it with a handsome prince who is . . . how did you describe him? Kind, intelligent and thoughtful. Oh, and a good sense of humour. But it's not real.'

'Jealous, are we?'

He leaned near, tugged gently on a milky lock of hair that had escaped my ponytail. 'If it was real, if you were genuinely happy, we wouldn't be having this conversation. The joy would be there in your eyes, Lucy. You'd be glowing, bubbling over with excitement at the prospect of spending the rest of your life with the man you love. You'd be talking nonstop about Adam, but you've hardly mentioned him. You'd never have left London without him. Instead, you're hiding out here in Edwin's dusty old guesthouse with me.'

I got to my feet, suddenly tired. The spark had vanished from the morning, everything seemed dull and jaded; the bare branches, the damp grass, the soft winter sunlight – all of it ruined. I hated what Morgan had said, hated that he could read me so well. Most of all, I hated that he might be right.

'Hey.' He was beside me, his hand gentle on my shoulder, turning me to face him. I tried to twist away again, but he stepped into my path. 'All I'm saying is there's no rush. Adam will understand.'

I thought of the last time I'd seen Adam. We were saying goodbye at Heathrow, both of us shuffling, not knowing what to say. Adam in his rumpled shirt, his mouth set firm, me in my red leather jacket, hair pulled back, steadfast in my resolve to leave. He had leaned close as if to kiss me, but had instead pulled me against him and whispered into my hair.

Come back to me, Lucy. I couldn't bear to lose you.

I had clung to him then, crushing him against me. Adam, with his pure heart and utopian dreams, his hiccupping laugh and gentle touch, his tireless work to save the world; I loved him more at that moment, on the brink of goodbye, than I had in all our two years together. I kissed him tenderly on the mouth, and with tears choking off any words I might have mustered, left him standing alone at the gate and hurried away.

'Come on,' Morgan said, glancing at the sky. 'It's time to go.'

My thoughts of Adam dissolved. My sullen mood ebbed, replaced by alarm. I clutched Morgan's wrist as if to restrain him by force. 'You're leaving?'

'We both are. It's Friday.'

I stared at him, baffled. 'Which means—?'

'Which means that Stern Bay Historical Society is open for business.'

Stern Bay, June 1993

The old church hall had barely changed since 1930. Paint peeled from its weatherboard flanks, and grass had mostly swallowed the stepping-stone path to the front entryway, but the outlook – a paddock dotted with paperbark trees, with a small graveyard tucked into the back of the block – was still exactly as it appeared in the photo.

My gaze went to a sheltered nook beside the apse. There was the leadlight window, its coloured glass panes glowing crimson and green and amber in the sun. Sixty-four years ago on that spot, my grandmother Clarice Briar had stood beside Edwin, the sun in her eyes, her lips downturned as the camera captured her in a moment of anger.

Morgan joined me on the grassy verge. 'Look up.'

Native ravens, black and glossy in the winter sunshine, perhaps twenty of them, gathered behind the hall in the branches of a dead tree. They startled suddenly, and lifted into the blue sky, filling the air with disgruntled cries.

Chills flew over me. I rubbed my arms, thinking of the photograph in the envelope I carried. Those birds might be descendants of the ones that had flocked here the day Clarice had her picture taken.

I gazed at the ravens, pulling my coat tighter about me. 'She hated him, didn't she? Edwin, I mean. You can see it in her face in the photo. She's unhappy about something, and I get the feeling it's to do with Edwin.'

'We can't know that.'

The ravens circled overhead, their cries sounding so desolate that I shivered again. 'Why else would she leave? Why else would she abandon her baby and run away? She couldn't stand to be around him a moment longer.'

Morgan stared at me, his eyes hard. 'Speaking from experience are you?'

I stepped back, defences prickling, the denial already on my lips. Then I noticed the rawness in Morgan's eyes, the subtle tightening of his mouth. It hadn't been a reproach, I realised. For the first time, I saw myself through Morgan's eyes: a wilful girl who had kissed him and declared her love, and then fled when things hadn't gone her way. In that moment, he was no longer my old love, Morgan, but rather a man whose family had just come undone at the seams, a man who was probably hurting and confused . . . and now putting himself back in the firing line with someone who could disappear again without warning.

I nudged him with my elbow, found my smile. 'I'll say goodbye next time, Morgan. That's a promise. Now let's see if anyone remembers Clarice.'

As we entered the cool open space of the hall, a big-boned woman in her sixties hurried over to greet us. She introduced herself as Brenda Pettigrew, and when I explained about the photos and my quest to discover more about my grandmother, she patted my arm.

'I was sorry to hear of old Edwin's passing. Dulcie had been one of my mother's friends, a lovely woman, devoted to Edwin. I suppose they're together now.'

I glanced at Morgan, and he lifted a brow. I knew better than to get my hopes up, but I slid the photos from my envelope and passed them to Brenda. She shuffled through them, stopping at the one taken outside the church.

'I've never seen this before. The old hall looks so well loved. I'm afraid these days we haven't much funding to attend to the paintwork. I can't make out the date—'

'1930,' I told her. 'Actually, it's Edwin's first wife we're interested in. That's her there.'

Brenda examined the image more closely. 'I know someone who might remember her. Mildred Burke and her husband had a big farm that once adjoined Bitterwood. Of course, they subdivided the land and sold it all off, but Mildred still lives in the original farmhouse. She's in her nineties, but her memory's as sharp as a tack. If anyone knows about the Briar family, it'll be her.'

She sketched a map and gave me directions to the Burkes' old farm, then paused, tapping a finger against her lips. 'I wonder . . .' Going over to a display of books, she retrieved a slender volume. The cover was well thumbed, the pages dog-eared. On the front was a black and white photograph of a smiling man with Brenda's large square face. Beneath it was inscribed *The Story of Stern Bay, by LM Pettigrew.*

'My father's memoir,' she explained, pressing the book into my hands. 'He was a grocer by trade, ran the corner store for years, so he knew everyone.'

Morgan had wandered over to a large painting. It showed a ship caught in the midst of a violent storm. 'It reminds me of an early Turner,' he told Brenda. 'It looks valuable.'

Brenda laughed softly, rubbing her palms together. 'I can't wait to tell my husband you said that. My uncle painted it. We always said Ken had a great talent, but he never had the confidence to follow it up. I think he painted that one from a newspaper clipping. It's an English ship, the *Lady Mary*. It was Ken's obsession. I've another picture very similar at home.'

'Obsession?' Morgan wanted to know.

'The *Lady Mary* foundered north of here along the coast, only about thirty clicks from Bitterwood. Sadly, there were no survivors. Back in 1929 they didn't have the communications we enjoy these days. A big storm blew up, according to Ken, and when the ship failed to dock in Melbourne, they sent a search party. The only evidence they found was a beach littered with debris . . . and bodies,' she added quietly.

We found Mildred Burke's farmhouse a few miles west of Stern Bay, at the very end of a steep street that led up into the hills. Its weatherboards were buckled and peeling, the gutters dangling loose, but the surrounding steep acre of grass was trim as a bowling lawn. As we approached along the drive, I saw why: a herd of white goats ran towards the van, bellowing in apparent excitement.

A woman pushed through the screen door, and waved the goats away. She was short and stout, her pink face obscured behind large glasses that magnified her blue eyes. Her thick hair was pure white, restrained by a squadron of hairpins.

'You're the Briar girl, then?' she asked, dusting her hands on her apron and peering up at me. 'I've just got off the phone to Brenda from the historical society. She said you'd be popping in. Come through. Don't mind the mess. I'm baking for the CWA fundraiser next week. I hope you like scones.'

She ushered us along a narrow hall and into a generous country-style kitchen. A huge wooden table sat central, cluttered with mixing bowls and wooden spoons, packets of sugar and raisins. A fine layer of white dust coated every surface. Flour, I realised, seeing the mound of bread dough proofing under plastic wrap. The oven blazed and warm aromas filled the air.

'Baking keeps me sprightly,' Mrs Burke said, clearing

a corner of the table and dragging out chairs. A cloud of flour wafted around her, puffing from her cardigan as she collected a leaning tower of mixing bowls. 'But like all of life's pleasures, it comes with a price.'

Morgan came to her rescue. 'Let me get those, Mrs Burke.'

Mrs Burke adjusted her glasses and peered up at him, beaming. 'Thank you, dear boy. Just on the sink, if you don't mind. And please call me Mildred.'

I brought out the envelope of photos and placed it on the table. While the kettle boiled, Mildred took a batch of scones from the oven and put them on a cooling tray. She made tea, and Morgan helped her set the table with cream and homemade jam.

'Dig in,' she said cheerfully, plating up the fragrant scones. 'Don't be shy.'

While we ate, she launched into the story of her family. I prepared myself for a polite interim of boredom before getting to the point of our visit, but was quickly intrigued.

Her husband had started life as a shearer, she said. As an eight-year-old, he'd entered the shearing shed, where his hard-headed father expected him to pull the weight of a grown man. Young Jensen lost the tips of two fingers before he was ten; the shears had been sharp, carving through his young bones like butter.

I let out an involuntary murmur, but Mrs Burke seemed oblivious, caught up in the momentum of her story.

'I met him at a dance after the war. Love at first sight, I suppose you'd call it these days. He wasn't much to look at – a burly, red-faced lad with shaving cuts on his jaw, and ears too big for his head. But he was kind, and he brought me flowers and fresh eggs, a luxury in those days. He wooed me for an entire year before my father finally gave his blessing. Sixty-seven years we were married.'

Morgan gave a soft whistle and reached for another scone. 'What's your secret?'

Mildred smiled. 'To a lasting marriage? Friendship, of course. Don't let Hollywood fool you into believing it's all about passion. Passion doesn't last.' She sighed. 'Poor Jensen died more than a decade ago. He'd gone out hunting. Meat for us, bones for the dogs. He was climbing through a fence and the wire snared him. He must have been struggling to get free, and bumped the rifle. A shooting accident, the police called it. Bled to death, poor man.'

'How awful,' I said. 'I'm sorry.'

'I missed him terribly when he went. That's why I bake, I suppose. It keeps my mind on other things.' She shook her head as if to dislodge the memory. 'Listen to me, rabbiting on. Memory is the curse of old age, you know. You can wander around for hours looking for your glasses, only to realise you're wearing them. But the past is all there. Thirty, forty, sixty years ago, all clear in your mind as the day it happened.' She sighed. 'Brenda said you have some snaps you'd like me to look at?'

Sliding the prints from the envelope, I placed the church fete photo on top of the pile, and slid it across.

'The woman is my grandmother, Clarice. Next to her is my grandfather—'

'Edwin Briar.' Mildred clucked her tongue. 'I always

thought he looked more like an undertaker than the landlord of a fancy guesthouse. Look at him there, so young.'

I shuffled through the photos and pulled out the enlargement, buckling a corner in my haste. 'What about the girl with them. Do you remember her?'

Mildred fumbled off her glasses, cleaned them on her apron, and then carefully examined the photo. 'It must be their daughter. Edna, I think her name was. No, it was Edith.'

I leaned forward, 'Edith,' I whispered, eyeing the photo. 'Is she still alive?'

Mildred shook her head. 'She died, poor little thing. Of course, I never knew the particulars, just what I heard in town. We didn't have much to do with the Briars, you see.'

'Oh.' I sat back heavily.

Morgan refilled Mildred's teacup. 'I get the feeling you didn't much care for Edwin.'

Mildred sighed. 'Not much. He and Jensen had a quarrel years ago. I never knew what it was about, probably leftover issues from the war. But it rattled Jensen. He was always nervy after, although I suppose that was just coincidence.' She looked at me. 'I'm sorry, my dear. I don't mean to speak ill of your grandfather, but you deserve to know the truth.'

She stood and retrieved the proofing dough, peeling off the cling wrap. 'My Jensen served with Edwin in the Great War. A bunch of them joined up together, local lads mostly. Jensen was thick with Edwin's older brother. Ronald Briar was a fine young man, high-spirited, very handsome. I can still see him and Jensen standing on our front porch, proud as punch in their crisp uniforms. Full of swank and swagger, cracking jokes about how they'd have Fritz on the run and be home before we knew it.'

She punched the dough flat and began to knead it up again. 'I was sad to learn of Ronald's death. I sent a card to his mother up at Bitterwood. She took it hard. Ronald had always been the favourite. It would have killed her to know the truth.'

I sat forward. 'What happened?'

Mildred turned the dough with a thump. 'Friendly fire, they call it. It happens a lot in warfare, although you rarely hear of it. Jensen once told me that friendly fire accounted for twenty-five per cent of wartime fatalities. In those days, if someone ran towards you, friend or foe, you were under orders to shoot. Cowards were every bit as much the enemy as the other side, according to Jensen. But anyone who'd ever met Ronald Briar knew he was no coward.'

Morgan searched her face, thoughtful. 'Ronald was killed by his own men?'

'By *one* of them, yes.' Mildred dropped the dough into a tin and dusted it with flour. Setting it aside, she wiped her fingers on her apron and looked at me. 'Jensen was there when it happened, he saw everything. Poor Ronald was wounded, you see. He'd managed to drag another hurt soldier out of the firing line and back towards safety. Edwin was nearby. Ronald called for help, but Edwin didn't acknowledge him. Instead, he raised his pistol and took aim. Jensen yelled a warning, but Edwin paid it no mind. He fired, taking down poor Ronald with a single shot to the chest.'

I pressed back in my chair, gripping the table edge. An image flashed to me: two young soldiers standing proudly with their mother in the orchard at Bitterwood. The woman's hand rested protectively on the shoulder of her older, better-looking son. While Edwin, with his bony features and dark hopeful eyes, stood slightly apart.

My voice was a whisper. 'Why would Edwin do that?'

Mildred's frown softened. 'How well did you know him?'

I stared at her. I wanted to say that Edwin had been my grandfather, *of course* I'd known him. But the sad truth was that I hadn't, not really. After Dad's breakdown, I had lived with Edwin at Bitterwood for three months. I'd sat at the dinner table with him, ignoring his attempts to engage me in conversation. I shunned him, avoided him – escaping into the orchard or losing myself in the library at the top of the stairs, or trawling for shells in the little cove at the foot of the headland. The last thing I'd wanted at the time was sympathy from a man I barely knew, a man my father had despised. In the end, when the going got too tough for me, I abandoned Edwin – just as everyone else had.

'Not that well,' I admitted.

Taking up a tea towel, Mildred draped it over her bread dough. 'Then you won't know that he had a ruthless streak when it came to getting what he wanted.' She lifted the loaf tin, but then seemed to change her mind, replacing it heavily on the table. She looked across at me. 'Ronald was engaged to a lovely girl. They had planned to marry after the war. When Ronald died, Edwin wooed her instead.'

I exchanged a glance with Morgan. When I looked back at Mildred, my heart was racing. 'Clarice.'

Mildred nodded. 'Yes.'

The kitchen was suddenly stifling, the air too hot from the oven. I stood and went to the window. The goats were congregating along the far fence. One shook itself and skittered away from the herd, bleating noisily.

I turned back to find Mildred's blue gaze trained on my face. Her smile trembled at the edges.

'I didn't mean to upset you, dear.'

I let out a breath. 'I'm not upset. Taken aback, maybe. I never knew Edwin well. He and my father didn't get along. I've only just discovered Clarice. She intrigues me.'

Mildred nodded thoughtfully. 'If only I could tell you more about her. For the most part, we moved in different circles. Before the war, I saw her frequently in the twelve months or so that Ronald was courting her. She was clever and kind, a thoughtful girl from a good family. Once she married Edwin, all that changed.'

'In what way?' I asked.

'She cut herself off from all her old friends, became quite reclusive. We lost touch. I blame Bitterwood. Such a dreary place, stuck out along that isolated stretch of road, nothing but the sound of the ocean and the cry of gulls. And Edwin's dull company, of course – enough to drive anyone nutty. I saw her once, walking along the old coast road. Away from Bitterwood, although town was a fair hike, about fifteen miles. It was early one morning, just on sunrise. I'd been in Apollo Bay with my sister, and was on my way home for the lambing. I stopped to offer Clarice a lift, but she ignored me. She seemed distracted, almost wild. The wind lashed her hair about. I'll never forget it, bright as polished copper in the dawn light. Her face was chalk white. She was barefoot and wore a man's old coat. I drove halfway home, but then started worrying and went back for her. By then, of course, she had probably found her way back to Bitterwood.'

She fell silent.

I placed my palms on the sides of my face. My cheeks burned. The story of Edwin and his brother, and now this glimpse of Clarice, wandering along the road, seemingly quite out of her mind, were doing strange things to my head. The kitchen was suddenly airless. I glanced at the door.

Morgan's chair scraped as he got to his feet. He gathered the tea things, carried them to the sink, returned the milk to the fridge, and then joined me at the window.

'You've got a lovely herd of little Saanens there,' he said, squinting out into the brightness. 'Goats are good company, aren't they?'

'I'd be lost without them,' Mildred agreed. She dusted her hands and opened the back door, then ushered us out onto the verandah. She whistled and the herd swarmed towards us. Several goats had curved horns growing from their knotty heads, others were coated in long whiskery hair; all had strange slitted pupils that seemed to regard us with grim curiosity.

As we wandered along a path and around the side of the house, the air was deliciously cool on my burning face. It cleared my head. I thanked Mildred for her hospitality and then thought to ask, 'That morning you saw Clarice on the road, do you recall what year it was?'

Mildred took a moment to consider this. Sunlight danced on her glasses as she shook her head. 'It would have been springtime, on account of the lambs. But other than that, I don't—' She stopped. Looking at the sky, she rubbed her throat. 'My sister was laid up with morning sickness, that's why I'd gone to stay. My niece was born in '32, so I must have seen Clarice late in 1931.' She shook her head and smiled. 'As I said, my dear, memory is the curse of old age.'

Bitterwood, June 1993

We drove back to Bitterwood in silence. My mind was flying. I needed time to organise my thoughts, to allow what I'd learned that morning to sink in. I wound down the window, but the salt air caught in my throat. The cobalt dome of the afternoon sky, the windblown trees and the bright chatter of birds, the glittering ocean. None of it seemed real.

Mildred Burke's words replayed in my mind.

He had a ruthless streak when it came to getting what he wanted.

As Stern Bay receded behind us, I burrowed deeper into my thoughts, trying to reconcile my quiet, bookish grand-father with the young man Mrs Burke had described. A man who had killed his own brother, and then married the woman his brother had loved.

After lunch, I immersed myself in clearing a couple of upstairs bedrooms, while Morgan carried boxes of junk down to the garage. Later, as the sun drifted closer to the horizon, he suggested a walk on the beach. We crossed to the headland and climbed down the stony path to the sand below. I tried to focus on my surroundings – the clearness of the water, the miles of wintry blue sky, the scuff of sand beneath my shoes, Morgan's quiet company beside me – but my thoughts kept returning to my grandmother.

The past is gone, Adam always said. *Brooding over it only makes you crazy.* But as the afternoon ebbed away and shadows began to edge across the beach, Morgan walking silently beside me, I realised that the past was never completely gone.

I still wore Clarice's dress under my coat, and though it was probably my imagination, I could feel her presence rippling through it, a whisper in the silk as the wind ruffled it around my legs. While we walked, I saw her clearly in my mind: beautiful, distracted; rushing barefoot along that long-ago road, her red hair whipping in the sea wind.

'Do you think it's true?' I wondered aloud. 'That he shot his own brother so he could marry Clarice?'

Morgan looked at me. 'We know the two brothers enlisted together, we've got the photo. But everything else could just be the imaginings of a lonely old woman.'

'Mildred Burke didn't really strike me as lonely. Besides, why would she invent something like that?'

'Ron might know.'

I thought of Dad's aversion to talking about his father, and his secrecy about Clarice. 'I get the feeling he knows more than he's willing to tell.'

'Why do you say that?'

'That photo of the two brothers got me thinking. There's a soldier in Dad's latest story, and an old king who reminds me of Edwin. There's also a restless young woman. Dad's always telling me that writing is therapy for him, a way to mull over things he doesn't understand. Maybe he's using this story to understand his parents. He's done it before with his characters.'

Morgan seemed surprised. 'Based them on real people?'

I glanced at him, unable to stop a smile. 'I can't believe you read Dad's version of Peter Pan and failed to see yourself in it.'

An eyebrow went up. 'What, now I'm the eternal child?'

'Actually, Dad sees you more as a pirate.'

His hint of a smile widened, turned into a laugh. 'Crazy old fool. I never should have told him about my childhood dream of owning a boat.'

'A boat?'

'Yeah, well. More of a pipe dream for a landlubber who suffers chronic seasickness. Whenever the yearning for adventure strikes, I usually end up buying another volume on maritime history.'

I considered him thoughtfully. 'Just when you think you know someone . . .'

Morgan went quiet, apparently absorbed in watching the sand roll away beneath his feet. The wind picked up, blowing a whirlwind of grit and icy sea spray across our path.

A shiver went through me. Morgan shrugged out of his jacket and settled it around my shoulders. I went to refuse, but the sudden cocoon of warmth held me captive. Morgan's scent drifted around me: motor oil and wood smoke, cloves and beeswax, delightfully male, intimate. I breathed it in and then wished I hadn't. Intoxicated, my bones loosened, a sigh escaped. I glanced quickly at him, hoping he hadn't noticed.

He was frowning at me. 'What's up?'

I hugged myself deeper into the coat, regathering my thoughts. 'I can't get that image of Clarice out of my mind. I keep wondering where she was going the morning Mildred saw her.'

Morgan stopped walking, raised his face to the sky. Examined the cloudless blue for a while, and then looked at me.

'Your father was born in October 1931, wasn't he? If Mildred was right about the date, then Clarice was either heavily pregnant or she'd recently given birth. Either way, she was in no state to be out walking along the road at dawn.'

'Then why was she?'

Morgan's frown was deceptive. Behind that brooding face, I knew the history-buff brain was relishing the mystery of it all. I could almost see the cogs turning. We continued along the beach in silence for a way, but then Morgan stopped again.

'What if that was the morning she left?'

I shrugged. 'It's possible.'

'Mildred didn't mention a suitcase.'

'Maybe she left suddenly.'

Morgan shook his head and continued walking. 'She might've just had a row with Edwin. Gone out to cool her head.'

'Barefoot?'

He considered this. 'It might've been a doozy of a fight.'

'At dawn?'

Morgan's mouth tightened and he looked out across the dark ocean. 'Don't you and Adam argue?'

I thought about this. 'Not really.'

Morgan fell silent. The wind whipped his white shirt. It made a fluttery sound that I found distracting. He must be cold. I wondered if he regretted giving up his jacket, but I was too cosy now to offer it back.

The beach curved inland a little way. I recognised the sand hills I had played on as a kid. Our old holiday cottage came into view. Late sunlight reflected off the windows, and the tall pine tree swayed gently in the sea air. The place looked inviting, a friendly haven on the edge of the otherwise deserted shore. Ahead of us in the distance, a low formation of rocks disappeared into the water. I stopped walking. My fingers drifted to the charm I wore around my neck, patting it beneath the layers, checking that it was still there. That it was real.

Morgan must have noticed my hesitation. He touched my shoulder, indicating with a tilt of his head that we turn back. He stayed close, gently colliding with me from time to time. I was grateful for his silence as we retraced our sandy footprints to the headland. I had hoped the cold sea breeze would clear my head after the morning's revelations – but instead I was beginning to withdraw into myself, become thoughtful.

I kept seeing two soldiers. One was broad-shouldered and handsome, his confident smile drawing me in, making me wish I had known him. The other boy, Edwin, was similar to his brother, yet his features seemed put together all wrong. His face was bony, compelling only for its strangeness. The large wet eyes with their dark soulfulness, the stubborn downturn of the mouth, the elfin chin. It was a gentle face, yet sombre and guarded. The face of a person who brooded silently, avoided confrontation. No matter how I tried, I just couldn't see him pointing a gun at anyone and pulling the trigger.

Yet he had completed combat training and gone to war. And if Mildred was right, he'd committed an act of unspeakable malice. Was Ronald's death an accident, or had Edwin acted with intent?

We reached the headland. The tide had gone out, so rather than climb the narrow track up the bluff edge, we picked our way around its base. The rocks were slippery, and once I almost lost my footing, my shoes splashing in puddles of seawater. We found a little cave just out of the wind, and sat for a moment to admire this new, rare perspective of the sea.

I shifted on my rock. Wet sand squelched beneath my shoes. Hugging deeper into Morgan's jacket, I watched the waves. 'Adam says brooding over the past makes you crazy. Do you think that's true?'

Morgan continued to watch the dark water. 'You're asking a history professor?'

'I'm asking a friend.'

He looked at me then, leaned in and really looked. The edges of his eyes crinkled up but he didn't quite smile.

'I believe we're products of our past. For me, there's nothing more intriguing than digging it all up, mulling it over. Finding out what makes a person tick.'

Maybe it was the warmth of the two coats, my torso over-hot while my face and hands and ankles froze in the icy blast of sea spray, but I found myself mimicking his body language, leaning nearer, my gaze locked to his.

'What makes *you* tick, Morgan?'

For the longest time, the only sounds were the rush of the waves, the cry of gulls circling overhead.

The half-smile finally reached his eyes. 'Love,' he said at last, and then shrugged. 'The idea of it, at least.'

'You're a romantic,' I accused.

'Guilty as charged.'

My brow inched up. 'A cat-rescuing, bike-riding history professor who's also a chronic romantic.'

'*And* has a good sense of humour. What more could a girl want?'

That made me smile. I looked back at the sea. From this angle, the horizon arched hard against the pink-streaked sky. Dark waves lapped the shore, their crests gilded by the setting sun. A fragile kind of peace settled over me. Morgan's solid presence felt grounding, while my thoughts flew out over the ocean like a bird searching, searching . . . but never quite finding the elusive thing it sought. Then, an image: a woman hurrying along a lonely windswept road, her bare feet bruised by the gravel, her hands numb with cold. If she had been running away, where were her bags, her shoes? Why had she refused Mildred's offer of a lift into town?

An argument, Morgan had said.

I tried to picture my grandfather arguing heatedly, but somehow the mild-mannered man I remembered would not cooperate. Yet hadn't Edwin once argued so violently with my father that Dad had run away from home . . . and stayed away for nearly three decades?

Dad never spoke about why he left home. Whenever I asked, my normally articulate father would waffle on about Edwin's aloofness, his inability to connect with people. As if these humble failings were, in my father's eyes, unforgivable crimes. *There are worse things than being bookish and quiet*, my mother used to say in Edwin's defence. *Murder, for instance.*

The soft sigh of the waves buffeted the cliff-face behind us. Overhead, a lonely sea eagle soared silently above the headland. My mother's voice gathered force in my mind, competing with the sound of the wind and waves. A window opened in the back of my mind. Through it, I glimpsed a battlefield where two brothers fought side by side. Then, superimposed across the scene like a reflection in glass, was a woman's face. At first, I thought it my own – but the hair was red-gold, while mine was fair. Clarice, I realised, my grandmother, the woman they both had loved.

I looked at Morgan. 'What if she discovered that Edwin shot his brother? That he killed the man she'd once loved?'

Morgan considered this. 'It explains a lot.'

His white shirt rippled in the wind, clinging to his chest and arms. A shiver went through him, and a thought bumped against my racing mind: *He's cold, give back the jacket.* But my brain only had room for one idea.

'She might've confronted Edwin. Things might have turned nasty. She would have been in shock, hating him. Maybe even scared of him.'

Morgan regarded me, his eyes full of shadows. 'It still doesn't quite add up. What about the baby?'

'Mothers leave their children, you know.'

'Not without good reason.'

I dug my hands into the pockets of Morgan's jacket. 'Like discovering your husband shot a man you once loved? His own brother? Seems to me that's reason enough.'

'To leave Edwin, maybe. But not to walk away from her little boy. Your theory might be right, but I'm not convinced it's the whole story.'

The wind invaded our shelter, swirling up icy gusts of sea spray. Dusk had fallen; it was time to go. We picked our way across the rocks to the trail that led up the side of the headland. The climb in the twilight took concentration, and we were silent for a while. When we reached the crown of the headland, I expected Morgan to make a beeline for Bitterwood, for the warm fire glow of the kitchen. Instead, he turned and pondered the ocean.

'There's something we're not seeing.'

I followed his gaze. Ten minutes ago our view had been vastly different; sitting on the rocks below, we had been almost eye level to the waves. Now we were birds gazing down on the endless water that stretched away before us into the dark.

'Maybe she never bonded with the baby.'

Morgan became thoughtful. 'When Coby came to live with us, he was shy and nervous. A scared little kid who jumped at shadows. Gwen loved him instantly – we both did. This one time, we took him shopping in the city. One minute he was there, the next he wasn't. This look came into Gwen's eyes, a look I've never forgotten. Fierce. I've no doubt she would have killed to get our boy back. He'd lived most of his childhood without us, he barely knew us . . . but already he was part of us. That's how strong the bond can be. You'd do anything to protect your child. *Anything . . .'*

I studied him, surprised. His face had gone ragged in the twilight. I thought I saw a gleam, but before I could be sure, he shook it off.

'What I'm trying to say is that Clarice must have had good reason for leaving her son.' He rubbed his hand across his face. 'Damn good reason.'

I slumped. 'So what was it?'

'We may never know.'

Sea spray chilled my face. Gusts of cold air found their way between my warm layers, made me shiver. I gazed back at my grandfather's guesthouse. It rose from the landscape like a great dark castle, surrounded by tortured tree shadows in the falling dusk. It appeared to breathe sluggishly, a living thing trapped inside the illusion of bricks and mortar, stone and shingle. Beyond it, on the other side of the orchard, was a place of even deeper darkness, a door that led down through narrow passageways into the ground, where once, as a child, I had imagined seeing something terrible . . .

There in the corner. A jumble of bony shadows that look, if I squint through the dark, every bit like the crumpled, mouldering shell of a person . . .

Morgan stood beside me, and together we gazed at the old house. Images of Clarice bombarded my mind. Smiling at the fair-haired girl in the garden. Glowering at the church fete beside Edwin, her eyes unable to disguise her displeasure. And hurrying along the windy road that long ago morning, barefoot, oblivious to a neighbour's offer of help.

A giddy stillness fell around us, like the eye of a storm. The wind stopped blowing. The ocean forgot to breathe.

'What if she didn't abandon her baby?' I murmured.

'How do you mean?'

The eerie calm lingered a moment longer. But then, as though stirred by the sudden whirl of my thoughts, the wind picked up and howled along the headland, making me shiver. When I finally spoke, my words were barely audible.

'Maybe she never left Bitterwood.'

21

Bitterwood, 1930

He found Orah in the orchard, sitting on the bench beneath the cherry tree. She was carving into the trunk with a small penknife, absorbed in her task. Flecks of sunlight danced across her hair, picking out dots of gold, giving her the elusive air of a magical fairytale creature.

Edwin should have said something about defacing the tree, or about the inappropriateness of a girl her age possessing a knife, but how could he? When she glanced over her shoulder, her eyes were dark with grief. Edwin would have gladly taken the axe and hacked the tree down himself, if only to bring back her smile. He settled beside her on the bench, his heart heavy.

He had seen Clarice comfort her young ones, even Nala on occasion; pulling the child against her softness, whispering a meaningless jumble of words that somehow, surprisingly, had the power to soothe. Edwin had always considered this womanly trait a weakness. Using words to soften the blow of unhappiness or pain seemed to him pointless. After all, words could not bring back the dead.

Today, he would have given anything to have Clarice's ability to weave comfort from words.

Instead, he had brought a gift, a golden bracelet from which dangled a small heart charm. He held it in a shaft of sunlight so it glittered.

Orah glanced at it, then away.

'It belonged to my mother,' Edwin told her. 'Her father had it specially made. You see, there's a tiny padlock for a clasp, and a pretty charm for luck.'

Still, Orah made no response. Her face was tear-streaked and grubby, and she stared at the swirl of letters she was carving with dull eyes.

'It's yours now, my dear,' Edwin said softly. He would have liked to put it around her wrist, show her how to attach the tiny safety chain, how to flick the clasp with her thumbnail to open it. Instead, he placed it on the bench beside her. She didn't look at it. She didn't look at him. She just sat, digging the knife tip into the bark, apparently lost in the savage *flick-flick* rhythm of her task.

Edwin shifted on the bench. 'I'm sorry about your father.'

Orah continued to ignore him, her lips pressed into a grim line. Anger, Edwin supposed, or grief. Whatever the reason for her silence, he understood it.

'This won't bring him back.' Edwin adjusted the bracelet beside her, and then searched her profile for the longest time. 'But I just want you to know that we care for you very much.'

Springing to her feet, Orah snapped shut the little knife and stowed it in her pocket. Without a word, without even looking at him, she dashed away down the hill, disappearing into the shadows beneath the trees.

Edwin stood up, gazing after her. The girl's mood clung to him, a sticky cloud of sorrow and reproach. He brushed at his legs and shirtsleeves, at the seat of his pants, as though in the hope of dislodging it. Only then did he think to glance down at the bench where he had left his mother's gold bracelet.

It was gone.

As the months passed and summer faded into autumn, Orah spent most of her time in the orchard with Warra and Nala. Picking the last of the fruit, collecting spoiled berries from the ground, inspecting tree trunks for borers to kill. The leaves were beginning to turn. Mottled yellow now, but Warra said they would soon fade to gold and fall, leaving the branches bare as bones.

The day of the church fete finally arrived. Orah had been looking forward to the fete, buoyed by Clarice's glowing account of previous fairs. *Our mulberry jam has won blue ribbons for the past seven years. Just you wait, Orah. When you see all our jars lined up with their labels – I declare, you'll burst with pride.*

Orah slid into her petticoat, the starched cotton crackling softly as it fell around her. She had ironed it specially, laid it out last night on the chest at the foot of her bed. She had chosen her dress, polished her shoes, and even taken the buffing cloth to the bracelet Edwin had given her. She'd never owned anything so pretty. It should have enchanted her, delighted her with its soft golden gleam against her skin. But it only reminded her of those dark days after learning about Pa's death.

Poor Pa. Orah could not bear to think of him dying under a pile of rubble. She had tried her hardest to forgive Edwin. It wasn't his fault Pa was dead. Edwin and Clarice had been so terribly kind, taking her in, showering her in gifts and love, treating her like their very own daughter.

And yet . . . And yet . . .

Still the heartache, the yearning for her own family.

'It could have been the orphanage,' she reminded herself sternly.

Times were hard. Often, she heard Edwin and Clarice talking in low, worried voices. The guesthouse had been mostly empty over summer. Even so, they were luckier than most. They had hens for eggs and meat, vegetables from the garden, goats for milk. Tattered men often came to the door looking for work or a meal, and always left with little bundles of Clarice's cake, butter, bags of tea.

Orah turned this way and that in the mirror. A pink flush clung to her cheeks. Clarice said she was pretty, but Orah couldn't see it. She didn't like her freckles. They ruined her skin. All those gingery speckles marring the peaches and cream she'd inherited from Mam. Orah tried to see Mam's face in the mirror, to find her mother's features in her own. With a jolt, she realised she couldn't remember what Mam looked like. Her pulse quickened. She searched her reflection – the wide-spaced blue eyes that seemed too large for her face, the straight nose with its splash of freckles, the broad cheekbones and arching brows. She could see nothing of her mother, nothing of her father; it was all just her.

'Mam,' she whispered. 'Oh Mam, where are you?'

An image flashed into her mind's eye: a jumble of bones half-buried by sand on the ocean floor. An open trunk from which spilled their chemises and bloomers and petti-coats . . . only now the garments were torn and tattered, their hems frayed, the fabric darkened by water stains.

'Orah?' Clarice poked her head into the room. The heat had flushed her face and her smile was luminous. 'Darling, are you ready? Edwin's finished packing and he's impatient to get going. Oh pet, you look adorable. Just as well we're taking the camera.'

Orah retrieved her hat from behind the door. Then, she did something that she'd never done before. Pausing again in front of the mirror, she smoothed her hair, patted her cheeks, brushed at her sleeves, and then delicately adjusted the gold bracelet so it hung just so around her wrist. Lifting her chin at her reflection, she gave a prim little smile. It was something she'd seen her mother do, this last-minute attention to detail, this stolen moment of preening. It made her feel grown-up, and it made her believe that somehow, however impossible it sounded, Mam was with her, ushering her now towards the door, smiling at her in that old familiar way that dimpled her rosy cheeks, and briefly kissing the top of her head. *My bright girl*, her ghostly mother whispered. *My bright and clever Orah-girl, how lovely you look.* And Orah suddenly found herself quite ready to face the day.

Clarice watched the girl as they drove along the winding road towards Stern Bay. Orah stared through the windscreen, her features empty of emotion like those of a doll. Edwin was no better, gripping the wheel with his long pale fingers, his eyes fixed rigidly on the road ahead.

This was not how Clarice had envisioned their new life together. Earlier in the day, she'd been brimming over with happiness, looking forward to the fete. But Orah had been chilly to her in the Ford. Not quite ignoring her, but near enough. And now Clarice felt the slow creeping in of her old despair. *Time will heal*, she kept telling herself. *Orah will recover and learn to be happy again.* But nearly two months had passed and Orah was still withdrawn. Clarice stole another glance, hoping to catch a glimmer of the girl's old spirit, but there was nothing. Orah's light had gone out. She was hollow as a shell. Would she come back, Clarice wondered, smoothing her shaky fingers over her skirt. Or would she resent them forever?

As they pulled onto the verge outside the churchyard, Edwin spoke for the first time.

'Remember, Orah dear, you're our niece visiting from Melbourne. We don't want tongues wagging.'

Without replying, Orah shoved open the door and jumped from the utility. She ran across the grass towards the church and waited by the gate, her back to them as she watched the stallholders setting up their tables of goods.

Edwin walked around to the back of the utility and unlatched the tailgate. Lifting a box of preserves and jams from the tray, he hoisted it into his arms. His gaze went to Orah. 'She just needs time,' he told Clarice gently, but his words had a flatness that betrayed his own fears.

Clarice retrieved the basket of cakes and slices she and the girls had baked. She glared at her husband, and said under her breath, 'This is your doing, Edwin. If we lose her, you only have yourself to blame.'

He looked at her, shock widening his brown eyes. 'I thought you'd be relieved to have her father out of the picture.'

Clarice wanted to rage, to lash out and strike him. But she kept her voice low. 'She was happier while there was still hope. Now she blames us. You realise that, don't you? She blames us for her grief and pain.'

'She'll recover.'

Clarice breathed a ragged sigh. 'I pray you're right. Because if we lose her, Edwin, I'll never be able to forgive you.'

Orah had feasted on toffee apples and ridden a pony, had her picture taken, and helped sell preserves from their stall. Clarice had been snappy with Edwin, and Orah was secretly glad. Glad too, when the Ford had finally rattled them back to Bitterwood. Back to Warra and Nala.

Now, walking along the clifftop with Warra, her knees got the wobbles. As they climbed down the side of the headland that overlooked the sandy inlet, her breath hitched. She tried not to look at the sea, but it was suddenly all around. She fought the childish urge to take Warra's hand, to draw strength from his strong grasp the way she had done after the shipwreck.

Far below, the water frothed and foamed as the waves crashed against the foot of the cliff. The sea-spray air was salty, and sunlight splashed bright flecks of gold on the swell.

Warra must have noticed her frown, because he took her hand. 'Look at that water. Beautiful, eh? And all that sunshine, friendly as a smile. Nothin' round here to worry about, is there?'

She looked at him, shocked and pleased all at once by the contact of his skin on hers, the strength in his fingers, the smoothness of his palm. Warmth flooded her, and she felt a twinge of almost painful gratitude at his words. He was right, too. There was nothing to fear. At least, not with him at her side.

'Where are you taking me?' she asked, feigning suspicion.

Warra's dark eyes were alight. He led her down towards a grassy embankment that overlooked the tiny beach below. Here grew wildflowers, big loose rings of them, protected from the wind. The ocean's roar became duller, the wind dropped away. The sun warmed Orah's arms. When they reached a patch of native daisies, they stopped.

It was odd, she thought, that of all places he had brought her here. Many miles in a westerly direction along this very coast, her ship had wrecked. Warra knew she still had nightmares. Soon after her arrival at Bitterwood, Warra had asked about her dreams and she had told him. He had nodded, as though dreams were a serious matter, and said, 'It's your spirit talking to your mum's spirit.' She hadn't really understood, but afterwards her dreams had faded a little, not pressed quite so sorely on her mind.

Warra released her hand and crouched at her feet, plucking daisies from the grass. They were white with yellow centres, and made a rustling papery sound in Warra's fingers. Orah sat on the soft grass next to him.

'What are you doing?'

'Making a memory chain.'

She gave a little snort. 'What's that?'

'You'll see.'

Warra settled himself beside her, and dropped his collection of flowers in her lap. Taking one, he split the stem with his fingernail and poked the stem of a second flower through the tiny gap. He split the second stem, threading a third flower into that.

Orah shut her eyes. She drank in the scent of sunlight, of grass and wildflowers, the salty sea. The world might have been perfect, but for the knot in her heart. She could feel it drawing her inwards, a dark shape that bunched and strained, cutting off her breath. For one horrible moment, she was alone. Her head spun, she was falling through time, back to that night in the water—

Her eyes shot open. Warra was beside her, watching. His smile was gentle, his gaze almost black in the sunlight. He held up one of the flowers.

'Paper daisy. Each link is a good memory. Can you think of something?'

She rubbed her eyes, embarrassed by the sudden wetness on her cheeks. 'Right now. Sitting here on this grassy patch with you. It's not exactly a memory, but it will be one day.'

Warra threaded more flowers, using up all the daisies until they formed a chain, fixing together the ends so it made a long necklace. He placed it around Orah's neck.

'It'll keep you safe,' he said with a grin.

'Truly?'

He nodded, then tore away his gaze and looked down at the little inlet below them. 'Me and Nala used to make them when we were kids. One of our aunties showed us.'

Orah settled back on the grass. It was finally making sense, why he'd brought her here; brought her to the ocean on a magical sunny day to make wildflower chains and happy memories. Until now, she had tried to avoid the ocean – shunned those rooms with sea views, refused to accompany Warra and Nala on their fishing trips, and generally tried to block out the pulsing, rushing roar of waves that defined their life at Bitterwood.

Today, though, Warra had shown her another face of the sea. A gentle sunlit face whose salty breath murmured not of death but of daisy chains and firm friends, of happy memories and life.

'Today's a good day,' she said. Then, on a whim, she leaned over and kissed his cheek. 'Thank you.'

Warra seemed startled, but hid his surprise behind a smile. A smile that grew wider as he looked at her. He sat up suddenly. 'I know what'd top it off.'

'What's that?'

264

'I reckon if I asked Mr Briar if you could come home with me and Nala next week, he'd say yes.'

Orah's heart swelled. 'You think so?'

Warra nodded. Jumping to his feet, he reached for her hand. 'Come on. Let's ask him now.'

'What about your family?'

Warra beamed. His dark gaze captured hers, full of pleasure. 'Don't worry, Orah. They'll love you, just wait and see. Mum and them, the aunties and uncles. The other kids. All of 'em, they'll love you. Just like me and Nala do.'

Giving her hand a gentle tug, Warra led her up the embankment. They walked back along the side of the headland towards Bitterwood. All the while, his fingers squeezed warm and steadfast around hers, as the daisy chain he'd made for her danced lightly over her heart.

22

Bitterwood, June 1993

Wintry morning sunlight flooded the bay windows. Without the ragged curtains, the sitting room had opened up. The timber floor gleamed honey-dark, echoing underfoot as I went to the phone. I dialled Dad's number and waited. When he finally answered, it took me a moment to realise it was him. His voice was frail and shaky, old-mannish.

'Dad, are you okay?'

'All good, kiddo.'

'You sound tired.'

He grumbled something inaudible, and then said, 'Stop worrying, love. I already have Wilma fussing over me like a mother hen. How's the clean-up going?'

'Fine.' I hesitated, hoping he was strong enough to cope with what I had to say next. Taking a breath, I plunged in. 'I've been hearing stories about Edwin.'

My father sighed. 'That's nothing new.'

'Did you know he had a brother?'

'Ronald, yes.'

'What do you know about him?'

A pause. 'Not much. He died in the war. Why are you asking?'

I recounted Mildred Burke's story about Clarice's engagement to Ronald before the war, and her claim that Edwin was responsible for Ronald's death.

'She implied that Edwin killed him so he could marry Clarice himself.'

There was another gap of silence.

'Dad—?'

'Nothing Edwin did would surprise me.'

'So you think it's true? That he was capable of—' *Murder*, I had meant to say, but the word stuck in my throat. This was my grandfather, a man related by blood. Privately mulling over all the possibilities was one thing, but voicing the question aloud made it all too horribly real.

Dad coughed. 'If you're asking me if he was capable of killing someone, then yes, I believe he was. Don't forget he served in France during the war. They gave him a gun and taught him to kill, then sent him off to fight. I expect he was responsible for his fair share of deaths. His brother might've been among them, and Jensen Burke might even have witnessed it. But war is war, Lucy. Things happened over there that we won't ever understand.'

I hung on his words. I'd never heard him speak about his father that way. Even when we holidayed at Stern Bay, he'd been dismissive of Edwin. My mother had been the one to fuss over the old man, listen to his stories, chuckle at his jokes. Dad had always been in the background, stony-faced, glancing at the clock, wanting only to be away.

Just now, though, he had defended his father. It made me wonder if he had known, or at least suspected, all along that there was another side to Edwin's story.

'He had all your books,' I said quietly. 'An entire shelf of his bookcase dedicated to your stories. All of them, even the ones before I started illustrating.'

Dad let out a cough. I feared that he was up to his old tricks, trying to fake a coughing fit to escape the conversation. I hurried on. 'They were all well-thumbed. He read them, Dad. Over and over, it seems—'

A strangled wheeze. 'Got to go, Lucy.'

When we hung up, I replayed our conversation. Dad hadn't been surprised when I'd hinted at the possibility of murder. The idea wasn't new to him, I realised. Did he have his own suspicions about Edwin? If so, why was he reluctant to share them with me? A darker thought drifted in. Dad was protecting me. Perhaps his suspicions were not about Clarice at all.

My fingers went to the gold charm.

The last time I saw my mother, she had been standing in the dining room of our holiday cottage, her hair escaping its ponytail, her eyes wide and distracted. Scratches on her arms, her jeans muddy and ripped at the knee. Something had rattled her. Deeply.

Where's your father?

The cogs in my mind began to turn. Had Dad known,

or at least suspected, that something had happened to her that day at Bitterwood? Perhaps an argument with Edwin that ended badly. After all, Dad himself had once quarrelled so grievously with Edwin that he'd left home. All along, Dad might have been keeping his concerns about my mother's fate to himself. Which made me wonder what else he was hiding.

Morgan had ridden off to find the beach where the *Lady Mary* had foundered, so I took the opportunity to escape into the orchard with *The Story of Stern Bay*. The day was a little overcast, but the sun poked through as I returned to my favourite spot beneath the old cherry tree. Basil curled on the grass at my feet in a shimmer of dappled sunlight, while I settled on the bench and began to read.

LM Pettigrew's outline of his own life was straightforward. He had been born at the turn of the century, above the shop where he would spend the larger part of his life. He survived four years of war, and returned home to take over his father's grocery business. He lived a humble life with his family at the back of the shop until his retirement in the late 1960s. Most engaging about his memoir were the colourful cameos depicting people who came and went from his shop. His short glimpses into other people's lives were surprisingly detailed.

He had devoted an entire chapter to the Briar family, but much of it was about Edwin's mother and the history of Bitterwood. There were only a couple of paragraphs about my grandfather, summarising how he and his older brother Ronald had enlisted together. Ronald had died in France in 1917, earning himself several medals for bravery. On Edwin's return to Australia in 1918, he married a young woman from Kyneton.

They had a daughter, such a bright chirpy girl. Little Edith used to come into the shop with Edwin on occasion. She loved boiled sweets, her face would light up as she gazed around at all the jars and tins. When Edwin wasn't looking, I'd let her dip into the lolly jar. My own darling daughters hadn't yet come into the world, but my wife and I adored children, we couldn't wait to have our own. We were ever so sad when Edith died in 1927. Diphtheria, she was only nine. Worse, we learned later that Edwin's wife – I can't recall her name, she so rarely came into town – had given birth to a second child, another little girl, who tragically died on the same day as Edith, barely three days old. They buried their girls in the same plot.

I sat back. Two girls. Sisters my father had never known, who had died on the same day. I couldn't begin to imagine Clarice's grief, or Edwin's. Somehow, it added another layer of understanding to why Edwin had always seemed shrouded in a fog of melancholy. I closed the book and gazed up through the bare branches at the sky.

The girl in the photo was not their daughter. By 1930, Edwin and Clarice's two girls were gone and buried, existing only as an aching void in the lives of those they'd left behind. A void later filled by another young girl with golden hair and a dark, anxious gaze. A girl who may have grown up and moved on, but who most certainly would still remember the couple who had welcomed her into their seaside home.

'It would have been dark when the ship went down.'

Morgan's gaze roamed the grey expanse of water. 'The sky moonless, black with clouds. The sea violent enough to throw them off course. No lighthouse to guide them past the rocks.'

We were standing on the spine of a rocky headland, twenty minutes by bike west of Bitterwood. The fragile sun had vanished behind a veil of grey. The air smelled metallic, and brooding purple clouds gathered on the horizon. Far below, waves crashed onto a narrow beach, frothing and foaming as they rushed up the shore then retreated, littering the sand with flags of black kelp.

Morgan pointed beyond the rocky front of the headland. 'Look over there.'

I squinted, making out a shadow beneath the water. As the swell retreated, the shadow grew blacker, more jagged. It was a bank of submerged rock, extending beyond the headland for a mile or more.

'The tide has come in,' Morgan said, 'but earlier this morning those rocks were above the waterline. Can you imagine how terrifying it must have been? To be so close to land, but the sea too rough to get ashore.'

'No survivors,' I whispered.

Morgan looked at me. His eyes reflected the violet-grey clouds, and the cold wind had flushed his cheeks. His dark hair stood on end from where he'd raked it free of the bike helmet.

'What if someone did survive?'

I frowned, searching the water with renewed interest. In the hazy afternoon light, between the heavy bank of storm clouds and the grey ocean, I fancied I could see a ghostly ship capsizing. Its hull breaking apart, its mast lines tearing free, its cargo spilling overboard. The passengers and crew, panicked, going under. Then, a lonely little figure clinging to the remains of a lifeboat, shivering in the water.

'The girl.'

Morgan nodded. 'We're not so far from Bitterwood. A few days' walk, at most. She might have washed up on the beach, climbed the headland and found her way through the bush.'

I stared down at the beach below. How could a teenage girl survive the wreck, while everyone else perished? Part of me wanted to doubt, but a stronger part insisted anything was possible. Clarice and Edwin had lost two daughters. They might have warmly welcomed a little orphan girl into their hearts.

'Come on,' I said, heading for the path that led down to the beach. 'Let's take a closer look.'

On the way down, we found a cave. It was protected from the wind, yet the narrow entryway provided a clear view across the sea. In a sheltered corner near the entry were traces of a one-time fire. Any ash or cinders had long since blown away, but fire had blackened the cave floor and someone had bundled a stash of dry wood into a crevice. The wood was sandy and woven through with spider webs and dead insects. It had clearly been there a long time.

Leaving the cave, we climbed the rest of the way down to the beach. We walked along the hard sand, watching the storm clouds draw closer. After a while, I looked back the way we'd come. The cave was invisible, the cliffs dark with trees and afternoon shadows. Beyond the headland point, the embankment of submerged rock lurked beneath the waves.

We continued walking. The windblown sand stung my face, and the sea spray was cold, but I barely noticed. 'Can you imagine what it must've been like for her? The ship falling apart, the cries and panic, the terrifying crush of bodies. She might have spent hours in the water. It would have been freezing. She would have felt alone, helpless.'

'You paint a vivid picture.'

'I can see it in my mind, almost as if I was there.'

'That's why you're such a talented artist.'

I smiled at this, and then found myself going on. 'Adam reckons my imagination controls me. He says I worry too much about things I can't change. That's why I . . . well, you know. Get the urge to run.' I waited a beat, but Morgan didn't respond. I pushed my windswept hair from my face so I could look at him. 'He says that sooner or later I'm going to have to stop running and face reality.'

Morgan regarded me. 'Adam doesn't know you as well as he thinks he does.'

A prickly flush of warmth went to my face. 'And you do?'

'Maybe.'

I squared my shoulders. 'Really?'

The storm clouds reflected in his eyes as he looked at me. 'I know you lost your mum too young. I know you skipped childhood to care for an alcoholic father. And I know something happened at Bitterwood that changed you from a bright young girl into a jumpy wreck.'

He tried to hold my gaze, but I moved away from him, went to the water's edge where thin wavelets lapped the sand. Picking up a pebble, I threw it into the swell. *Something happened at Bitterwood . . .*

I rubbed my arms. A breeze touched my skin. Not the fresh wintry sea air, but air that was dank and mouldy as though drifting up from underground. *The darkness is icy. It makes me shiver. Chills rush up my arms, up the back of my neck. She's in here. I can hear her—*

My face flooded with heat. My fingertips tingled.

Morgan came up beside me. 'What was it, Luce?'

I sighed. 'It was nothing.'

He bumped his arm gently against mine. 'Tell me anyway.'

I opened my mouth, but then shut it again. I glanced along the beach, and the open expanse beckoned me. *Run*, said a voice in my head. *Run as far and as fast as you can and don't look back.* But I didn't run. I was getting tired of running. Besides, of everyone I knew, Morgan was the person I trusted most.

'I used to like small spaces,' I told him. 'Escaping from the world, I guess.'

Morgan didn't quite smile. 'Why doesn't that surprise me?'

'There were lots of places to hide at Bitterwood. Up in

the library, nooks and crannies in the guest rooms. The big shed where Edwin raised his moths. But the one I liked best—' I took a breath, eased it out '—was the icehouse. It was creepy and dark. It intrigued me. I used to prop the door open, and feel my way down the stairs and into the blackness. It was like existing in the perfect night, no moon or stars, just utter nothingness.'

Morgan shifted nearer. 'Didn't Edwin keep it locked?'

I let a tiny window open in my mind. 'He hid the keys in the pantry. I spied on him once, saw where he put them. One night, I unlocked the icehouse and went in . . . but the wind caught the door and slammed it shut. I got the mother of all frights.'

Morgan watched me silently. The wind fluttered his jacket collar, tore at his hair.

'What did you do?'

'I couldn't get the door open. So I took out my little keyring torch and went in search of another way out.'

'Did you find one?'

'Yeah, there was . . .' *It's colder, the deeper I go. So dark. And over there . . . I try not to look, but can't help it, because huddled against the wall . . . in the corner . . .* I swallowed, pushing away the memory, faking a laugh. 'There was this old drain in the floor, I must have climbed down and crawled along it. I don't really remember that part.'

'How long were you in there?'

'All—' I shut my eyes. *In the corner, I know it's her, I can hear her whispering to me, calling . . .* I remembered to breathe. 'All night, as it turned out.'

'Hell. Where was Edwin?'

'Asleep.'

Morgan caught my fingers. 'You're trembling.'

I tried to pull away. 'Just cold. The storm's nearly on us. We should head back.'

'What was in there?'

My mother . . . huddled there in the corner. 'Nothing.'

'You saw something, didn't you?'

I shrugged. 'You know what kids are like. Put them in a dark room and their imagination grows wings.'

'What did you *think* you saw?'

The sand seemed to drop away beneath my feet. I pressed my lips together, finally meeting Morgan's gaze. 'A body.'

Morgan didn't react. He continued to watch me, his eyes thoughtful. 'Was it real?'

I shook my head.

'Did you tell Edwin?'

'Of course not.'

'You didn't tell anyone, did you?'

'What was the point? I knew what it was.'

Morgan waited.

I gazed out to sea. Storm clouds muscled at the edges of the sky, rolling closer. I burrowed my hands deeper into my pockets. 'When they found my mother's body, Dad didn't cope.'

'I remember.'

'The day he went to the morgue to identify her, he said something. It really spooked me.' My voice was barely audible over the wash and sigh of the waves. The wind blew against my back, and I felt the first spots of rain. Absently, I brushed them from my face. 'He said they'd made a mistake, that the woman on the table wasn't my mother. Of course, it *was* her – but Dad's reaction shook me. I started obsessing. Worrying about where she might have ended up.'

Morgan gave a soft whistle. 'So what you saw in the icehouse . . . you thought it was her?'

I nodded.

'And it's haunted you all this—'

Before he could finish, the sky opened. Raindrops fell in a deluge. Within moments, we were soaked. I gladly shoved away all thoughts of the icehouse and my mother, and turned to look back the way we'd come.

We were miles from the headland. I could see it through the grey curtain of rain, a dim elephant-like blur in the distance. Morgan grabbed my hand and we ran across the beach towards an overhang of rock, a natural shelter carved out by generations of king tides. It wasn't quite a cave, rather a long narrow shelf at the base of the cliff. I could stand upright, although Morgan had to stoop. The rain blew in on the wind.

'We're going to drown!' I yelled over the din.

'If we don't freeze to death first.'

The wind blew harder, and Morgan looked out at the sky. 'We can't stay here. This isn't going to blow over anytime soon. We need to get back to that cave.'

'It's miles away,' I pointed out.

Water streamed down his face, dripping from his hair, clinging to his dark lashes. He smiled widely and hunched deeper into his jacket. 'Got any better ideas?'

The cave was dry, sheltered from the wind and rain. Outside, thunder cracked and I saw a glimmer of lightning. While I stood shivering in the entryway, hugging myself to keep warm, Morgan gathered an armload of driftwood and small branches that had blown into the cave. He broke the branches into pieces, then fashioned them into a pyramid on the scorched rock where once, a long time ago, someone else had built a fire too.

Morgan removed his jacket and found a jutting rock to hang it from at the back of the cave, where it seemed driest. I pulled off my sodden coat and jumper, and draped them nearby. Shoes and socks came off next. I was already shivering, but squelching around in my wet clothes was worse.

I stood by the fire Morgan was building, watching him. Soon the fire blazed. I sat on the sandy cave floor in front of it, toasting my hands.

'I'm impressed.'

'Pity we don't have a billy to boil. I could use a pot of tea.'

'I'd kill for a cocoa.'

Morgan palmed the water from his hair, his face glistening. He joined me at the fireside, and we sat watching the flames consume the wood. The warmth was delicious.

'What about the Harley?' I wanted to know.

Morgan warmed his hands. 'It's been through worse.'

'How long do you think the storm will last?'

'At the rate it's blowing now? It might go all night.'

'Oh.' I glanced at the entryway. Waves boomed on the shore, and rain hissed off the rocks outside, eclipsed at intervals by the distant crack of thunder.

Morgan snapped a stick and fed the pieces to the fire. 'Back there on the beach, you were telling me about what you saw in Edwin's icehouse.'

'I was hoping you'd forgotten.'

'You don't have to talk about it if you don't want to.'

'Okay. I don't want to.'

'Maybe Adam's right.'

I tried not to take the bait, but I could already feel the question reshaping my features. Knotting my brow, narrowing my eyes. I sighed.

'Right about what?'

'Sooner or later, you have to stop running.'

'Running is what I do.'

'It's making you miserable. And it's hurting everyone who tries to get close to you.'

I said nothing. A sandy gust blew through the cave entrance, guttering the flames.

Morgan fed a branch into the fire and then watched me for a while in the shifting light. 'I know what it's like to be on the run.'

'You do?'

He sat back, turning his attention to the smoky updraft gathering against the cave roof. 'After my brother died, I was angry. At sixteen, I bought my first motorbike and hit the road. Tried to outrace what I was feeling.'

'I never knew you had a brother.'

'His name was Dylan.' A pause. Morgan studied the flames. 'I still think of him as my big brother, but he died when he was twenty-three. Younger than Coby is now.'

'What happened to him?'

I half expected brooding silence, so I was surprised when he scrubbed his hands over his face and continued.

'Dylan was a bright kid. He wanted to go to university, study medicine. Dad used to scoff at the idea, tell him he didn't have the brains to be a doctor. That he was useless, would never amount to anything. Dylan was desperate to impress him, so when he was old enough he followed Dad's footsteps into the army. Then in 1966 he went to Vietnam.'

Morgan sat a long time in silence, elbows on his knees, staring into the flames. I was like a statue, observing him, willing him to keep talking. He had never spoken to me of his past, and I was burning to hear more. But as the silence stretched, I worried that he had withdrawn from me.

'What happened?' I prompted.

Morgan lifted his eyes and held my gaze for a moment, before looking back at the fire.

'Soon after he got home, he took an overdose.'

'Oh. I'm sorry.'

'The following year, Dad succumbed to liver disease. He was a big man with a liking for books and whiskey, not necessarily in that order. He had the habit of flying his fists around when he was drunk. Mum made her position clear earlier on by divorcing him. Later, after Dylan died, I left home too. The following year, Dad went into hospital.'

'Did you ever see him again?'

Morgan shook his head. 'I didn't even go to his funeral. I hated him for the way he'd treated my mother, but especially the way he'd been with Dylan. I carried that anger with me for years. It made me reckless, stupid. I thought I could outrun my grief, but of course, you never can. It's a miracle I didn't end up wrapped around a tree on the edge of some godforsaken road.'

'Actually,' I reminded him, 'you did.'

He raised his face and looked towards the cave entryway. 'Ron made me see sense, in the end. He said, "The Buddhists have a saying, son. Being angry with someone is like taking tiny bites of poison. The only person you hurt is yourself."'

'So what did you do?'

'A few years ago, I went to Dad's grave. I was feeling a little lost. You were in London, worlds away.' He paused, gazing into the darkness beyond the firelight.

I wanted to ask what he had meant by lost, and what, if anything, it had to do with me being in London – but before I had the chance, Morgan continued.

'It was a grey day. The cemetery was deserted. This'll sound nuts, but I stood ranting at his headstone, flinging insults and accusations for an hour or more. Then I sat on his grave exhausted. Too weary to stand up and go home. Sometime later, he spoke to me.'

'Your dad?'

He nodded. 'Clear as day. He said, "I did the best with what I had."'

'Did you reply?'

Morgan looked at me and something passed between us. Not quite a smile, more a softening of resistance, an invisible barrier falling away. He inhaled deeply, and when he breathed out again the years fell away from his face. In the firelight sat the angry young man from the Polaroid, the one in grease-stained jeans who had once leaned against his bike with such attitude. But his scowl,

I now understood, had been concealing the grief he felt after losing his brother.

Finally, he smiled. Hesitantly, almost warily. 'I promised him I'd try to do better. Be a better man than he'd been. Suddenly, I had this feeling. Like slipping into warm water. Like relief, only more intense.'

I leaned nearer. 'You forgave him.'

Morgan bowed his head, and when he looked up again he was his old self. Dark hair raked about, lines around his mouth, creases at the corners of his eyes.

'I guess I did.'

The wind whistled through the entryway. The ocean roared as it thrashed against the rocks below. I imagined the tremors travelling up through the heart of the cliff, vibrating beneath me. I shifted closer to the fire, and to Morgan, where the ground seemed somehow more stable.

'I understand what he meant. Your father, I mean. By doing the best we can with what we have.'

Morgan watched me across the flames, waiting for me to continue.

'My mother's death seemed too big to process. So, I just tucked it away in the back of my mind. Planning to bring it out one day, deal with it when I was older and wiser. But I'm still waiting.'

'It's never too late.'

I wanted to laugh. 'That's just the problem, though, isn't it? Not dealing with something becomes a habit. When you discover how to avoid the big things, you start avoiding the little things too. One day you wake up and find that your whole life is built upon a lie.'

'I know exactly what you mean.'

I looked at him, taking in the damp hair, the cheeks flushed from the fire. The eyes lost in shadow. 'You're the most forthright person I know.'

'And yet for so long I was living a lie.'

'What lie?'

'Gwen and me.' He searched my face and seemed surprised by what he found there. 'You don't know?'

I shook my head. 'Know what?'

'We were quite a team. We hit it off the moment we met at university. We both came from humble beginnings. Both wanted a stable family, and kids. We had similar beliefs and values.'

'You still love her.'

Morgan only smiled, his eyes on me, thoughtful.

A shadow tied itself around my heart. The wind cried in the entryway, trying to get in. Talk of Gwen and the history she and Morgan shared, the life they had built together, felt like a wedge between us. Suddenly I couldn't look at him. My attention drifted to the cave roof. The stone was shrouded in darkness and smoke, but I let my imagination paint stars up there, a moon with a golden aura and a city below. The moon over London. I pictured Adam gazing up at it, thinking of me. I tried to summon feelings of longing, of missing him – but felt only emptiness. Then I tried to envision myself over there, pottering about the Camden Town apartment, sitting in my little studio room, bent over a sketch.

It wasn't working. London seemed a million light years away. My only reality was this cave, the firelight and the wind sneaking over the rocks. And the man sitting on the other side of the flames, silently watching me.

'You know,' he said carefully. 'There were no secrets between Gwen and me.'

He got up and went to the wood stash, brought back an armful of driftwood and laid them by the fire. He placed one on top of the coals, dusted his hands, and settled back on the cave floor.

'Gwen was upfront from the beginning, even before we got married. She wanted a family, she wanted stability.' His tone changed, to something close to regret. 'But she also wanted freedom.'

I looked at him. 'Freedom?'

'Over the years, Gwen had friends. Intimate friends, women. Back in the 1970s, the lifestyle she craved was still considered scandalous. So, having the smokescreen of a husband and child gave her enormous independence.'

I stared at him, grappling to process what he was saying.

'You mean Gwen . . .?'

'Yep.'

The world spun off centre. For the briefest moment, some chaotic force took hold, pulling me out from myself and into uncharted territory. A woman I had known most of my life and loved dearly, a woman who had been a sometimes-mum and friend, was suddenly not who I had believed her to be.

'That's some smokescreen,' I murmured. 'So, did you and she ever—' I bit my lips, mortified that I'd actually spoken the question aloud.

Morgan laughed. 'Sure we did. She was only human.'

'I can't believe you're joking about it.'

He shrugged. 'Gwen and I joked about it all the time. If we hadn't laughed at ourselves, our marriage wouldn't have lasted as long as it did. Remember that, won't you,' he added quietly, 'when you tie the knot with Adam.'

I was still getting my head around Gwen.

'So, that's why you split? Because of her affairs.'

'The affairs weren't the problem. While they were casual, the marriage coped. But once she got serious about someone, she couldn't bear to be around me. We persevered for Coby's sake, but the strain eventually got too great.'

I shifted closer to the fire, my thoughts still flying. 'What about you?' I asked after a while. 'How did you cope?'

'I had what I wanted. A family. A stable home for Coby.'

'That's not what I meant.'

'I wasn't exactly heartbroken, if that's what you're asking.'

'Did you ever . . . I mean was there someone else?' I hadn't meant my voice to sound so small.

He sat very still, his gaze steady on my face. The faintest of smiles appeared, and he seemed to glow softly in the firelight.

'I guess I was waiting for the right girl . . .'

'To come along?' I blurted, and then bit my tongue.

There was a long silence as Morgan watched me. 'To grow up,' he said quietly. 'I was waiting for her to grow up.'

The wind whispered through the rocks, making a hollow sound. I stared at him, barely daring to breathe.

'Oh.'

Morgan continued, his voice low and mesmerising. 'But then when she did, it happened so fast, I wasn't prepared.

Suddenly there she was in my arms, all grown up and more beautiful than I could ever have imagined. Before I could collect myself, she kissed me. Wham, just like that. My head was reeling. I started rambling some stupid crap about her being too young, trying to talk her out of it.' His gaze was steady on my face. 'Letting her go was the worst mistake of my life.'

I froze, unwilling to move and break the spell. I must have misheard. My brain must have twisted his words, giving them meaning he hadn't intended. My heart raced, my limbs quivered. My hands were suddenly damp. Morgan was right, I realised. I saw only what I wanted to see, heard only what I wanted to hear. Because right at that moment, I was hearing words I'd often dreamed but never thought possible.

Letting her go was the worst mistake of my life.

I drew a long breath. 'Why did you . . . let her go?'

Morgan sat a long time in silence, elbows on his knees, staring at the sandy cave floor beneath his feet.

'My son was crazy about her. It would have been cruel to cut in. Unforgivable. So I held back. Besides, my marriage was crumbling, and I still hoped there might be a way to keep it afloat. If just for Coby's sake.'

I got to my feet. Went to the entrance, stared out into the storm. It was cold away from the fire. My clothes were still slightly damp. Rain blew in, and somewhere out across the ocean lightning lit the night sky.

'I'm freezing.' The words hadn't meant to be a challenge, but they came out more harshly than I'd intended. I heard motion, but I didn't look around. I sensed him behind me.

Finally, I turned around. He was near, his gaze burning me up. He watched me for a moment and then tilted back his head, a subtle beckoning.

Slowly, I trod the few steps between us.

'This girl,' I said softly. 'If she was here right now, what would you tell her?'

Morgan moved closer. His fingers traced the side of my face. 'I wouldn't have to tell her anything. She'd know what I wanted to say.'

He was right, she did know. She knew exactly.

Placing my hands flat on his chest, I lightly shoved him. The rebuff registered in his eyes, just a tiny flicker, enough to give me hope. To give me courage. Gathering the front of his shirt in my fingers, I drew him back to me.

And pressed my mouth to his.

Morgan murmured softly. Or maybe it was me. He took hold of me and my body ignited under his touch. I smoothed my hands over his fire-warmed skin, lost my fingers in his rain-damp hair. His arms went around me, tightening, pulling me hard against him. Through the thin wetness of his shirt, his skin was warm and alive. Overhead, a thunderbolt cracked the sky and I felt its electric charge in my bones.

When his kisses travelled along my jaw and then down over my throat and neck, I found myself giggling, breathlessly drunk with the pleasure of being near him. I took his face in my hands, searched his grey eyes, found my own spark reflected there. *Love*, I wanted to whisper. *Always have, always will* . . . but my lips were on his again, tasting, committing him to memory—

'Lucy, promise me.'

'What?' I murmured.

'Don't run away again. Come home and be with me.'

I searched his face, wanting to believe. Wanting this to be a beginning, rather than an end . . . yet knowing in my heart that something this good, this perfect, could not last.

I sighed, and pulled away. 'I can't promise that.'

'I'm rock steady, Luce. I won't waver. I pushed you away once before, but that won't happen again.'

'I can't.'

Morgan caught my hand and drew me back against him. 'Why not?'

I opened my mouth, but the words – the right words – would not come. I wanted to tell him that for a while we would hum along nicely, perhaps even blissfully, just as Adam and I had done, but that sooner or later the cracks would appear and I would have no choice but to vanish into them. The nightmares, the guilt, the need to run. Morgan may be steady, but I was like the great ship that had foundered on the headland point out there on the dark sea. A vessel blown off course, lost in the night, ever wary of the dangers that lurked unseen in the water below.

23

Bitterwood, 1930

They set out along the track at dawn. Nala skipped ahead, her bare feet kicking up eddies of dust, Orah and Warra walking behind, not talking, but occasionally sharing a glance. The further they walked inland away from the sea, the cheerier they became, Orah about to bubble over in anticipation of meeting her friends' family.

Chattering birdcall broke the stillness.

'That was the first sound I heard,' Orah said. 'The morning after you saved me. I heard the birds laughing.'

Warra's dark eyes shone in the sunlight. 'Kookaburra. He's not laughing. He's tellin' his friends it's breakfast time.' He pointed to the glint of water through a grove of trees. 'He'll fly to the creek. When the insects come out, he'll start swooping. He's a big fella too, hungry. Look over there,' he added, pointing across the valley. All around were thick trees and ferns, damp gullies. And beyond that, miles of rolling ridges. 'Our family lives on the other side of that hill.'

'It seems a long way.' Orah hoped he hadn't noticed the wobble in her voice.

'We'll stop this afternoon and make camp. Don't worry, it's not as far as it looks.' Warra's gaze travelled over the landscape. 'You see that rocky hilltop, up there?'

Orah nodded.

'When I was a little kid, I learned to hunt in those trees. I know every stone, every gully and fern. Every anthill. The birds, all of it. It's part of me, this land. When I see myself reflected in the water, or in a glass, I don't see a face. I see—' He gestured across the treetops. 'All this.'

Orah tried to tear her gaze off him, but his words had cast a spell. Curious, magical words that summoned a night sky full of stars, a drift of fire smoke, and a sunny morning filled with birdsong and the strange harsh laughter of kingfishers.

'How can a person look at their own reflection and not see a face?' she said at last.

Warra's mouth twitched. 'You don't look with your eyes.'

Orah blinked at him. A million questions rose inside her mind like a froth of bubbles. 'What do you mean, not look with your eyes?'

The early sunlight illuminated his face, burnishing the proud cheekbones and full mouth, painting shadows around his eyes. Orah liked his face. There was strength in the way his bones sat beneath the skin, but his smile was always changing. Sometimes it was cheeky, teasing. Other times it seemed almost sad.

'You open up,' he said, turning to her. 'Like dancing, feeling free. A good feeling inside. Then you look around with soft eyes, not at any one thing, but all things at once. Forget what your eyes see. See with your heart.'

A tingle flew up her spine. Her froth of questions ebbed away. A strange knowing stillness settled over her. His words – his beautiful, mystifying words – had not made sense. At least, not rational sense. But behind the words, perhaps carried by the solemnity of his voice, she sensed a deeper meaning. It did not yet unfold for her, remaining closed like a dark flower, its petals folded tight, its nucleus hidden from sight. Yet she could *almost* see it. Almost grasp it.

'See with your heart,' she whispered, marvelling over the mystery and beauty of the words. *I will learn*, she decided. *I will remember this moment. Make it a part of me. I will set aside everything I know about the world, and instead learn to see this way.*

Goose bumps prickled on the back of her neck and spread over her scalp. She shivered, her determination of a moment ago giving way to a sense of premonition. *See with your heart.* The words rang in her mind, no longer a mystery . . . but a sign.

Closing her eyes, she thought of Mam, and instantly Mam was there. Then she thought of Pa, but was disappointed when he failed to show. She sighed and opened her eyes.

'I suppose I need practice.'

Warra's warm laugh echoed in her ears. His smile was friendly, and Orah found herself looking at him and away, then back again as if she'd never really looked at him before. Yes, she liked his face, with its deep brown eyes and strong features. Most of all she liked his smile; it was wide and forthright and gave her tingles, and it made her want to smile back. Perhaps that was what he meant by seeing with your heart.

'Come on,' Warra said, nudging his arm against hers, 'let's catch up with Nala. She'll be wondering where we are.'

Nala was waiting by a fence. It was post and wire, and ran in a straight line alongside a bushy stand of gum trees, travelling parallel to a dirt track for a way, before cutting across it.

'Old Mister's land,' Warra said, as they joined Nala at the fence.

Nala pointed to a distant ridge, dark purple against the shimmering blue horizon. 'That's where we want to go. Less than an hour's walk if we cut through Old Mister's place. Almost a full day if we go around.'

Orah was dismayed. 'Another day?'

Nala nodded, but she was smiling. 'Two, if we dawdle.'

'What'll we do?'

Nala's smile widened. 'Cut through, of course.'

Orah hesitated. 'But isn't it—'

Dangerous, she had been about to say. The last time they had come this way, Warra had woken her in the night, dragging her from her grass bed. They had left behind their camp and fled into the dark, away from gruff men's voices. And gunfire.

'Come on,' Nala said, giving her a mischievous smile. 'Race you.' She darted through the wire, and began to run on the other side, dodging saplings and shrubs as she headed for the dirt track. Warra was already ducking between the wires. He beckoned to Orah as he followed his sister.

Orah gazed first one way and then the other along the fence line, as if it were a busy city street she was about to cross. They were miles from civilisation, a long way from any houses or roads. The only sounds were birds and insects and the occasional distant thump as a wallaby pounded unseen through the undergrowth somewhere nearby.

Swallowing her unease, she slipped through the fencing wire as her friends had done and raced after them.

Some time later, the track widened and they rounded a bend. The trees thinned, and the sun climbed the sky. The morning grew hot. Orah dawdled a little way behind her friends, stopping occasionally to inspect a wildflower or fallen cluster of gumnuts. She was removing her cardigan when a deafening shot split the quiet.

Gunfire.

She stumbled, and in the moment it took her to steady herself, a terrible quaking engulfed her. Wide-eyed, she looked at Warra, who had frozen on the path just ahead of her, his shoulders tense, his face set in a frown. Orah could tell he was listening, because he began to swivel his gaze, taking in the open ground around the track and then sweeping across the trees behind them. Only his head moved, while his body remained rigid.

Orah could hear nothing. Her ears still rang from the echo of the shot. Instinct told her to run and hide, but her legs trembled so violently the best she could do was keep herself upright.

Warra lifted his arm and beckoned to her with his fingers. Orah began to move quietly along the track. She had only gone a few steps when another shot shattered the stillness, followed by what sounded like thunder.

Orah whirled around. Through the trees, she glimpsed a horse charging along the fence line. Its hoofs kicked up clods of grass and earth, and the musky animal odour of its sweaty flanks was sharp in the pine-scented bush. The horse was too far away to see the rider clearly but as she watched, the man raised his rifle and took aim. Orah stumbled backwards, knowing she must get to her friends, but when she turned to run she tripped on a clump of grass and crashed to the ground. Pain tore through her ankle and she clenched her jaw to stop herself crying out.

There was another shot, frighteningly close, followed by a scream. Orah flinched, pressing herself as low as possible against the ground, clawing her fingernails into the dirt. Her body trembled so badly she was unable to draw breath. In her head, the scream echoed. She couldn't be sure whether it had been her own or someone else's.

The thunder of hooves grew fainter. Orah's heartbeat hammered in her ears. Powdery dust filled her nostrils and mouth and stuck to the wet patches around her eyes. Moments later, a fourth shattering report echoed across the sky. Orah cringed into herself, weak with relief when she realised that the sound had come from further away.

Then, in the silence, another scream.

Orah sprang up, but her ankle blazed with pain, forcing her to lurch shakily along the track. Ahead, two figures huddled in the shadow of a giant ironbark tree.

Not huddled, she saw now. One lay prone. Warra, on his back, and his shirt, the one Edwin had given him, the shirt he had been so proud to own, was no longer white, but stained with large wet blotches of reddish black.

'No. Oh please, no.'

Warra lay so still. Nala huddled over him, crying his name. By the time Orah reached them, Nala had slumped onto Warra's chest, her muffled cries cutting gashes in the brightness of the morning.

'Warra!' Orah went to her knees, shaking him.

'Warra, wake up. Please, Warra . . . wake up.'

Nala was weeping more quietly now, a low keening. Orah dragged in a frightened breath. Warra needed help. He needed a doctor. The patches of blood on his shirt were quickly spreading, soaking the fabric, joining into one enormous wet stain over his heart.

Oh no. Please, no—

Orah forced the words through her clamped jaw.

'Run and get Edwin,' she instructed Nala. 'I've hurt my ankle. You'll be faster. Tell him what's happened. Tell him to come at once.'

Nala stared as if she'd never seen Orah before. Her eyes were blank with terror, wide and dark as those of a trapped possum. Orah wanted to shake her, to make sure she understood, but she didn't want to release her hold on Warra.

'Nala,' she said more slowly, desperate to make her friend understand. 'Run to Bitterwood. Do you hear me? Run as fast as you can. Tell Edwin to come.'

Finally, Nala nodded. She bent over Warra, pressing her lips to the side of his face. Orah thought she meant to kiss him, but instead she began to murmur, her tears dripping on his cheeks, streaking through the dust like rain. Nala released her brother and got to her feet. Without looking back, she staggered along the track for a way, and then veered into the trees.

It was only when she disappeared behind a dense thicket of scrub that Orah realised the girl was heading the wrong way. Not back towards Bitterwood at all, but westwards towards her home.

'Nala!' she yelled, clutching Warra's motionless arms. 'Where are you going? Come back, you have to get Edwin. Nala! Please, come back!'

Nala did not return. The sky grew bright, and one by one, the lorikeets and finches, the wrens and butcherbirds began to fill the air with their song. Orah might have slept. An uneasy doze, where shadows pressed in from all sides and the smallest sounds – falling leaves, the shiver of wind-blown grass, the furtive call of a raven – echoed loudly in her ears, keeping time with the ragged thunder of her pulse. It seemed wrong to shut her eyes, but shock and fear had immobilised her. All she could do was wait – for Nala to return . . . or for the men with guns to circle back along the track.

For Edwin.

She drifted in and out of wakefulness. Warra's hand was clutched tight in her own, her head rested on his chest. His blood felt sticky against her cheek, mingling with the hot wetness of her tears. Her ankle throbbed, a white-hot ball of pain, but it seemed inconsequential compared to the horrible knotting, writhing thing that had taken up residence in her chest.

Warra stirred. 'Orah?'

His voice was a dry leaf scratching on sand. At first she thought she'd imagined it. Then his fingers curled ever so gently around hers.

Propping up on an elbow, she looked at him. His eyes were open. She released his hand, and placed her palms on either side of his face, gazing down at him.

'You're alive,' she whispered. 'Oh Warra, I thought . . . I thought you were—' Her voice choked off. Leaning over him, she brought her face close to his. Her hair formed a curtain around them, its golden strands clotted with Warra's blood. Dappled light touched his skin, painting honey-coloured streaks on his jaw and throat. Orah drank in the sight of him, before locking her gaze with his. She could see the small oval of her face reflected in the dark depths of his eyes.

'Orah,' he said again.

'You'll be all right, Warra.' She took a breath, praying with all her might that she spoke the truth. 'Nala has gone for help. She's gone to your family, Warra. Do you understand? She'll bring someone to help you. You'll be all right.'

'I'm cold, Orah. Will you—' His lips moved, but no sound left his mouth. It didn't matter. Orah understood.

Gently, she kissed his cheek and then lay down beside him, her face resting against his. She slid one arm under his neck and draped the other carefully over his ribs, below where the ragged wound continued to bleed its darkness into the fabric of his shirt.

'I'm here, Warra. I won't ever leave you. I promise.'

Orah.

He may have whispered her name, or it might have been the wind ruffling the grass, or the leaves in the trees sighing in sorrow. At that moment, it seemed to Orah quite natural that the world around them grieved, just as she grieved.

'I'm here,' she said again, her throat thick. 'I won't leave you, Warra. I'm here. I'll always be here. With you, my dear friend. Always with you.'

Somewhere in the canopy above her, a kookaburra alighted in a high branch. The branch creaked as the heavy bird came to rest, and a shower of dry leaves rained down. Throwing back its head, the bird began to laugh . . . the same crazed laughter Orah had heard that first morning after the shipwreck. She huddled protectively over Warra. If only another type of bird had come to serenade them. A magpie or a butcherbird, whose songs were sweet and melodic.

A shiver rippled through her. As if in answer, Warra shivered too. He let out a sigh that sounded like her name. He shivered again, and then stillness settled over him.

Orah clasped his body tight against hers. She shut her eyes.

She'd been wrong. The bird in the branches above them

wasn't laughing. There was no joy in the sound, no gaiety. Rather, it seemed to shriek in distress. As she cringed, trembling over Warra's body, the bird's strange call seemed to her the saddest, most desolate noise she had ever heard.

The afternoon was slipping away. Shadows crowded under the trees and the air grew cold. A group of men approached Orah, but did not look at her. They were very dark, and wore dusty faded clothes. Gathering around Warra's body, they murmured among themselves. Orah watched one of the men kneel by Warra's head and touch the patch of shirt where blood was seeping. He let out a moan, and covered his eyes with his hand. After a while, he gathered Warra into his arms and staggered away.

Orah followed, crying out, but a strong hand gripped her shoulder, forcing her to stand still. She tried to tear herself away, but the steely fingers, strangely gentle despite the force on her shoulder, held firm. When the man carrying Warra's body disappeared into the trees ahead of her, she crumpled onto the ground.

A man kneeled beside her. His skin was very dark, a terrain of wrinkled folds dotted with freckles and grey patches of beard. The wiry hair that framed his face was the colour of ash, giving him a strange fierceness that made Orah afraid.

'Who did this?' the man asked.

Orah shook her head, struggling to find her voice, but all she could think of was Warra disappearing into the bush ahead of her, and the gap widening between them, and her fear that they would take him far away and she would never see him again.

Please, she wanted to say. *I want to go with him. Let me follow, don't leave me here.*

The man shook his head, as though he had heard her silent words. 'Go home.'

'I can't walk.'

Orah pointed to her ankle, which had swollen into a purple lump. The man studied her foot for a long time.

'Who did this?' he asked again.

Orah swallowed, a bitter taste filling her mouth.

'I don't know,' she said hoarsely, but then added, 'Old Mister.'

The man's face turned hard. He glared around at his companions, and murmurs rippled among them. Yet when he looked back at Orah, his eyes were kind again.

'You have to go home.'

He stood and strode away into the trees and began to walk in circles, looking down at the ground as if searching for something. Finally, he crouched and plucked something from a small bush. A handful of stems and leaves, Orah thought. These he pushed into his mouth and began to chew.

He hurried back and crouched beside Orah. Spitting the contents of his mouth into his hands, he gently massaged the green pulp into Orah's ankle. He took a strip of what looked like animal hide from the pouch at his waist, and wrapped it neatly over the poultice, binding it around Orah's foot.

He spoke in his language to the other men. They seemed

disgruntled, frowning and talking angrily, glancing uneasily at Orah. Then, to Orah's surprise, the ash-haired man lifted her easily into his arms and, with a nod to his fellows, strode back along the track in the direction of Bitterwood.

Several hours must have passed, Orah could not be sure. She dozed, and when she awoke, the sun had rolled across the sky and settled on the horizon, and they had reached the edge of the orchard.

24

Bitterwood, June 1993

The storm had vanished in the night. The sea was calm, the sky cloudless blue. Driftwood and kelp littered the shore, but they were the only signs that the storm had ever been. As we rode back to Bitterwood, I held tight to Morgan, resting the side of my helmet against his back, watching the ocean appear and disappear between the trees as Morgan manoeuvred the Harley around the sharp bends of the road.

My lips felt bruised, my body strangely heavy. Images of the night before – of Morgan's face in the firelight, his grey eyes and hesitant smile – flooded my mind's eye, but I pushed them away. In the flickering darkness of the little cave, held warm through the night in Morgan's arms, it had been easy to pretend that the rest of the world did not exist. But now, as the sun began to rise into a flawless blue sky, the illusion vanished.

Passion doesn't last.

On the other side of the globe in London, Adam would be brewing his last coffee of the day, thinking of me as he always did before bed. Gazing out his window at Camden Lock, perhaps remembering the day we had stumbled laughing from the markets and eaten lunch on the canal side, tossing chips to the overfed seagulls. That fragile blue summer day beside the water had been one of our happiest. It seemed forever ago, but was just a few months before Edwin's letter arrived. Before I had allowed the first doubts to chip away at the solid foundations Adam and I had worked so hard to build.

Friendship is what makes a marriage.

Last night, in the cave, I had forgotten Adam, forgotten the life we had planned together. A good life, where we would rub along and find contentment. There would be no fire-lit nights in a cave above the ocean where once a ship had foundered on the rocks; there would be no velocity, no fast rides to clear the head. No giddy sense of flying, no cat rescuing, no magic . . . Yet nor would there be the crushing insecurity that came from utterly, helplessly losing your heart.

I dug my fingers into Morgan's ribs, felt him flinch.

It made me feel better to hurt him, even just a little. The person I really wanted to hurt, of course, was myself. But the ache in my heart was already so intense, I feared that heaping on any more guilt would cause actual physical damage.

When we reached Bitterwood, I climbed off the bike and dragged open the gates, waited for Morgan to ride through.

I gestured to him that I would walk the rest of the way. By the time I had pulled shut the gates behind me and walked on shaky legs to the verandah, I knew what I had to do.

A fire blazed in the kitchen. The air was delicious with the smell of buttery toast and scrambled eggs, melted cheese, bacon and tomato.

Morgan thumped around in search of a teapot, and then set about making tea, sending me thoughtful looks across the table.

As I watched him pour, I flashed back to another morning. It seemed a lifetime ago. I had been breakfasting at Morgan's before a school excursion. Coby and Gwen bantered as they made last-minute sandwiches. Morgan skimmed the newspaper while he waited for the rest of us to get our act together. I was fifteen, old enough to know that what I felt for my best friend's father was bad. All the other girls at school had crushes their own age, which seemed normal and healthy; trust me to get it wrong. Trust me to be the one standing there in that sunny kitchen, feeling like a traitor as the friendly clatter of plates and soft voices and the rustle of newspaper washed around me. *All right, Lucy?* Morgan would say, and smile in that irreverent way he had, adding a half-wink that made my teenage heart do cartwheels.

Now, a decade later, here I was in another kitchen, feeling just as lost and out of my depth as I had been back then.

'A penny for them,' Morgan said.

'They're not worth a penny.'

'A ha'penny, then.'

'Ha'penny?' I smiled, trying to lighten the mood. 'Careful, Mr Roseblade, you're showing your age.'

'Ouch.'

Our eyes met, and just for a moment, we were back where we had begun, all those years ago. Friends, caught up in our teasing banter, comfortable. But then Morgan's face softened, became serious. He settled in the chair beside me and reached for my hand. 'I meant everything I said last night. I don't regret a minute of it. But you clearly do.'

There was so much I wanted to say. So many questions, too. But I found myself unable to voice any of it. I studied the ring on my finger.

'I made a promise to someone, Morgan.'

Morgan gave my fingers a gentle squeeze, and then let them go. He sat back, raked his fingers through the dark mess of his hair.

'If Adam is right for you, then you should be with him. Whatever my selfish reasons for wishing it wasn't so, I love you too much to try and stand in your way.'

He got to his feet and then pulled me up beside him. He let his palm rest against the side of my face. Leaning in, he pressed a feather-light kiss against the corner of my eye and then drew me against him, whispered into my hair.

'Goodbye, Lucy.'

He said it so easily, so casually, that he might have been mentioning what a fine day it was, or that the ocean looked calm in the sunlight. But the word echoed in my brain with quiet finality.

Goodbye.

He went to the door, and it was only then that I saw his bag was already packed. He had known what I would say. Or perhaps, he had sensed my hesitation and drawn his own conclusion about where we were heading.

He went out and without looking back, shut the door silently behind him. His boots thumped along the verandah, and then he was gone.

I told myself not to go to the window. Not to watch him leave. I stood very still, staring at the tea grown cold in my cup. Then the Harley started up, the motor revved into a growl. I heard tyres crunch along the gravel at the side of the house, heard the engine purr while it idled at the gate.

I stood very still, alone in the kitchen, listening.

The gate squealed shut. The Harley's engine roared. Even from the back of the house, the noise seemed deafening, amplified by the cold clear air. It jarred me from my trance. Suddenly I was running along the hall, my footfall echoing loudly on the floorboards. Through the sitting room, to the bay window, its panes strangely naked without the ragged curtains. Both palms on the glass, I stared across the yard to the gate. I could still hear the bike motor rumbling, but the sound faded quickly. Then, there was just the silence.

Morgan was gone.

You've made the right decision, I told myself. *You're doing the right thing.*

But another, smaller voice whispered defiantly in the back of my mind. *If this is the right thing, then why does it feel so wrong?*

Melbourne, June 1993

The Hennessy Avenue letterbox was overflowing after my week away. Grabbing the bundle, I headed into the house. The air was stuffy and cold, but I was too tired to bother lighting a fire. I opened a can of fish for Basil, and then emptied a tin of soup into a saucepan and heated it for myself. I ate in the kitchen, the book on my lap unread, a snowstorm of thoughts whirling in my mind.

My night with Morgan. The emptiness after his departure. My promise to Adam, and the shadow of my guilt. I knew what I had to do, but my resolve was shaky. No matter which way I turned, someone was going to get hurt. The snowstorm was quickly becoming an avalanche, so I shoved it away and tried to focus instead on the reason for my return.

I had arranged to meet with Dad the following day and hand over the photos. He would be emotional, perhaps even try to withdraw from me. It might not be the perfect time to press him further about Edwin's history, but I was burning to continue our conversation about my grandfather's wartime experiences, and the possibility that Clarice had met with foul play.

The chill of the house settled around me.

Arriving back in Melbourne had shaken me from whatever fantasy world I'd inhabited this past week. Camping in my van at night, a big old cuddly cat warming my feet. Spending the better part of my days trawling through my grandfather's collection of curios and treasures, chasing ghosts. It all seemed such a long way away from reality. From the life I'd built for myself in London. My life with Adam. The life I was making such a mess of.

'I can see why Edwin hid from the world,' I told Basil. 'The idea of becoming a hermit seems very appealing right now.'

Basil glanced up from his food. The light from the hallway caught his eyes and he seemed otherworldly, a spirit creature whose purpose was known only to himself. Then he went back to lapping up his fish, a cat again, scarred and battle-weary, with torn ears and a permanent crimp in his tail.

Setting aside my bowl, I shuffled through the mail: mostly bills addressed to the woman who owned the house. One, however – a postcard of Hyde Park in London – made my heart skip. Somehow I knew, even before I started reading the neatly printed message, what it would say.

Dear Lucy,
Don't be angry, I know I promised you space, but I miss you terribly. Since you left, I've been going out of my mind. Things haven't been great with us. We need to talk. I can't wait any longer to see to you, and I'm useless on the phone. I've booked a flight and will arrive at Tullamarine on 15 June.
Adam xx

Still clutching the postcard, I got up and looked at the wall calendar, needing visual confirmation. Locating today's date, I traced my finger towards the fifteenth.

Two days.

Checking the clock, I calculated London time: just after

7 a.m., Adam would be rushing for the tube, grabbing coffee at the kiosk, on his way into the office. I rang anyway, waited for the answering machine to beep on. My own voice echoed from the other side of the world, inviting me to leave a message. A dullness washed over me, as though I'd fallen through the cracks of my life into a netherworld of shadows. I felt disconnected, torn between two realities, belonging in neither.

'Adam, it's me. I got your postcard. I wish you could have waited until I get back. Now's not a good time. My grandfather died, I'm halfway through clearing his house for Dad. Can you cancel your ticket? I'm not—' I broke off on a sigh. Tried to regather my thoughts, but failed. 'Look, if you must come . . . fly safe.'

I hung up and went back along the hall, upstairs to the bedroom, and climbed into bed with my clothes on. Dragging the covers up to my chin, I stayed that way until the ache in my chest grew so bad I had to sit up. Hands over my face, I breathed through my fingers. When Basil meowed from the doorway, I came to my senses.

'Come on, boy.' I patted the bed. He jumped up beside me and lowered his head for an ear rub. The cuts on his face were healing, leaving pale patches of skin where the fur had yet to grow back. I smoothed my palm over his thin body. Moments later, he tucked himself against the mound of my feet, and settled into sleep.

Two days.

Adam would look at me and know. Just as I'd known what he'd written on the postcard before I read it, he would take one look at me and know there was someone else.

Closing my eyes, I sank deeper into the bed. My hair tangled over my face, and as I breathed slowly through it, I smelled the ocean and wood smoke and the salty dampness of the cave where we had taken shelter. Rain-soaked clothes, wet skin, the crackling fire. Me melting against Morgan, yearning for him, all my old feelings rekindled.

I took deep breaths. The wild reckless joy of that night was about to cost me dearly. Adam would know; Adam, who had only ever been kind and good to me, would know that I had betrayed his trust in the worst possible way.

Yet even as the first tears began to leak from my eyes, I couldn't stop the yearning. I could still taste Morgan's skin on my lips, could still feel the soft length of his hair between my fingers ... and I wanted to taste and feel him again. Even if I could travel back through time to change what had happened between us, I knew that I wouldn't.

Basil began to purr. The soft vibrations tickled the soles of my feet, and strangely, despite the agitation that had taken hold of me, I began to calm.

In two days, Adam would be here. But I couldn't think of it now. I would rest my exhausted brain in sleep, and worry about the rest of the world in the morning. Rolling onto my side, I snuggled into the pillow, and it was only then that I realised I was still clutching the postcard, damp now from my tears, and rumpled into a wad between my fingers.

The Stork Cafe was right on the beach. Dad was waiting when I arrived. He sat on the far side of the cafe near the wall of windows that overlooked a spectacular ocean view. His crutches were propped against a chair, his face pale and anxious. I kissed his cheek and gave him a quick hug before settling myself opposite. I placed the envelope on the table between us.

Dad eyed it warily. 'I've already ordered. Poppy-seed cake all round, that okay?'

I nodded to the envelope. 'Open it, Dad.'

He drew it across the table, but then rested his hands on it and looked at me. 'You must have questions.'

'Only about a million.'

His smile seemed a little shaky. He turned his face to the window. The water in the bay was steely, the waves flecked with dirty white foam. The greyness of the day seemed a fitting backdrop for our meeting. Dad sighed and looked back at the envelope.

'Where to begin?'

'You could start with the row you had with Edwin when you were fifteen. It was about Clarice, wasn't it?'

The wind blew across the sandhills and rattled the big windowpanes. The air inside the cafe was still, but Dad shivered.

'Edwin was always distant,' he began. He clasped his hands tightly on top of the envelope, and then gazed back at the window. 'When I was younger, his aloofness hurt me. I suppose that was why, when I learned the truth about my real mother, I found it so easy to resent him.'

'Why do you think he never told you about her?'

'I guess for the same reason I never told you.'

'To protect me?'

He nodded. 'Edwin would have wanted to spare Dulcie's feelings. And his own. My father was a very private man. Secretive, even. Mum – Dulcie – knew that Edwin had been married before, but in those days it was one of those topics people never discussed.'

'What about the row you had with him?'

'A few days before Dulcie died, she called me into her room. Said she didn't want to go to her grave with a burden on her chest.' Dad let out a ragged sort of laugh. 'Then the bombshell. She told me how Edwin's first wife, Clarice, was my natural mother. She said that Clarice had run away and left Edwin with a new baby – me – and that she'd broken my father's heart, which is why he never spoke of her . . .'

Dad looked up as a waiter arrived at our table with a tray of cake and tea. When he'd gone, Dad continued.

'I remember thinking that Dulcie must be delirious, that the medication was affecting her brain. She gave me this old photo album, but before I had a chance to go through it, Edwin took it back. Mum said Edwin was wrong for hiding the truth from me. I wanted to ask more, but she drifted into sleep after that.'

Dad picked up his fork and broke off a corner of cake. He chased it around his plate for a while, and then sighed. 'Of course, there was a row over the photos. Edwin refused to hand them over. He didn't deny Dulcie's story, just told me to forget it. To forget Clarice.'

'That seems harsh.'

Dad nodded. 'I flew off the handle. I said some things I'm not proud of, ranted and raved at him for an hour

312

or more, but in typical Edwin fashion, he barely said a word. Dulcie died in her sleep that night, and for a time our argument was forgotten.'

He stared at his slice of cake. 'After the funeral, I tore the house apart looking for those bloody photos. I began to doubt if they even existed. Then I started bombarding Edwin with questions. Why had Clarice abandoned us? Where had she gone, was she still alive? I blamed him for chasing her away, accused him of being unlovable, a bore. Then my own doubts set in. Had she left because of me? Maybe she never loved me, never wanted the burden of a child. Finally, worn down by my hectoring, Edwin turned on me. I'll never forget the look in his eyes – the wild, desperate look of an animal hunted into a corner. He said, "She left *because* she loved you." Then he slammed the door behind him and I didn't see him again for nearly thirty years.'

'What did he mean?'

Dad shook his head. 'I've spent a lifetime asking myself the same question. Now I'll never know. Whatever secret Edwin was protecting has gone with him into the grave.'

My fingers found the ribbon around my neck. Now was the perfect time to tell Dad about my mother's charm. About Edwin's letter, and his promise.

I've something for you that will explain everything.

My father frowned at me across the table. His shoulders were hunched, his collar ruched up around his ears. His face was pale, but twin blotches of livid pink burned on his cheekbones. My gaze drifted to the crutches, and I flashed back sixteen years: Dad lurching along the hallway at our old house, thumping his hand along the wall as he went, spilling wine from his flagon.

I couldn't tell him, I realised. Giving him the photos today had burdened him enough. If I unloaded anything more, he might crack under the strain.

My appetite had deserted me, but I picked at my cake, washing it down with hot tea. Dad watched me for a while, and then started on his own poppy-seed wedge, but didn't get far. Pushing away his plate, he picked up the envelope.

Drawing out the photos, he shuffled through them, pausing from time to time to examine one more closely. When he got to the church fete photo, I leaned over and pointed out the fair-haired girl.

'Who's that?' Dad wanted to know.

'I was hoping you could tell me.'

'Is she one of my . . . my sisters?'

I held myself still. 'How did you know about them?'

'Lionel Pettigrew once gave me a copy of his memoir. I thought he might know something more, but he said he'd put everything into the book. It saddened me to learn I'd once had sisters. I felt robbed. If only Edwin had told me, things may have turned out differently between us. I discovered more about my family background from Lionel's little book than I ever learned from my own father.'

I reached out across the table and touched his hand. 'She isn't your sister,' I said quietly. 'They both died three years before this photo was taken.'

Dad was silent. He spread a couple of photos on the table, and then chose one of the children in the orchard.

'There she is again, the fair-haired girl. What about those Aboriginal kids with her . . . any idea who they are?'

I shook my head. 'Maybe their parents once worked for Edwin.'

Dad shuffled the photos back into a pile, but then he paused and went back to the orchard shot of the kids. He studied it again at length.

'What is it?' I asked.

'There's something about the little Aboriginal girl with the basket. I don't know . . .'

'Do you recognise her?'

Dad examined the print again, but then sighed. 'My head's all over the place. I'll be seeing Clarice in my dreams tonight. I had hoped that the photos would somehow put an end to the questions, the wondering. But . . .' He gave a defeated sort of shrug. 'They've only made me more curious.'

Replacing the photos in the envelope, he set them aside. His cheeks were flushed, his eyes watery bright. There were crumbs in his beard, and a worried knot between his brows.

'All my life,' he murmured, 'she was a thorn in my happiness. No matter how good it got – meeting Karen, having you, getting my books published – no matter how happy or successful I tried to be, Clarice was always there in the background, haunting me. If only I'd known why she left, why she abandoned me. Even if her reasons had hurt me, it would have been better than not knowing at all.'

I gazed through the window. If anyone knew about thorns, it was me. I touched the charm that hung around my neck and saw my own mother's face: her kind blue eyes, her freckled nose and wide smile. She had loved me, I'd always felt it. Yet a child's lie had cost her everything, and there was no undoing that. I understood my father's sorrows because they so closely echoed my own.

'Dad,' I began carefully. 'Do you think Edwin had it in him to hurt her . . . Clarice, I mean?'

My father shook his head, but seemed unable to meet my eyes. 'I don't know. It's possible, I suppose.'

'Then maybe she didn't leave, after all? Maybe Edwin . . .'

Dad fixed his gaze on the scene outside. The windswept beach, the brackish water in the bay, the hollow sky. 'What does it matter now, Luce? There's no way we can ever be certain. It's only going to cause us more pain.'

He was right on all but one count. Clarice's fate did matter. It mattered to me. And if I wanted the truth, I was going to have to chase it alone.

From where I sat, the grey sea and bleak white sky seemed endless. I turned my back to it. The cafe had emptied; we were the only remaining patrons. Our little corner in front of the window was an island detached from the larger continent of tables, bathed in watery light, serenaded by the whistling wind outside. The air seemed to shimmer around us, thin and silvery, as though some rare sort of magic had taken place, leaving us both raw and fragile.

'Adam is arriving tomorrow,' I said softly. 'He's decided to come over after all.'

'You don't sound too thrilled.'

'I'm not entirely sure that I am.'

'Lord,' Dad muttered, not removing his gaze from the sea. 'It never bloody rains, does it?'

The Queen stood on the headland. Wild wind lashed her hair, and sea spray drenched her gown. Wringing her hands, she cried out to the seething ocean, 'I cannot give her back! I will not.'

—*The Shell Queen*

25

Bitterwood, 1930

'Why did Warra die?' Orah demanded. 'He never hurt anyone.'

They were sitting in the orchard, on the bench beneath the cherry tree. The dying afternoon light lingered high above them in the treetops, but here below, the cool fingers of night had already begun to gather.

Edwin cleared his throat. 'I don't know.'

Orah's gaze lifted, and for a while, she seemed mesmerised by something that lay out of sight in the densely growing trees at the far edge of the orchard. 'He could see himself in the land and sky,' she murmured. 'Like looking in a mirror.'

Edwin felt the need to respond, to say something about Warra's intelligence, his kindness, his honesty, his capacity for hard work – but the burden of the boy's loss seemed suddenly unbearably heavy. He shut his eyes. 'A shame,' was all he said. 'A terrible shame.'

Orah bowed forward, pressing her fingertips into her eyes. 'He saved my life. But I couldn't save his.'

'It wasn't your fault, Orah. There was nothing you could have done.'

She looked at him sharply. 'Mr Burke should hang.'

'We've no proof it was him.'

'He should be punished.'

Edwin sighed, and then nodded.

Her voice rang of defeat. 'He won't, though, will he?'

Strange, how she reminded him of Clarice. Her loyalty, her instinct to protect those she loved; yet she had a strange fragility, as though she clung to life by a thread. He had begun to see Clarice in her gestures too, in the way she walked, the way she fixed her hair on the side, the way she screwed up her nose when she laughed. Had she always been that way, or had she fallen under Clarice's spell, unconsciously emulating Clarice in the way that every daughter learned from her mother?

She was watching him expectantly. His heart clenched. He groped for words, finding only a short quotation his mother had favoured.

'Sin makes its own hell.'

Disappointment registered in Orah's eyes. She looked away quickly, as if embarrassed for him.

Edwin had seen that look before, many years ago, a look bordering on pity. He'd been sitting in the mud with his back against the trench wall, staring fixedly at – a button, he recalled suddenly, a shiny brass button fallen in the mud, its grey thread still attached like a torn-out hank of hair. The captain had been calling his name. He had dragged his eyes away from the button, but only for a moment . . . Just long enough to register the gleam of contempt in the man's eyes.

He blinked away the memory to find himself alone on the bench. Shadows lapped at his feet, and as dusk began to settle, the ocean's roar seemed loud, the waves crashing in time with his pulse. He stood stiffly and walked further down the hill. He could see the grassy mound, beneath which lay the icehouse. He thought of its cool dark passageways, its blind silence, and he drew strength from it. He had only intended to look, but then Orah's words rang around him again, accusing.

Burke should hang for what he did . . .

He rattled the keys from his pocket, weighing them in his hand. Men like Jensen Burke saw themselves as untouchable, immune to the laws that other, lesser men abided by. He had been that way in France – young and bullish, full of his own importance. He and Ronald had been thick, two of a kind; swaggering among the men like lords, quick to jeer and point the finger at anyone they considered beneath them – Aboriginal soldiers, or those under-fed diggers of smaller stature, or bookish loners like Edwin . . .

He should be punished.

Later, in the central chamber of the icehouse, Edwin lifted the iron grate from the drainage culvert and reached for the wooden box concealed inside it. He prised open the lid. His old service revolver gleamed in the lantern light, still smelling faintly of oil and cordite. His mind conjured the image of young Warra lying in the bush, his blood leaking away into the dirt; the senseless waste, the sheer horror of loss seemed, in that moment, unbearable. In his ear, a tiny mosquito-like buzz.

For the love of God, hold your fire . . .

He swatted away the buzz, clicked open the barrel. Took six rounds from a small carton at the bottom of the box, and loaded them into the chamber. Then he hurried back through the icehouse, out into the cold air of the night, and towards the garage.

Stern Bay, 1930

Jensen Burke stepped from the shadows of the barn. He was tall and stringy, red-faced with a thick neck. If he was surprised to see Edwin, armed or otherwise, he failed to show it.

'What are you doing here?' he asked gruffly.

Edwin hesitated. The sound of the other man's voice sent him reeling back through time. A gravelly drawl, spoken with just the right hint of nastiness that had once turned Edwin's legs to jelly. Edwin gritted his teeth. He wasn't that scared kid any more, and Jensen was no longer his captain.

He raised his weapon. 'A boy was shot last week. On your land. I believe you know something about it.'

Burke's jaw began to work from side to side, and he sent a glance across the green paddock towards the farmhouse.

'Nothin' to do with me.'

'You're wrong. It has everything to do with you. Especially since you're the one who shot him.'

'You can't prove anything.'

'I don't need to.' Edwin lowered his voice and stepped closer. He was now little more than an arm's length away. He noticed, as though viewing himself from outside his body, that he was strangely calm. 'I know it was you, Burke. I can see the guilt written all over your ugly face.'

Edwin thumbed the firing pin, heard the neat click as it locked into place. Burke took a few stumbling steps back.

'Just a minute,' he said, pushing his palms against the air as though to ward Edwin away. 'You can't come here threatening me.'

'That boy was part of my family.'

'So what?' Burke's voice turned raw. 'He was thieving my stock. I've got every right to defend what's mine.'

Edwin could smell the man's sweat. It jogged a memory. Jensen Burke after the war, crouched over Edwin's prone body, his knuckles slick with blood, his big fists pounding and pounding until Edwin blacked out.

'Those kids weren't doing any harm, and you know it.'

Burke's face crumpled into a grimace. 'They were trespassing.'

'They were on their way to see their people. Harmless kids. One of them witnessed the whole thing. And she's keen to tell the authorities what she saw.'

Burke's eyes grew small, his mouth turned down. He made a coughing noise in the back of his throat, and then, without warning, lunged at Edwin, swinging his fist. Edwin was ready. Thrusting the weapon forward, he drove the mouth of the barrel into Jensen's throat and backed him against the barn wall.

'You'll pay for what you did to that boy.'

Burke tipped back his head, his eyes wide. 'What are you planning to do,' he rasped. 'Put a bullet in me . . . the way you put one into your brother?'

'It's a tempting idea.'

'You wouldn't have the guts.'

Edwin slackened his grip, lowered the gun. 'We'll see.'

Burke moved away, rubbing his throat. 'If I get so much as a whiff of interest from the cops, I'll go straight to Clarice. Tell her what sort of man you really are, Briar. I'll tell her what you did.' He coughed and wiped his mouth. 'Poor bloody Ronald, what did he ever do to you?'

Edwin disengaged the firing pin. He tried to back away slowly, as though with confidence, but Burke's words struck at him, filling his veins with ice.

'You know nothing about it.'

Burke was trembling now, his big hands fallen limp at his sides.

'She loved Ronald, you know,' he said almost regretfully. 'Really loved him. She only married you out of pity.'

Edwin had heard enough. He turned to go, but then looked back over his shoulder.

'One dark night I'll be waiting.' He spoke quietly, but his words echoed in the stillness with chilling authority. 'It might be tomorrow. Or I might let you sweat it out for another fifty years. But I promise you this, Jensen. You'll pay for what you did to that boy. However long it takes, in the end, I'll make sure you pay.'

26

Melbourne, June 1993

The fire blazed as I stirred the embers and added more kindling. I warmed my hands a moment, and then turned back to the room.

Adam sat on the lounge, watching me. He looked tired after the flight. Black circles under his eyes, stubble darkening his jaw. I had collected him from the airport earlier that afternoon, and the drive back to Hennessy Avenue had seemed to take forever. Adam updated me on his job and our friends in London, while I talked about Nina and Coby, my grandfather's death, Dad's broken hip. Everything, it seemed, except my time at Bitterwood. Then, back at the house, I had settled Adam on the sofa, uncorked a bottle of wine, and told him what I'd decided.

Crossing the room, I sat beside him. 'I'm really sorry.'

He scrubbed his hands over his face, reddening his eyes and leaving flush marks on his cheeks. 'What if I was willing to move to Melbourne? Would that change your mind?'

I shook my head.

'Lucy, we were so good together. We can be again.'

'No, Adam. We can't.'

'You sound very certain.'

I gazed at my wineglass, the wine inside catching the firelight, dark as blood.

'I am.'

He looked at me for a long time, and must have seen that I meant it. He dragged his fingers through his sandy hair, and then tried without luck to flatten it down again.

'There's someone else, isn't there?' he said quietly.

My mouth was suddenly dry. I considered draining my glass, avoiding the truth for a few minutes more, but then decided I needed a clear head. I met Adam's eyes.

'Five years ago, I ran away from him. He didn't love me the way I wanted, and he broke my heart. So off I went, all the way to the other side of the world. To London. I was a terrible mess. Until I met you. You made the pain go away, made me want to stop running.'

'But you did run. In the end you ran back to him.'

I wanted to deny this, but a flash came to me. The cave nestled in the headland, the storm raging over the sea. The grey eyes watching me from the flickering shadows. Our night beside the fire had eventuated from a chain of unrelated events – or so I'd thought. Now I wasn't so sure. Maybe there was such a thing as fate or the universe leading a person along the path they most needed to travel.

'I didn't come back for him,' I told Adam. 'At least not

intentionally. Anyway, we're not getting together. Things are . . . complicated.'

'So who is he?'

'I've known him since I was a kid. He's like family. Only,' I glanced at Adam from the corner of my eye. 'Only, you know. *Not.*'

'Let me guess, the boy next door?'

'Actually . . .' I took a breath. 'He's more like the father of the boy next door.'

'Hell.'

'Tell me about it.'

'You love him?'

I shut my eyes a moment, and then looked back at him. Nodded.

Adam slumped. 'Did you ever really love me, Lucy?'

'I still do. Just . . .'

'Just not enough.' Adam sighed heavily and sank back against the cushions. 'I always knew you were running from something. Some*one,*' he corrected. 'I suppose a part of me knew that sooner or later you'd have to come back here to face them.'

I hugged myself, wishing Adam would get nasty, start shouting, calling me the names I probably deserved. But that wasn't in his nature. Adam was a peacekeeper, and even now, while his heart was breaking, he did not have it in him to start a war. He reached for my hand, slipped his fingers around mine. His skin was warm and dry, his touch familiar.

It made me think of the warm July afternoon he had proposed, almost a year ago. We were strolling along the

Serpentine in Hyde Park, laughing at a family of geese as they splashed in the water. Adam had tugged me into his arms, whispered he loved me, and then pulled the little box from his pocket. The diamond inside had dazzled me, catching the summer sunshine like a prism, exploding into a rainbow of shimmers.

I twisted the ring on my finger, slid it off. Placed it on the coffee table between us. I searched Adam's eyes, found them brimming with more questions. I'd always believed that he couldn't hurt me, but I realised now how wrong I'd been. The pain creasing his face, the confusion in his kind brown eyes, cut me to the core.

'Where did we go wrong?' he murmured.

I thought back across the two years we had been together, trying to find the thorn that had come between us. Our meeting at the charity dinner, our instant chemistry. All the funny times we had in London, all the good times. With Adam at my side, I had drifted along, happily ignoring the shadows swarming under my skin. The nightmares, the guilt, and the way my feet got itchy whenever life took a complicated turn. But now, in hindsight, I understood that the shadows had never left me. They had been there all along. Adam's presence in my life had merely pressed the pause button, held them at bay for a while. I had let myself believe that life in London – the new friends, the hectic pace, the giddiness of constant distraction – had banished the past. That running away had finally worked. Now I saw how mistaken I had been.

I looked at Adam. 'After I lost my mother, I built a wall around my heart. It was how I coped. Then when I met you, the wall seemed to crumble away. For the first time in years, I felt free as a bird. But I wasn't free at all. I'd just built another wall around the old wall.'

'Double indemnity.'

'Something like that.'

'So what did I do?'

I thought of my grandfather's letter, and the golden heart charm it had contained. I wondered if things would have turned out differently if I had never written to Edwin, never felt the compulsion to invite him to our wedding. Would fate still have orchestrated a way to lure me back?

'It wasn't anything you did, Adam. The past found a chink in the wall and slipped through. My old nightmares started up again, my old fears. I guess that's what really brought me back here.'

Adam took my hand again. 'I don't want to lose you, Lucy. Whatever you have to face here, you don't have to do it alone.'

I gave his fingers a squeeze, and then pulled away. My gaze drifted to the diamond ring on the coffee table, the red glint of the wine, and then finally the crackling fire.

'That's just it, Adam. I *do* have to face it alone. I've been on the run most of my life, but running away isn't the answer. You taught me that. I have to take a stand, face my problems head on. The only way I can genuinely do that, is alone.'

At seven the following night, I arrived on the doorstep of a tiny worker's cottage in the colourful inner suburb of

Prahran. The narrow house sat at the end of a cul-de-sac, a leafy haven that seemed worlds away from the nearby bustle of shops and cafes on Chapel Street.

Nina opened the door, hugged me hello, and then peered over my shoulder. 'Where's Adam?'

'He's not coming.'

'Oh. Where is he?'

I bit my lip. 'On his way back to London.'

'Without you?'

I nodded, blinking hard. 'We've split up.'

Nina searched my face. The crease between her brows deepened, but then her expression went soft and she gave me one of her upside-down smiles.

'Come inside, little Bub. Curry's still twenty minutes away, but the wine's chilled. I'll tell Coby we're eating outside tonight. Seems like we're going to need the fresh air.' She gave me her hanky, clean and smelling faintly of lavender, and then ushered me inside.

The house was warm, a gas heater burning quietly in the lounge room. Nina's cats swarmed me at once, four sleek bodies coiling around my legs; the Siamese leaped onto a chair as I passed and extended its ear for a scratch.

The place had hardly changed since I'd last been here. Aside from Coby's obvious presence – a guitar propped in one corner, several posters for the Natural History Museum, and a stack of textbooks on the coffee table – the house was purely Nina. Huge colourful paintings covered the walls, a dramatic backdrop to the black lacquered furniture and cabinets full of collectibles.

Coby burst from the kitchen. For a moment, we stood

facing each other like a pair of chess pieces. He was wearing one of Nina's vintage aprons over a bulky mohair jumper and jeans. He seemed taller, more at ease with himself than I remembered. With his broad cheekbones flushed from the heater and his cropped dark hair, he was strikingly gorgeous. But the old Coby, my childhood friend, was still in there, and I could see the familiar hesitation in his eyes.

I handed him the wine I'd brought. We had parted on shaky terms, and hadn't spoken in so long. Was it enough just to shake hands, or should I attempt a quick peck on the cheek?

Neither, as it turned out. Smiling widely, Coby came at me, gathered me into a bear hug and swung me around, making me laugh, making me drop my guard and let the tears – that until now I'd been trying to hold in – pop from my eyes and splash down my cheeks. For so long I had visualised our first meeting: chilly, reproachful, perhaps even involving harsh words. But Coby's warmth threw me off kilter and I realised that I'd blown the situation entirely out of proportion.

I heard a strangled sound behind me and glanced around.

Nina was wiping her eyes. 'Ignore me,' she said, half-laughing through her tears. 'I'm hormonal. I'm allowed to be an emotional mess. So is Lucy, she's just broken up with her boyfriend. What's your excuse, Coby?'

Coby released me and swiped at his eyes. 'Damn it Nina, I haven't seen her for five years.' He turned to me. 'I'm sorry about Adam. Is it something you can patch up?'

'I gave back the ring.'

He winced. 'I guess that's pretty final.'

Nina muscled between us, linking her arm through mine. 'Distraction is what you need tonight, Bub. We're going to eat, drink and be merry . . . At least,' she added, 'you and Coby are going to drink and be merry. I'm just going to eat.'

We went through to the kitchen. Coby busied himself at the stove. One large copper pot was almost bubbling over with deep red pumpkin and tofu curry; another was brimful of fluffy white basmati, steaming gently beneath a tea towel. I shut my eyes and breathed in the delicious aromas, which made my stomach rumble.

'You can't fool me, Bub.' Nina's words tickled my ear, and as she slid her arms around my waist, I braced myself for what she'd say next. That day in her shop, she had pressed me about unfinished business. *You know who I'm talking about*, she'd said. *Someone you used to love.* Nina had a special talent for sniffing out the truth. She claimed she'd learned it from her mother, who had worked for a notorious divorce lawyer. But Nina's gift was unequivocally her own; she loved people, and her heart was a bottomless well of compassion. Truth and lies, she often said, were easy to see if you only looked close enough.

The way she was looking at me now.

'There's more going on than you're saying, Bub. Isn't there?'

I nodded.

She patted my arm. 'Don't worry, I won't interrogate you tonight. But if you get the urge to spill all, then I'm your girl, right?'

'Right.'

Linking her arm in mine again, she ushered me through a set of glass doors and out onto the back verandah.

A vintage club lounge and chairs were arranged around a burning brazier. While Coby served big plates of curry and rice, Nina uncorked the wine and updated me on five years of gossip. Who among our old friends was getting married, falling pregnant, filing for divorce. I marvelled at how easily we picked up where we'd left off. The years I'd been away no longer seemed a breach between us, but rather another layer embroidered into the larger fabric of our friendship.

Between delicious mouthfuls, I told them about my life in London, the endless thrill of art galleries and dinners, the dazzling distraction of a city that seemed never to sleep. They wanted to know all about Adam: how I'd met him, what he was like. I expected sorrow to swamp me – after all, I was still raw after our breakup – but talking about him seemed to help. When I related the story of the charity dinner and Adam's £50, Nina smiled and took my hand.

'He sounds like a really cool guy, and it's clear you love him.'

I knew that look in her eyes. 'But—?'

'You don't light up when you talk about him.'

'No spark,' Coby agreed.

I thought of Mildred Burke and her secret to a long marriage. 'Passion doesn't last,' I told them, but it suddenly sounded lame, even to my own ears.

Nina leaned in. 'But nothing lasts, Bub. Not forever. We're all going to die one day . . . but in the meantime, if you're lucky enough to find someone who lights you up, then you owe it to yourself – and to them – to cherish it while you can.'

We sat in silence for a while. The brazier crackled and Coby added more wood. The noises of the city rose and fell beyond our verandah haven: trucks rattled along Dandenong Road, car horns blared in the distance. Stars twinkled above us; the faint smokiness of wood fires scented the night. Flying foxes chattered in the garden, and Miles Davis played on the stereo inside, weaving his hypnotic magic through the winter air. The magic caught me and, for just a moment, held me spellbound. *Cherish it while you can*, Nina had said, and I found myself doing exactly that. The warbling trumpet lifted me, tugged me back to the narrow cave overlooking the shipwreck beach. Through bird's eyes, I looked down upon the scene unfolding below in the firelight: two lost people opening their hearts, finding each other in the smoky darkness. Had it been so very wrong?

Our conversation drifted onto other things: Nina's plans to source vintage baby clothes and new mum goodies for her shop, Coby's upcoming promotion at the museum, how the arrival of their little munchkin would change the scheme of things. When Coby described his parents' thrill over soon having a grandchild to fuss over, again I thought of Morgan. This time, the confusion and chaos of my feelings ebbed away, leaving just a warm glow. A grandfather, I muse. A cat rescuing, Harley riding, maritime history enthusiast of a grandfather – what more could a child want?

'What are you smiling about?' Nina wanted to know.

'Nothing, it's just . . . good to be home.'

She looked at me, letting my words sink in. She blinked, and a tiny smile touched the edges of her perfect lips. 'Does this mean—?'

I sat back, circling my finger around the rim of my wine-glass. 'Well, I'm heading back to London as planned. But once everything is tied up there, I'll be coming home. For good.'

Nina squealed. I heard Coby mutter, 'Oh, thank God.' And then more quietly, almost to himself, 'Dad'll be over the moon.'

Later, when the curry was gone and the last of the wine consumed, Nina and Coby farewelled me at their front gate. As I drove away, I looked back over my shoulder. Nina's arm was raised in a wave, while Coby stood solidly beside her. Just before my van turned the corner, I saw him lean against her, perhaps to whisper something in her ear.

Cherish it while you can.

A pang of longing wound itself around my heart. I tried to imagine standing on some future porch with Adam, the two of us a picture of domestic contentment – but my brain betrayed me. Rather than slim, elegant Adam, I saw a differ-ent man: a man with windswept hair and a smile that lit a fire in my heart, but who seemed, at least for now, as distant to me as the stars.

By the time I got back to Hennessy Avenue, it was after midnight. The house was in darkness, cold inside, the fire long since burned out. When I stepped into the lounge room and saw the wineglasses left on the coffee table, I slumped.

The distraction of curry night and the pleasure of reuniting with my friends ebbed away. The sting of my breakup with Adam rushed back. He would be in a hotel room somewhere, perhaps with a bottle of whiskey, wishing like crazy that he'd never paid anyone to sit next to me.

Basil came running, greeting me with a short sharp yowl that I now understood to mean, *I'm so happy you're home but what the heck took you so long?* I bundled him up in my arms and cuddled him, kissed the impossibly soft fur of his ears. After a while, the emptiness subsided and I released Basil gently onto the floor. Gathering up the wineglasses and bottle, I took them out to the kitchen and poured the dregs down the sink. Then I stood in the semi-dark, listening to the emptiness: the murmur of traffic in the distance, the sighs and creakings of the house, the guttural chatter of possums in the trees outside.

This is what it feels like to be alone, I told myself. *Get used to it.*

I took a hot shower, and retreated to bed with a mug of cocoa. Basil jumped up beside me, chirping contentedly as he pressed his paws into the blanket and curled against my leg.

'Distraction is what we need right now,' I told him.

Retrieving Dad's manuscript from the bedside table, I found my place. I had left Fineflower in the dungeon with the angry king, about to be separated from her baby son forever . . .

I sat up, suddenly wide awake.

My father's face flashed before me. The way he'd been at the cafe, pale and anxious behind his beard, his eyes dark with emotion as he spoke of his rift with Edwin. A rift caused by the discovery that his birth mother had abandoned him as a tiny baby.

I looked down at the sheaf of pages with fresh eyes. As the first threads of understanding began to lace together in my mind, I couldn't help wondering if Dad had woven deeper truths into the fabric of his story. Perhaps the answers I wanted had been right here in my hands all along.

The King's face turned from purple to black, his frown dark as a thundercloud. 'I will not abide a wife whose heart belongs to another.'

Fineflower stood tall. 'Release the soldier. He's committed no crime.'

'Too late,' the King replied. 'The vultures are picking over his carcass as we speak.' He leaned near, his old eyes hard with hatred. 'Without a doubt, my dear, your soldier love is already dead. Now you'll spend the rest of your days in this dungeon. You shall join my other treacherous brides beneath the window, eyeless, bloodless and alone. Your only companions will be the worms, and when you die – from starvation or loneliness, or perhaps from a broken heart – they will feast upon your flesh until there's nothing left but bones.'

While the King spoke, Fineflower glanced about the cell. The spinning wheel creaked softly as a moth fluttered through its spokes. The other wives swayed back and forth in the darkness. Silky white threads littered the floor, and there at the edge of the lantern light, Fineflower noticed the gleam of a blade: her soldier's blade.

She looked back at the King. 'What about my son?'

The King regarded her coldly. 'I will raise him without you. And when he's old enough, I'll tell him that his mother never loved him. That she left in the night like a thief. He will learn to hate you, and your name will be like ash on his tongue.'

Fineflower pictured her little boy's bright button eyes and snowy thistledown head. She thought of him growing up without her, taking his first steps, learning to read and write, going through life never knowing how much she loved him. Stricken, she covered her face with her hands and crumpled to the floor.

'Let me see him once more,' she begged the King. 'If only to say goodbye.'

'Impossible.' The King narrowed his gaze. 'Unless . . .'

Fineflower looked at him hopefully. 'Unless what?'

'Unless you can guess my true name.'

Fineflower was weary of the King's cruel games. She was weary of the chilly dungeon, heartsick for the brilliance of the outside world. She longed to feel the sun on her face, to breathe the perfumed flowers of her garden, to dig her fingers into the soil and watch things grow. Most of all, she ached to hold her beautiful son once more in her arms, to kiss his downy head and hear him laugh. She would give anything, anything at all to see him again.

She looked up at the King. Guessing his true name was no challenge, because she had known it right from the start.

'Your name is Greed.'

The King's face turned crimson. In a whirl of fury, he drew his sword and rushed at her, raising the weapon aloft above his head to strike.

Early the next morning I packed the van and drove over to Dad's house. I was still thinking about his latest chapter when I pulled into his driveway. Anyone could see that Fineflower's story contained echoes of my father's story. The little boy abandoned by his mother, raised by an uncaring father, coming to believe that he was unloved. But did Dad really think that Edwin had forced Clarice away? Perhaps even harmed her out of jealousy, believing she still loved someone else? Or was this story simply Dad's own private wish fulfilment, his way of dissecting a situation he was still trying to understand?

Dad was in the kitchen, trying to work the toaster.

'Damn contraption. The minute Wilma leaves, all the appliances go rogue.'

I unplugged it at the wall and then used a fork to dislodge the croissant he had jammed into the slot. 'You might want to try toasting these under the grill,' I advised. 'Or at least slicing them in half.'

Dad ignored me and hobbled over to the table. Propping his crutches on the back of the chair, he struggled into his seat. I offered to help, but he waved me away.

'Where's Adam?' he wanted to know. 'I thought he'd be here by now.'

'He was.' I buttered two croissants, spread one with jam and placed it on Dad's plate. I smothered mine in honey and then stared down at the gooey mess. 'But he's gone back to London.'

'Already?'

'We broke up.'

Dad's eyebrows shot up. He stared at me a moment, as though hoping it was a joke. Then his shoulders slumped. 'Kiddo, I'm sorry. What happened?'

'There was no spark.'

Dad searched my face. When he finally smiled, the gleam had returned to his eyes. 'I thought you said sparks were overrated?'

'I changed my mind.'

His smile turned hopeful. Then suddenly he was beaming. 'Does this mean you're coming home?'

'Maybe.' I bit into my croissant, devouring it in a few sticky bites, and then reached for my teacup. Dad was still watching me, probably waiting for me to elaborate. I had already tossed and turned the night away replaying the breakup, so decided on a change of topic.

'I'm heading back to Bitterwood today. There's still quite a bit to do. Under all that clutter, it's turning out to be a lovely old place.'

Dad nodded, but he seemed distracted. 'That reminds me. I finally twigged about the little Aboriginal girl.'

It took me a moment to backtrack, but then I remembered our conversation at the cafe. 'In the orchard photo, you thought you knew her?'

'I finally realised who she reminds me of . . . Do you

remember Mrs Tibbett? She worked for Edwin on and off over the years, mostly housekeeping.'

I smiled, recalling the woman who had taken me under her motherly wing during my chidhood stay at Bitterwood. When I left there, I had done my best to forget Edwin and his gloomy old house, but I had forgotten kind Mrs Tibbett too. Suddenly I was eager to talk to her. Getting to my feet, I collected our dishes and took them to the sink.

'How do I contact her?'

Dad pulled out a handkerchief and dabbed his lips. 'You know that old cottage we used to stay in, the one along the road from Bitterwood? Mrs Tibbett bought it a few years ago. She lives there with her daughter.'

Gull Cottage, June 1993

The last time I'd walked along this path, I had been ten years old. My mother was missing, and my father silent with worry. They had been hollow days, passing in a dream, a shadow on my memory of the place.

As I pushed through the gate and approached the little cottage, those old shadows scattered. The gentle winter sunshine drew the sappy smell of pine from the towering tree, and as I breathed it in, a memory came: My mother had found some old jacks – 'knucklebones', she called them – and was teaching me how to play. 'Toss them up and catch them on the back of your hand . . .' My pudgy fingers fumbled, but she showed me how to splay them slightly to catch more jacks. We sat under that old pine for hours in its fragrant shade, playing and laughing, chatting happily, the sea at our backs. The sun shone brightly overhead, but Mum's smile was always somehow more luminous.

The cottage seemed smaller than I remembered, but was in good repair. The paintwork was fresh and the small garden brimmed with native shrubs. A classic Mini Minor was parked in the driveway, so I was hopeful – and a little trembly – as I strode up to the door. I knocked, shuffling from foot to foot as I waited.

The door swung open, and a tall woman stepped onto the threshold. She looked to be in her mid-fifties, her olive skin offset by soft silver-grey hair that fell to her shoulders. She regarded me with eyes that were deepest brown, almost black.

I introduced myself, and was about to launch into an explanation of why I was there, when the woman cried, 'Heavens, Lucy!' and pulled me into a hug.

'Look at you,' she said, holding me at arm's length. 'Edwin's little granddaughter all grown up. Oh, I wish Mum was here.' She beamed into my face. 'You wouldn't remember me, I met you a few times at Edwin's when you were little. I'm Len Tibbett. My mother was Edwin's housekeeper on and off over the years. Come on in.' She stepped aside and threw open the door. 'I'm afraid I'll have to dash off in twenty minutes, I'm rostered at the cultural centre this afternoon. Have you—' She winced apologetically. 'Sorry, I'm a bit of a babbler. With Mum away, I've no one to talk to. Can I offer you a pot of tea?'

Inside, the cottage was just as I remembered. A short hallway bypassed three compact bedrooms, and led through the lounge room to a light-filled dining room and kitchen. I hesitated here, flashing back to the last time I had seen my mum. She'd been standing on this same spot in the doorway, her clothes soaked by rain, covered in mud and grazes, her face ashen. *Where's your father?* she had asked. A shiver ran along my arms. Shaking off the memory, I breathed away my guilt and followed Len towards the back of the house. The timber floor gleamed, and Indigenous artworks adorned the walls. Len ushered me in to the lounge room, and offered me a seat.

Between sips of scalding milky Darjeeling and bites of shortbread, I explained to Len that I was keen to talk to her mother about her time at Bitterwood as a child.

Len nodded. 'Mum'll love that. She often talks about you, you know.'

I had a flash of a tiny, birdlike woman bustling along Bitterwood's hallways, carrying bundles of folded sheets or breakfast trays for the guest rooms. I had followed her around like a pale little ghost, her constant happy chatter filling the hollows in my heart created by my mother's sudden absence.

'She was always kind to me,' I remembered. 'She took me under her wing.'

'That's Mum for you.'

'When are you expecting her back?'

'She's visiting my brother Warren in Daylesford. I was expecting her home by now, but she called last night to tell me she's decided to stay longer.' Len rolled her eyes and smiled. 'Which, knowing Mum, could mean a few hours or a few days. She doesn't own a watch, never has. She tells the time by looking at the sun or stars. Reading between the shadows, she calls it. She grew up in the bush with her mother and aunties, in a little community north-west of here. She started working at Bitterwood when she was twelve, which sounds terribly young, doesn't it? But that's what it was like, back in the 1920s. She wore hand-me-down clothes and spent most of the time barefoot – but she gets a glow about her when she talks about those days, you know? She says they were the happiest of her life.'

'Makes me kind of envious.'

'Me too. My brother and I grew up in Stern Bay, but things had changed by then. Back in Mum's day, there was tension between the black community and the whites. Mum doesn't like to talk about it, but we'd occasionally hear whispers in town. Of course, by the time Warren and I came along, all that business had settled down.'

'Business?'

Len drained the last of her tea and got to her feet. 'I'll let Mum explain, it's her story. She tells it better than I could. Besides,' she added, grabbing her keys off the coffee table, 'I'm going to have to be terribly rude, my dear Lucy, but I must dash off. I've so enjoyed our talk. We must do it again sometime.'

'I'd like that, Len.'

As we went back along the hall, light spilled from an open doorway, a bedroom, my old bedroom. I couldn't help looking in. A pretty chenille bedspread brightened the narrow iron bed, and a floral rug warmed the polished floorboards. I was about to continue past, when I spied a large framed photograph on the wall near the door. It was a creased and spotty old print of three kids: two girls in their early teens had crowded into a wheelbarrow, while an older boy pushed them along. All three were smiling broadly, their faces blurred a little by the motion. Two of the children were dark-skinned, but one of the girls was fair.

A thrill of recognition went through me. It was the girl from the church fete photograph.

Len joined me. 'Gorgeous photo, isn't it? We keep it in here so we can shut the door if need be. Some of our relatives are sensitive about old pictures, it can upset them to see images of those who've left us.'

'Beautiful kids. They seem so happy,' I said, looking closer, rubbing the sudden goose bumps on my arms.

'Yes, old photos are usually so formal and stiff. Your grandfather took this one in 1930. He had a knack for photography. The boy is my Uncle Warra, Mum's brother. Sadly, he died the year this was taken. That's Mum in the middle, and the fair-haired girl was her best friend.'

My yearning to identify her, my hunch that she was the key to Clarice's story made me want to rush ahead, ask the questions. *Who is she? How do I get in touch with her?* But as my gaze travelled over the old photo with its cracks and age spots, its sepia haze, I realised that much time had passed and the girl may have moved on, or no longer be alive.

I took a breath. 'The fair girl, do you know who she is?'

'I should.' Len smiled. 'I'm named after her. My full name is Lenorah.' She looked back at the photo, and her expression turned wistful. 'Her name was Orah, and Mum never forgot her.'

'*Was?*' My hopes plunged. 'Then she's gone.'

Len searched my face. 'Mum never knew what became of her. Orah may well be alive, but she left Bitterwood while Mum was away and never returned.'

27

Bitterwood, 1931

Winter blew in one breezy afternoon, bringing with it a whirlwind of fallen leaves and an icy chill. Orah rubbed her arms to warm them as she gazed down at the orchard. More than a year had passed since she last saw Warra. Since that day on the track beneath the ironbark tree, when he had closed his eyes for the last time.

He would be bones by now. Ash and bones. She knew it was morbid to think that way, but she couldn't help it. There were now more people she loved in the land of the dead than there were among the living.

If only Nala would return. Orah had wanted to go to the encampment, but Clarice forbade her. *Nala's grieving for her loss, Orah. Her whole family is. You must be patient. She'll return when she's ready.*

Orah had drifted half-heartedly through her chores, escaping when she could to her special places. The bench beneath the cherry tree where she'd cut her name with Warra's penknife; the bushland where she collected wattle seeds with Nala; and, most favourite of all, the grassy bank where Warra had once fashioned her a necklace from wildflowers.

Then a few months ago, Clarice had come to her with news.

'A miracle,' she told Orah, her eyes brimming with joyful tears. 'Edwin and I are having a baby. Just think, Orah. Another little son or daughter. A little brother or sister for you.'

Orah had tried to smile and be happy for Clarice, but a new baby seemed wrong, a betrayal. A year and many months had passed since that day on the track, but Orah had not finished grieving for Warra. She could not forgive that Edwin and Clarice had forgotten him so easily.

A little brother or sister . . .

The words depressed her, made her uneasy. She had settled into life with Edwin and Clarice, had begun to feel part of their family. A special daughter, dearly beloved. Yet if another child came along, a child who shared their blood – would they forget her?

Since Clarice's announcement, they were being especially kind to her. Edwin brought books from his trips into town or along the coast, despite money being scarce for such luxuries. They fell into the habit of stories before bedtime, Clarice reading on the bed with her, while Edwin listened from the doorway.

Lately, Clarice had begun inventing her own tales. Stories of romance and adventure that bewitched Orah and left her hungry for more. She was almost fifteen, which seemed too old for fairytales. She didn't care. She looked forward to bedtime. Clarice's stories cast a spell on her, made her forget the nagging darkness in her heart.

Orah hugged herself as another gust of dry brown leaves stirred in the wind. Shadows crawled along the ground beneath the mulberry trees, and the sight of them made her shiver. Bitterwood had become her home. Edwin and Clarice were now her family. Yet there were times, like now, when not even the promise of a bedtime story could ward away the emptiness that seemed to creep in with the night.

At first, Edwin thought Clarice's stories charming. Princesses lost in the forest, brave young woodsmen who battled beasts or saved their ladyloves by outwitting the evil old king. When bedtime rolled around, he had loved nothing more than to lean in the doorway and smile in on the enchanting scene.

Orah, beautiful Orah, snuggled next to Clarice on the bed, tucked under her arm like a little bird; her blonde head nestled on Clarice's shoulder, the lamplight gilding her hair. They might have been mother and daughter, and the rightness of that always filled him with longing.

The scene reminded him of earlier bedtimes, earlier stories – happier times when it had not been Orah under Clarice's motherly wing, but another girl. The stories

Clarice spun now were darker, and in them, Edwin began to glimpse familiar characters and themes. Lost children taken in by a kindly woodsman, or two little girls imprisoned in a deep well. And once, the strange sad tale of a seahorse trapped in a bottle.

Clarice's imagination both awed Edwin and filled him with a deep disquiet. For the longest time he couldn't pinpoint the origin of his unease. He had not minded that Clarice wove snippets of their life into her tales; what story-teller didn't? There was no single story that spelled out their private secrets. Rather, it was an accumulation of tiny threads woven so tightly together that even he could not see exactly where fiction ended and fact began.

Until that night in August, at the tail end of winter in 1931. A cold night, the fire blazed downstairs, filling the house with the scent of wood smoke.

At nine o'clock, they bundled up to Orah's room at the top of the stairs. Clarice climbed into bed beside the girl, while Edwin took up his usual post at the door. That night, Clarice wove the intricate tale of a queen who lived alone in her castle. Haunted by the loss of her children, she often walked along the beach below her home, despairing. One day, a fisherman found a little girl in a seashell, and gave her to the Queen. The Queen came to love the child dearly. But her love was possessive and smothering, and in time, the child withered and wasted away.

Edwin tried to assure himself it was just a story, that the symbolism of any fairytale was far-reaching. That was its nature; you could pick any tale and find within it echoes of your own life. Yet the tale of the Shell Queen shocked Edwin and filled him with dread.

Clarice looked up from the bed and smiled at him. A devastating smile, she seemed barely more than a girl herself: her face freshly scrubbed and bare of make-up, her hair pulled back, she looked guileless and more breathtakingly beautiful than Edwin had ever seen her. He realised that she had become so caught up in the telling of her story that its resonance with their own lives eluded her.

Orah's head had grown heavy. She was almost asleep. Clarice rested her lips on the shiny hair, and murmured quietly, almost wistfully, against her scalp.

'Oh my darling Edith, I'm so happy you're here with us.'

Orah bent back her head and looked at Clarice. 'Orah,' she said sleepily. 'It's Orah.'

'That's what I said, love.' Clarice cupped Orah's cheek and kissed her again, this time on the nose. 'Sweet Orah, how precious you are.'

A simple mistake, a slip of the tongue, yet Clarice had not appeared to register her blunder.

Edwin did not sleep that night. He lay in the bed next to her, breathing through his teeth. He let his thoughts wander into forbidden territory: little Edith, and the void she had left behind; tiny Joyce and her whisper-short life. Perhaps he and Clarice had tried to fill that void too soon. He pictured the beautiful child who had come to them, even before Edith's bones had fully crumbled back into the earth. The golden-haired girl who had appeared in their lives as if by magic. She had transformed them, healed them. But was she like the Shell Queen's child, trapped in the prison of their love, doomed to wither and waste away? Had they, like the Shell Queen in Clarice's story, chosen badly – would they too pay a price? Yes, Edwin believed they would. And the gnawing in his gut told him it would be a steep one.

Edwin shivered. Rolling on his side, he curled into himself, trying without success to will away the hollowness in his chest. When the dark time before dawn sent its chill into the room, he got up and padded barefoot to his study.

Taking out paper and pen, he drafted a letter. It took several tries, and by the time the first rays of sunlight were peeping through the study window, a scattering of crumpled rejects lay about his feet. Daylight returned his reason. His final draft joined its predecessors on the floor, and Edwin swept them all up and took them downstairs to the fire grate. As he watched the pages burn, the gnawing in his gut subsided, but did not leave him completely. It lingered, barely there, a reminder that in life, just as in stories, no price ever truly went unpaid.

Nala did not return to Bitterwood. Every day Orah went to the gate and watched the road, hoping to see a wisp of dust, wishing hard that Nala's small figure would appear, striding towards her. She envisioned her friend seeing her there at the gate, lifting her skinny arm in a wave as she ran to greet her.

But Nala never came.

Spring arrived. New green leaves unfurled and mulberry

blossoms filled the air with their sweet scent. Seven new lambs had joined the flock, and the mulberry trees were full of nests and fledgling birds.

As Clarice's time approached, she became more beautiful. If Orah had not seen it with her own eyes, she would have thought such a thing impossible. Edwin had noticed too. Orah watched him sometimes, gazing at his wife as if at some wondrous vision. Clarice seemed to glow with an inner fire. Her lips were always on the brink of a smile, and roses bloomed in her cheeks. She laughed at nothing in particular, and when she caught Orah glaring at her she would sweep the girl into her arms and coddle her like a baby, kissing her hair and trying to tickle her into a better mood.

Orah refused to be drawn into Clarice's orbit of joy. The happier Clarice became, the more resentful Orah grew.

When the baby comes, you'll forget me.

By October, the weather grew a little warmer. Although the newspapers reported a worsening economic climate, Bitterwood seemed like another world. Leaves were greening up the bare branches, and jonquils poked their yellow heads from the grass. The house was beginning to wake, a creature stirring after long hibernation. In preparation for the summer guests they hoped would arrive, Orah and Clarice had spent the past few months cleaning the guest bedrooms, airing blankets and sheets, scouring the floors, polishing the windows until they shone. They rarely saw Edwin, who had thrown himself into his usual routine of buying supplies, chopping wood, writing and rewriting inventories and accounts and then transcribing them into his ledgers late into the night. Without Warra and Nala to help with the workload, and now with Clarice needing increasing rest and care, the pace would be hectic.

'Orah?' Clarice's voice drifted from the kitchen.

Orah was in the rearing house. She had been escaping there a lot lately, and had just collected a box of silkworm eggs from the icehouse. She ignored Clarice's call, concentrating on her task. Picking out a paper sheet of the fine grain-like eggs, she placed it carefully inside the warming boxes and covered it with a soft mantle of new leaves. In twenty days, the eggs would hatch, and feeding would begin.

'Orah, are you there?'

She still had two boxes of silkworm grain to lay out, and hated to be disturbed. The eggs were fragile. At this crucial stage of their development, they needed steady temperature and quiet.

'Orah?'

She sighed. Returning to the icehouse, she stowed the boxes, dusted her hands on her apron, and then went towards the house. She could hear Clarice clattering in the kitchen, muttering to herself. Edwin had gone to Apollo Bay and he would not be back until dark. Whenever he left the house, Clarice became more fretful, worrying that the baby might come while he was away.

As Orah stepped into the kitchen, she heard someone knocking at the front door.

'Would you get that, love?' Clarice said, as she packed away the box of old preserving jars she'd been sorting. 'I'm covered in dust.'

Orah frowned. 'We're not expecting guests tonight.'

'Ask them to wait. I'll be out in five minutes.'

Orah hurried along the hallway to the sitting room and peered through the window. A man stood on the verandah. His back was turned to her, but instantly Orah knew that he had not come for a room. This was no holidaymaker, no solitary soul seeking fresh air and ocean views.

His grubby trousers were shiny with wear and patched around the cuff. The tops of his shoes had separated from the soles, the leather scuffed and broken. He wore an ill-fitting coat, and his dull fair hair curled over his collar, greasy at the roots, in need of a wash.

Most likely he was hoping for a meal, perhaps in exchange for some light labour about the yard. Occasionally men like him turned up at Bitterwood. Half-starved, empty-eyed men desperate for work.

She opened the door. The man turned. When he saw her, his mouth dropped agape. Behind a red-veined nose, his face was chalky-pale, and he was wringing a frayed woollen hat in his hands. He smelled of grog.

'Can I help you?' Orah asked.

The man shuffled forwards. He searched Orah's face, shaking his head, his lips trembling.

'My name is Hanley Dane,' he said hoarsely. 'God forgive me . . . You must be Orah?'

28

Ballarat, 1930

On the edge of the goldfields, a shantytown of sorts had sprung up. Edwin stood at a narrow crossroads, scratching his head, trying to make sense of the directions Mrs Mallard, the barmaid, had given him. The maze of tents and shanties and dirt lanes between them seemed too chaotic to navigate.

Edwin gave the Scotsman's description to a toothless old gent, who pointed to a little dwelling on the far side of the camp. Edwin approached.

There was no door to knock on, just a heavy burlap curtain fixed to the lintel with a row of rusty nails. Edwin stood in the doorway, despairing. The man was alive after all. He had not expected the disappointment to be so raw. He almost walked away right then, but only his promise to Orah stalled his retreat.

'Mr Dane?' he called. 'Mr Hanley Dane?'

A grunt from inside. A moment later, a scarred hand wrenched aside the burlap and a leathery face peered out. He wore a filthy woollen hat on his head, its grey and red stripes forming a curious symphony with his mottled skin and red whiskey nose.

'Who's askin'?'

Edwin cleared his throat. Hastily he gave his name, and was about to explain his visit . . . *Your daughter is alive and well, she's been living with my family on the coast and she's keen to find you—*

But the words died on his tongue. Hanley Dane had clearly once been a large man, but his big frame was now emaciated. His cheeks were hollow, his face ashen. He reeked of drink. His living quarters were not simply humble, but squalid. Edwin had tried to overlook his abandonment of Orah and her mother back in Glasgow, but seeing him now brought home the truth with a jolt. Had he really thought he could give her up so easily?

'If you're from Immigration,' Hanley said hastily, 'then my papers are all in order, never you fear. I suppose you'll want to have a squiz, though, won't you? Of course, you will. Hang on then, they're about here somewhere.'

'Oh that won't be—' Edwin wanted only to escape, to flee this horrible place and never look back. He had come with noble intentions, but now saw that he'd been a fool.

Hanley narrowed his gaze, and then grumbled again. 'Come on in while I look for it. It's too damned hot to be lurking out in the sun.'

Edwin had to stoop to enter. It was dark inside, the tiny cabin windowless, lit only by strands of sunlight that made their way through the wonky corrugated iron roof. The floor was trampled earth, and the smell of perspiration and tobacco smoke hung heavily in the air.

Hanley poured water into a tin mug and placed it on the table in front of Edwin. 'Forgive me,' he said, more to himself. 'A man's not prepared for company.'

He retreated to a corner and pulled an old cigar tin from a hole in the floor. For a while he rummaged, then produced a grubby fold of paper. Carefully smoothing out the creases, he placed it on the table for Edwin to inspect.

'Just as I said, all in order.'

Edwin gave the papers a fleeting glance. 'Having any luck finding employment, are you?'

Hanley shrugged. His scarred hands hung limply at his sides. For the longest time he looked at Edwin, his gaze brimming with desolation. 'There's always hope,' he said at last, chasing his words with a soft snort.

Edwin felt a jolt of recognition at the sound. He had heard Orah inhale that way when disbelief or amusement took her. He looked more closely at the shabby man hovering uncertainly in the shadows, and shuddered. How he hated to see his precious girl's features reflected in that grey, leathery face. The tilt of the chin, the proud arc of the brow. The wisps of gold that threaded the man's beard, and the eyes – the blue of a summer sky, identical in hue to those of his daughter.

His daughter.

Edwin backed towards the makeshift door. 'I can see your papers are in order. I'm sorry to have troubled you. I'll see myself out.'

At the doorway, he paused and looked back over his shoulder into the room. Hanley Dane had his back to him, bent over his cigar tin, shuffling the contents to make room for his dog-eared papers. Edwin felt a rush of pity for the man.

He took out the knotted bank notes Clarice had given him and placed them on the table's edge. Two pounds, as if that came anywhere near compensating for the lie he had just spun. The lie that would, from that day forth, burden him so heavily that every waking breath would be a struggle.

Emerging from the hut, he gulped a mouthful of cold air and hurried away, his heart crashing against his ribs as he fought the urge to run.

29

Bitterwood, June 1993

With most of the clutter gone, the bones of the old guesthouse were beginning to emerge. The high ceilings and wide floorboards gave the space an air of serenity. Light flooded in and the shadows retreated; the old place now felt almost welcoming. On Friday morning, I found myself standing beneath the art deco light fitting in Edwin's room, breathing the atmosphere, gazing around with fresh eyes. Since I'd pulled down the derelict old curtains, the views – ocean to the south, glimpses of winding road to the east and west, and tree-covered hills to the north – were breathtaking. I had little flashes of how my own belongings would look here: my huge cast-iron bed in place of Edwin's sagging single, my vintage Tiffany lamp on the bedside table, my framed paintings hiding the hairline cracks in the walls. *Not going to happen*, I reminded myself. *This place once featured in your nightmares, remember?*

The shrilling phone cut into my thoughts. I tried to ignore it, but my body was already moving towards the door. Downstairs in the sitting room, I picked up. The woman on the other end introduced herself so hurriedly that I missed her name – but not her organisation.

My pulse began to race. 'Salvation Army, did you say?'

'Yes, you rang a week or so ago about some correspondence your grandfather received? The man you should talk to is one of our former senior officers. Henry is his name. He still comes in to headquarters from time to time, a lovely old chap. Retired decades ago, but stayed on as a volunteer. He's got an elephant's memory – if anyone recalls your grandfather, it'll be him. He's out at Riverview Nursing Home, not far from here. I have the address, if you'd like it?'

Geelong, June 1993

As I travelled eastwards along the Great Ocean Road, the van rattling around the sharp turns, the wide blue-green expanses of the water yawning below me, my thoughts returned to the contents of the letter I had found half-burned behind the stove.

How was it for her, Edwin? At the end, her last breath – how was it? Did she slip peacefully into the next world? Did she, perhaps in a moment of forgiveness, speak my name?

I didn't hold out much hope that the old ex-Salvo officer would even make the connection to the person who had written the letter, but I had to try.

It was mid-morning when I arrived at the nursing home. The clatter of plates and cutlery drifted from the tearoom as I passed, and the aroma of coffee followed me along the corridor. I found the office, and knocked lightly on the door. A voice beckoned me in. A stout grey-haired woman glanced around as I entered. She finished securing the door of a clunky old wall safe, and crossed the room to greet me. She introduced herself as Marge, and asked how she could help.

I explained that I had come to visit one of the residents.

Marge frowned, smoothing her fingers over her jawline. 'We don't have anyone here called Henry. What's his surname?'

'I'm afraid I don't know. The Salvation Army officer couldn't tell me, but she seemed certain he was here.'

Marge's frown melted away and her face opened up in a smile. 'Salvation Army, why didn't you say? It's Hanley you're after, not Henry . . . Hanley Dane. I'm sure he'll be delighted to have a visitor. Follow me.'

We went along a carpeted hallway, brightly lit and deco- rated with framed posters. At the back of the building was another corridor of numbered doors. Marge knocked lightly on one door and opened it into a neat, self-contained bedsit.

On a chair by the window, tucked beneath a mountain of crocheted rugs, was an elderly man. He appeared to be sleeping, his head fallen forward, his pale bony hands clasped on top of the rug. His wispy white hair floated out from his scalp as though electrified, and his large freckled old face, composed in sleep, was a roadmap of folds and furrows.

'Hanley,' Marge called softly. 'You've got a visitor.'

The old man emerged from his nap with a start. He

squinted towards us and then reached onto the nearby bedside table to retrieve his glasses. Poking them onto his face, he scrutinised me with a steady blue gaze. His mouth downturned, his eyebrows knotted together.

'Is it you?' he queried, with a hint of a Scottish accent. 'Have you come for me . . .?'

Marge ushered me into the room. 'Hanley, this is Lucy Briar. She's travelled all the way from Stern Bay to visit you. How about I bring you some coffee, so you can properly wake up?'

Despite Marge's reassurances, the old man's expression did not change. He recoiled at the sound of my name, his fingers unlocking themselves from each other and burrowing into the crocheted holes of his blanket.

'What's she want?' he asked crossly.

'Just a chat.' Marge smiled encouragement. 'Perhaps you can show her your snails?'

The old man's gaze darted across the room to a small aquarium sitting on a narrow table.

I couldn't see any inhabitants, just aquatic plants and a stream of bubbles generated by a pump. Whatever was in there seemed to have a soothing effect on Hanley. His face relaxed, his fingers loosened their grip on the rug. Marge nudged my arm, nodding at a vacant chair. Then she bustled off along the corridor, leaving us alone.

Hanley looked at me. 'Briar, you say?'

I nodded. 'Lucy.'

Settling onto the seat, I took a box of chocolates from my bag and handed it across to him. He frowned suspiciously, and then sat clutching the box while he scrutinised me.

I dredged up a smile. 'When I came in just now, you thought you knew me.'

'Someone else,' he muttered. 'She wore her hair long, too.' He shook the box, wrinkling his nose. 'I don't like chocolate.'

'You can always use them to bribe the nurses.'

He considered this, and then brightened. 'Do you like snails? Freshwater gastropods, they're marvellous creatures. It soothes the nerves to watch them.' Depositing the chocolates on the bedside table, he dragged off his blankets, struggled to his feet and lurched across the room. When he reached the aquarium, he looked around and beckoned to me.

Together we peered through the glass into the water. The plants fluttered in the slipstream of bubbles. Hanley's bony finger pointed to a round gold-coloured shell, and as we studied it, the creature emerged. It was twice the size of a common garden snail, its sinewy body creamy-pale, rippling along the gravel. A pair of long whitish tentacles emerged from its head and began to wave around in the current.

'She's my favourite,' Hanley told me. 'A marvel, isn't she? A man has to have a bit of joy in life. Gloria, I call her.'

'She's certainly beautiful. She likes those bubbles.'

Hanley chuckled. 'They're addictive to watch, the old gastropods. Such peaceful creatures. Sometimes I spend hours with my nose pressed against the glass, observing them. They calm me.' He sent me a sideways glance and then said, almost under his breath, 'I once knew a man called Briar.'

'You did?' I waited for him to elaborate.

He looked back into the aquarium, but said nothing more. I heard a clatter along the hall outside. A moment later, Marge appeared in the doorway with a tray of coffee and biscuits. She smiled encouragingly as she laid the tray on a side table, then she went out.

Sweet coffee smells filled the room, but neither of us moved away from the aquarium. Hanley's earlier reaction had made me wary. If I rushed into an inquisition, I would lose him. Yet his admission that he had once known some-one called Briar intrigued me, gave me hope; convinced me that he may have the answers I wanted.

'My grandfather was a Briar,' I began. I let the name hang in the air, gauging Hanley's reaction. He continued to watch his snails, pointing out another one as it emerged from its golden shell.

After a while, he cleared his throat. 'Uncommon sort of a name, isn't it? Briar. Makes a man think of thorns and unpleasant scratchy things.'

'I feel sure you knew him.'

'No,' Hanley said quickly. Reaching to a shelf below the aquarium, he retrieved a glass jar of what appeared to be dark green herbs.

'Spinach,' he explained. 'Gloria prefers the frozen variety. It's nice and mushy, easy to eat. But this dry stuff lasts longer.' He sprinkled some flakes on the water, and we watched them slowly sink. Screwing the lid back on the jar, he replaced it on the shelf.

I tried again. 'My grandfather ran a guesthouse out along the Great Ocean Road past Stern Bay. A big old place called Bitterwood Park – you might have heard of it. There's an orchard and huge garden, wonderful ocean views. The woman I spoke to at the Salvation Army in Geelong told me you might remember him.'

Hanley stayed silent. His mouth had taken a downward turn again, his freckled cheeks pulled taut. His blue gaze darted around the aquarium, corner to corner, as though he was trapped in there, searching for a way out.

'Why would she tell you that?'

'She thinks you've got an elephant's memory.'

Hanley looked at me suddenly, his frown deepening. 'I don't know him, I already told you.'

'But you said you knew someone called Briar?'

'I was mistaken.'

Something warned me not to press him further, but I couldn't help myself. 'My grandfather died recently. I've been clearing out his house; Dad's keen to put it on the market, get it sold. That's why I'm here, really. I found a letter—'

Hanley began to blink rapidly. Then he jerked away from the aquarium. The snails we had been watching snatched back their tentacles and withdrew into their shells.

'I'm sorry,' I said hastily. 'I didn't mean . . .'

Hanley lurched back to his chair and retreated under his mound of woollen rugs, pulling them to his chest. With shaking hands, he took off his glasses, folded them into his pocket. Then he shut his eyes and squeezed them tight, like a frightened child.

'Please,' I urged. Instinct told me to walk away, leave the old man alone, and perhaps return another day, give him time to adjust to the idea of me . . . to the idea of my grandfather. But I couldn't. I was so close, the answers were here; if only I could draw him back, make him see I meant him no harm. 'Please, Hanley. It's important to me.'

'Go away,' he whispered.

I took the letter from my pocket, unfolded it and shook out the creases, held it out to him. 'You wrote this, didn't you? You knew Edwin, and he did something to hurt you. I think he may have hurt my grandmother, too. And possibly my mother. Please, I only want to understand—'

Hanley's nostrils flared as he shakily inhaled. 'Get out!' he bellowed. 'Get out.'

Footsteps whispered along the hallway carpet. I refolded the letter, slipped it back in my pocket. Grabbed my bag.

'I'm so sorry,' I told the old man. 'I truly am. I didn't mean to upset you.'

I hurried out, passing Marge on the way, murmuring more apologies, hating the painful way my heart thumped against my ribs. Almost running back along the hall, I emerged outside into the yellow winter sunshine, breathing the cold air deep into my lungs.

My visit to the nursing home had left me with a sour taste. I had liked Hanley and felt sorry that the visit had ended badly, that I had pushed him too far. It was clear the old man had lost someone dear to him, and the pain of that loss was still fresh. He still blamed my grandfather for the wrong he had done him, and now, I suspected, that blame had passed to me.

I spent the remainder of the day sifting through more boxes of paperwork. I was beginning to give up hope of finding the explanation my grandfather had pledged me in his letter. As the afternoon progressed, I kept thinking about the burned album, and then about the kerosene smell in the icehouse. Edwin had clearly tried to cover his tracks. I couldn't help wondering if that meant he had also destroyed the 'something' he'd promised me.

It was late afternoon. Sunlight began to retreat. Shadows crept in, dragging themselves under furniture, into corners, sliding across floors until all the house lay in darkness. At five o'clock, I made my way to the kitchen and stoked the fire. I fed Basil, and then placed a pot on the Warmray, lingering at the window while I waited for my soup to heat.

Adam would be back in London by now. Whenever I thought of him, my fingers clenched into fists, as if some primal part of me regretted letting him go. Regretted losing the permanence and stability he represented. I was doomed, it seemed. Doomed to spend my life alone. Because how could I build a future with someone – least of all a self-possessed man like Adam – when my own foundations were so shaky?

Night came down outside. Colour faded out of the garden, replaced by a thousand shades of black. Shadowy shapes flitted through the treetops, bats on the hunt for insect prey. I stood in the quiet, listening to the sea pounding the base of the cliffs. Windblown branches creaked outside the window, and the flue ticked softly as smoke rose from the belly of the Warmray and chased the updraft.

Basil curled himself around my feet, his long whiskers tickling my ankles. I bent and gathered him into my arms, cuddled him against me. He purred, his green eyes aglow in the dimness.

'I've got one foot stuck in the past,' I admitted, resting my face in the soft fur of his neck. 'That's why I can't move on.'

Basil chirped, forming a question mark with his tail.

'Nina called it unfinished business. But what if I'm like Clarice, what if it's in my blood to bolt at the first sign of trouble?'

My soup was ready, so I took it off the stove. I noticed the fire had burned low, so I opened the Warmray door and fed in another stick of wood. As I was securing the heavy door, I flashed back to the nursing home. Marge, in her office, pushing shut the door of her clunky old-fashioned safe.

A safe. Lots of places had them: nursing homes, hotels. Guesthouses.

Soup forgotten, I ran down to Edwin's office. His walls were still cluttered with paintings – grim old faces scowling imperiously from the distant past. There was only one face that really spoke to me, so I went up to it. The solid frame looked heavy, but I managed to lift the painting down and prop it on the floor.

And then I turned to stare at the rectangular metal strongbox set into the wall.

It was the size of a small television set. The reinforced iron door had once been green, but age had darkened the paint almost to black. On the door was a heavy-duty brass plate set with a small keyhole.

I tried all the keys on Edwin's house ring. In desperation, I even clawed my fingers around the edge of the door and tried to force it. I rang Dad's number, to see if he knew anything about it, but no one answered. Then I returned to the office and sat on Edwin's desk chair with the cat in my lap, swivelling from side to side, staring at the safe, scheming about how I was going to open it—

A distant knocking interrupted my musings.

I waited, ears alert. The knocking came again. Releasing Basil onto the desk, I ran along the hallway past the stairs, through the big echoey sitting room. Unlocking the deadlock, I swung open the front door.

A woman stood there. A tiny woman with a halo of curly grey hair, and large black-rimmed glasses. I knew her instantly.

'Mrs Tibbett?'

'Hello, Lucy. And please, call me Nala. My daughter Len said you wanted to see me?'

The rush of emotion took me off guard, and when she smiled – her face lighting up, her eyes filling with the warmth of recognition – I quite forgot myself. Letting out a little cry, I pulled her into a hug.

30

Bitterwood, 1931

larice took the man's shabby coat and hung it behind the door. Then she ushered him along the hallway to the kitchen. Orah trailed behind them, her legs wooden, and her heart beating unsteadily. While Clarice made sandwiches and a pot of tea, Orah kept stealing glances at the man.

It was a mistake, of course.

He wasn't her father. Wasn't Pa.

Clarice set the table, but seemed reluctant to take her leave. She rested her hands on her swollen belly, hovering near the doorway. 'I'll let you two to get reacquainted, then. And Mr Dane,' she added, smiling tight-lipped at the man, 'please make yourself at home.'

She had spoken kindly, but the gleam in her eyes said she was not at all pleased. She kept looking at Orah, trying to catch her attention. Orah fixed her gaze grimly on the teapot and waited for Clarice to go.

But Clarice would not be ignored. She grasped Orah's arm and tugged her back into the hall. 'I'll prepare one of the guest rooms,' she said quietly. 'If he needs a place to stay, tell him he's welcome here as long as he wants. As long as *you* want,' she added. Then she hurried away and went upstairs.

Orah stood in front of the kitchen door. For so long, she had yearned for this moment. At least, she had until nearly two years ago. Learning of Pa's death had crushed her. Now that he was here, her heart was empty. Pa was a stranger. Whatever would she find to say to him? Her fingers trembled as she reached for the door handle. Her palms were dry and her head clear, but her senses raced out of kilter. She had already weathered so much heartbreak, and felt ill prepared to endure any more.

The man stood facing the window, a shadow against the dying afternoon sunlight outside. He turned when he heard Orah's shoes on the floorboards. His face was pasty grey, his eyes the colour of slate. Even his clothes were grey. The only colour was the red blotching his cheekbones. He gazed back at her with the startled apprehension of a rabbit caught by spotlight.

Orah stared back. This was not her father. How could it be? Her father had travelled to Melbourne to make his fortune. Pa would most certainly be wealthy now, standing tall, square-shouldered and proud, the way she remembered him. No, she decided. This was not him. Her real Pa would be in his grand house, sitting with his feet up reading the paper, puffing on his pipe. Not here, shuffling in the kitchen, wringing his hands and peering at her through the helpless eyes of a hobo.

'Will you have some tea?' Orah gestured to the teapot and cups, the plates of sandwiches and oatmeal biscuits laid on the table.

'Thank you.' The man made no move. 'That's very kind.'

In the stillness of the kitchen, his voice sounded different to the harsh croak he had offered on the doorstep. The tone, the polite way he spoke his gratitude, the genteel tilt of his head—

No, Orah told herself again. It's not him. The jovial bear-like father she had created from her store of memories and the man before her now were two different people. Her Pa would not be standing so meekly, wringing his hat. *Her father would stride towards her and take her in his arms,* and she would smell the inky tartness of his black waistcoat, the one she had clung to so tearfully that long ago day of his departure. He would push back his thick fair hair with his fingers, and the air around him would be rich with the sweet smell of his pomade. His full beard would rest on his chest, threaded with pure copper like a Viking's. His eyes would be bright with merriment.

Orah searched his face, gathering her courage to utter the words. *I'm afraid there's been a mistake. You're not my pa. There is no resemblance, no sense of recognition. I don't believe we have ever met before—*

The man's hand lifted, his fingers hovered as though tracing her image into the air. A smile dawned, and his features reassembled into a face that was ever so vaguely familiar. For one quavering moment, the ghost of her father peered out.

His mouth trembled. 'Is it true? Are you my little Orah?'

Orah couldn't breathe. The ache of tightness around her lungs constricted her. She took a step back. Nodded.

Tears began to spill freely from the man's eyes, leaving tracks in the grime.

He dashed a hand across his eyes. 'When I saw you last, you were a wee girl. Now you're all grown. A real little lady.' He licked his lips and glanced hopefully over Orah's shoulder at the door. 'Your mother, did she . . . is she here too?'

Orah stared. He didn't know. Of course he didn't, how could he? He hadn't received their letters. He hadn't known they had bought two berths on the *Lady Mary*. He didn't know about the storm or the rocks, or that Mam had . . . that she was—

She gestured for him to sit, and found herself dragging out a chair from the opposite side of the table, slumping into it.

'I thought you were dead.'

The man – that was how she thought of him, because to name him Pa was simply too great a leap for her mind – took the chair she offered.

'How long have you been here?' he asked hesitantly. 'I mean to say, when did you leave Scotland?'

'Two years ago.'

'And you are lodging here, you and your mother? It's a very fine place indeed.' He glanced around the room and a pained expression came upon him. He seemed to shrink into himself, as if the kitchen with its warm smells and abundance of food and cosy homeliness was more than he could bear. 'You must be doing well for yourselves. I'm glad for it, truly glad.'

Orah reached for the pot. She couldn't remember if she'd already asked, so she asked again. 'Tea?'

The man looked at the pot with wide eyes, as if he'd never seen one before. 'Water will be most welcome, thank you kindly.'

Orah recoiled at his formality, his horrible downtrodden humility. She filled a glass with water for him, and then returned to her seat. Eight years had passed since he left her and Mam. In that time, she had imagined every scenario possible. He had died. Been imprisoned. Struck down by sickness. Then, two years ago, the news of his death. Through all her fears and imaginings, one question had continued to torment her.

'Why did you stop writing to us?'

His smile fell away. He swiped at the tears on his cheeks, leaving smudges of grime.

'I meant to. I wanted to bring you and your mam out here in style. But the riches didn't flow as freely as they did in the stories I'd heard back in Glasgow. Within a month of my arrival here, I was deep in debt. Failure dogged me. I could barely scrape together enough to eat, let alone two fares to bring my wife and daughter across the sea.'

'You should have written. At least put our minds at ease by letting us know you were alive.' She bit her lips before she could blurt what was really on her mind. *If only you had considered us. We would have waited for you in Glasgow. We would never have bought the tickets on the* Lady Mary, *never have travelled across the sea, never have encountered the storm. And Mam would still be—*

Unshed tears swelled into a hard lump in the back of her throat. She would not cry. The damage was done.

'Mam might have been angry with you,' she said quietly, 'but she loved you. She would have forgiven you in the end.'

Hanley got to his feet and shuffled over to the window.

'Shame is a terrible thing,' he murmured, his gaze lost in the brightness outside. 'It cripples a fellow, makes him want to run and hide. I left Scotland a proud man, full to the brim with ambition. But within months, that man was gone. Along with the entirety of your mother's money.'

'You might have let us know.'

Hanley gazed around the dim kitchen. After a while, he coughed. The rattle in his chest sounded loud and brutal.

'I understand that I have no right to ask,' he said when the fit ended. 'Not after the way I left you both. Yet I must ask. How is your dear mam? Not a day goes past that I don't think of her. Did she . . . remarry?'

Orah said nothing. The lump had re-formed in her throat. She wanted to tell him everything, wanted to open her heart and let the pain pour out of her. She looked at the man opposite, and knew that he was barely strong enough to hold his own sorrow at bay. For a moment, she could not breathe. Finally, she shook her head.

'She did not remarry.'

Hanley seemed to brighten. 'My dear Posie,' he murmured. 'True as ever, just as I knew she would be. I'd give anything on earth just to see her beautiful face one more time.'

Orah noticed the gaps of missing teeth, the shrunken gums. She noticed the pale unhealthy colour of her father's skin. His eyes were red-rimmed, his lashes crusty with conjunctivitis. He began to cough again, and this time the rattle made him buckle over and press his fist against his chest.

Orah found her voice. 'You're unwell.'

He shook his head. 'The cool weather is nearly gone. I'll be right as rain come summer. Tell me, where is your dear mother?'

Orah shifted on the chair. 'We were worried when we didn't hear from you. We saved the money, and bought passage on the *Lady Mary*. We came to find you.'

Hanley brightened. He returned to the table and sat forward on his chair. 'So, it's as I hoped. Posie is here with you. My Lord, who would have thought it. I've struck gold at last.'

'There was a storm.' Orah hated the way her voice shook, but she forced herself to go on. 'The ship foundered and sunk. We made it into a lifeboat, but the sea was too rough. We hit some rocks. Mam went overboard.'

Hanley stared. The little colour remaining in his face drained away. The silvery stubble on his cheeks and the faded blue of his eyes seemed stark compared to the grey pallor of his skin. His lips moved silently. He shook his head, his eyes fixed questioningly on hers.

'Mam didn't survive the wreck,' Orah told him. 'She drowned that night.'

Hanley's head dipped, as if he'd taken a blow. His face buckled, and he reached across the table towards her. When

Orah did not make a move to grasp his hands, he slumped against his chair back, his hands palm-up on the table, his fingers trembling.

'Oh Posie,' he said wetly. 'All those years alive and well in Glasgow, and me caught up in my selfish quest . . . an empty quest and foolish dreams. I wanted to redeem myself in her eyes, make her proud. Now it's too late.' He looked at Orah suddenly. 'I'll make it up to you, my girl. Only this morning there was talk of another find, to the west of where I'm camped. A big nugget the size of a baby's fist. It's only a matter of time . . .'

Orah stood and went to the window, gazed out at the garden. 'We never wanted your money. Mam cared nothing for wealth. Love was all she wanted. Did you never wonder how different our lives would have been if you'd stayed?'

Tears ran down her father's face. This time he didn't wipe them away. His eyes were strangely naked. 'Every day of my life, Orah girl. That question haunts me every single day.'

Shadows moved across the window as the sun drifted towards the western horizon. A fly flew into a spider's web in the corner and buzzed angrily for a time, but soon its protests dwindled to a hopeless grizzle.

Orah frowned at her father suddenly. 'How did you find me?'

Hanley rubbed his stubbly cheeks. 'Several weeks ago, a letter arrived. Addressed to me, care of the hotel in town. It was from your Mr Briar. He said you were staying with him and his wife. I borrowed a truck and got on the road . . . and here I am.'

Orah stood very still. 'A letter – from Edwin? Several weeks ago?'

'Aye, that's right.' He patted his pocket and took out a rumpled grubby paper. 'Here, read it for yourself.'

Orah took the page. She recognised Edwin's neat script, but when she tried to read the letter her gaze danced all over the place and she could make no sense of the words. Only one line stood out to her, the date. Just three weeks ago.

Orah's fingertips turned cold and she threw the letter on the table. Her father collected it and poked it back in his pocket, then sat looking at her, as if waiting. Orah could not speak.

The cold spread from her fingers, up her arms, finally settling over her heart. Edwin had told her Pa was dead. He had never mentioned the possibility that he'd been wrong, that Pa had survived. So why had he not told her he'd written to Pa? Had he wanted to spare her more disappointment? Or had he known her father's whereabouts all along?

'How did Edwin know where to find you?' she murmured.

Her father nodded. 'A couple of years back, a man came to see me, claiming he was from Immigration. He left money, so right away I knew something was off. I couldn't recall the name he gave, so I made some inquiries in town, and a woman at the hotel in Ballarat recalled that a well-dressed gent had travelled from the coast, apparently keen to locate me.'

Orah felt a chill. 'Edwin.'

Her father nodded. 'He left no forwarding address, and so I thought I'd hear no more from him. But then he sent the letter and told me about you. The one thing I can't fathom,' he added thoughtfully, 'is why took him nearly two years to write.'

Orah settled her father upstairs in the smallest of the guest rooms, the one at the other end of the corridor to her own. There was no ocean view, only a pretty outlook over the garden. She brought a jug of hot wash water and laid out clean towels and a block of soap. She wished him good night, and then hurried downstairs.

Clarice was tidying the kitchen, packing away the remains of Hanley's supper.

'Did you know?' Orah demanded.

Clarice paled. 'Orah, dear . . . please try to understand—'

'Edwin said Pa was dead, killed in the mine. But he lied!'

Clarice placed a hand over her belly. She glanced at the ceiling, as though fearing Hanley might overhear them, and then moved nearer to Orah, her voice low.

'Edwin thought it for the best, love. He found your father in a terrible state. Sick and destitute, barely able to care for himself let alone a daughter. He was living in a shanty. Broke, surrounded by disease. It shocked Edwin deeply, and he couldn't bear to think of you going to live in such a place. You were better off with us.'

Orah clenched her fists. 'Then you knew? All along, you both knew but you kept it secret. For nearly two years?'

Clarice's hand drifted towards Orah, as though to touch her, but then she drew it back. 'We only wanted what was best.'

'But that's not up to you. You're not my parents.'

Clarice drew herself a little taller. 'Edwin smelled the drink on your father, Orah. I'm sure you smelled it yourself this evening. Hanley's in no fit state to care for a young woman. What sort of life would it be for you if you went with him?'

'You had no right to lie.'

'We were only protecting you.'

Orah felt a whirlpool rising up in her. She had trusted Clarice, come to love her. But now, everything was unravelling. The sea roared in her ears. The waves crashed, the dark water lapped at the edges of her mind. She slapped her hands over the hotness in her cheeks.

'I don't need your protection.'

'But Orah, that's what families do. Protect one another.'

'You and Edwin are not my family.' Her fingers curled into fists against her cheeks. 'You're nothing to me!'

'Oh, Orah.' Clarice grasped the table edge to steady herself. 'Love, of course we are. You're a daughter to us, and we love you. Please don't say those things, darling. You love us too, you know you do.'

'You're wrong. You've lied to me about my pa and I hate you!'

'Please, sweetheart.' Clarice's voice cracked. Her eyes were large, her gaze pleading. 'Get some rest tonight. It's been an emotional day. You'll feel different in the morning—'

Orah turned and ran from the kitchen, not wanting Clarice to see her tears. Up the stairs she fled, stomping along the upper landing, pushing into her room, slamming the door behind her. She glared around at all her lovely things, the things that Edwin and Clarice had given her. Pretty clothes, new shoes, lace shawls and filigree clips for her hair. Nothing mattered now. She could not stay, how could she? She fell onto her bed, and lay stiffly for the longest time. Her tears dried, but she didn't bother summoning any more. What was the point? She just glared at the shadows on the ceiling, a million thoughts burning through her mind.

Edwin and Clarice didn't love her. They had betrayed her, tricked her, trapped her with their lies. Bitterwood was ruined for her. The only choice she had now was to leave.

After a while, she sat up. Roughly unclasping her golden charm bracelet, she threw it onto the floor. Then she grabbed her satchel and began to pack the few things she would need to start her new life with Pa.

When she knocked on her father's door, there was no answer. She knocked again, and waited. Then pressed her ear to the door.

'Hanley?' she called softly. 'Pa . . . are you awake?'

Floorboards creaked under her feet, but only silence came from her father's room. Rattling the door handle, she pushed open the door.

The bedclothes were undisturbed, the pillow plumped just as she had left it. The wash water in the jug was cold, and the towel she had laid there sat pristinely white beside it. Orah's father had left no trace of himself – not one grubby fingerprint, no smear of dust or muddy footprint.

Orah grabbed the little bag she'd packed and raced

downstairs. The kitchen was empty. She stood for a moment in the dark warmth, her knuckles pressed to her lips. Bitterwood wasn't her home, Edwin and Clarice weren't her family. Not her true family – that was Hanley, and she belonged with him. Blinded by tears, she rushed to the doorway, stumbling on the step, the doorframe catching her shoulder. She felt the bruise instantly bloom beneath her skin as pain moved through her. Violent, white-cold pain. Her limbs began to quake. Stumbling back, her only thought was to put as much distance between herself and Bitterwood as possible. With Nala gone and Warra dead, there was nothing for her here. The shockwave of hurt reached her heart and her mind greyed. Any love she'd had for these people drained away, leaving her empty and desolate.

She had to find her father. Travel with him to Ballarat, do the best she could with whatever they had. It was right, she told herself, hurrying through the dark house. After all, Hanley was her family, and she belonged with him.

31

Bitterwood, June 1993

Nala declined my offer of a cup of tea in the warm kitchen, admitting that she would feel more comfortable on the headland, with the fresh darkness of the sea and hills around her.

I grabbed my coat and we walked along the drive, crossing the road and onto the headland. Nala pointed to a sheltered spot further down the embankment. The waning moon glowed brightly in the starry sky, lighting our way down the slope. The sea stretched away into the darkness, and breakers washed and sighed against the shoreline below. As we settled on a grassy bank out of the wind, Nala's reedy voice lifted above the roar of the waves.

'Len rang me yesterday, told me you dropped by the cottage. She said you were asking about Clarice Briar?'

I snuggled deeper into my coat, nodding. 'Dad told me

Clarice walked out soon after he was born, and that she never came back. I'm trying to understand why. How well did you know her?'

Nala pushed up her glasses and looked at me thoughtfully. 'After she lost her daughters in 1927, she went into a dark place, poor thing. Edwin employed my brother and me to help her at Bitterwood. Edwin knew our mum, and we were glad of the work. Back then, kids like us didn't go to school. You could either work or starve, and Bitterwood was better than other places we'd been. The Briars made us part of the family. Edwin taught us to read and write, and Clarice insisted we eat our meals at the table with them. Looking back, I think we helped fill the hole left when they lost their little girls.'

'It must've been unbearable for them.'

Nala's dark eyes gleamed. 'It was . . . until Orah arrived.'

'Your friend.'

Nala nodded, gazing out across the dark water. 'The first time I saw Orah, she was a pale little speck clinging to an upended lifeboat. My brother Warra swam out and saved her. Orah lost her mum in the wreck that night, but she was so brave. We brought her back to Bitterwood, and she won Clarice's heart. Edwin's too. Anyone could see she reminded them of the daughter they'd lost, the older girl, Edith. Orah was clever and goodhearted, you know? We all loved her. But I think Warra loved her most of all. They had a bond, you see. But in 1930 . . .' Nala brushed her fingers over the grass, and sighed. 'My brother was shot and killed.'

'Oh,' I murmured. 'I'm sorry.'

'We never found out who did it,' she said softly. 'Of course, we had our suspicions, but not any proof. There was no enquiry. The police never even questioned any suspects.'

I frowned. 'No enquiry?'

'That was the '30s for you. A year or so earlier, in Central Australia, two Aboriginal men supposedly killed a white farmer who'd been abusing some women. In the months that followed, a local Constable led patrols to deal out "justice", although what happened was anything but just. It turned into a massacre. Sixty or more Warlpiri people lost their lives. Stories like that are far-reaching. Even here, people were nervous afterwards. My family never pushed for an enquiry because they feared what may come of it.'

I searched the dark water, thinking of all the young men I knew – Coby and Adam; the boys I'd grown up with in St Kilda; my London friends. If someone had shot and killed one of them as a teenager, there would have been an uproar. I couldn't imagine the scars left by losing a brother so tragically, and with no punishment for whoever had killed him. I thought of the boy whose face grinned from the photo on the Tibbetts' wall. Kept alive in his sister's heart, but when Nala was gone, he would be forgotten.

Waves crashed along the foot of the headland, and the wind delivered a gust of sea spray that sprinkled us like rain.

I shivered. 'Do you know why Clarice left Bitterwood?'

Nala hunched in the wind. 'I'm afraid I don't. After my brother died, I went home. I was gone a couple of years. By the time I came back to Bitterwood in 1932, everything had changed. Clarice had gone. Orah's dad had taken her to live with him. Edwin had a baby boy, and he employed a woman to care for him.'

Nala looked at me and smiled. 'Dulcie Frost was her name, your grandma. Anyone could see how she adored little Ronnie, and she was fond of Edwin, too. I helped in the guesthouse for a while. Then in 1936, the year I turned twenty, I left to get married. My kids were born, and the war came. Things got a bit harder after I lost my Charlie, so in the late forties I returned to Bitterwood for a spell. Business picked up for Edwin, and I was glad of the work. But I had another reason for being there.'

She looked down at the grass again, plucking a daisy, twirling it in her fingers. 'I was waiting for Orah.'

'You thought she might return?'

Nala nodded. 'It niggled me, the way she left. So sudden, you know. Orah thought her dad was dead, but then he turned up out of the blue and she went off with him. It struck me as . . .' She sighed and tossed the daisy back into the grass. 'I don't know. Maybe I was just being wishful.'

'Did you ever see her again?'

Nala shook her head. She brushed her fingers over her face, and dabbed her knuckles beneath her eyes. 'Funny, isn't it? Sixty-three years later, and I still miss her terribly. My brother, too.'

The wind rose up. Beside me, Nala shivered. I leaned against her, sharing what little warmth I had. 'Do you think Orah's still alive?'

Nala sighed. 'I hope so. I often think of her out there somewhere with a family of her own, maybe some grand-kids. I like to think she's had a happy life.'

'You said she left with her father. I don't suppose you knew his name?'

Nala looked around at me, her dark eyes framed by the black rims of her glasses. 'I should, I heard it often enough. For a time, he was all Orah talked about. His name was Hanley Dane.'

I froze a moment, staring at her. My pulse began to fly, the roar of the waves filled my head. 'Dane,' I whispered, 'are you sure? He was a Scotsman?'

Nala nodded, eyeing me curiously. 'How did you know?'

'Because I've met him. This morning. He's in a nursing home in Geelong.'

Nala sat up straight, her eyes suddenly sharp. 'Did he mention her? Did he say how she is, where she's living? Oh Lucy,' she added in a whisper, pressing her fingertips to the sides of her face. 'I'd love to see her again, do you think . . . ?'

The waves boomed beneath us, the wind murmured over the grass. Bats circled overhead, sly shadows swooping against the night sky. I thought of the letter I'd found. Hanley's words, written almost a decade ago, finally made sense. *I can't bring her back, but I simply must know how it was for her at the end.*

I looked at Nala, and the desolation I felt must have showed in my eyes.

She slumped, and returned her gaze to the sea. 'Did he . . .' she began in a barely-there voice, and then cleared her throat. 'Did he tell you what happened to her?'

'No,' I said softly. 'But I hope he will.'

My thoughts flew in circles as I returned to the house. Retrieving Hanley's letter from its place among my collection of clues, I sat by the fire to reread it. But I couldn't concentrate. I kept remembering Hanley's face when he'd seen me in the doorway, kept hearing the tremor in his voice.

Is it you? . . . Have you come for me?

Later, when I queried him, he had tried to dismiss his reaction. *Someone else,* he'd muttered. *She wore her hair long, too.* I refocused on the letter, but the words seemed to jump around. I rubbed my eyes, and tried again, hearing Hanley's voice in my mind as I read. *I can't bring her back, but I simply must know how it was for her at the end.*

At the end.

I sat back in my chair.

Hanley had written to Edwin about his daughter.

The daughter whose death he blamed on himself.

I rested my head in my hands. Was it cruel of me to pursue this? Was it worth causing more heartbreak to an old man who already seemed deeply tormented? Besides, after my visit to Riverview that morning, Hanley would not want to see me again. Marge might be waiting at the door to bar my entry. Yet I couldn't help feeling that Orah's fate was linked somehow to my grandmother's decision to leave Bitterwood, to abandon her husband and newborn son.

It was after midnight. Good sense told me to go to bed. But my mind was racing, my heartbeat echoing like a drum in my ears. Going over to the table, I looked over my collection of puzzle pieces. The icehouse keys, the drawing of my mother, Edwin's spidery letter, and my selections of the photographs – from which peered the face of a lost girl with eyes as large and fathomless as the sea. I pictured her out there in the cold water, clinging to the upended lifeboat, waiting. Waiting through the long night to die. Only she hadn't died. A brave-hearted boy had dived into the stormy waves and swum through the wreckage to save her.

I searched Orah's features, hoping to find evidence of the inner strength, the stubborn streak she must have needed to cling to that lifeboat and survive. Yet the harder I looked, the more insubstantial she seemed to become. Almost ghostlike, as though she was vanishing right before my eyes.

I rummaged in Edwin's utility drawer for a pair of scissors, and took them back to the table. Picking up the photo, I cut out the girl's figure so she was separated from the other people in the picture. Then, to distract myself, I settled Basil onto my lap and picked up my father's manuscript.

In the moment before the King's sword came down, Fine-flower closed her fingers around the soldier's knife. Springing to her feet, she raised the knife and pricked its tip against the King's throat. A single droplet of blood trickled onto the King's collar.

The King let out a bellow and dropped his sword. He did not dare move, but his eyes glared into hers with such hatred that she began to tremble.

'Let me go.'

The King sneered. 'My men will soon return, and

when they do I will order your execu—' He broke off. His attention darted over Fineflower's shoulder. With a cry, he staggered backwards, knocking over the spinning wheel.

Fineflower whirled around. Beneath the window, the shadows twitched and fluttered. One by one, the other wives unravelled themselves from the darkness and dropped to the floor. They swarmed towards the King, reaching out their shadowy little hands. In the lantern light, their waxy faces gleamed with fierce pleasure, and as they surrounded the King, their thumbprint eyes sharpened in triumph.

Fineflower turned away. The door was open and she slipped through it. Behind her in the cell, the old King howled like a struck dog. For one long terrible moment, the scream echoed through the castle, cut short at last by a whimper.

Fineflower ran on. Up the damp stone steps she went, past the burning torchlight, past the dripping walls, past the rats who scuttled under her feet. The ocean roared beyond the walls, and the cold prickled around her, but Fineflower only ran harder.

When she reached her chamber at the top of the castle, she went straight to the cradle. Her baby boy gurgled when he saw her and reached out his chubby arms. She gathered him close against her, wrapped him in his little blanket, and then fled the King's castle. In the stables, she chose a sturdy roan stallion and quickly saddled him. With her baby strapped to her chest, she mounted the horse and rode through the castle grounds, towards the high stone fortress walls. The guards at the gate recognised her and smiled, waving her through. Leaning low over the pommel, Fineflower was about to kick the horse into a canter, when a dark shape in the shadow of the wall caught her eye.

Tugging lightly on the reins, she turned the horse back to investigate. It was a man, beaten and bloodied. His face was purple with bruises, but she recognised the torn blue coat with its brass buttons and ruined gold sash.

Dismounting from her steed, she went to him, kneeled at his side. She took his hand and pressed a kiss to his forehead. He flinched away at first. He had grown pale, his strength and spirit wasted away. Yet when he looked into her face, he seemed to brighten.

'Here you are at last,' he murmured.

Fineflower stroked his matted hair. 'Let us leave this place,' she told him gently. 'We can start a new life together. You see here, I have my son.'

The soldier smiled at Fineflower's little boy, and climbed to his feet. Fineflower mounted the horse, and helped her soldier up behind her. They rode away from the castle, not once looking back, and many leagues vanished behind them. They passed towns with little walled gardens, and crossed streams and bridges and acres of parkland. They rode along the edge of a vast glittering ocean, and then inland past rivers and mountains. Finally, a dark mass of trees came into view.

In the deepest part of the forest, they arrived at a cottage. The soldier dismounted and took a key from his pocket, and let them inside. From the pantry, he brought bread and ale and sweetmeats, and they shared a meal while Fineflower nursed her baby.

Later, in the crackling firelight, while the little boy slept in his mother's arms, the man of shadows settled himself close by. Poking from his pocket was a corner of fine crimson.

Fineflower smiled. 'I see you still have my heart.'

The man nodded sadly. 'I was wrong to demand it. My love held you prisoner, just as surely as the King's dungeon. Can you forgive me?'

Fineflower lifted a brow. 'You'll give back my heart?'

'Only guess my name,' he told her on a sigh, 'and I'll willingly return it.'

Fineflower's body filled with warmth. She might not be any good at spinning silk thread into gold, but she had a knack for seeing behind a person's mask.

'Your name is Love,' she replied.

The man of shadows smiled. Reaching into his pocket, he drew out Fineflower's handkerchief. It was crumpled and grubby, the edges worried by his fingers, the corners damp with his tears. When he held it out to her, the cloth began to glow like a tapestry of burning cinders.

Fineflower understood then that the man of shadows had been right. The human heart was truly a treasure, far more valuable than diamonds and emeralds, far more precious than gold thread. Nothing in this world or the next existed that was of greater value . . . unless, of course, it was a heart that glowed with love.

She reached for her soldier's hand and closed his fingers around the scrap of crimson cloth.

'Keep it,' she said. 'It's yours now.' Then she drew him near, and when their lips met, the forest beyond the cottage door came alive with the sound of birdsong.

For a long time after finishing the story, I wandered through the house. I didn't bother with the lights; the glow of my torch seemed enough. The rooms were vast and echoey without their mantle of clutter, and I found myself shining my light around into every corner, every cupboard and crevice, searching – although not entirely sure what I was searching for. Keys, perhaps. A parcel from Edwin with my name on it. Or maybe I wasn't searching at all, but simply letting myself disappear for a while in the emptiness and dark, so that my tangled thoughts could unravel.

Basil trotted at my heels, occasionally darting off to investigate a mouse, or running ahead into the darkness, whiskers twitching. *Writing stories*, my father had once told me, *is how I work through things I don't understand*. His tale of Fineflower, I now felt certain, was his own story. Through it, he had worked the threads of his wish fulfilment. The mother defying the old king, returning for her little boy, saving the soldier and riding off to a better life. A life that glowed with love given and love received. As I stalked through those empty corridors and hallways, I carried with me the image of a woman: tall and willowy, her curves swathed in red silk, her copper-gold hair gleaming gently in the torchlight. Several times I turned, expecting to see her . . . but there were only shadows.

I would have liked to ask her if my father had gotten it right in his fairytale – if, in the end, she had found her happy ever after. I hoped she had. With all my heart, I hoped that she had. Yet something told me Dad's story was simply that: a story.

Geelong, June 1993

Hanley did not seem surprised to see me. He nodded resignedly, and then beckoned me over to his bedside. Gestured for me to sit, and then reached for me. His fingers trembled as they circled my wrist. His skin was warm, dry as paper, the old bones beneath fragile as those of a bird, but there was strength in his grip.

'Can you see them?' he asked. He directed a glance to the other side of the room, to his aquarium. 'Are they moving around in there, Lucy? Do they look happy?'

I could see nothing from where I sat, just the aquatic plants swaying in the artificial current, and the overhead lights reflected dimly in the glass. There was no movement on the snail front, but the old man seemed to need reassurance.

'Gloria's waving her tentacles,' I told him. 'Almost as if she's dancing.'

That made him smile. Releasing my wrist, he lay back on his pillow and let out a sigh. 'You said you found a letter.'

I took it out of my pocket. 'The one you sent to Edwin, it's here. Hanley, who was the woman you wrote about?'

Hanley didn't look at the letter. Instead, he closed his eyes and began to speak, stumbling over the words, his voice a wheezy rasp.

'Not a woman, at least not quite. A beautiful girl, clever and funny, kind-hearted. So like her mother. Back in Glasgow . . . we had a little house. My wife, Posie, had come from money, but she swore our modest life made her happy. After the war I was restless. I took a job in an accounting firm, started off small, working my way up, and for a while it was enough. Then I started hearing tales about Australia . . . streets paved with gold, nuggets free for the picking. I envisioned my wife and daughter in finery, saw the three of us living like royals . . . and couldn't wait to pack my bags.'

Without his glasses, his eyes looked naked. He rubbed them with shaky fingers. 'It was quite a different story when I arrived, of course. I went up to the Ballarat goldfields, but they'd abandoned the mines so I panned the creeks for a while. A wretched time, it was. Near starved to death, froze in winter. Even caught a lift down to Wonthaggi to the coalface, but the rotten conditions there, and gold fever, I suppose, drove me back to Ballarat. For a while, I worked a stint on the sewers. Ironic, isn't it. I came to dig for gold, and ended up shovelling drains. All the while, dreaming that the next lucky nugget might be mine. I was a Scotsman, I declared. It wasn't in my blood to give up. But truth be known, that old tin shanty had become my home. I had nowhere else to go.'

He drew a handkerchief from his pyjama pocket and wiped it over his face, then took a rattling breath. 'Late in 1931, I started heavy on the grog. A man had a mind to drink himself into an early grave, didn't he? A brutal time. There were no jobs. Everyone was hungry and destitute. Somehow I scraped through, although countless didn't. Then the Salvos found me, cleaned me up. Saved me, so they did. In return, I offered back the only thing of value I possessed – my life, though there are many who'd say even that was worthless. I trained as an officer and spent the next thirty years doing the Lord's work. Counselling anyone who needed a kind word.'

He coughed, reaching for the water glass beside his bed. After a noisy drink, he replaced the glass and settled back into his pillows. He looked at me. 'But you didn't come all this way to hear that, did you?'

I shook my head. 'Could you tell me about the letter?'

His mouth tightened, turned down. Then he nodded. 'I'll be glad to get it off my chest. Perhaps then I'll find peace.'

There was a silence. I waited, but Hanley did not go on.

'In the letter,' I prompted, 'you asked Edwin about someone's final moments. Someone you loved.'

He nodded, but made no attempt to elaborate.

I slid my hand into my bag, retrieving the section of photo I had cut from one of the enlargements. It showed only the girl, her face framed by long fair hair, her eyes large and dark, almost reproachful. I placed it on the bedside table.

'She was your daughter, wasn't she? Orah.'

Hanley's gaze flicked to the photo, then away. He nodded, and seemed about to speak. But then his chin pushed up, began to tremble. A long silence followed. The old man seemed in the grip of an internal battle, his lips drawn against his teeth, his eyes squeezing shut. Finally, he flared his nostrils and drew a shaky breath.

'I failed her . . . in the worst possible way.'

'How do you mean?'

He sank deeper into his pillows. His eyelids fluttered. 'If only I hadn't gone to see her. If only I'd stayed away, let her be. A man doesn't know, though, does he – what the future will bring. He thinks only of the moment. So when I got Edwin's letter saying she was alive and well, living right here in Australia, I had to see her.'

He paused and wiped his eyes with shaky fingers, looked across the room. 'Is Gloria still there?' he asked anxiously. 'Still dancing?'

Mid-morning sunlight filtered through the curtains, and a solitary beam shone into the fish tank. Even from here, I could see her: a golden shell the size of a finch's egg, twirling in the slipstream of bubbles, her pale tentacles waving about in the water.

'Yes, she's still dancing.'

Hanley nodded and then, pulling in a raspy breath, continued. 'When I left my girl in Glasgow all those years before, she was just a tiny wee thing. Eight years had passed since then, but when Edwin's letter arrived, I only saw that little child . . . had visions of her trailing after me around the shanty, cute as a button, brightening the place with her golden curls and quick blue eyes. But the girl I found at Bitter-wood was almost a young woman. I got a shock. She looked so much like her dear mam. Clever, too, and politely spoken. Immediately I saw she was better off with the Briars. Edwin and his wife clearly loved her. They'd provided a comfortable home, education, food on the table – far more than I could have offered in a month of Sundays at my humble shanty. So I decided to leave the next morning. I planned to explain my situation to the lass, and then say my fond goodbyes . . . Lord,' he added in a strained whisper, 'if only I'd stuck to my guns, instead of listening to Edwin—'

'What happened?'

Hanley collected himself. 'Later that night, his lordship knocked on my door and suggested I leave immediately. Without a word to the lass, he advised. He slipped me a bundle of notes – almost thirty pounds, I counted later, a king's ransom. A man was torn, wasn't he? I found myself over on the headland with a bottle for company, trying to clear my head. It was a crook business, sneaking off in the night like a thief. Wrong, you know? Funny about that . . . Leaving her should have been easy. After all, I'd done it once before. But it tore me apart all the same.'

He drew a shuddering breath. His gaze roamed the room, and then finally came to settle on the photo. His mouth shook and tears began to seep from his eyes.

I couldn't stop the words. 'What happened to her?'

Hanley didn't seem to hear. 'I spent my life chasing riches,' he murmured. 'All the while failing to see that the grandest treasure of all had been right there before me all along.'

'Your daughter.'

He seemed to shrink into himself, somehow grow smaller. With trembling fingers, he reached for the photograph. He fumbled, unable to pick it up. I passed it to him, and he held it up close to his eyes for the longest time. He began to cry, noisily, wetly . . . and with the unself-conscious abandon of a small child whose heart was breaking. Then, in the faintest rasp of a voice, pausing occasionally to regather himself, he resumed his story.

32

Bitterwood, 1931

Orah hurried along the road, glad of the bright moonlight. She noticed an old utility parked beyond the hedge, and ran towards it, her satchel banging against her side, her shoes sliding around her feet.

'Pa?' she called hopefully. 'Pa, wait!'

The vehicle was empty, and the only reply was the swish of waves on the beach far below. She was trembling, out of breath. Stopping, she rested her hands on her knees and tried to breathe slowly. Her hair had escaped its ribbon and whipped her face in the wind, blinding her. She paused to retie it. That was when she saw – at least, *thought* she saw – the solitary figure on the seaward edge of the headland. She started running towards him. Her body felt stretched out of shape, as in a dream; her legs too long for her body, wobbling all over the place, her arms weak and trembly. She wanted to call out, but her breath was trapped in her throat.

She ran along the headland, hearing the boom of water on the rocks below. She staggered, almost tripped. Her head ached horribly. She had been so angry, so hurt. Edwin had lied, and Clarice had been part of the lie too. They had betrayed her, and she hated them, hated their woeful excuses.

Your father was in a terrible state, ill and destitute, barely able to care for himself, let alone provide for a daughter—

Orah didn't care. Soon she would be living with her father, helping him find his pot of glorious gold. She was clever, hadn't he said so? She could cook for him, look after him, make his bed and shine his shoes. Use the skills she had learned at Bitterwood to restore him to the pa he had once been, with his rosy face and scratchy beard and bear hugs.

'Pa!'

He turned, seemed to freeze on the spot.

Orah ran the last few feet and flung herself into his arms. 'Pa, why didn't you wait? I was so worried. I thought—' She stopped. Her father's face was ragged. Orah became aware of the smell, a tart unpleasantness that made her eyes water. She took a step away, searching her father's face, seeing – not the joy she'd hoped for, but alarm.

'What is it?' she asked.

'How did you know I'd be up here?' There was no warmth in his voice, no pleasure.

'I just . . . found you.'

His face twisted. 'You're no different to your mother. You'd hound a man into an early grave, wouldn't you? I only came here to see that you were all right, lass. That's all. I'd not intended to take you back with me. The shanties are no place for a young woman. You'd be a hindrance, a liability.'

'Liability?'

Pa seemed to wilt. 'You're nearly fifteen now, Orah. A pretty thing, too,' he added in a softer voice. 'A man would have to spend all his time fending off unwanted attention. You see how it is, girl? I can't take you with me, I won't.' He seemed about to take a step towards her, but then staggered sideways.

That was when she saw the bottle. It was almost empty, just the dregs of a brownish liquid at the bottom. She looked back at her father. His pale hair was stark against the shadows of his face, and his whiskers were now as white as those of an old man.

'Pa?'

'You shouldn't have come after me,' he said harshly. His lips drew back from around his teeth, and he spun away from her. Orah feared he meant to fling himself from the cliff edge – but his arm swung out, and he hurled the bottle. Orah watched it arc over the waves and then drop, disappearing into the water without a splash.

Pa turned to face her. 'Go back to the house.' Then he said, more softly, 'I can't take you with me, Orah girl. It's madness out there, a man can barely fend for himself, let alone take care of a lass. Go on with you now, get back to your people. Back to where you belong.'

Orah gritted her teeth. 'They're not my people. I belong with you, Pa. I'm not going back, I'm coming with you. I don't care about the madness, as long as we're together.'

He pushed past her and began to stalk back along the

headland, the reek of drink and sour sweat gusting around him in the wind. Orah ran after him, grabbed onto his sleeve, not letting go when he tried to shake her off.

'Please, Pa—'

He yanked hard and tore free, shoving away from her. Panic rose up, pounding its fists against her ribs. She sobbed, tasting the salty breath of the sea, the fusty dampness of the sand somewhere below.

She ran at her father again and seized his arm. 'I don't want to stay here! Please take me with you. I don't belong with them; they're not my family. Pa, please, it's what I want. Don't make me stay, don't leave me behind.'

Her father let out a sob – harsh and ragged, not even human, more like the cry of an animal – and the sound turned Orah's heart to stone. She let out an answering cry of her own, a wordless plea snatched away all too quickly by the wind.

'Please, Pa. Take me with you.'

She tried to embrace him, but he veered away with a shout. Too near the edge, but that didn't stop her lunging again. She had to make him see reason, had to make him understand. The salt air stung her eyes, and she felt the ocean breeze lick its hungry tongue along her skin. Her legs shook beneath her, but she couldn't give up; wouldn't. Pa was escaping, more than a body length ahead of her now. She ran after him, barely noticing the loose stones beneath her feet, the slide of her shoes.

'Pa, please—'

Thrusting out her arm, she launched herself at her father's hunched shoulders and grabbed a fistful of his shirt. Pa roared and swung around, his arm raised as if he meant to strike her.

It happened so quickly. One moment there was solid ground beneath her feet; the next, her foot met no resistance, sinking into nothingness, its momentum pulling her with it, plunging her downwards into the dark. The sea roared in triumph, its booming cry swallowing the scream that tore from her throat. The world split open, the starry sky spun, and the rocks below whirled up to greet her.

The Queen had only to name the girl. Give her a name, and the child would be hers. So many lovely names, they crowded her mind, teetered on the tip of her tongue . . . but each time she tried to utter one, any one, a face popped into her mind's eye. A small face with faded freckles, and eyes once as dark as the wild kelp that grew beyond the shore, now as dull as a spent penny.

—The Shell Queen

33

Bitterwood, June 1993

A storm blew in as I drove back to Bitterwood. Black clouds rumbled across the sky, turning afternoon to night. I barely noticed. Hanley's account of Orah's fall had shaken me and I couldn't settle. For a while I stalked around the house, trying to pull myself together, but as the sky darkened and the storm closed in, the uneasy thump of my heart only grew louder.

After collecting the icehouse keys from their hiding place in the pantry, I took my flashlight and went into the garden. The sky was mottled now, crowded with deadly looking black and purple clouds. Rain began to fall around me, and a freezing wind caught leaf drifts and whipped them into the air, blinding me.

Thunder cracked in the distance, and by the time I reached the hollow beneath the dead oak, I was wet to the skin. I hesitated there on the brink of the orchard, but the wind strengthened at my back, pushing me forward. I took a few reluctant steps, then halted again.

The old oak creaked in the gale. As I watched, one of its upper branches splintered from the trunk and shattered onto the mound below.

Taking a breath, I walked towards the icehouse.

Unlocking the door, I went in. The din of rain faded. As I trod into the cold darkness, shining my torch around, the calm seemed eerie, abrupt after the wildness of the storm outside.

My light fell on broken bottles and the ruined shelving from which they had fallen. I noted blackened concavities at the base of some support beams. Edwin had tried to burn the icehouse, but the damp air and solid constriction had prevented its destruction. I thought of the album, and his attempt to burn that too, and wondered again what tracks he'd been so desperate to erase.

The air smelled sour. Burned wood, ash, stale smoke. A hint of kerosene. I pressed my hand to the wall, touching the cold stone, taking comfort from its solidness.

I reached the steps and trod down.

At the bottom, the air was noticeably colder, damper. I rested my palm on a support beam. It was rough and splintery, and as I lingered, spidery legs darted across my wrist, ticklish on my skin. I gasped, and then huffed out a laugh. A cockroach, a spider. The stuff of nightmares for some, but not for me.

I continued along the passageway. Veils of cobweb loomed in the light. I was staring so hard into the blackness that sparks flashed behind my eyes.

Deeper underground I went. The weight of cold pressed around me. No one had breathed this air for a long time, perhaps decades. The smell of earth and stone, a greasy odour, faintly mouldy, sat heavily in my lungs. I fought the urge to rush back outside into the freshness of the storm and expel it from my body.

At the end of the passageway, I followed the bend around to the right. The ground sloped down, and the low ceiling forced me to stoop. The support beams were closer together, and I wondered how my grandfather, with his impossibly tall frame, had manoeuvred his way through this cramped narrow space.

I paused, shining my light ahead into the dark.

The passageway ended. The cobwebs thickened here, as though I was entering a large subterranean web. Directly above me, muffled by many feet of stone, thunder boomed.

The support beam nearest to where I was standing shuddered. Earth rained down from the ceiling. I stepped out of its way, brushing sandy dirt from my hair, but another deafening crack overhead startled me and I dropped the torch. As I bent to retrieve it, something glittered on the ground. A shard of glass, I thought at first. Kneeling, I looked more closely.

A tiny padlock.

Tarnished, encrusted with dirt, half-buried between the flagstones. I tried to pull it loose with my fingers, but it was stuck fast. I patted my pockets, found Edwin's keyring, and used the end of the large key to scratch away the solid packed earth. Thunder rumbled overhead, and as I kneeled on the ground intently digging, I became aware of a faint shrieking sound, perhaps the trees outside bending in the wind.

The padlock loosened. It was attached to a chain. I tugged on it gently, scratching around it with the key until finally it came free. Holding it in my palm, I examined it under the torchlight.

The chain was broken, but there was no mistaking it. The delicate links, the padlock clasp. I breathed a shaky sigh, and felt the hairs stand up along my arms. My mother's bracelet.

'You were here,' I whispered.

I shut my eyes and my mother appeared before me. Her fair hair floated out from her face, rippling in the current. Her eyes were open, blue as the water in which she drifted. She was reaching for me, her large freckled fingers so near that all I had to do was lift my hand and grasp them. But something held me back.

It's not her, my father said from the darkness. *That's not my wife in there . . . You've made a mistake.*

I shook my head to clear it, and got to my feet. Weighed the broken gold bracelet in my palm, and then slid it into my pocket. I knew she wasn't down here. I knew that when my father had seen her body that day at the morgue, he had been in denial, his ability to grasp what had happened diminished by grief. The woman whose ashes we had farewelled at the crematorium, really had been hers.

So why did my old fears suddenly feel so real?

I shone my torch to the end of the passageway. Bending low to avoid knocking my head on the overhead beams, I walked towards the cavity in the wall where once my grandfather had stored the ice.

34

Bitterwood, 1977

As Karen hurried along the beach towards the shadow of the headland, her argument with Ron replayed in her mind. She hadn't meant to cause friction, but that was precisely what she'd done. Worse was Ron's reaction. Rather than discussing the matter like a reasonable adult, he'd flown off the handle, attacked her as if she'd created the whole episode just to provoke him.

She sighed. They'd been together long enough for her to understand the deep hurt Ron had suffered after his mother – Dulcie – had died. Edwin had withdrawn from the world, making himself unavailable to the teenage son who desperately needed him. Karen understood, but she was also a firm believer in forgiveness. No family was perfect; no one escaped the chaotic rollercoaster of interpersonal relationships. The secret, she had learned, was to roll with the punches, avoid taking anything much to heart, and above all else, be willing to forgive other people's foibles and move on.

He had a doting wife and a son who idolised him, but do you think you noticed?

Without breaking stride, she glanced back along the beach towards their holiday house. In the morning light, the red tin roof was a tiny speck in the distance, and somewhere beneath it she imagined her daughter's dark head bent over her colouring book, the girl happily lost in her current obsession as the TV blared in the background. Ron would be at the kitchen table, probably still red-faced after their argument, gorging on the pastries he'd brought back from the bakery. After their episode in the kitchen, Karen feared that he would go to the pub, drink away the day in the company of the casual friends he'd made there over the years. Instead, he had barrelled back through the door half an hour later, arms laden with paper bags.

Karen wanted to smile. Though the day was sunny, a storm brewed in the distance, black clouds pushing bruises along the horizon. On days like today, hot bright days caught on the brink of a storm, she itched to take out her paintbrushes and paper. Seeing Lucy this morning bent over her colouring book, Karen had stifled the temptation to join her.

Funny how things worked out. Since she could walk, Karen had dreamed of being an artist. She'd gone to art school, but had only lasted a year. Her interests changed, that's what she told everyone; she kept the real reason to herself: lack of talent. Instead, she'd enrolled at Melbourne University to study history, in particular the art of medieval and Renaissance times. Which was how she met Ron.

She reached the headland, and was glad to step into its cool shadow. Climbing the steep path seemed more torturous today than it had last night, and she couldn't help wondering how she'd managed it in moonlight, without a torch. She was tired, she realised. The combination of sleeplessness and her niggling worries about Ron's drinking – not to mention the increasing frequency of their arguments – was wearing her down. She paused, and glanced back along the beach. She could see her footprints in the wet sand, weaving all the way back to the foothills. Nestled behind the grassy sandbanks, the cottage would now be in shadow; she could no longer see any sign of it, not even the roof. Far out at sea, the storm clouds had grown darker, and she thought she heard the first rumblings of thunder.

When she reached the crown of the headland, she took another breather. Further up the slope, Bitterwood Park loomed on the other side of the narrow road. Trees obscured the lower half of the building, but its peaked roofline seemed to rub against the clouds, severe and imposing.

She crossed the road and followed the trail between the hedge of twisted trees and around the side of the house, as she'd done last night. She made a beeline for the back door.

'Edwin, are you there?' There was no reply, but the door was wide open, so he couldn't be far. Karen ducked her head inside. The kitchen smelled of toast and fresh coffee. 'Ed, are you about? It's Karen.'

Strange. He must be in the garden. She followed the path that wound between the flowerbeds and down into the orchard. The trees were heavy with fruit, large succulent purple mulberries that hung in clusters like babies' fingers.

They would end up taking bucketloads back to Melbourne with them, and Karen would spend the next two weekends stewing them or making her specialty mulberry tarts.

'Edwin?'

She emerged from the other side of the garden, but still there was no sign of him. Odd, that he hadn't heard her. She hoped he was all right. She began to worry. Perhaps he'd seen her last night, after all; perhaps he was hiding from her. Ron's words echoed in the back of her mind.

Mad old buzzard.

Now she was picturing Edwin, concealed somewhere in the shadows, his lanky frame buckled like a concertina into some impossibly tiny bower. Perhaps he was watching her now as she gazed around. Part of her wanted to laugh at the image, but the more compassionate side of her nature felt sorry for the old man.

'Ed, I just wanted to see if you're all right.'

When she saw the icehouse door ajar, she let out a relieved sigh.

As she went closer, a shadow swept across the garden. She looked up, realising that the storm had blown in more quickly than she had anticipated. The sky was black overhead, the clouds settling in for a long spell of rain. She'd get soaked if she went home along the beach. She didn't mind, only that the track down the headland would be slippery. She would have to ring Ron to drive up to collect her, and he wouldn't be happy.

The wind gathered around her legs, and the icehouse door creaked. She saw that the keys were still in the lock. Going to the threshold, she listened. It wasn't like Edwin to disappear like this, maybe he was hiding from her after all. Or worse, he might have slipped and fallen.

Pushing through the door, Karen ventured into the icehouse.

So dark. In the distance, she heard the slow rumble of thunder. As she felt her way down some steps, the air got colder. She might have turned back, but the idea had lodged in her mind that Edwin might be in trouble. Poor Edwin. She could still see him, hunched over his book of photos, his frail body gripped by sobs.

The passageway grew narrower. Karen touched the wall beside her. The surface was crumbly, and her fingers came away damp. Perhaps she should go back to the cottage and return with reinforcements. Despite Ron's lack of compassion for his father, even he wouldn't ignore the old man's disappearance.

She was about to turn around, when a glimmer of light caught her attention. At first, she thought it was lightning, but of course, she was too deep into the icehouse for any outside light to reach. It was coming from up ahead. Feeling her way along the wall, she hurried towards it.

The passageway ended. A narrow opening led into a small rectangular room. Near the opening burned a candle, the source of the light she'd followed. It fluttered as she stepped into the room, her shadow cavorting madly up the walls and across the cobweb-infested roof beams. Karen drew a breath when she saw the figure huddled in the far corner.

'Edwin!' she cried, and lurched towards him, but as the candle guttered violently in the breeze of her passing, she saw that it wasn't Edwin at all. It wasn't even a person, not really, just a bundle of—

The candle went out. Her nostrils filled with smoke.

Impossible . . . Just seeing things.

She stood a moment, hoping her eyes might adjust, but the darkness seemed only to grow denser. It didn't matter. The thing she'd seen had imprinted itself on her mind, as crisply detailed as a photograph.

Slowly, she felt her way back through the dark, out into the passageway. As she groped along it, her arm snared on something, probably a nail, and she felt the sting of torn skin. Up ahead she saw the stairs, faintly illuminated by the watery light from outside. She hurried towards them. A moment later, she was through the open door and out into the rain. She ran towards the house, but bypassed the verandah and made her way around the front, through the trees and along the crown of the headland. The pathway was wet and slippery. Halfway down she fell and slid. She was more careful, after that. When she reached the sand at the foot of the headland, she paused to catch her breath.

Each breath burned. She tried to tell herself she'd been mistaken, but the thing in the corner had seared itself into her mind's eye – the dark, tattered thing that looked like a person, but wasn't. She was not entirely sure what she had seen in Edwin's icehouse, only that it had no right to be there. Something was amiss, terribly amiss. Ron's words rang in her ears.

Mad old buzzard, there's likely more than one skeleton hiding in his closet.

She had to talk to Ron – to articulate what had happened

so she could make sense of it. He might still be grouchy after their row that morning, but Ron never sulked for long. He was always there when she needed him. She brushed the wet sand off her jeans and ran back along the beach towards the cottage.

Stupid, to have left the candle burning. How much easier it would have been just to snuff the flame between his fingers, plunge the place into darkness. She hadn't had a torch, hadn't been expecting to enter any dark place. The candlelight had given away his presence; it had attracted her, drawn her into the innermost chamber of his secret world, and now she had seen—

Stupid.

Edwin manoeuvred himself in the cramped cavity beneath the floor. There was barely room to flex his arms, let alone roll onto his back, but flex he did, and, reaching up, managed to lift the iron grate set into the floor. Slowly, with concentrated effort, he pushed the grate away from the opening. As a boy, he had fitted into the drainage channel with relative ease; he'd been slender and surprisingly strong, agile as a monkey. Ronald had teased him about his physique, calling him a string bean, a human twig. Edwin had burned inside at the taunts, but his secret had made the jeering easier to bear. A secret place within a secret place – even his mother hadn't known about the icehouse culvert. During Bitterwood's heyday at the turn of the century, the well-insulated inner chamber of the icehouse had taken almost a ton of ice. Slowly, as summer reached its peak, that ice would melt away. Edwin's grandfather, Colman Briar, had been to America and viewed famous icehouses in Washington and Philadelphia, where he'd learned about the importance of installation, proper storage, and drainage.

Edwin climbed stiffly out of the trench. Due to the proximity of bedrock to the surface, Colman Briar had been unable to make his icehouse culvert as deep as he would have liked; instead, he had created a wide, shallow drain, with just enough capacity to cope with the flow of meltwater that inevitably accumulated at the end of summer.

Rubbing his legs, Edwin cursed his age. He was no longer the agile string bean who could fold his lanky body into the smallest of spaces. He was eighty now, his joints arthritic and swollen, his tendons dried up, his muscles withered.

Relighting his candle, he shuffled through the narrow opening into the passage, and was about to head for the stairs when he paused. On the ground near his feet, he caught a glimmer. At first he thought it was just another shard of broken glass, but when he bent to investigate he found instead a small golden heart. He knew it instantly. It was the charm from the bracelet he had given Karen. She must have dropped it here in her rush to get away. He shone the candle about, but did not find the rest of the bracelet. It was very old, he reasoned; perhaps the link attaching the charm had broken, while the rest of the chain remained around Karen's wrist.

He slipped the gold heart into his pocket. He must return it to her. Immediately, he decided.

Pausing on the icehouse threshold, he looked around the garden. She was gone, no doubt to report to someone – Ron, the authorities, perhaps even the police – what she'd seen. He would go after her, make his way along the road; take a jar of the mulberry jam she loved. Pray that he was not too late to stop her.

Locking the heavy door behind him, he stood for a moment in the sunlight. He was so weary, so tired of keeping secrets. It seemed he had kept them his whole life. Suddenly he wished them gone. Every secret had its use-by date. He had carried this one close to his chest for over four decades. Perhaps it was time to pass the burden to someone else.

Gull Cottage, 1977

Back at the cottage, the dining table was a mess of drawings: green owls flying across a purple sky of yellow stars; tiny red boats bobbing on black oceans; blue cats and big white dogs with brown spots; houses spewing streamers of orange smoke from their chimneys. In the midst of this rainbow of chaos sat Lucy, head bowed over her page, furiously colouring.

Karen called to her, but the girl didn't look up.

Ron wasn't in the kitchen or lounge room, so she ran along the hall and checked the bedrooms. When there was no sign of him on the back porch, she went back into the dining room.

'Honey, where's your father?'

Lucy shrugged, intent on her page. 'Gone out.'

'He left you alone?'

'I'm ten, remember.'

Karen's frustration sharpened the already brittle edge to her voice. 'Where did he go? And please don't say the pub, or I'll scream.'

Lucy looked up, and her eyes widened. Karen glanced down at herself. Her T-shirt was filthy, her bare arms scratched where she had run carelessly through the hedge at Bitterwood. She had badly grazed her elbow, and a thin worm of blood wound down her forearm.

'Mum, what happened?'

For a moment Karen couldn't speak. Lucy rarely called her Mum these days, claiming it was too babyish, and arguing that if Coby got to call his parents by their Christian names, then why couldn't she? For the past few months, Lucy had been calling them Ron and Karen, but that wasn't what made Karen pause. It was the girl's tone: worried, with an edge of alarm.

She took a breath and let it out. Cleared her throat. 'I'm all right, love. I got caught in the rain.' She tried to laugh, lighten her voice. 'What a goose, I slipped over on the headland, skated halfway down on my bum.'

Lucy fixed her gaze on Karen's forearm, frowning at the thread of blood. 'You'd better get something on it.'

For an instant, Karen felt trapped. Such an ordinary moment, here in the dining room with Lucy, the air still sweet from Ron's pastries and the coffee he'd brewed to go with them. Yet it was far from ordinary. Her discovery had left her shaken. She didn't know what it meant, only that it cast a terrifying shadow over her family that would remain until the situation was resolved. And to do that she needed to speak to Ron. They would have to go to the police; there might even be an investigation.

Her legs were suddenly wobbly. Dragging a chair out from under the table, she sat heavily, palming her face, breathing through her fingers.

'Where is it?' Lucy asked.

It took her a moment to make sense of the question. 'Where's what?'

'The bracelet.'

Karen's mind whirled. She glanced at her wrist, saw the streaks of dirt, the scratches; vaguely remembered her arm catching on something as she fled along the dark passage—

'You promised,' Lucy accused. 'You promised I could have it, and now it's gone. Did you give it back to Grandad?'

'Give what back?'

'The bracelet he gave you. Did you give it back?'

'No, I—'

'You lost it, didn't you?'

Karen stood up, shaking off her wobbles. 'Where's your father?'

Lucy pouted, snatched up a pencil and bowed her head back over her drawing. 'Dunno. Out.'

'Out where, exactly?'

There was a long pause, and then Lucy sighed. 'He went fishing.'

'I don't recall seeing him on the beach.' Nor would she have, she realised. She'd been so distressed that a full circus parade could have passed by and she wouldn't have noticed.

'Which way did he go – west towards the headland or east to the rocks?'

Lucy shrugged, Karen's impatience squirmed inside her. She wanted to shake the girl, hurry her up. She considered just running out onto the foreshore and screaming Ron's name until he heard her. Crazy thoughts, stress always did that to her. *Stay calm*, she warned herself. *There's no need to panic. Ron will know what to do. Take a deep breath and stay calm.*

Lucy's attention went back to Karen's wrist where the bracelet should have been. Her eyes narrowed, and finally she looked up.

'He went to the rocks.'

35

Bitterwood, 1931

Edwin was undressing for bed when he heard the hammering on the door. He groaned and sought the clock, grimaced at the time. A quarter to eleven.

He had returned home late from Apollo Bay to discover a stranger's car parked along the verge. He had a sinking feeling, so when he found Clarice in bed, crying and not making sense he feared the worst. Clarice told him that Orah's father had turned up, and was, at that moment, asleep in one of the guest rooms. She said Orah had gone to her room upset, and that there'd be hell to pay in the morning.

Edwin cursed himself for sending the letter. He had written it in a moment of weakness, overcome by guilt and remorse. Now, he'd have done anything to be able to turn back time and rip the damn note to shreds.

He gazed at Clarice's sleeping form. She'd been restless of late, but had found relief with the help of Doctor Vetch's sleeping draught and a cup of hot milk. Soon, the baby would come, but the thought brought Edwin no joy. In the past months, Clarice had grown frail. A frown line had begun to show between her brows, and she had chewed her nails to the quick. She bustled around the house, her face aglow, her eyes bright. This was her last trimester, the baby was due any day and the doctor had given her a good prognosis. Yet Edwin could see the cracks, the forced cheer.

His beautiful Clarice was afraid, and nothing he nor a battalion of well-meaning doctors could do or say would put her mind at rest. When the baby came, she would improve. That's what he kept telling himself. Once she held that tiny healthy bundle in her arms, she could stop worrying. Her fear was only natural, after what she'd been through with Edith and baby Joyce, and Edwin had made it his life's mission to protect her.

The hammering came again.

Clarice did not stir, thanks to the potent draught. Orah would still be sleeping. Her room was tucked away at the top of the stairs, out of earshot of the front door. On any other day, he may have ignored the ruckus, let the intruder go on their way and return at a more reasonable hour, but if Clarice woke, she'd be wan and fretful all day. Besides, Edwin had a restless feeling in the pit of his stomach.

It was probably Hanley. Edwin had knocked quietly on his door just after ten, and slipped him a tight bundle of notes; more money than Hanley Dane had seen in a month of Sundays, evidenced by the widening of his greedy eyes. He had blustered and tried to push the money back, but Edwin would not take it.

'Leave now,' he'd cautioned. 'While the girl's asleep. She's happy here with us. We can provide for her, give her a decent home. Can you honestly say you could do the same?'

Hanley had stared back at him, his weather-beaten face a picture of sorrow. Edwin's heart went out to him, but what could he do? They both knew he was right.

The hammering had stopped.

As Edwin descended the stairs, he heard an engine cough to life somewhere on the other side of the hedge. It quickly faded, lost to the crash and boom of waves against the rocks. On nights like this, when the tide was high, the roar of the sea was all you could hear; a bomb might go off and they'd be none the wiser.

In the sitting room, Edwin went to the window, but could see no sign of the automobile. He waited, and then caught a glimmer of it speeding along the narrow strip of road back in the direction of Stern Bay. Edwin breathed a sigh. It was over. Life could return to normal, he could carry on with a clear conscience now, and best of all – and here a spark of joy began to burn brightly in his heart – Orah was theirs at last. Not stolen, not theirs by devious means, but truly theirs. She would forgive them in time. She was a sensible girl, she would come to see that they had lied only to protect her. Now that she'd seen with her own eyes the sort of man her father was, she would understand their motive.

In time . . .

He considered going back to bed but something drew him to the front door. He told himself he wanted to be sure that Hanley had really gone, but it wasn't just that.

Something niggled. A shabby coat hung on the rack, reeking of smoke and grime, but it wasn't that either. Nor was it his irritation with himself about the letter.

Opening the door, he glanced down.

The cry that shot from his mouth left him winded. He prayed that he was mistaken, that his eyes were playing tricks – even as he fell to his knees and gathered her into his arms. *A mistake, please. Let it be a mistake. It can't be her, it can't be—*

As he carried her inside and laid her gently on the couch, careless of the blood that seeped onto the fine silk cushions, he continued his silent pleading. *It can't be . . . It can't be.* It kept on long after he knew that it was no mistake, that the broken and bloodied creature in his arms was indeed his beautiful Orah, the sweet golden-haired girl who had brought his family back from the brink.

'Clarice!' he roared. Curse the sleeping draught. Why had he given her so much? 'For the love of God, Clarice!'

Orah made a mewling sound. She was crumpled like a broken doll, her skin slick with blood, her poor head crushed. He could see the black stain above her ear, growing larger, eclipsing the bright gold of her hair. Edwin's mind spun. He wanted to race into the hall and telephone the doctor, but dared not leave her. What if she slipped away while he was gone? And then the wait for help to arrive. Thirty minutes from town, possibly an hour at this time of night. Did she even have that long? What if she—

'Clarice, get down here!' Orah couldn't die. He wouldn't let her. He would keep her alive by sheer force of will. 'Clarice! Oh . . . God.'

A murmur, a sigh from his sweet girl. He lowered his face to her. 'Orah, love, can you hear me?'

'Edwin?'

'I'm here, little one.'

'Where's Pa?'

Hot tears stung Edwin's eyes. 'Did he do this to you, Orah? Did your father do this?'

'I tried to go with him,' she murmured. 'But he . . . oh, Edwin, he didn't . . . want me. You were right . . . Clarice said . . . he didn't—'

Edwin began to weep silently. He longed to gather her against him, to hold her tight and make the pain go away, but he was terrified of hurting her. Jumbled words clamoured in the back of his mind, words of comfort and explanation, words of encouragement – but he could not give voice to any of them. He was losing her. He recognised no particular sign of that loss, just a dark foreboding that pushed against his mind. After the female silkworm moths laid their eggs, they only lived a few hours; he had often watched them fluttering on the windowsills, their movements growing erratic as the strength ebbed from their wings. Many thousands of times he had witnessed the dying of the moths . . . and the presence of death never failed to chill him.

Just as it chilled him now.

'He's here,' Orah whispered. Her eyes widened, focusing on something over Edwin's shoulder. She smiled. Her fingers fluttered weakly, and then her hands lifted from where Edwin had placed them on her chest. They hovered in the gloom, a pair of moths beginning their death dance.

'Orah, stay with me,' Edwin breathed. He grasped her hands, kissed the knuckles, willing her fingers to tighten, even for an instant, around his own. Instead, as though melting under the heat of his terror, her fingers relaxed and the sudden weight of her arms dragged them from his grasp. Her eyes, a moment ago so bright, trembled shut. A sigh whispered from her, and then she vanished into a stillness so profound that Edwin felt his heart vanish with her.

'He's here.'

Orah could see him clearly, just behind Edwin's shoulder. Standing in his proud way, his dark eyes fixed to hers. *Warra*, she called. *Warra, am I seeing you with my heart?*

A breath, or a sigh. *Yes.*

Heaviness settled over her. She reached for Warra with both hands, expecting to feel his strong fingers grasp hers, but there was only emptiness and shadows. She was no longer in the sitting room at Bitterwood. All was dark.

Warra, where did you go?

A whisper nearby. *I'm here, Orah.*

She saw him then. Dear, beautiful Warra. He wore a wallaby skin at his waist and a necklace of wildflowers. His dark hair formed a halo around his head, and he was smiling so sweetly that it made her heart squeeze.

Put your arms around my neck and hold on, he told her. *Climb on my back. Hold tight. Don't be afraid. I'm a good swimmer.*

She knew he was a good swimmer, she'd seen him in action. But why was he telling her now? There was no water here . . . Yet even as the thoughts formed in her mind, she heard a soft whooshing sound nearby.

It's the ocean, Warra whispered, his breath warm on her cheek. Now his hand grasped hers and pulled her lightly to her feet. To Orah's surprise, they were standing on the headland. Not the gravelly embankment high above the rocks where she'd been earlier, but the gently sloping grassy hillside Warra had taken her the day he'd made the daisy chain. It was early morning. The sandy path that led down to the beach meandered around the headland like a white ribbon. The cloudless sky shimmered a perfect shade of blue. Below them stretched the indigo sea, trimmed with foaming waves. *Look at that water*, Warra said. *Beautiful, eh? And all that sunshine, friendly as a smile.*

All around them, paper daisies raised their white and yellow heads between tufts of soft green grass. Above them soared a pair of sea eagles. Orah smiled and thought her world complete. Here was the place she'd dreamed of, a place where everything – every stone, every tuft of grass, every tree – was a mirror, in which she could see herself reflected.

Someone called her name. She looked around, and joy exploded in her heart, for there was Mam, her very own dear mam striding towards them along the sandy path, her arms outstretched, her lovely face flushed pink from the sun. Orah let go of Warra's hand and ran towards her mother. The last of the heaviness left her limbs, she was now as light as a bird. Flying free, she thought, as free as a cloud.

But the notion only lasted a heartbeat. Here was Mam at last, weeping for joy. Orah's own glad tears streamed from her eyes as she threw her arms around her mother's neck and felt herself disappear into that warm, strong, loving embrace that she knew so well.

He lifted her with infinite care, adjusting the slight weight of her in his arms. Through the dark house he went, out the back door and into the garden. Picking his way across the grass, he followed the path downhill into the orchard. It was a starless night; shadows seemed to gather around him in the garden, as though paying their last respects. He walked past them, trying not to think of what lay ahead.

When he reached the icehouse, he paused to fumble out his keys and open the door. Pushing into the deeper darkness, he entered the damp passageway that smelled of earth and stone and staleness. The cool breath of the icehouse wafted around him.

He knew his way by memory, had ventured here so often since he was a boy that his internal compass was finely tuned to the number of paces he must take, the exact moment to turn, when to duck his head to avoid the lintel over the narrow entryway into the heart of the icehouse. In the room that had once stored blocks of ice throughout the long summertimes of his childhood, he finally laid her down. He tucked her back against the solid sandstone wall, her body on her side, the way she liked to sleep, and then, as an afterthought, he took off his cardigan and rolled it into a pillow under her head.

Fumbling in his pocket for a box of matches, he lit the old kerosene lamp. The cool yellow glow sent fingers of light exploring into the corners, chasing the shadows, making them dance sinuously up the walls. There was nothing left to do, but still he lingered. He wanted to hold her one last time, but how could he bear her deadweight again, when the act of carrying her here had almost finished him?

A shadow of cold. He and Clarice had wanted only to love her, but instead they had smothered her. Both of them, wanting so desperately to keep her safe, protect her, give her the life they envisaged, a good life. Instead, they had clipped her wings.

And now . . .

The ice room had become hollow, the air around him unearthly still. He could hear the soft whistle of his breath, the heavy thump of his heart – and, as though from another world, a muffled voice calling his name.

Pausing in the narrow entryway, he looked back.

The glow of the kerosene lamp washed her hair gold. Her small hands lay folded beside her face, her brow as smooth and white as a pebble. If he half-closed his eyes, he could imagine that she was only sleeping. That the stains on her skin and clothes were nothing more sinister than shadows; that her deathly stillness was only that briefest of moments before the next intake of breath.

He cursed himself. More tricks, he told himself. Nothing more. Yet that fleeting, knife-jab moment of hope held more pain than he believed anybody – least of all a man like him – had the capacity to bear.

'I'm sorry,' he whispered. His voice bounced off the walls, tight with pain. 'Can you ever forgive me?'

With the echo of his words turning to dust in his ears, he ducked beneath the lintel, along the passageway, through the door and out into the brilliance of a frosty dawn.

36

Bitterwood, June 1993

Ducking through the low doorway, I continued on my way into the heart of the icehouse. The air was so cold it felt moist on my skin, the darkness so dense it deadened my torchlight. I shuffled into the room, pushing aside strings of cobwebs. Thunder echoed dimly through the thick walls. Earth and grit sifted from between the roof beams. I trained my light on a spot near the entryway.

Long ago, I had spent the night in this place. A dark night, in the company of spiders and cockroaches, rats. And . . .

The torch wavered in my hand.

Memory froze me in place.

That distant night, I had stumbled backwards and come to rest on that spot, sliding down the wall to sit on the floor. Scrabbling my legs, trying to disappear, arms locked

433

around my shins, my face pressed into my knees. I had not cried, hadn't made a sound. Was too scared. Just breathed, and tried to think, think of anything. Tried to think lovely thoughts. I had told myself a story, I remembered. One of my father's fairytales from the days before he got published. Picturing myself as the fearless princess who disguised herself in a bearskin to rescue her prince. Over and over I told it, as though it had the power to ward off the terrifying vision on the opposite side of the cramped room.

In a way, it had.

I shone my torch at the centre of the floor. Set into the flagging was a large rectangular grate. Beneath it was a shallow drain which had once carried away the meltwater produced by stored blocks of ice. Once allowed me to escape this place.

The torch beam crawled. Slowly, to the other side.

There, in the corner.

Not a pile of discarded bricks after all. Not a bundle of old rags.

But someone. A small someone, slumped on the floor, back against the wall as though sleeping.

I went over. The skeleton was delicate, the jumble of small bones blurred by dust, collapsed within the decayed confines of what had once been a girl's dress. There were shoes, and a long thin strip near the skull that might once have been a ribbon.

I kneeled beside her. 'Orah.'

My voice whispered around the walls. As though in answer, muffled thunder cracked somewhere overhead. The tremor that followed drew a shudder from the support beams around me. More earth rained down from the ceiling, drawing my gaze upwards. Solid, I told myself. The icehouse had already endured more than a hundred years. It would not collapse now.

I looked back at the girl.

A network of spider webs, as fine and white as silk, shrouded her bones – connecting a shoulder blade to the wall, lacing between delicate finger bones, creating a veil over her ribs and spine.

Who was she, really? She had survived a shipwreck, lost her mother in the dark water. Clung to a lifeboat until the early hours of what must have been a terrifying night. She had been rescued by a boy she came to love. She had gone to live at Bitterwood, and filled two empty hearts with hope. How glad she must have been to discover her father alive, only to plunge into bitter disappointment when he left in the night without saying goodbye.

And then, her fall.

I could see Hanley gathering her from the rocks below the headland, rushing with her back to the house. Weeping quietly over her stillness as he laid her on the doorstep, promising that everything would be all right. But it hadn't been all right. She had died of her injuries, and Edwin had brought her to this icy crypt, locked her in the darkness, kept her here for more than sixty years. He had guarded her memory, and then, when he knew that his own death was near, he'd burned the album containing her image. Burned away all trace of her – or so he'd thought – to stop anyone wondering, asking questions. To stop them uncovering what he'd done.

Thunder rumbled outside and more rubble sifted from the ceiling. Still, I lingered. It seemed infinitely sad to think of this bright girl entombed here, while year after year and only a few feet above, butterflies danced in the wildflowers, and the song of the ocean drifted up from the cliffs below.

My fingers tightened around the ruined bracelet in my hand.

Understanding came in a rush.

Mum had been here that day. She'd been inside the icehouse. Located the keys, perhaps, or simply discovered the door unlocked and gone in.

Where she had found the remains of a young girl.

She would have known it was Edwin's doing. Because who other than my grandfather had keys to this subterranean place? No wonder she had been in such a rush to find my father; no wonder she had slipped on the headland in her haste to return to the cottage and find him. No wonder she'd been careless on the rocks where I had told her he might be—

I thought about my dream. About the crushing guilt it always inspired in me, bringing with it the echo of my mother's voice, drifting from far away.

I'm trapped here, Lucy. Why did you lie?

Loosening my fingers, I looked down at the bracelet in my palm.

It hadn't really been my mother's voice calling through my dreams. Just my own guilty conscience laying blame where no blame belonged.

Into the darkness, a whisper.

You only see what you want to see, Lucy . . . If you believe something to be a certain way, then that's exactly how it appears to you.

The truth, I realised, wore many masks. Eyes were deceptive, seeing what you told them to see. The heart, on the other hand, never lied.

Somewhere in the dark behind me, the wind murmured against the walls. I became aware of a muffled scraping and tearing. The wind picked up, and I wondered if it had caught the door and was preparing to slam it shut. But the tearing noise increased, as though the earth itself was splitting down the middle. Soil and gravel began to rain around me, falling faster and thicker than it had before. I shone my torch to the rafters and saw a steady stream of dirt and small stones sifting down.

It was time to go.

Lifting the ribbon from around my neck, I drew out the gold heart charm and placed it on the floor beside Orah. Next to it I laid the bracelet chain with its tiny padlock clasp. Then I got to my feet.

'I hope you found Warra,' I whispered. 'Wherever you are, I hope you're loved.'

Then I turned and, feeling somehow lighter in my spirit, I hurried out.

Taking the steps two at a time, I ran up along the passage towards the open doorway. As I reached it, part of the roof collapsed behind me and a beam swung down, striking my arm, knocking the torch from my hand. I staggered through the doorway, bursting out into the garden, only stopping when I got to the edge of the orchard.

Soaked to the skin with rain and whipped by the wind, I hugged my arms around my body and looked back. As I did, lightning lit the sky. The scene burned into my eyes. The verdant green hillock. The churning clouds behind. The rain lashing sideways, driven by the wind. At the centre was the dead oak, its silvery trunk leaning on an angle, its bare branches quivering. As the world went dark again, the great trunk groaned, listing further over. Roots split and tore from the ground, spraying soil and stone. The tree gave a shudder, and finally fell. With a violent crash that seemed to shake the world, it collapsed onto the hillock.

The rain began to lash harder. The wind hurled a cloud of leafy grit into my face, but I held my ground, transfixed as another lightning flash illuminated the wreckage.

Beneath the oak's heavy trunk, the knoll had collapsed. Where there had once been a mound, was now only a bank of rubble and shattered branches. The icehouse door lay on the path, its sturdy timber frame skewed around it. The icehouse was gone. The passageways under the hillock that had once led underground, the thick walls insulated with sawdust and stone, the rock ceiling upheld by support beams, and the silent chamber at its heart – all now buried beneath a heavy load of stone and debris.

Where the bones of a lost girl were finally at rest.

While the storm raged outside, I sat in Edwin's office by candlelight, staring at the strongbox set into the wall. The power was out, the telephone had gone dead. I had navigated my way through the dark kitchen by the glow of embers in the Warmray, found a stash of candles in the pantry, and then gone upstairs to change my sodden clothes for dry ones. I found a first aid box, using what was inside to disinfect and then bandage my arm. Nothing felt broken, but bruises were already blooming and the skin along my forearm was grazed where the beam had struck it.

All the while, Basil had trailed behind me, meowing fretfully. He now sat on the desk enjoying a wash, apparently unbothered by the rumbling thunder outside.

The icehouse keys were still in my pocket. I took them out. Crumbs of soil still clung to the large brass key where I had used it to dig the bracelet from the icehouse floor. I set that one aside – I wouldn't need it anymore. I had assumed that both keys belonged to the icehouse, but as I examined the smaller one, I couldn't help wondering.

It fitted perfectly.

I turned the strongbox handle, and with a whisper of metal on wood, the door opened. The emptiness inside was a shock. I wasn't entirely sure what I'd been expecting. Jewellery. Bundles of cash. Silver candelabras.

A box of secrets.

Anything but emptiness. I shone the candle into the cavity, just to confirm what I was seeing. Then the soft light caught the edge of what at first I thought was a book. On closer inspection, I found it was a slim bundle of papers tied with black ribbon.

A shiver of anticipation flew across my skin.

They were letters.

37

Bitterwood, May 1993

Some days his memories of Clarice were so bright and clear that he truly believed he was once again a young man. He could hear her laughter, see the glint of sun in her reddy gold hair, feel his body stir to her beauty; and always, when he blinked her away and startled back to reality with a wrenching shock, the ache of her loss was unbearable.

Edwin crossed his bedroom and went to the window, peered through the patina of grime at the sky beyond. The sun had set, leaving behind a trail of purple clouds. Soon, the day would lose its colour. How he resented that grey time before nightfall. Of all the lonely hours in his day, twilight was the loneliest.

He was an old man, while the woman he loved – still loved, despite the eternity that now lay between them – would remain forever as he had last seen her. Achingly beautiful, her skin smooth and free of lines, her sweet lips the colour of cherries.

He shook his head. He was privy to the terrible secret of those who grow old: that inside, he was still young. But the shell that concealed his youth was frail, a wrinkled carapace that shuffled hither and thither. Preserved, it sometimes seemed to him, only by the vinegar of his regret.

Taking the album from his bedside table, he flipped through the images until he found his favourite. Clarice, with her copper locks, and little Orah with her long golden waves. Sitting together on the garden bench, their smiles alight, the mulberry trees around them dotted with blossom. Happy times.

He had known they couldn't last.

Not *known* exactly, but rather sensed the approach of something large and overwhelmingly dark. He'd sensed it the way a dog detects the drop in barometric pressure before a storm. There was no logic to the feeling. He simply knew in his bones that the sky was too perfectly blue, and that any moment a cloud might drift across to obscure it. A cloud.

Or a shadow in the shape of a man.

He sighed and turned the page, gazed sadly at another snap taken in the orchard. Clarice and Orah seated under the blossoming cherry tree, tired after a long day, but still their faces glowed. He had pictures of Dulcie, and of Ron as a boy, but he always found himself returning to his favourites, the ones of Orah and Clarice. They were the ones he spent his nights bowed over, the ones whose pages he stained with his tears.

Today, it was finally time to let them go.

To erase them from the memory of the world.

From his memory.

He closed the album. Downstairs in the kitchen, he opened the Warmray. The fire had burned away, but the embers were still fierce. Without pausing, without giving himself the opportunity to waver, he thrust the album facedown into the fire and shut the hatch. Then he hastened through the kitchen door and locked it firmly behind him, determined not to weaken and retrieve his precious photos from the fire.

He passed the rearing house without a glance, following the path down through the orchard and around into the green hollow beneath the dead oak.

For a while, he stood at the icehouse door, unable to remember why he was there. Digging in his pocket, he took out a matchbox. Struck a match, and let the wind blow it out. A voice whispered to him from the past, a fragile murmur that might have been the rustle of leaves, or the rub of scarlet silk on soap-scented skin. He found himself tumbling back through time, to that dreadful night in 1931.

He could still see her huddled there, on the icehouse floor. Her head resting on the pillow he had fashioned from his cardigan, her hands tucked neatly at her face. She might have been sleeping. He had lingered, but only for a moment. A muffled voice had interrupted his farewell and called him back to the surface; it could only have been Clarice.

He had emerged from the icehouse, still trembling. He'd been right. Clarice's voice, muffled by the heavy walls of the icehouse, now seemed alarmingly loud in the cold air. Edwin hesitated on the edge of the orchard, trying to gather enough calm to face her. His earlier cries for help must have woken her, and now she wanted to know where he was.

He shuddered.

Clarice was so frail. So afraid of losing the baby she carried. So desperate for a little one to love that her old fears were creeping back, her old nightmares. Edwin glared up at the sky, cursing God, cursing Hanley Dane, cursing fate and the twisted string of events that had brought Orah into their lives and then snatched her away again. Most of all, he cursed himself. He had believed he was doing the right thing, keeping Orah from the wreck of a man who had once been her father; had believed he was saving her from a life of destitution. Now he saw that he had not saved her at all, but condemned her.

'Edwin?'

Clarice's cry trembled in the cold night air. It sounded to Edwin as though a window was open somewhere, and he imagined Clarice in her nightgown, shivering as the wind blew up from the sea.

He began to run. She was not at the window, but sitting on the edge of the bed. Edwin switched on the light. When he saw the blood, his knees buckled, but he forced himself to go to her. Crashing to the floor in front of her, he gripped her arms and searched her face. How pale she was, how gaunt. Her skin was slick with clammy sweat, her body trembling violently. Had she been that way earlier that night when he'd given her the draught of medicine? He couldn't remember.

'Dr Vetch,' she whispered, and grimaced in pain. Circling her thin arms around her enormous belly, she hugged herself, rocking forward and back, shivering. 'Hurry, Edwin. The baby's coming.'

Thirty minutes later the doctor arrived, and delivered Clarice of a healthy baby boy. Dr Vetch must have assumed the blood on Edwin's shirt was Clarice's blood; he barely glanced at it. Such a lot of blood. Edwin stripped off his shirt and threw it on the pile of soiled bedclothes with Clarice's blood-soaked nightdress. He dragged on his dressing gown and stood idly, watching as Vetch attended to the child, checking lungs and heart with his stethoscope.

Later, after Vetch had gone, Edwin washed the little boy and wrapped him in a soft blanket, then settled him into Clarice's arms. Edwin sat at the bedside. When Clarice's thin fingers sought his hand, he clutched them gratefully.

'A son,' she said, her voice gentle with disbelief. 'Edwin, can you believe it? A dear little boy of our own.' Then she looked at him and the brightness left her face. 'Oh Edwin, where were you? I called and called, but you never came. I called until my throat was raw. Where were you? Didn't you hear me? Orah must be fast asleep. I called her too, but—'

Edwin began to weep. He was teetering on a knife edge. *I must not fall*, he told himself. *For her sake, I must not fall.* With a gargantuan effort, he forced a smile, wiped his face and murmured something about tears of relief. Part of him still lingered in the cool sanctuary of the icehouse, perhaps it always would. He was a ghost, a creature of such frail substance that he could barely breathe. Yet in that heart-beat of silence, he knew what he must do. Clarice seemed so fragile, her face ragged and pale, her lips bitten and bloody, her eyes brightly deranged.

'Look, Edwin, isn't he perfection? His tiny fingers, his dear little face . . . such a perfect sweetheart. Oh darling, I want to call him Ronald.'

Of course she did, and surprisingly, Edwin was glad. Joy flowed into his shrivelled heart. Too many years had passed since Clarice had called him darling. Her endearment electrified him. In that moment, he would have given anything, even happily died for her, if only to hear her murmur his name that sweetly again. As he gazed at the tiny bundle in her arms, the bundle they both had dreamed of for so long, he let himself believe, for one instant, that all was well in their world.

Then reality crashed around him. He could not tell her, he realised. Not about Hanley and the knocking on the door. And not about Orah. Nor could he tell her where he had put the girl. She must never know. Even the merest whisper of shock would send Clarice over the edge. The prospect of spinning more lies, of weaving a web of deceit between them, made his stomach churn, but what other choice did he have? Lies, as much as he hated to tell them, were really all he had left to give Clarice.

He realised then that this birth was not a joy. Rather, it was a curse. Each time he looked into his son's face, it would haunt him.

'Edwin dear, fetch Orah, will you? It's nearly dawn. I want her to meet her new brother.'

'Let's get you cleaned up first,' he said kindly. 'I'm sorry I wasn't here. I was . . . You see, there was—' He stopped, overcome by a helplessness he'd never known before. 'I'm so very sorry, my dear. But I'm pleased as well. Look at him.' He swallowed around the lump lodged painfully in his throat. 'He certainly is a handsome little fellow.'

In the days that followed – dark days sweetened only by the pink-faced little boy Clarice could hardly bear to let out of her sight – Clarice badgered him endlessly about Orah. Where was she, why hadn't she come to see the baby? Had she taken ill, as Edith had all those years ago? Was she all right? Then, on the fourth day, Clarice demanded that Edwin tell her the truth.

Edwin told her, as gently as he could, that Orah had gone to stay with her father for a while, a sort of holiday, really, and that she would return in a month or so. Clarice didn't need to worry herself; Orah was coming back, she was coming back. He hoped the lie would buy him time, stall Clarice's questions until she was strong enough to bear the truth, but he quickly saw that he was wrong.

Clarice asked repeatedly, *Why did Orah not come to say goodbye?* When Edwin could not answer, she withdrew deeper into herself. She refused to eat. She turned her face away when Edwin tried to make her drink. She could not sleep. Black shadows appeared around her eyes. When her milk stopped flowing, Edwin bought formula and heated it in a bottle, but Clarice waved it away. *He needs his mother's milk,* she insisted, squeezing the baby tighter in her arms. Edwin wanted to bathe the child, to wash away the smell of Clarice's sickness, but Clarice rejected his attempts to take the baby. For two days, the little boy cried from hunger or distress, perhaps both, until Edwin's heart could stand it no longer.

Dr Vetch returned several times that week. Administering injections, monitoring her pulse, speaking with a cheery voice in the hope of rousing Clarice's spirits. Edwin moved to the guest room along the hall, to give her space. Another day passed, then another. Still, Clarice rejected Edwin's offerings of soup or tea, or dry toast and honey, even the warmed milk with brandy that Dr Vetch recommended. Still the baby cried.

And then, the letter.

Edwin palmed his face as the ink-stained page drifted into his mind's eye. He wished he had the power to block it from his memory, but it had seared itself there, indelible as a scar.

Bitterwood, 1931

Her fingers were numb; she could barely hold the pen. Ink splatters covered the paper. *Dear*, she managed to write, but then another wet splodge fell from the nib, and in her haste she dragged the side of her hand through the mess, making it worse.

Making everything worse.

Dear Edwin, she wrote. Then stalled. The words she had intended to say jumbled in her mind. She grabbed the tail end of a sentence and scratched it across the page, but the nib flicked up more ink spots. Screwing up that attempt, she took out a fresh leaf.

Dear Edwin, she began again. Her fingers trembled, her shoulders shook with concentration. Just as she was forming the words in her mind, the baby began to cry. She glanced over her shoulder to the cot. The child had a fragile tearful smell that made her think of the ocean. He had small gooey fingers like starfish tentacles, and his grip on her was surprisingly strong—

The room was suddenly hot. She couldn't breathe. She ran to the window and flung it open, gulped in the cold air. Her head pounded. For a moment she couldn't remember what she had been trying to do.

The wind blew hard and she gripped the sill, steadying herself. Letting her thoughts untangle. For a while, there was only the delicious cold air, damp with sea spray, and the fresh salt-seasoned darkness. She wished she could stay adrift in that moment forever.

Once, when she was a child, a relative had given her a tiny seahorse preserved in a specimen jar of alcohol. It fascinated her, but it had also instilled a trembly sort of terror. An animal so mysterious and rare did not belong in a bottle. She had lain awake at night, watching it on her bedside table. It was a question mark of a creature drifting in its glass bubble, its pale body catching the moonlight. After a week, she could stand it no more. She crept out of the house into the garden and smashed the specimen bottle with a brick. She scraped the seahorse into her mother's roses with the toe of her boot, and then hurried back to bed.

Years later, when she was nineteen, she had received a letter from Ronald's mother. She had known, of course, even before she opened it, what it would say. She knew Ronald was gone, knew by the emptiness, the ache in her chest.

Sitting very still in her mother's parlour, she had torn open a corner of the envelope, but then stopped. The image of the seahorse flashed into her mind. With it came her old terror, her old fascination. She saw herself as though from a faraway place, a curious specimen poised in a single sorrowful moment that would, for the rest of her life, define her.

The memory passed.

Behind her in the room, the baby's cries dwindled, ebbed away. The child made a hiccupping sound, and Clarice held her breath. *Don't look at him. Don't go near.* Instead, she fixed her gaze on the world outside. Searching, praying to glimpse a slight figure with a trail of fair hair slipping through the shadows of the garden, perhaps on her way to see Clarice, to visit the new baby—

The ache in her chest made her gasp.

It was cruel, to torture herself. Orah was not coming. Edwin had lied about the girl's whereabouts, but Clarice did not have the heart to press him further. To endure what he might say.

She clung to the windowsill, forcing her gaze outwards. The headland was a grey blur. Waves crashed against the rocks at the base, and overhead a lone sea eagle wheeled in the predawn sky. Below her in the garden, the trees swayed in the wind. Somewhere, a branch cracked.

A cry answered from the cot, a gurgle. Then the baby filled his lungs and let out a bellow that rose in pitch until it became a shrill wail. Clarice ran back to the writing table, snatched up her pen, and dunked its nib in the ink.

Dear Edwin . . .

The words came then, gushing from her in a hectic flood. The nib sped across the page, splashing words and ink and dark regret in a jumbled mess that she prayed Edwin would somehow decipher.

She folded the note once, and then slid it beneath the inkbottle. Her heart began to buck against her ribs like a frightened horse, and she stood for a moment in the centre of the room, lost. Her only lifeline was the baby's thin wail, lifting around her like a thread of hand-spun silk, and then unravelling into a cry so desolate that it stole away her breath. She wanted to snatch that cry from the air, pull herself along it and find, at the other end, the loving mother she had once been . . . but that was an illusion. There was nothing left of that person. There were no soft arms, no soothing voice, no enchanting stories; no part of her being that a small child might burrow into and call home.

She looked at the window.

Down behind the orchard, the first pink fingers of dawn touched the sky. Soon the sun would rise. Edwin would stumble from his bed in the guest room and creep back to see why the child was making all that noise.

Hurry, the seahorse whispered in her mind. *Hurry, or all will be lost.*

Running from the room, she half-fell down the stairs. She opened the front door and a gust of freezing air blew in. She saw a coat hanging on the stand, and grabbed it. It smelled of rum and sawdust, male smells that sickened her, made her think of a craggy face topped by fair wispy hair, sorrowful eyes. She shuddered. Thrusting the image away, she dragged the coat around her and went through the door.

The baby's cry followed her outside, down the verandah steps, along the gravel drive and all the way to the front gate. She unlatched the gate and slipped through, running and walking and then running again until her breath was ragged. Her feet hurt and a vague thought came: *Where are my shoes?* No matter. All she cared about was that the house disappeared behind her, far behind. The wind tore at her hair, and sea spray stung her cheeks. Breathless, she slowed to a walk. It was only when she reached the edge of the old coast road that the crying – the thin, pitiful crying of her baby son – finally died away behind her.

They found her huddled in a ditch, barely more than a mile from Bitterwood's gates. Cuts and grazes covered her feet, and the cold had stiffened her fingers, but she was alive.

'She's in good hands now,' Vetch had promised. 'She'll get the finest care. Treatments these days are marvellous. Never fear, old man, she'll be back home with you and baby before you know it.' He must have seen something in Edwin's eyes, because he added, 'Take heart, dear fellow, my absolute discretion is assured.'

Edwin had nodded, grateful for the reassurance, but as the taillights disappeared along the road that led back to Stern Bay, he feared the worst. In his mind's eye he followed the car's progress all the way along the winding Ocean Road and then through the deserted streets of Geelong. As he lay in bed that night, baby Ronald gurgling and babbling happily in the cot next to him, his little belly full of formula, Edwin imagined a host of faceless doctors in white coats bundling Clarice into a sterile room with grey walls and windows that looked out onto nothing. How she would hate a room like that. Edwin tried to picture her surrounded by trees, the tall willowy poplars she loved, the maples and eucalypts of her home in Kyneton. Better still, he tried to picture her arriving home to Bitterwood in a flurry of excitement, her cheeks rosy with health, her eyes as brilliantly blue as the sea, and her smile just for him.

Darling, darling . . .

He never saw her again. The doctor spoke of blood loss and complications, worsened by Clarice's fragile state of mind. But Edwin knew what really killed her: a broken heart. After she died, her parents drove from Kyneton and collected her, took her back to the family plot. Clarice would have hated that. She had often told Edwin that when she died a satisfied old woman she wanted to be buried near her girls, and – although she never voiced it aloud, Edwin knew in his heart it was so – near her beloved Ronald.

Memory faded.

Edwin broke from the reverie to find himself shivering on the threshold of the icehouse door. An old man holding a burned-out matchstick, the box of matches clasped in his fingers. The edges of the box bit into his palm, but he could not release it. No matter how hard he willed his fingers to let go, they would not obey.

Twilight had turned to night. He was cold. So terribly cold. A thready pain spread up his arm, into his chest, where it blossomed into something large and unwieldy.

It began to claw at him, and vaguely, in the back of his mind, he thought, *There you are, at last. You have found me. Finally, you have found me—*

The pain increased. A shadow fist clenched vice-like around his heart. He tried to take a breath, but his lungs had thickened, closed off, become useless. He fell against the icehouse door, and then slid soundlessly onto the paving stones. For a long time he rested there, waiting for his strength to return. He could only flex his fingers. Tiny, jerky movements.

With immense concentration, he slid open the matchbox. Fumbled out a match. Then he used all his remaining willpower to strike it, once, twice, three times against the side of the box.

When the sulphurous match-head burst into flame, the light radiating from it seemed so intense that Edwin's eyes filled with tears. Overcome with awe, he watched the match flame blur and grow larger, bursting outwards until it engulfed the night like a single, brilliant star.

38

Bitterwood, June 1993

Taking the letters over to the desk, I settled into Edwin's chair. Unfolding the top sheet from the pile, I began to read.

16 May 1993
Dearest Lucy,
Please find enclosed the documents as promised in my letter. I hope they will explain enough, if not to help you and your father find forgiveness, then perhaps simply to bring a degree of peace.

I had hoped to hand them to you in person and tell the story in full, but if you're reading this letter then I am gone. I couldn't risk sending them by post. I've kept them safe for over sixty years and now I entrust them to you. I know that you, dear Lucy, will judge how best to use them.

454

I regret not being a part of your lives. Your wonderful books have brought me much consolation. Ron's mother was a storyteller too, and I'm glad that something of her lives on in him.

I regret so much. There were times when the burden of my mistakes seemed too heavy to bear. But your father, and then later you, made me realise that good has come from me, after all.

Your grandfather,
Edwin

I read the last line again, and glanced over at the portrait. My fingers trembled a little, and I realised it was sorrow. He had always been kind to me – when we holidayed in the nearby cottage, and then later during the three months I stayed with him while Dad was at Banksia House. To hear his voice echo up from the spidery writing on the page was bittersweet. Out of a lifetime of regret, Edwin considered only two truly good things had come: my father and me.

I unfolded the second letter. It had been typed on letter-head paper, and as I gleaned the contents, a deeper shadow of sadness fell over me.

Alberton Psychiatric Hospital, Geelong
12 November 1931
Dear Mr Briar,
In response to your telephone call about your wife, who we admitted as a patient at Alberton two weeks ago, I regret to confirm that she passed away in her sleep on Tuesday night.

Soon after her admittance, Mrs Briar requested that we release her into the care of her parents. Her father, Mr Gerald Hopeworth, has informed us that he is arriving tomorrow to collect her for burial in their family plot at Kyneton.

Please accept condolences from all of us here at Alberton.

Sincerely yours,
B. Matheson
Head of Psychiatry

Folding the letter, I returned it to the envelope and rested my elbows on the desk. I looked again at the portrait of my grandfather, wondering why he had allowed his wife to die alone in a psychiatric hospital. Had she gone willingly, or had Edwin forced her there? Fineflower in the dungeon, I thought. Except in Clarice's story, there had been no soldier's knife, no open cell door, and no baby son awaiting her upstairs in the light. My grandmother had died in the dungeon, far from the rocky cliffs and boundless blue-green ocean that surrounded her home. Far from her loved ones.

I tried to picture her last moments in the hospital, but the effort bruised my heart. Instead, I saw a woman hurrying along the beach road, the wind lashing her red-gold hair, the old coat flapping around her legs. Her bare feet dusty and cold as they carried her away from Bitterwood.

Away from Edwin and her child.

As I opened the last letter, an unexpected lump came to my throat. Clarice had written it ten days after my father was born. The writing paper looked expensive, thick and creamy white – but it was covered in ink splotches and small holes gouged by the pen's nib. The handwriting was erratic, the words scrawled large and elaborate in parts, while some sentences were so small I had to tilt the page nearer the light to decipher them. As I read, as understanding dawned, my heart grew heavy.

28 October 1931

Dear Edwin,

I've done a bad thing. I am so ashamed. I don't ask forgiveness – how can I expect it of you when I can never forgive myself? But something dark rushed up in me and I couldn't find the strength of will to hold it down. You have always been so very good to me, but in return I've been more trouble than perhaps I was worth. That's why I lost them all, isn't it? My girls, and Orah. Even Ronald. The darkness inside me consumed them, took them away.

This morning, it came close to taking little Ronnie, too.

I promise you Edwin, I never meant to hurt the boy. Never meant him any harm. He's more precious to me than the moon and stars, than all our lives rolled into one – but it was there in my mind to do it, and I fear what will happen if I stay.

I'm not myself. My head is full of black clouds and rain. My heart is choked with shadows. My thoughts frighten me. Violent thoughts. I picked him up to cradle him, hold him tenderly, kiss away his grizzling and cuddle away his cries. I don't know how it happened. I shook him, Edwin. Hard. Only the once, I promise. But his little eyes rolled back, and he made such a desolate sound like the mewling of a kitten trodden underfoot by one who means to love, but hurts instead.

I'm not myself. The right words aren't coming. The rain and clouds in my head won't let them. He's crying again now. I ache to go to him and hold him near, I love him so dearly. All of him. His wise little eyes, the way he tilts his head when I tell a story, as though he's taking in every word. My little prince, I called him, do you remember, Edwin?

One day, tell him his mother loved him ever so much. And if he asks you why she went away, just smile and say it was because she loved him so. Will you do that for me, darling?

One last thing. Promise me, dear heart, swear on my life that you will never breathe a word of what I've told you. Please, love, let my darkness die with me.

Goodbye, Edwin.

My love always,
Clarice

Kyneton, June 1993

Dad was wordless in the passenger seat, watching the landscape rush past his window, his hands fisted on his knees. The Volkswagen rattled and creaked, its little motor noisy, its grumbling roar filling up the silence between us that might otherwise have been unbearable.

We stopped once so he could stretch his legs and ease the stiffness from his hip, but he was keen to reach our destination. Two hours northwest of Melbourne, we turned off the Calder Highway and went through the township of Kyneton. Out of Kyneton, we drove along a country road towards the cemetery.

I parked on the verge, and we walked into the grounds, Dad careful on his crutches. We followed a gravel path to the furthest edge where the plots were tall and imposing. Hemmed behind a wrought iron surround, stood a large granite angel, her head bowed over the dove in her hands as though deep in thought. Kneeling at her base, I brushed away the crumbling lichen from the inscription.

Clarice Hopeworth Briar
28 May 1896 – 10 November 1931
In Our Hearts for All Time

We settled on a nearby bench, in the shade of a sprawling black-trunked cyprus. The sun was warm, infusing the air with the scent of pinesap and fresh cut grass. My skin began to tingle. I took the letters from my bag, held them on my lap.

I had told my father exactly what Edwin had told me. That I had something, which would explain everything. Of course, by *everything*, my grandfather had meant that the letter would clarify just enough to let us understand that things were not as they had seemed. He had made a promise to Clarice. Not in person, because by that time Clarice was gone. Rather, he had promised in his heart, and honoured his promise to the end.

I handed the letters to Dad. A look passed between us, and then Dad untied the ribbon and bent his head to read. When he reached the note written by his mother ten days after he was born, his plump shoulders began to shake. He removed his glasses and rubbed his eyes, then went back to the letter. His fingers trembled so hard he crumpled the paper. When he finished, he lifted the page to his eyes and sobbed into it.

I had never seen him cry. I had seen him pale with self-pity, drunk and depressed, crimson-faced with anger. Once I had watched him slam down the phone so hard after a conversation with Edwin that the receiver broke away from the handpiece. Yet in all the years of my father's emotional rollercoaster of a life, I had never seen him shed a single tear.

Until now.

Not knowing what else to do, I leaned against him. And waited. A breeze murmured through the branches overhead. The melodic song of a magpie drifted from the other side of the cemetery. I waited.

Finally, Dad folded the letter, tied the ribbon back around the bundle, and looked up. His dear moonface was blotched pink, his eyes wet. He patted his pockets for a hanky, and when he failed to find one, I gave him mine.

'My word,' he murmured.

'I know,' I agreed.

Stillness settled over us. My father took a great deep shuddering breath, and then slowly let it out. Finally, he said, 'Thank you, kiddo.'

'For what?'

'For standing by a foolish old man when his world fell apart.'

'It was my world too.'

He sighed and palmed his eyes. 'Edwin carried quite a burden, didn't he?'

I nodded. 'You can't know, can you? What makes other

people behave the way they do. He was keeping his promise to Clarice. Protecting you.'

Dad's eyes went misty again. Small spots of colour reddened his cheeks. He gazed at the bundle of letters in his hand.

'I thought Edwin blamed me for her leaving. I thought he resented me. The things I said to him . . . Oh, Lucy. What I'd give now to take them back.' He polished his glasses on his shirtfront and sighed. 'Poor Clarice. I really believed she didn't love me. Seems I was wrong about her, too.' He fell quiet, and for a while, there was just the stillness. Birds chattered high in the branches overhead, and the tree creaked gently in the breeze. Then Dad sighed. 'You know, Karen suffered the same thing when you were born. Postnatal depression, we call it these days.'

'What happened?'

He shrugged. 'She talked to a counsellor. Learned meditation. After a while, the depression passed. She went back to her happy old self.'

'That's how I remember her.'

He looked at me suddenly. 'You were our golden girl, you know. Karen was forty-two when you were born. We'd been trying to have a baby for years. I'd never seen your mother so close to despair. Time was ticking away from her; she was desperate. Then one day, suddenly there you were. A tiny heartbeat . . . a blip of hope. We wept for joy, and our joy was so great, so overwhelming, that it never truly left us. It may have been hidden for a time,' he added. 'But I expect that wherever she is now, Karen still feels it. I know I do.'

I hid my own tears behind a shaky laugh. 'Dad, "a blip of hope"?'

He laughed too, more of a sniffle really, but it got us back on solid ground.

'I miss her,' he said. 'Every day.'

'Me too.'

A delicious peacefulness settled over us. A light breeze fluttered the letters Dad still held. The afternoon grew warm, and shadows began to lengthen across the cemetery. Sunlight shimmered through the feathery cypress leaves, and the magic I had sensed the week before in the cafe returned, this time cocooning us, drawing us from the shadowland of the past and out into the brightness that waited for us ahead.

39

Melbourne, October 1993

There was a wedding, after all. A night-time celebration with fairy lights and candles hanging from the trees in jars, white roses that Wilma had cultivated especially. A celebrant came to my father's garden, and read from a book of poetry. One of my favourites, by Emily Dickinson – the same quote, as it turned out, that my grandfather had once sent to me.

> *Exultation is the going*
> *Of an inland soul to sea,*
> *Past the houses – pass the headlands –*
> *Into deep eternity –*

An odd sentiment for a wedding, I'd once thought. But now it made me think of wide-open seas and endless new possibility. It made me think of braving the rain and thunder and finding beauty in the storm. It made me think of Fine-flower escaping the dungeon to be with her soldier love, and venturing into the magical blue unknown where all things were possible.

Loud music nudged me from my musings.

Dad had cranked up the stereo. He was off his crutches, had shaved his beard and become a new man. I saw him catch Wilma about the waist and lure her onto the patio for a romantic waltz.

Nina was stunning in a vintage lace wedding dress that showed off her large baby bump. Coby took his bride's hand and led her down to the lawn, where they kicked off their shoes and danced on the grass.

I kept glimpsing Morgan from the corner of my eye. One minute he was chatting to Gwen, the next he was collecting empty wine bottles and a while later, having a yarn with one of the elderly guests. The next, he had vanished.

I hadn't seen him in the months since we said goodbye at my grandfather's guesthouse. I had returned to London to farewell my life there, and once that was done I'd come back to Melbourne. I had moved out to Bitterwood, and was still settling in. Still trying to get my head around being there. The weeks I had spent there over winter had changed me. The place I had shunned for so long had gotten under my skin. Now, I couldn't imagine a better home for Basil and me.

Morgan was avoiding me, I felt sure, so I went to investigate.

I found him sitting alone at the far end of the garden, back in his old place on the bench against the shed wall.

It was October, a starry night with a full moon. It felt unusually warm for this time of year, but that might have been the wine and the dancing. Morgan had stripped off his formal shirt to the snug T-shirt beneath, and the sight of him gave me tingles. He'd raked his hair into disarray and the cool night air had flushed his cheeks.

He looked around as I approached. 'Who's this gorgeous creature?'

I had planned what I would to say when I saw him. I'd been rehearsing for a week, but the minute he spoke, I forgot myself.

Gorgeous creature.

He patted the seat beside him. 'I thought you might've absconded back to London by now.'

I stayed standing. I wanted him to see the dress. My grandmother's scarlet silk, figure hugging and just a little bit sinful when worn with heels.

'I'm hardly going to miss my best friend's wedding.'

He looked up at me and time unravelled. Suddenly, we were back in the cave with the ocean pounding the rocks below and the storm raging outside. That night he had asked me not to run, but I had. I'd run along the path that fate or the universe had set before me. And as I ran, the memory of our time in the cave stayed with me. In the smoky blackness, in Morgan's arms, I had slept deeply. No dreams washed against my subconscious. No whispers, no cold ghostly hands. Just Morgan's warm body beside me, his breath rhythmic as the sea, his heartbeat steady beside mine.

Passion might not last, I had realised. But love was eternal.

He must have seen the gleam in my eyes because he got to his feet, fixed his pale gaze to mine. He traced his fingers lightly over the tiny mermaid tattooed on my shoulder, then drew away.

'Luce?'

I was possessed, I must have been. My arms went around his neck and I drew him near, pressed so close I could feel the warmth of his breath on my lips.

'I'm home, Morgan. To stay.'

Morgan smiled. He captured my face in his hands and kissed me. The world slid away. The garden faded, the fairy lights dimmed, the stars went out one by one. There was just the two of us, cocooned in the darkness together, right where we had always belonged.

Acknowledgements

Writing a novel can be a fairly isolating activity, but I'm lucky to have a brilliant network of people who all play a part in getting it over the finish line and into the hands of my readers.

Selwa Anthony is always first on my list to thank because without her my stories would still be languishing in a dusty bottom drawer. Selwa does so much to help me, I feel very blessed to have her in my life. She's been my rock in hard times, and is always there to inspire and counsel, and I love her dearly for that.

I would also like to thank my steadfast crew at Simon & Schuster Australia, who always go out of their way to look after me. Larissa Edwards who saw the spark in my first novel, I'm forever grateful. Dan Ruffino for his faith in this book. My dear friend Anna O'Grady, a fellow bushwalker and camper, who always takes such care with detail and with getting my books noticed. Many thanks as well to the hard working sales team who really get behind my books and always do such an excellent job.

Special thanks to my editor Roberta Ivers who is always so generous with her time and expertise. I've learned more from Bert about writing than from a mountain of how-to books. She always works incredibly hard to get my story to its best, and I'm so grateful to her for everything she does. She is absolutely a treasure.

I'm hugely indebted to my copyeditor Claire de Medici and proofreader Clara Finlay for their skill and hard work. Thanks as well to my patient typesetters who, for this novel, have gone far beyond the call of duty. And many thanks to Christa Moffitt for her beautiful cover artwork, which has turned each of my books into a delicious treat.

My overseas publishers, especially Goldmann in Germany, Presses de la Cité in France, and Penguin Random House in Spain, who believe in my books and put so much thought and love into getting them out there. I'm eternally grateful.

Thank you to Bolinda Audio for always bringing my stories to life so beautifully, and to Hannah Norris for her outstanding narration.

Many thanks to Brian Dennis, the magical man behind the scenes who's always there to make things flow more smoothly. Drew Keys for his enthusiasm over the years. Linda Anthony for all her tireless help and for her insights about the furry loves of our lives.

Russell Taylor for our spine-tingling conversations, especially the one that inspired this book. Dan Mitchell for enriching my stories and my life with his knowledge and passion. Bet Mitchell always for her love and friendship.

My lovely Weirdo (Peter Wears) for many memorable and much-needed cups of tea. Ron Southern who taught me that history is in the eye of the beholder; I miss you, you mad old buzzard!

Thank you to my friend across the sea Vera Nijveld, for our sparkling connection and for getting me hooked on the best band EVER! Aunty Nancy (Hannah Banister) for a lifetime of family anecdotes that so often find their way into my books. Bob Ruthven and Stuart Ruthven for help with research, and Hailey and Luke for turning out to be such cool people.

A really special thank you to my mum Jeanette for inspiring me with her courage and resourcefulness, and for all our wonderful talks about books, history, and life. My dad Bernie, for the tall tales he told me growing up. My sister Sarah for all her help and support, and for loving me even when I'm a babbling overworked wreck. My sister Katie for bringing fun and sparkle into my life, and for continuing to remind me what's important.

Lastly, a heartfelt thank you to my readers all over the world who brighten my writing journey with their good wishes and encouragement.

My love and thanks to you all,
Anna Romer

Book Club Questions

1. What did the silkworms symbolise?

2. Do you think Lucy's fear was justified?

3. How did Lucy change by the end of the book?

4. Do you think that uncovering the truth can really bring about lasting transformation? In real life, does change take more time?

5. Why do you think Lucy didn't just send Morgan into the icehouse to see what was in there?

6. Do you feel the underlying theme of the story has more to do with fear, or with love? Why do you feel this?

7. Ron says, 'Everyone's a hero in their own story, even the crooks.' Which of the characters acted selfishly but believed they were doing the right thing?

8. Do you think Edwin eventually kept his threat to Jensen Burke?

9. Whose crime do you feel was the most unforgivable?

10. How might events have turned out if Edwin had told the truth about Orah's father?

11. Why you think Edwin kept his promise to Clarice, even though it meant hurting his son?

12. Did you see Edwin as good or bad? In what way might he have been a mix of both?

13. What do you think the book's title is referring to?

Anna Romer was born in Australia to a family of book-lovers. She led a nomadic life for many years, travelling around Europe and Britain in an ancient Kombi van where she discovered a passion for history.

These days she lives in a little old cottage surrounded by bushland, writing stories about dark family secrets, rambling houses, characters haunted by the past, and settings that feature the uniquely beautiful Australian landscape.

You can find more information about Anna and her books at www.annaromer.com.au